ZERO
COUPON

Also by Paul Erdman

The Swiss Account
The Palace
The Panic of '89
The Last Days of America
The Crash of '79
The Silver Bears
The Billion Dollar Sure Thing

PAUL·ERDMAN

ZERO COUPON

*A Tom Doherty
Associates Book
New York*

ZERO COUPON

Copyright © 1993 by Paul Erdman

This book is printed on acid-free paper.

A Forge Book
Published by Tom Doherty Associates, Inc.
175 Fifth Avenue
New York, N.Y. 10010

Library of Congress Cataloging-in-Publication Data

Erdman, Paul Emil.
    Zero coupon / Paul Erdman.
        p.   cm.
    "A Tom Doherty Associates book."
    ISBN 0-312-85380-7 (hardcover)
    1. Commercial crimes—United States—Fiction. I. Title.
    PS3555.R4Z3   1993
    813'.54—dc20   93-11521
                                                                       CIP

First edition: October 1993

Printed in the United States of America

0 9 8 7 6 5 4 3 2 1

To the three young ladies in my life:
Helly, Conny and Jenny.

ONE

It was high noon at the Federal Correctional Institution in Pleasanton, California. It was hot. William F. Saxon was sitting on the porch outside the main building waiting to be picked up. He'd lived in Pleasanton for three years—in fact for three years and a day. His sentence had been for six years, but good behavior had cut it in half. Plus the fact that he had paid a fine of one hundred million dollars and chipped in another two hundred thirty-five million dollars to settle the myriad of lawsuits that had been brought against him.

So he was broke. Except for that little stash in Liechtenstein. But at least he was once again a free man. And the last three years sure as hell could have been worse. A glance across the grassy mall that lay in front of the porch confirmed that, yet again. For on the other side, just two hundreds yards away, was a Federal maximum security prison for women. It looked like a bunker designed to withstand an atomic bomb. It was surrounded by fifteen-foot-high fences, topped with double intertwined rolls of barbed wire. Guards armed with automatic rifles were constantly patrolling its perimeter in jeeps.

He would be dead by now if he had been put in a place like that.

He glanced at his watch, a Rolex. The Timex he had worn for the past three years he had just given to one of his roommates. At first it had not been easy living with three other guys. But after a few days he had decided that it was no worse than prep school. Even the daily routine was something like it had been at Choate. Up at six-thirty, breakfast at seven, work detail instead of classes at eight, lunch at twelve-fifteen, off work at five, dinner at six, TV at eight, bed at eleven. Weekends off.

But it soon became boring, deadly boring. He'd chosen outside work, and must have mowed the grass on the mall at least three hundred times. Then early last year he'd learned from one of his lawyers that the books from the library at the Presidio would be up for grabs when that army base was closed as a result of budget cutbacks at the Pentagon. So he found three men with carpenter skills, and one who was a bookbinder by hobby. Together they had built the library in Building B. But it was not intended just for the books; he soon had the *Times,* the *Journal, Forbes, Barrons, Fortune, Business Week,* and even the *Economist* and the *Financial Times* from London. The subscriptions were all arranged for through his lawyers. He managed to set up his own desk in his own private corner of the library. And then he had gone back to work— *real* work.

He glanced for the tenth time down the road that led into the prison complex from the outside. Frank was late.

Then he saw it coming. Saxon got up, left the porch and waved at the limo as it approached. Frank had never visited him, and the natural tendency for visitors was to overlook "his" prison, and head for the parking lot adjacent to the women's slammer across the way.

The limo stopped in front of him, and Frank jumped out. The two men embraced quickly, and awkwardly.

As Frank Lipper pulled away, he said, "Lemme look at you Willy. Christ, you've never looked better. What do you weigh?"

■

"A hundred and sixty-five." He was also six feet tall, tanned, and dressed in an Armani suit.

"How come you never let me visit here before?" Frank asked.

"I preferred it that way."

Frank started to look around. "Where exactly did you, uh, stay?"

Saxon pointed to the wooden barracks behind him.

"Where are the fences?"

"There are none. No fences, no locks, no guns. But also no swimming pool or tennis court."

"So why doesn't everybody just take a hike?"

"Because if you do, when they catch you, you get a mandatory extra five years. And not here. In a place like that." And now Saxon pointed to the prison across the mall.

Frank looked, and shuddered. "I think I've already had enough of this, Willy. Let's get out of here. The boys are waiting."

"Just hold on five minutes. I want to say goodbye to the warden. In the meantime, maybe the driver could put my briefcase and suitcase in the trunk. They're on the porch."

The warden was a woman, in her mid-thirties, and good-looking. For all of these reasons she maintained a cool distance from the two hundred eighty-five male inmates under her supervision. When Saxon entered her office, she rose to greet him, but did not shake his hand.

"Everything sorted out with the office?" she asked.

"Yes."

"Then I assume they told you that you're free to leave. Do you have transportation? Otherwise we can have you driven to the airport. I doubt that it will be the bus station in your case."

"Thanks. But there's someone waiting outside for me. I just wanted to come by to tell you how much I appreciated the civilized treatment I received here."

■

"You're welcome." She looked at her watch. "I'm lunching with someone in the cafeteria. Good-bye, Mr. Saxon. And by the way, thanks for organizing the library. Maybe someday we'll name it after you."

He knew he was dismissed, so he left. She had always gone out of her way to be "nice," but he knew that in reality she considered him dirt. The crack about the bus station could not help but once again evoke the memory of the look of utter disdain on the judge's face when he had given him six years—after reminding him of all the advantages he had enjoyed in life, and then misused. Or the smirk on the face of the bailiff when he had cuffed him immediately thereafter. Then the leg-irons he was forced to wear when they "transported" him to Pleasanton.

Five minutes later the limo was on Interstate 580, headed for the Bay Bridge.

"How's it feel?" Frank asked.

"Like it's not real," Saxon replied.

"Everybody says you got screwed, if that's any help."

"It's not."

"Did you spend much time with Michael Milken in there?"

"Not much. He stuck to himself. Anyway, he left Pleasanton quite a while ago. When you've got a half billion dollars left over like he did, you can afford lawyers like Dershowitz, and they get you out early."

"Milken's going around claiming he was just a misunderstood social scientist."

"Weren't we all."

They were passing the sign indicating that Mills College was somewhere up in the hills to the right when Frank again broke the silence.

"I've never had an opportunity to do this before, Willy, so I want do it now. To say thanks."

"For what?"

"For leaving my name out of it."

■

"Oh. You mean the parking operation? Your name was never in. I parked those shares with Ivan Boesky. Period."

"Yeah, but it was my idea."

"As I recall, it was Dan Prescott's idea."

"Well maybe, but I made the initial call to Boesky. And by the way, Dan's going to be at lunch, too. So will Bobby Armacost. Just the four of us, as you suggested when you called me."

"How're they doing?"

"Lousy. Like everybody in the financial business these days. It's nothing like the eighties, Willy. The rich are definitely not getting richer anymore. The fucking Democrats meant what they said when they talked about soaking the rich. Everybody thinks the same; why take a risk and invest in the future if they're going to take all your profits back in new taxes? I know you won't think this is funny, but if you had to take a couple of years off, you sure picked the right ones."

Now they were approaching the Bay Bridge and ten minutes later the limo was entering that part of San Francisco known as North Beach, formerly the destination of thousands of Italian immigrants, and still home to dozens of Italian restaurants.

"Ed Moose opened up another restaurant while you were away," Frank Lipper said. "The crowd that used to go to his old place have all switched. So we thought you'd like to go. For old times' sake."

TWO

The "old" place had been the Washington Square Bar and Grill, the hangout of San Francisco's financial hotshots. For years it had been a second home to the investment bankers who came there from their posh offices on Montgomery Street, to corporate lawyers from their suites in the Embarcadero Center, as well as to just plain stockbrokers on the make. They were usually the last to arrive, since they had to stay at their trading desks until one o'clock, when the markets closed in New York. But the minute the gong sounded on Wall Street, they were out the door headed for their first drink of the day at Moose's.

It was shortly after one o'clock when William Saxon entered the place. The bar was packed three deep. At first only a few heads turned. But as the whispered word spread, the muffled roar of conversation gradually subsided into an eerie hushed silence.

Then a loud voice yelled: "You got fucked, Saxon! Welcome back to the Den of Thieves!" A spontaneous cheer arose from the noontime faithful, and then the boys went right back to what most of them did best: drink.

Ed Moose, the proprietor, now appeared front and center to greet the guest of honor.

"Willy," he said, as he offered his huge Irish paw, "today

■

it's all on the house. But first a celebratory drink. Can I assume that it's still the same?"

Willy Saxon nodded.

The same was an ice-cold Sapphire gin martini with two olives. One appeared seconds later, and Moose presented it as if it were a gift of the gods. Saxon took a tentative sip, and then a real slug. The ceremony had once again caught the attention of the crowd at the bar. And from its midst it was a female voice that this time expressed their collective sentiments.

"Now all you need is a good piece of ass, Willy!"

At the urging of the boys the woman behind the voice—a commodities dealer at Dean Witter known affectionately as Betty the Barracuda—surged forward to plant a juicy kiss on the lips of Willy Saxon, while pressing her ample thighs and boobs against his Armani suit.

Another cheer went up. The proprietor, sensing that it was time to move on, rescued Saxon from the clutches of his admirer and led him into the adjacent dining room. Frank Lipper trailed behind.

"Your two friends are waiting," Moose explained. "I've got you at the family table."

Both men rose when they saw Saxon approaching. In turn they shook his hand, and briefly embraced him, while murmuring words of welcome.

"The champagne's on the way, gentlemen," the Irish proprietor of this Italian restaurant declared. "Enjoy."

"Let's sit down," Saxon said. "I think I've had enough of the clowning around."

"They all like you, Willy," Dan Prescott said, as he took his place opposite Saxon. "In contrast to Milken and Boesky and Levine you took your medicine and kept your mouth shut. They admire that. So do I."

"Thanks for the words," Saxon replied. "And thanks for

■

showing up. I can imagine that not all of your partners are going to be overjoyed when they hear about it."

The partners he referred to were principals in the investment banking firm of Prescott & Quackenbush, regarded as one of San Francisco's finest, ranking right up there on the local scene with Hambrecht & Quist, and Montgomery Securities.

"Ditto for you," Saxon said to Bobby Armacost, the other man who had been waiting at the table.

"As a lawyer, I can only echo the sentiments of my colleague from the investment banking community," Armacost replied. "What's done is done. Your slate's clean. That's the American way."

For the first time since entering the restaurant, Frank Lipper spoke up. "That sounds great, Bobby, but I'm not so sure the SEC will buy it."

Dan Prescott jumped in. "Now Frank, for Christ sake, why put a damper on . . ."

Saxon interrupted. "Leave him alone, Dan. I'm banned for life from the securities industry."

"Hold on," Bobby Armacost, the lawyer, said. "You're banned for life from acting as a broker or dealer in the United States. But you're as free as I am to invest, advise, consult— you name it."

"So do you think that Goldman, Sachs is going to beg me to join their board?" Saxon asked. "Or, for that matter, Prescott and Quackenbush?"

That produced a lull until Dan Prescott spoke. "I don't think you'd want to come on the board of Prescott and Quackenbush, Willy. We've got a lawsuit on our hands that's eating us up. When we settle—and we're not going to have any choice, as Bobby can tell you, since he's also involved— our capital is going to be totally wiped out."

"What's the problem?"

"We took a biotech company public two years ago. The

■

investors claim that we misrepresented their R and D in the prospectus. You know, stuff like their being close to a potential cure for AIDS, when it turns out that none of their products can even relieve a headache. We got led down the garden path by the company's founder, and now we're going to have to pay the price."

"What about the founder?"

"He shot himself."

"Then what about the law firm that did the due diligence?" It was the Willy Saxon of old who was now talking.

Dan Prescott, instead of replying, just pointed his right thumb to the man sitting beside him.

"That's right," Bobby Armacost said. "Me. We're chipping in with all we've got. And then some."

Willy Saxon's face did not mask his skepticism and Armacost saw it. "All right, Willy. There was more. Like outright fraud. The company booked income from licensing agreements they were making all around the world—Japan, U.K., Switzerland, you name it. Only guess what? All phony. They were just dressing up their financial statements."

"So how could anybody claim that you knew?"

"Dan and I were on the board."

"They told me it was a fucking jungle out here," Willy Saxon said, "but if I had known it was this bad I might have stayed a while longer in Pleasanton."

That got the mood back on track. The arrival of the champagne helped things further. When the speciality of the house, Fettuccine Alfredo, came shortly thereafter, accompanied by a chilled bottle of Pinot Grigio, they were all reminiscing about the good old days of the 1980s before it all fell apart.

"Remember, Willy, how we managed to flog that half billion in junk bonds issued by that fucking dog department store chain in Texas?" Frank Lipper asked. Frank had been Willy Saxon's right-hand man at Saxon & Co. before it

■

folded. Since then he had been working as a bond salesman with Dan Prescott's firm.

"Only because Dan helped us stuff half of it into that S and L in Denver."

"Was that the one where Bush's son was on the board?"

"No. That was Silverado Savings. Good name, actually. We used Mile High S and L for that one."

"And in the meantime, it blew up more than a mile high," Bobby added.

"Anybody go to jail?" Willy asked.

"Naw. They said it was your fault."

"Everybody forgets the ones that worked out," Dan Prescott said. "Look at Safeway. It's doing better than ever."

"But that was Milken's deal," Willy said. "And by the way, the chairman of Safeway didn't forget. Peter McGowen visited Milken in Pleasanton every single week. But that's all water over the dam."

Then he switched gears. "How much capital are you going to need to get Prescott and Quackenbush back on its feet, Dan?"

"First we've got to have the settlement in place. Otherwise it would be like throwing money down a bottomless pit."

"So when's that going to happen?"

"Ask Bobby."

"A month. Give or take," Bobby said.

"OK. Then how much?" he asked Prescott.

"Ten million. Fifteen would be better," the investment banker answered. "But these days, forget about it. Not even Houdini could come up with that amount of money in today's market. Anyway, even if we could raise it, we'd have to give away the store to whoever put up the new equity. After the settlement, we're all going to be broke."

"What about any other aftereffects?" Willy asked, addressing the question to the lawyer.

"You mean are we damaged goods? I really don't think so.

■

Everybody in the industry knows that we got taken," Bobby Armacost answered.

"All right, next question," Willy said. "Are there any laws or regulations against offshore money coming into an investment bank like Prescott and Quackenbush and assuming a controlling equity position?"

"None that I know of. If we were talking about a commercial bank, the law now says that the Fed must approve any foreign participation over five percent. But no such provisions apply to investment banks," Armacost replied.

"Even if the money came from Liechtenstein?" Willy asked.

" '*Pecunium non olit*,' " the lawyer answered, " 'Money has no odor.' But it wouldn't hurt if there was a good name attached to the money."

"Would that of a corporation whose chairman is the son of the Prince of Liechtenstein do?"

"Admirably."

"OK. Next question," Willy Saxon said. "Have any of you heard of a guy by the name of Sid—must be Sidney—Ravitch?"

"Sure," the investment banker said. "He rates bonds. Used to be with Moody's. He left there about two years ago and bought control of a smaller firm that does the same thing. In fact, he runs it."

"That's right," Frank Lipper, the bond salesman, said. "It's the Western Credit Rating Agency. Their head office is right here in San Francisco, in the Russ Building."

"His reputation?" Willy asked.

"Never been questioned as far as I know," Armacost answered. "Why?"

"A friend of his was—still is—in Pleasanton."

"For what?"

"Out-and-out securities fraud. He was selling options on gold bullion he held in a warehouse in Vancouver. If you sent him five thousand dollars, you had a claim on one hundred

■

ounces of gold. If gold went up a hundred dollars an ounce and you exercised your option, you doubled your money. And the beauty of it all was that the option never expired."

"What's illegal about that?" the lawyer asked.

"Nothing. Except that there was no gold in the warehouse. In fact, there was not even a warehouse. The only gold in the entire operation was that used for the embossment on the prospectus. It was a beauty. This guy was so proud of it he kept a copy in his room in Pleasanton and liked to show it around."

"How'd he get caught?"

"When gold finally moved up, a lot of his investors tried to exercise their options. Which prompted my former colleague in Pleasanton to take a hike. To Canada, where he came from in the first place. The Mounties picked him up in Toronto and sent him back."

"And what's Sid Ravitch got to do with it?"

"According to this guy, he wrote the prospectus," Willy replied. "Which made them silent partners, I guess. Very silent."

Low whistles all around.

"I don't want to go into detail now," Willy added, "but the whole thing gave me an idea."

Nobody chose to pursue it further.

Desert and coffee arrived just then, and while it was being served Willy Saxon leaned across the table and, in a low voice, spoke to Dan Prescott.

"Who's that lady in the red dress at the next table? For the past half hour she's been looking at us."

"I noticed it too," Prescott replied. "I'm surprised you don't know her. But then again, as I recall, you had little time for her crowd. Her claim to fame is that she's very big in San Francisco society. Naturally, she's loaded. Her late husband expired last year of old age and left her his company, plus, it's said, fifty million in cash and securities. That's on top of the

■

mansion in Pacific Heights, the ranch in Mendocino County, and the beach house on Maui."

"Why's she keep looking our way?"

"She collects interesting people. No doubt somebody told her who you were, after your tumultuous reception."

"What's her name?"

"Denise van Bercham. Her late husband stemmed from Dutch aristocracy. They were into chocolate and coffee—the Dutch East Indies and all that. His branch of the family settled in San Francisco at the turn of the century. Which qualified him—and now her—as old money."

"What about her?"

"Of less certain ancestry," the investment banker replied. "Rumor has it that she's the illegitimate child of a wealthy Eastern-European landowner's daughter and a member of the Romanian royal family. She vehemently denies this. Adding credence to the story, however, is the fact that before she first arrived here about ten years ago, she was often seen in the company of 'royals' in Europe."

"How old is she? She doesn't look much older than . . ."

Dan Prescott interrupted. "Look out. Her table is starting to break up and she's coming this way."

Prescott rose to greet the lady in red with the obligatory air kisses on both cheeks.

"My dear Dan," she said, "It's been ages."

She then looked directly at Willy Saxon, and, as he rose to his feet, said, "I don't believe we've met."

"Willy Saxon," he said, and took her extended hand in his. Hers stayed a brief moment longer than was normally called for.

"My late husband spoke about you on various occasions. I believe you are in finance."

"Was," Willy said.

Denise liked that.

"I'm giving a lunch tomorrow at Stars restaurant. One

■

o'clock. There were to be six of us. It will now be seven if you would care to join us."

"Why not? What's the occasion, if I may ask?"

"None in particular. Do be on time. I insist on that."

"I can assure you, Mrs. van Bercham, that I always come on time."

She chose to smile at the double entendre. She extended her hand once again to Willy Saxon, and ignoring everyone else at his table, turned and left.

"Who the fuck was that?" Frank Lipper asked, once Willy and Dan Prescott had regained their seats.

"Probably the most powerful dame in San Francisco," Prescott replied. "She makes 'em and breaks 'em in this town. I'm not so sure you were smart in accepting that invitation, Willy."

"I disagree," Armacost said. "If Denise van Bercham gives you her benediction, you'll be accepted all over this city, and beyond. That would be in *all* of our interests." And as he said this, he shot a warning glance at Dan Prescott.

"You're right, Bobby," Prescott now said.

"Let's get back to business for a minute," Willy Saxon said, "I'd appreciate your keeping me up-to-date on how Prescott and Quackenbush's settlement negotiations are proceeding. You said they should be wrapped up within a month. That's about right, where I'm concerned. I've got some work to do that will take me at least that long, too."

Then he looked at his watch.

"I've got to check into my hotel before it gets too late."

"Where are you going to stay?" Dan Prescott asked.

"The Huntington. Frank arranged it."

"If you're ready to go now, I've got the limo waiting right outside," Frank Lipper said. "I'll come along to make sure everything's all right, Willy."

"OK. Let's go."

The four men rose from the table.

■

"I think Bobby and I will stay for another coffee," Dan Prescott said.

"Sure," Willy said. "We'll keep in touch. I can't tell you how much it means to me having buddies like you. I've got a good feeling about the future. We've all had some tough luck lately, but from now on that's going to change."

With that, Saxon headed for the door. Frank Lipper, as usual, trailed slightly behind.

"What a guy," Bobby Armacost said, as he and Dan Prescott sat down once again. "Tell me, how did he rank in your business in the 1980s?"

"Right up there with the big boys. Smaller than Milken— everybody was—but a hell of a lot bigger than Boyd Jeffries or that guy Levine. Even Boesky. It got to the point where if Willie made less than a hundred million it was a really bad year."

"So there's got to be enough left over."

"Obviously. But now I've got a question for you, and I'd appreciate it if you'd tell me straight," Prescott said. "In your opinion as a lawyer, how big a *crook* would you say he was?"

"As compared to whom?"

"Let's say Boesky was a ten. And Milken an eight."

"How about Robert Maxwell over in England?"

"Probably an eleven."

"OK," Armacost said. "I'd put Willy Saxon at a three. He never stole, *really* stole, a nickel for himself. He just got carried away with playing the game. Had to outperform everybody in the business even if it meant cutting corners, like parking shares or slightly doctoring up balance sheets."

"So it was not a hell of a lot different than . . ."

"Than what we did? Or at least what we went along with. Right."

"One more thing, Bobby. How come you didn't tell Willy what you told me, before he got here?"

"Because it is just a very vague rumor."

■

"Still. If they really go after us on criminal charges . . ."

"They might try, Dan. But believe me, with a case this complicated, it will take many months, even years, before they could come up with anything close to an indictment that would stick. So there's no use our worrying Willy about something that remote. Right?"

"I guess so."

■

THREE

At one o'clock sharp the next day, William Saxon's taxi pulled up in the alley where the main entrance to Stars restaurant is located. Once inside he told the young lady who asked about his reservation that Denise van Bercham was expecting him.

That set off an inaudible red alert that almost immediately produced Jeremiah Tower, founder and chef extraordinaire of the biggest and best brasserie west of Paris.

"You must be William Saxon," Tower said. "Please follow me."

They walked through the packed main restaurant to the slightly raised terrace at the other end. This was obviously reserved for Jeremiah's special clients, a haven where they could enjoy semi-privacy reasonably remote from the middle class seated three steps below. Their final destination was the corner table, where Denise van Bercham and five other ladies were already seated. She was at the end of the table facing the entire restaurant. When she spotted Willy Saxon approaching, she pointed to the empty chair to her right. As he took his place she offered her cheek, and then took charge.

"This is my new friend, William Saxon," she announced. "He is very smart where money is concerned."

That caused a ripple among the ladies. They all had older husbands, in most cases much older, and knew that some day,

■

hopefully soon, the burden of properly managing their inherited millions would fall on their fragile shoulders. Thus any opportunity to get financial advice, especially free advice, was always welcome.

"He just got out of prison," she continued. "Yesterday."

That caused more than just a ripple.

"But as my dear husband told me before . . ." Denise paused out of respect before continuing, ". . . he left us, Mr. Saxon was no more guilty of criminal activity than he was."

His innocence having been established, Willy Saxon nodded his appreciation, and was saved from having to add anything further on the subject by the arrival of the waiter

"Drink, sir?"

"Sapphire Bombay gin martini, two olives," he said, an order which produced looks of respect for the manliness of his choice.

Denise van Bercham proceeded to introduce her other guests in rapid fire. The woman directly across from Willy then leaned forward and asked, "Do you mind telling us which prison you were in?"

"The Federal Correctional Institution in Pleasanton," Saxon answered, and he could immediately sense the table-wide disappointment. They had hoped for a *real* prison like San Quentin. So he added, "Michael Milken was there also."

That was better.

"Did you get to know him?" the woman asked.

"Actually, I knew him before. We both worked in the same field—junk bonds."

"How very interesting," the woman—her name, if Willy remembered correctly, was Sally—said. "My husband insists that Milken never should have gone to prison either. That he financed companies that couldn't get money anywhere else and that's one reason why everybody prospered in the 1980s. What do you think?"

"Sally's husband was in oil," Denise interjected.

■

"I guess one could make a case for that," Saxon answered.

Now the woman to Willy's right spoke up. "My husband says that they sent Milken to jail because the establishment on Wall Street couldn't stand a Jew moving onto their turf and making a half billion dollars a year."

"Lois's husband is in textiles," Denise explained.

Then a rather statuesque woman seated at the other end of the table spoke up. "That's all rubbish. Milken deserved everything he got, and much more."

She was the Episcopal bishop's daughter who had married the CEO of one of the largest mining operations in the United States—now also deceased. She never dressed in anything that had not been created by Karl Lagerfeld, Bill Blass, or Gianfranco Ferre; never rode in anything but a Rolls or a Ferrari. Yet, she was a screaming liberal who never missed an opportunity to demonstrate it.

"In the beginning," she continued, "Milken probably did some good. But after he ran out of good companies deserving of being financed, he started floating junk bonds for corporations that were already doomed to failure. That's why no respectable banking house would touch them. Then he dumped the junk bonds with his buddies who ran the savings and loans, like that Keating fellow. Everybody involved collected enormous bribes, disguised as fees, to go along with the game. And they'd still be doing it if the government hadn't shut them down. Now we taxpayers are stuck with a half-trillion-dollar bill to bail out the S and L's. And Milken is living somewhere in the lap of luxury after 'suffering' for a couple of years over in that country club in Pleasanton."

An embarrassed silence followed, which was, however, almost immediately broken by Denise van Bercham announcing that everybody was going to have salad niçoise and sole meunière for lunch. She told the waiter who was standing by to pour the wine, and, as soon as her glass was full, emptied half of it.

■

Then she leaned over to Willy Saxon and whispered, "Ignore that bitch. She hasn't been laid in five years, and this is how she gets her kicks."

To further demonstrate her sympathy, Denise's right hand moved and gave a reassuring squeeze to Willy's left arm.

"I hope you don't mind, Mr. Saxon, but I would like to ask another question about that place in Pleasanton." It was Sally again. "Do they allow conjugal visits?"

"Yes they do," Willy replied, "although in my case that situation did not arise."

Oh, oh. Was he . . . ?

"You see," Willy continued, "my wife divorced me shortly before I arrived in Pleasanton."

That was better.

"How often?" Sally asked.

Denise interrupted before Willy could answer. "I think that's quite enough on that particular subject, Sally." She looked around the entire table for emphasis. "Now I have some very important news about the opera. As you all know, I have assumed Jacob's place on its board of directors. We intend to open the season with *La Traviata,* but until now were not sure who would play the male lead. I can now tell you that Gordon Getty and I have managed to get Pavarotti."

That took them through both the salad and the fish. It also allowed Willy Saxon to just listen, and watch. He paid particular attention to Denise van Bercham.

She was probably just a shade under fifty—four or five years older than he was. Her flawless features—especially the absolutely perfect nose—had no doubt gotten a little help from a cosmetic surgeon. From the way her breasts filled out the white blouse, it was doubtful whether she had needed any help in that department. Her waist was tiny, but in contrast to at least two of the ladies at the table, there was no hint of anorexia in Denise van Bercham. She had a full head of dark,

■

flowing hair, and from what he had seen of her legs at the restaurant the day before, she had nothing to be ashamed of there either. Denise van Bercham was one hell of a woman, Willy concluded, and as feminine as they get—with one exception: the eyes. They were steely blue-grey, and didn't miss a thing. In fact, Willy was sure that Denise was fully aware that she was being subjected to a full body scan. He suspected that she was also enjoying it.

By the time coffee came along, they had finally exhausted the topic of Pavarotti and who would get to put on the lunches and dinners for him during his stay in town. Denise's imprimatur sealed any arrangements, since only she could be counted on to personally deliver "my good friend Luciano" at the appointed times and places. For, as she made amply clear, it was she who would be making Pavarotti's travel arrangements. Both her G-4 and Gordon's 727 would be put at his disposal. That raised the specter of Gordon's wife, Ann, trying to muscle in. But Denise had already anticipated that. She would make sure, she told the ladies, that Luciano flew *in* on *her* plane, and *out* on Gordon's.

She finally turned her attention back to Willy Saxon. "I'm afraid we've been boring you, William. Before we break up, I think we all would like to hear your opinion on the financial markets, wouldn't we?"

The ladies collectively agreed.

"May I ask a question?" It was the bishop's daughter.

Although she had fallen from grace as a result of her earlier tirade on Milken, Denise nevertheless nodded her assent.

"My broker says that the next general slowdown will probably begin next year, meaning that corporate profits are bound to fall off dramatically. When people start to realize what's happening, they are going to pull their money out of the stock market by the tens of billions. So he says, if you're smart, you'll get out now. Do you agree?"

"I agree with both the diagnosis and the conclusion," Willy

■

answered. "Although I would not necessarily sell all my stocks tomorrow morning. Make your broker earn his money. Tell him to come up with a plan."

"But," Sally said, "if you get out of the stock market, where do you put your money?"

"Into a money market fund," said one of the two anorexic women who had hardly said a word thus far, perhaps due to her weakened condition. "It's safe."

"And get less than four percent?" said the bishop's daughter. "Are you kidding!"

Denise stepped in. "Let William talk."

"Well, in a way, all of you are right," Saxon said. "Yes, we're headed for another recession. And yes, if you're smart you'll get out of the stock market before everybody else does. When you do, you'll want to play it safe, and a money market fund is as safe a place to park money as there is. But as was pointed out, you only get four percent. The rate of inflation is almost that. So, in essence, you'll make nothing."

"Then what about bonds?" Denise asked.

"You're getting close. Bonds, especially long-term bonds, are probably what you should be thinking about. But not corporate bonds. When the recession hits, if it's a deep one, a lot of corporations are bound to get into trouble, And when they do, their bonds—and I'm not talking just about junk bonds—are also going to get into trouble."

"So the place to be will be T-bonds," said the bishop's daughter.

"Partially right. You'll want to be in government-backed securities for safety, but the yields on T-bonds are not very exciting. Furthermore, the interest on them is taxable."

No one at the table was in favor of paying taxes, so he now had their undivided attention.

"Tax-free municipal bonds. That's what you want to be looking at. Most of them—the so-called general obligation bonds—have governmental backing, so they're safe. They have relatively high yields—a lot higher than anything you can get in a money market fund. And if you buy the right ones, you pay neither Federal nor state taxes. If you need further proof, just look where Ross Perot has most of his billions, or for that matter, Denise, your friend Gordon Getty. Tax-free municipals. Just ask them."

Having just paid for his lunch, Willy Saxon looked at his watch. Sensing what he was about to say, Denise beat him to the punch.

"Ladies, it's time to adjourn. But before we do, I think we would all like to thank Mr. Saxon for sharing his thoughts with us. We must do this again, don't you think?"

That evoked murmurs of unanimous agreement, as everybody began to rise from the table.

"Do you have a car here?" Denise asked Willy.

"No. I came by cab."

"Then you'll need a ride."

"That would be nice. I'm staying at the Huntington. Would that be out of your way?"

"Of course not."

Denise's driver had the Bentley waiting outside when she and Willy emerged.

"How long do you intend to stay at the Huntington?" she asked, as they left the alley and headed for Nob Hill.

"Until I find an apartment."

"Perhaps I can help."

"I certainly could use some help."

"In fact, we—or rather I—own a very nice apartment building right across the park from the Huntington. You get your own floor and elevator stop, and there's room for servants. My husband was very fussy about whom he would lease to. So you can be sure that only the right people live there."

"But would anything be free?"

"If not, something could be made free," she responded. "That's the apartment over there, on the other side of the

■

park," Denise said, as they pulled up in front of the Huntington hotel.

She leaned across Willy in order to be able to point it out. As she went on to extol the merits of the location—comparing it to the coops on Park Avenue and Central Park in New York, and those *appartements* overlooking the Jardin Luxembourg in Paris—her breasts remained pressed against him. He could not help but think back on what Denise had said about the bishop's daughter: that she had not been laid for five years.

For that matter, he hadn't been laid for three years. And although Denise's age might exceed his by five years, he had always wanted to see if what they said about older women was really true.

"Perhaps you would care to come into the Big Four bar for a drink?" he asked.

"I never drink in bars, my dear," she said. "I'll call about that apartment."

FOUR

At four that afternoon, punctual as usual, Willy Saxon walked into the head office of the Western Credit Rating Agency, which was located on the seventeenth floor of the Russ Building, on Montgomery Street.

In keeping with what the company did, its offices were anything but luxurious. They had been decorated and furnished in a way intended to give the initial visitor a feeling of clinical efficiency, of thorough, though low-key, professionalism. Even the receptionist was dressed in a rather severe grey suit that looked more like something you would get at Brooks Brothers than at a boutique.

"My name's William Saxon. I have a four o'clock appointment with your Mr. Ravitch."

"Yes, sir. He's expecting you." She rose from behind her desk and led him down a corridor into a spacious office at the end, one with a commanding view of San Francisco Bay.

Willy Saxon had been prepared to thoroughly dislike the person he was now to meet for the first time. But as the large man approached him, grasped his hand and pumped it three times—all with a huge smile on his face—he knew that it was not going to be easy. This feeling was reinforced by Sidney Ravitch's words.

"Lenny Newsom has told me all about you, Mr. Saxon. He says that, beyond any doubt, you were the best guy of the

■

whole gang over there in Pleasanton. So it's a great pleasure for me to finally be able to meet you in person. Take a seat."

They both took a seat at the coffee table, where a pot of coffee and two cups awaited them. Willy placed his thin attaché case on the floor beside his chair.

"No sugar or cream for me," Willy said, as Ravitch began to pour.

"I just talked to Lenny yesterday," Ravitch said. "He phoned to tell me that you left him your Macintosh computer. He's like a big kid, you know. For him it was like getting a new toy for Christmas."

"Now," Ravitch continued, "what brings you here, Mr. Saxon?"

"Strictly business. As you no doubt know, my whole background and experience is in finance. For the moment—because of what happened—it will take a while before I can get back into the game directly. So I'm looking for ways to do so indirectly."

"Like?"

"Like investing rather than managing."

"And you thought our company might be able to help you find such an investment?"

"No. I thought maybe you might be interested in having me as an investor in your company, Mr. Ravitch," Willy Saxon replied.

"Sidney, please. Or even better, Sid," Ravitch said. "What makes you think we need a new investor?"

"I did a lot of homework over in Pleasanton. You see, I helped organize the library over there, and was able to develop access to all the financial data I needed, if necessary by tapping into the Dow Jones Retrieval System, using a modem and the Macintosh your friend Lenny has just inherited."

"What did your research tell you about us?"

"First, that you are a member of a very elite club. That the credit rating business in this country—in fact, in the world—is

■

restricted to just a handful of companies. Everybody knows about Moody's and Standard and Poors. But some of the smaller ones, like Fitch Investor Services, or your company, are really only known by the professionals in the investment business."

"What else?"

"That rating agencies wield enormous influence. In fact, there was an article in one of last week's *Financial Times* that said that together you represent one of the most powerful groups in the international financial markets."

"But you must have realized that when you worked in the business," Ravitch said.

"You're right. I should have. But don't forget: my specialty was junk bonds. We couldn't have cared less about ratings. Junk is junk. Our stuff was light years removed from being rated Triple-A. We couldn't even get a rating on most of the bonds we took to market. People bought them for other reasons."

"Makes sense. Anything else?"

"Yes. It seems that your industry is completely unregulated. As I understand it, the fact that the SEC recognizes you gives your ratings such powerful standing that you can make or break a bond issue. But they never vet you—no audits, no nothing."

"That's right. And it's because we have a very good record. Maybe not impeccable, but nothing has ever happened that was bad enough to give sufficient cause for any governmental interference," Ravitch said. "But you still haven't answered my question. Why do you think *we* need a new outside investor?"

"Perhaps because of this."

Saxon reached down for his attaché case, opened it, and extracted a brochure that immediately caught one's attention due to the rather gaudy gold embossing on its cover.

Ravitch's face turned red the moment he recognized it.

■

"Lenny gave you that?" he demanded.

"No. I borrowed it. Lenny was so proud of it he always kept it in the top drawer of his desk. His room was across the corridor from mine."

"So you stole it."

"As I already said, Sid, I borrowed it."

"All right, let's leave that be for the moment. What exactly do you want from me?"

"I already told you. I want to invest in your company."

"I don't . . ."

Saxon interrupted him. "Please hear me out, Sid. As I said earlier, I've done my homework. And I don't mean what Lenny told me. Your strength has been that your agency has been a big fish in a small pond. You stick to California, Oregon, and Washington and leave the rest of the country and the world to the big boys. Right?"

"You've got it. We know every municipality—big, small, or tiny—in our territory like nobody else."

"But now you've got a problem," Saxon stated. "The big boys—your old firm, Moody's, as well as Standard and Poors—have begun to invade your backyard. Since Standard and Poors is owned by McGraw Hill, and Moody's by Dun and Bradstreet, they both have deep pockets. They can muscle into your territory even if it means running losses in the process. You don't have deep pockets, Sid. In fact, if my information is correct, you are running into a cash flow problem. I'm in a position to take care of that problem. And maybe come up with an idea or two that could make our firm a lot more money in the future."

"So it's already 'our firm,' is it?" Ravitch said.

"Sid, and I mean this sincerely, if you don't want to talk about it any further, I'm out of here. Right now. You can keep Lenny's brochure. And we will both forget this conversation ever took place. OK?"

■

Sidney Ravitch got up from the coffee table, and went to the window.

"How much are you proposing to invest?" He kept gazing out the window as he said it.

"Ten million."

"All cash?"

"All cash."

"All cash now?"

"All cash within thirty days."

"How much of the company do you expect to get for your ten million?"

"Forty-nine percent. And an option to buy the rest."

Sidney Ravitch now turned from the window to face Willy Saxon.

"You've really thought this through, haven't you?"

"All the way."

"All right," and now Sid Ravitch reassumed his place at the coffee table opposite Willy, "where's that money going to come from?"

"Abroad."

"In whose name?"

"Not mine."

"That's good. But then whose?

"That would depend where it came from. As long as my name is left out of it, does it really matter?"

"It matters, and I'll tell you why. You're right. We're not subject to regulatory oversight by the SEC. But that might change. There's a congressman from Michigan by the name of John Dingell pressing for it right now. He's chairman of the House commerce committee and one mean, suspicious son of a bitch. All I need is to get him on my back."

"All right. How about if I use a bank in the Bahamas?"

"Willy," Sid said. "You might not think so, but, despite your library and modem over there in Pleasanton, you're not yet fully back in touch with current realities in this business."

■

35

"What's that supposed to mean?" Willy asked.

"The Bahamas is a sieve. Look what happened to Dennis Levine. He thought he was completely safe using the Nassau subsidiary of a Swiss bank, the Bank Leu, as a front for the insider trading he engaged in while working on Wall Street. He assumed that he was covered by the bank secrecy laws of *both* countries. He found out differently. When they finally caught up with him, the Feds put the pressure on the Bahamian government and the bank, and both completely caved in. They not only turned over every nickel Levine had made—and if I recall correctly, it was about eleven million dollars—but they also provided the paperwork that put Levine in Lewiston for seventeen months. It would have been a lot more, but Levine cut a deal and finked on everybody he'd ever dealt with."

Sidney Ravitch was obviously a student of such matters.

"If you need further convincing," he continued, "go back to Pleasanton and have another talk with our mutual friend, Lenny. He used the Cayman Islands' branch of the Royal Bank of Canada's subsidiary in Nassau and suffered exactly the same fate as Levine. They took all his money, and sent him to prison for three years."

But, Willy thought, they didn't get *your* money, did they. You must have stashed your share of the "profits" from that gold options scam somewhere else. And then used it to buy into this credit rating company.

"All right, how about using a British corporation domiciled in the Channel Islands?" Willy asked.

"That's better. What about board representation?"

"The company's secretary is a senior partner with one of the most prestigious firms of solicitors in London. I'm told they advise Prince Charles. I assume he would be acceptable."

Ravitch liked that. "You're one smart cookie, Willy. I'm surprised they caught you."

■

"So was I, Sid. We all used to joke and say it could happen to any of us, but . . ."

"Yeah. 'There but for the grace of God go I.' "

Willy was starting to genuinely like the man. Ravitch knew that *he* knew about his entanglement with Lenny and their phony gold scheme. Yet rather than come out with some bullshit, Ravitch was willing to admit that he had just barely dodged a bullet of the same type that had sent both Lenny and him to Pleasanton.

There probably was something else too. He had tried to find out why Ravitch had left Moody's so abruptly before coming to this much smaller agency. But everybody had clammed up.

"All right," Ravitch said. "I think we have the elements of a deal, Willy. Let's talk timing."

■

FIVE

By the time Willy got back to the Huntington hotel it was almost seven in the evening. He stood for a few moments in the lobby thinking over his next move. He decided it would be a drink in the hotel bar, which was named after the four robber barons who had struck it rich in San Francisco in the late nineteenth century.

The bartender in the Big Four was an ex-cop by the name of Bob. He was usually into sports, and, depending on the season, would entertain bets on anything from the Giants to the A's to the Warriors to the '49ers to the Sharks. This evening he was into his other specialty, trivia. The subject: obscure capitals of countries, states, provinces, cantons—you name it. Challenging him were the regulars.

"Prince Edward Island," said one, as Willy slid onto the only empty stool, at the end of the bar.

"Charlottetown," came the immediate response.

"Vermont."

"Montpelier."

"Liechtenstein."

Pause.

"Vaduz," Willy said.

Everybody at the bar looked at him.

"All right," Bob said, "your turn to ask one. By the way, what's your name?"

■

"Willy."

"OK. Shoot, Willy."

"Upper Volta."

The bar lay silent.

"We give up," Bob said.

"Ouagadougou."

"Spell it," Bob demanded.

Willy did, as Bob reached into a cupboard below the cash register, pulled out a dog-eared atlas, and began to page through it.

"You're right," the bartender finally said.

"Give the man a drink," said one of the men at the other end of the bar.

"By the way, Willy, you wouldn't by any chance be Willy Saxon?"

"That's me."

"No shit," the man said. "I'm Jerry McGrath. Used to be with Dean Witter when you were doing your stuff. You've been away for a while, right?"

"Three years and one day," Willy replied.

"Give the man two drinks, Bob."

It was eight o'clock before Willy was able to finally excuse himself from his newly-found fan club. He now knew what his next move would be. Except that it was four o'clock in the morning in Vaduz. Plus, he'd had a bit too much to drink. Furthermore, he didn't want to make a phone call to Liechtenstein that could be traced back to his room. So he picked up the phone and dialed room service instead, ordering a ham sandwich and a Beck's beer. It arrived ten minutes later. After he had eaten, Willy set the alarm clock for 11:45 p.m. and lay down for a nap.

It was just before midnight when Willy left the lobby of the Huntington hotel and headed down California Street. The fog had come in, and the temperature must have plummeted into the forties, so it was hardly the night for a lengthy nocturnal

■

stroll. There were four other big hotels on Nob Hill: the Mark Hopkins, the Stanford Court, the Ritz Carlton, and the Fairmont. Willy wanted the one that was close, preferably also one with lots of late night lobby traffic. His mind was immediately made up for him as he approached the Fairmont. There were four tour buses in front of it, disgorging hundreds of noisy conventioneers.

Halfway down the corridor that led from the main hotel to the Fairmont Tower, there was the phone booth he'd been looking for. He took a slip of paper our of his wallet, and, consulting it, began dialing: 01-41-75-433-4981-#.

"May I help you?" the international operator in New York asked.

"Please. A collect call to Vaduz, Liechtenstein. For Dr. Werner Guggi, spelled G U G G I."

"And your name?"

"William Randolph Hearst." It was the first one that had come to mind when, years ago, Guggi had suggested he use a false name when communicating with him by phone from the United States.

The line went dead as the operator began to do her stuff. Ten seconds, fifteen, twenty. What if Guggi was dead? Twenty-five, thirty. Then the phone came alive again.

"Willy! This is Werner Guggi. What a surprise!"

"I hope not an unpleasant one."

"No, no, no! Just unexpected. Where are you?"

"Not where I was. I want to come and see you, Werner."

"But of course. When?"

Willy made up his mind right then. "Thursday."

"That's very short notice, I must say," the Liechtenstein lawyer replied. "Let me look at my agenda."

I entrusted him with sixty million dollars of my money and he's got to consult his fucking agenda!

A few seconds later: "I'm afraid Thursday's a full day for me, Willy."

■

"Then let's meet in the evening." Willy said, trying to hold on to his temper.

"That should be possible, yes. Let's have dinner together. Say at seven. At the Gasthof zum Sternen in Vaduz. You must remember it."

"Of course. Could you book a room for me there?"

"Certainly. Anything else?"

"Not now. I trust you will have some numbers to show me."

"But of course. At least the numbers that will concern you."

"Good. Then, until Thursday night at seven at the Gasthof."

"Auf Wiedersehen."

There was a bar featuring Dixieland music off the corridor, and Willy Saxon headed right for it. There was nobody there but the bartender.

"Sapphire Bombay gin martini straight up, two olives."

For the first time since he'd left Pleasanton, he had a queasy feeling in his gut. What had Guggi meant by that last crack? He would bring the numbers "that concern you." What might the numbers be that would *not* concern him?

It was not as if he'd picked Dr. Werner Guggi out of the Liechtenstein Yellow Pages. He had been put onto him by no less than Dr. Rudolph Schweizer, the Chairman of the Board of the Union Bank of Switzerland, Switzerland's largest, and, since he was now into credit ratings, only one of five banks on earth given a AAA rating by both Moody's and Standard & Poors.

Over the years, he'd built up a good working relationship with that Swiss gnome, as well as a hefty balance with his bank. The balance came from underwriting fees related to the issue of offshore junk bonds, an area in which he, Willy Saxon, had been a genuine pioneer.

The opening had come in 1985, when the Swiss authorities decided to allow non-Swiss banking entities to form under-

■

writing syndicates in their country. Before that the Big Three Swiss commercial banks had had a monopoly on the issuance of bonds denominated in Swiss francs, and a policy preventing all but the highest-quality issues from being launched in Switzerland.

With the arrival of Willy Saxon on the scene in Zurich, that monopoly, that policy, and that quality were soon things of the past.

Willy had immediately established a *Finanzgesellschaft,* a form of banking corporation that, under Swiss law, could do anything a commercial bank could do except solicit deposits from the public. Then he had gone to Rudolph Schweizer. His pitch: you put up the seed capital, and provide some customers for my wares, and I'll provide the junk bond know-how, and the client companies that want to issue them. We'll split the profits fifty-fifty. If you want to remain a silent partner to protect your unsullied reputation for quality, that's fine with me.

UBS had done the deal with him immediately, and had chosen to go the silent route. Willy Saxon had likewise decided to be as invisible a beneficiary of the new joint venture as possible. That had led to Liechtenstein and the good Herr Doktor Werner Guggi.

Their first meeting had occurred in early February of 1985, in the restaurant of the Gasthof zum Sternen in Vaduz.

"It is a great pleasure to meet you," had been the first words of the Liechtenstein lawyer. "You must realize that you come with the highest possible recommendation."

"Herr Doktor Schweizer asked me to give you his regards," Willy had countered.

"You drink wine?" Guggi had then asked.

"Certainly."

"Would you like to try a local one?"

The local one was a not-too-bad Johannesberg Riesling.

■

"Now, I assume you are familiar with our situation here," Guggi had begun.

"Not really. I studied for two semesters at the university in Zurich in the late 1960s—my mother was Swiss, so I had no problem getting in—but never even visited Liechtenstein. It did not seem very important, frankly."

"You're right. It's not. In fact, for centuries, Liechtenstein was just an obscure, agrarian, backwater principality on the periphery of the Austro-Hungarian empire. Things were never good here, but they got a lot worse, at the end of World War One. The empire collapsed, and we found ourselves as a people without a country.

"All that changed dramatically on January first, 1924, when Liechtenstein entered into a sweeping agreement of association with Switzerland. The Swiss borders and tariffs became our borders and tariffs. The Swiss franc became our legal tender. And Liechtenstein's banks, all two of them, were fully integrated into the Swiss banking system, bank secrecy laws and all."

"So what can you offer here that's not available in Zurich?" Willy had asked.

"Another entire layer of protection," Guggi had answered, adding, "protection against prying eyes."

Then Guggi had explained how it worked.

The key was a unique "corporate" entity called the *Anstalt*. It loosely translated into English as "foundation," but a Liechtenstein *Anstalt* had about as much in common with an American foundation as Madonna had to the Virgin Mary, as Guggi had explained with a rare flash of humor. It was an institution that was neither required to list its true ownership, nor to reveal any of its financial dealings or records to anyone, even the government of the principality. And no matter how much it earned, its taxes would always be the same: five thousand francs a year, or just over three thousand dollars.

It was not for nothing, Guggi had pointed out, that some of

■

the most powerful men in the world—like Robert Maxwell, the British press lord and financier extraordinaire—used Liechtenstein as the hub for the "private side" of their businesses.

To be sure, there were also the fees that had to be paid to the men who fronted as the directors of the corporation. They did not come cheap. Nor did the lawyers who administered these "foundations," almost always under a blanket power of attorney. The granting of such sweeping power to a lawyer bothered some people, Guggi had admitted, especially Anglo-Saxons. But such an agreement lay at the very heart of the system, a system which, in the final analysis, was based on trust.

Willy had spent the next morning in Guggi's office. He got his *Anstalt*. It came with a board, headed by the second son of the Prince of Liechtenstein. He signed the power of attorney, appointing Dr. Werner Guggi as his alter ego in charge of the *Anstalt*. He executed the papers which transferred ownership of his Swiss *Finanzgesellschaft,* as well as his account at the Union Bank of Switzerland, to the *Anstalt*. And he also signed a piece of paper authorizing Dr. Werner Guggi to deduct an annual fee of one million Swiss francs to cover all services, expenses, and board fees.

In return, Werner Guggi had promised to faithfully protect Willy's interests as if they were his own. And so far he had. Neither the American courts nor the IRS had a clue about the stash he had built up in Vaduz from the profits siphoned off from his offshore underwriting operations.

But absence does not make the heart grow fonder, nor lawyers in distant lands more faithful.

Willy paid for his drink and was back in the Huntington by twelve-thirty. In a series of phone calls, he booked the 8 a.m. United to New York, the 7 p.m. Swissair to Zurich, and a rental car at Kloten airport for the last leg of his trip to Vaduz.

Six

It was raining when he landed in Kloten on Thursday morning. A Mercedes was waiting for him at Hertz. It had been years since he had last been in Switzerland, so Willy asked the woman behind the counter to trace the easiest route to Vaduz on one of their maps. Minutes later he was on the N1 Autobahn headed east, and by noon he had arrived in Vaduz.

It rained all the way, and was still doing so when he pulled up in front of the Gasthof zum Sternen. It was built in chalet style, and had the same Swiss-calendar look as did the small town of Vaduz itself. Willy decided to find out if his German, a remnant of his two semesters in Zurich, was still in reasonably good working condition.

"*Grüss Gott,*" he said to the desk clerk. "*Herr Doktor Guggi hat für mich ein Zimmer reserviert. Ich bin Willy Saxon.*"

"Welcome to Vaduz, Mr. Saxon," came the reply in English. "We have the reservation, and your room is ready. Do you have any luggage?"

"Just what I've got here," Willy replied. And so much for my German, he concluded.

His room was so rustic it could have been used in a Heidi movie. On the ancient oaken table in front of the window there was a bottle of wine—a Johannesberg Riesling—with a note attached.

■

"I hope this brings back fond memories of Liechtenstein," it said, and was signed, "Your good friend, Werner."

Outside the window there was the obligatory box of geraniums, and beyond, as the sun finally began to come out, he could see the mountains beginning to emerge through the mist. The knot he had had in his stomach for the past twenty-four hours, and the doubts that had created it, finally began to abate. Not everybody in this world was necessarily a crook, although during the past three years it had sure seemed so.

Willy decided that another nap was in order, and with the help of the mountain air and the serenity of the surroundings, Willy Saxon was fast asleep within minutes. When he awoke five hours later, for the first time in years he looked forward to what would happen next.

Willy's newly-found confidence was not disappointed.

Dr. Guggi arrived in the restaurant of the Gasthof at seven o'clock on the second. Willy was already waiting at a table. Guggi had barely finished with his greetings, when he reached into his briefcase, extracted an envelope, and handed it to Willy.

As they sat down, Willy opened it.

The lone piece of paper inside—no letterhead—contained but a single number: $74,768,411.76.

"That's your balance as of right now," Dr. Guggi said.

Willy's mind worked it out immediately. Ten million for the investment bank. Ten million for the ratings agency. More than enough left over to grease whatever wheels needed it. Leaving a hefty sum as his fallback position.

Willy Saxon was back in business.

"I assume our mutual friend, Dr. Rudolph Schweizer, is still running the Union Bank of Switzerland?" Willy asked.

"Of course."

"And I further assume that he still is a mutual friend?"

"He always speaks highly of you, Willy. You've got to understand that none of us over here could understand why

■

the American authorities did what they did to you. It was absurd."

"Maybe. Well, I intend to buy a piece of an investment bank in San Francisco. The American authorities you just alluded to might not like the idea. So I was thinking of establishing a holding company in Switzerland, in the canton of Zug, to act on my behalf, so to say."

"I can easily arrange that," Guggi said.

"Now I hope you'll understand, Werner, but I think it best if your name is also kept out of it," Willy said. "Keeping our little arrangement to ourselves has worked very well so far, so I see no need to change anything."

"Agreed."

"OK. What I've got in mind is this. We're talking about ten million dollars. I want the money channeled to Zug through UBS in Zurich. Ideally, the board in Zug would include some UBS executives, and a few "friends" of Dr. Schweizer. We'd, of course, need a local lawyer, who would be our nominee, where ownership of the holding company is concerned. Now what can we offer Schweizer and friends? First, we'll have to put up some front-end board fees. I'm thinking about maybe a million dollars or so. Then, at least where Schweizer's concerned, we're going to have to offer a piece of the action, just like last time around with the junk bond operation, though hardly anything approaching fifty percent. What do you think would be appropriate?"

By midnight they had worked out all the details.

■

SEVEN

At noon the next day, Willy was back at the Zurich airport, in time to catch a one o'clock flight to London. His ebullient mood was not only intact, but buoyed by that fact that he was now headed for one of his favorite cities, armed with adequate pocket money. He had arranged through Dr. Guggi to have ten thousand pounds and fifty thousand dollars in cash delivered to his hotel before he left. He had also phoned ahead to Claridges to have their Rolls waiting for him at the airport.

Claridges' manager was there to personally greet him in the lobby, murmuring how nice it was to have him back, and asking whether there was anything that needed arranging.

"Dinner," Willy replied. "I'm caught between Christopher's and Harry's Bar."

"I'd go with Christopher's," Mr. Bentley replied. "It's a favorite of both the Queen Mother and Princess Margaret, but the food is nevertheless still the best in town. And afterward?"

"I guess Annabel's. Unless some place new has come along. It's been over three years, you know."

"There's still only one. Tramp. It attracts the most beautiful girls in London."

"I'm not sure the girls will be necessary, but one can never go wrong having a backup position. Shall we say dinner at

■

eight, and Tramp at eleven? For two. And I'll need transportation."

"It will be waiting outside at seven-thirty."

The first thing Willy did when he was in his room was to extract the little black book from his briefcase. Under "N" he found the telephone number of Nuffield, Weatherspoon and Latham, the august firm of solicitors he had retained at the time he had introduced junk bonds to Europe. They were known in the City for being insufferable, but flexible. Mr. Nuffield's secretary informed him that her boss was engaged, but, yes, despite it being a Saturday he had made an exception and was expecting him at eleven the next morning.

After he hung up, Willy went back to his black book and, after skipping through a few letters, stopped at "Doreen." He dialed, only to find out the number had been disconnected. He went on to "Liz"—tall, dark, and big breasts, if he recalled correctly. Nobody answered. And so it went through "Marty," "Patricia," and finally "Shirley." Shirley at least answered the phone, but said that she was busy that evening. Perhaps tomorrow? He said he'd get back to her.

Now what? The bar at Claridges was not exactly fun, but it was at least close. On his way to it, he had no sooner stepped out of the elevator into the lobby than he saw a familiar figure—also tall, of dark hair, and with very big breasts. It was the bishop's daughter, watching her luggage being brought in and counting to make sure that it had all arrived. There must have been ten pieces already.

Should he or should he not? He decided to step up to the plate.

"Remember me?" he asked.

The question drew a look of instant dismissal.

"Stars in San Francisco," he continued, "Denise van Bercham's lunch."

The look became a puzzled frown. "Of course. You're the

■

49

clever financial man. How odd that we should meet again so soon. And here.''

"Well, I just thought I'd say hello," Willy said, concluding that it had been a big mistake in the first place.

But as he turned to leave, she spoke again. "You're staying here too? It's William, isn't it."

"Willy. Willy Saxon. And yes, I'm staying here."

"I'm just checking in, as you can see. Daddy's attending a bishop's conference here, and I decided to accompany him. Daddy's going to be in Lambeth for the next three days, so I'm going to spend the time here shopping, doing the theater, the usual. And you?''

"Probably just tonight. Then right back to San Francisco."

"What a pity. Otherwise, we might have been able to find a new restaurant together, and drive Denise crazy when she can't claim it was her discovery.''

"If you're game, we might drive her crazy with an old standby, Christopher's. I have a reservation there for eight o'clock.''

"You mean tonight?" There was some hesitation. But not much. "I would barely have time to unpack. But the maid can do that, can't she?''

"I would think so. Then let's say just before eight down here in the lobby?''

Minutes later, over a Pimm's No. 1, which he considered appropriate given the setting, Willy wondered what had prompted him to invite the fifty-year-old-at-least daughter of an Anglican bishop to dinner on his first night in London in over three years. On top of that, she was a big girl. The English had a naughty saying about such women: when introduced, one is not sure whether to shake hands or throw a saddle over them.

But he changed his mind radically a few hours later. What stepped from the elevator at five to eight was indeed a lady of statuesque proportions. But as the green gown she was wearing made amply clear, the distribution of her 140 pounds was flawless. Her legs seemed to never stop; her bosom was straining the Givenchy to the limit; and her jewelry—all emeralds— set off her "English" complexion to perfection.

"Wow!" he said, as he—yes—shook her hand.

"Thank you, sir," she replied. "Is the carriage waiting?"

The carriage was a Daimler, and the driver a snob.

"Christopher's," Willy told him.

"Sir?"

"Wellington Street," Willy said, "and step on it."

The bishop's daughter liked that.

"Willy," she said, as the Daimler crept away from the curb, "I want an honest answer to what I'm about to ask you."

"Sure," he said.

"Do you remember my name?"

"In a word, no," Willy replied. "But I certainly didn't forget your face, did I."

"You are a clever one. All right, guess."

"First or last name?"

"First."

"Penelope."

"Guess again."

"Prudence."

She laughed. "Wrong name, but good thought. All right, it's Sara. Sara Jones."

Willy reached across the backseat of the Daimler and shook her hand. "A pleasure to meet you, Sara. In fact, a great pleasure."

Inside the restaurant it was Christopher himself, Christopher Gilmore, who led them to their table, chatting amiably with Willy the entire time.

"You certainly seem to know your way around here," Sara said, when they were seated. "How come?"

"It would bore you to tears," Willy replied.

"Try me."

■

"All right. Here's the abbreviated history of Willy Saxon. Undergraduate at Georgetown's School of Foreign Service. Then Zurich University, for two semesters. Why Zurich? Because my mother was from there. Then L.S.E., London School of Economics, where I took a Masters. Back to the States, where I joined First Boston. They taught me the investment banking business, first in New York, then London, finally San Francisco, where I jumped ship and started my own little merchant bank."

"Hold on. How old are we at this point?"

"Thirty-four."

"Why San Francisco?"

"Its proximity to Silicon Valley. I put together investment groups that provided seed capital for hi-tech startups, nursing them along with further financing, in the hope of later taking them public and making a bundle. The first three deals I put together clicked. Then by chance I attended a lunch put on by Jerry Kohlberg and George Roberts. It was at the Villa Taverna."

"Who are they?'

"KKR. The second K is for Henry Kravis. I'm sure you probably know his former wife, Carolyn Roehm. I understand that she's to New York what Denise van Bercham is to San Francisco. Anyway, Kohlberg, Kravis and Roberts—George Roberts is from San Francisco, that's why the lunch there—invented the leveraged buyout. It sounds a lot more complicated than it is. In essence, all they did was entice management of undervalued companies to take over their own outfits by buying out the public shareholders. KKR provided the financing by issuing junk bonds, in return for a big piece of the action. They then cleaned up the companies and sold them back to the public, at double or triple the share price they had paid in the first place. KKR made billions, literally billions, in the process."

"And you copied them."

■

"Exactly. But I also took it one step further. I opened up offices in London and Zurich and introduced junk bond financing to Europe."

"Clever Willy."

"As it turned out, too clever by half. Ten years later I ended up in prison."

"How did you manage that?"

"I got involved with men like Ivan Boesky and Michael Milken. We all kind of helped each other. And the way we did it was sometimes illegal."

"Weren't you ever afraid of getting caught?"

"Never even gave it a thought. You know the old joke about the drunk. After three drinks he thinks he's omniscient; one more and he's omnipotent; another and he's invincible; a nightcap and he's invisible. Except in my case—and in the case of the whole gang in the 1980s from Boesky to Milken to Boyd Jeffries—it was not drink. It was the power that money gives you today in our society. You made enough money, and no one would dare touch you. In the end, we got what we deserved."

"At least you admit it, Willy," Sara said.

"I admitted it in court. I also provided full restitution and more to anybody that was hurt in the process. But I absolutely refused to fink on anybody else. So they gave me the limit in prison time."

"What about the others. Did they all betray their friends?" Sara asked.

"Every single one of them. The courts even invented a euphemism for these Judas Iscariots. They called them "cooperators." Boesky was the biggest crook of all, but also the biggest cooperator. So he served just two years and eleven days. Milken turned "cooperator," and served twenty-four months instead of ten years. Marty Siegel, who was Boesky's most important supplier of information for insider trading, took his payoffs in suitcases full of cash. After they caught

■

him, he "cooperated" to the hilt, and got two months. Two months!"

"And you?"

"I served full time. Three years and one day, because I refused to rat on my pals. I hate people who fink. And I hate even more a system that rewards people who fink. So my attitude now is very simple: Fuck 'em all!"

"I fully concur," Sara said, "and now let's change the subject."

They did, and after dinner went on to Tramp and danced until two in the morning. When they got back to Claridges, Willy Saxon and Sara Jones both agreed that they had had the best time in years. Willy never even broached the subject of spending the rest of the night together. Why? Because she was a "nice" girl, and his wildly outdated prep school system of ethics dictated that you don't try to sleep with nice girls on the first date. It was like finking on a classmate. You just didn't do it.

EIGHT

Ethics had never been the strong point of Nuffield, Weatherspoon and Latham, solicitors. But they never claimed it was. Their mission in life was to make enough money to support an apartment in the West End, a home in the country, a Jaguar, and, as one approached the pinnacle of the legal profession, a girlfriend in Paris. A prerequisite was that all this could be accomplished during office hours that started no earlier than ten a.m., and ended no later than three p.m, with ample time for lunch in between.

All this depended upon having satisfied clients. And that, sometimes, required a wink and a nod where the strict niceties of the law were concerned. To be sure, in their own minds Nuffield, Weatherspoon and Latham were not there to help clients *break* the law, but *bending* was all right.

When Willy walked into their offices promptly at eleven, the only person there was a receptionist. His solicitor had not yet arrived. When he finally did, twenty minutes later, he was not a pretty picture.

"Sorry, dear chap," Lionel Latham said, in his somewhat fruity voice, "but I'm not accustomed to coming in on Saturdays. Slept in. Late night. A bit of a hangover. But some coffee should cure that. Let's go to my office."

When the coffee arrived, Latham gulped down its entire

■

contents. "That's better," he said, and then gave Willy what seemed to be a quite deliberate once-over.

"You look fine. In fact, you're in a hell of a lot better shape than I am, that's for sure. No liquor in that prison, eh?"

"Nope. Three years on the wagon."

The solicitor shuddered. "I read about some of it in the papers at the time, but the press here didn't give it a very big play. Between us girls, what exactly did they get you on?"

"Stock manipulation was one count. It involved the shares of one of the companies involved in a takeover we were arranging. The drill was simple, and oft repeated, I might add. We'd get a friend to buy shares of Company A, bidding up the price, so that when Company B bought the rest it would have to pay more. The more they paid, the more we made. The problem arose from oral agreements between the "friend" and us, stipulating that we would buy back Company A's shares at cost, no matter whether the merger went through or not. That's illegal in America."

"Here too. That's what they nailed the Guinness people on. They had similar arrangements with Swiss banks. And still got nailed. Didn't go to jail for very long, though. Ernest Saunders, who was Guinness's CEO, got out really early by pleading Alzheimer's. Rather imaginative, I thought. What got you out?"

"Nothing. I stayed for the full stretch."

"Well, that's all water over the dam, isn't it. What can I do for you now?"

"I'm buying a piece of a company in the States, but I need to muddy the waters."

"You thinking about anything in particular?"

"I want a British company up front, with some good names on the board, and impeccable bank references."

"Who'd own it?

"I thought about using an entity in the Channel Islands."

"Fine. And who'd own it?"

■

"Maybe a Liberian company?"

"Excellent. How much capital are we talking about?"

"Ten million dollars."

"Where will it be coming from?"

"Luxembourg." And before that Liechtenstein, which was none of Latham's business.

"The company you're buying into. What's it do?"

"Rates bonds. Like Moody's, or your IBCA."

"I see. What about the authorities? The SEC?"

"Not to worry. The SEC doesn't vet them. Nobody does."

"Strange. And surprising that nobody thought of it before."

"Now we're going to have to round up some "nominees" for the board of the British company. By the way, any ideas for a company name?"

"Veritas, Ltd."

Willy liked that. "It's perfect. We will offer the truth, but in a limited sort of way."

"One chap immediately comes to mind for chairman. Sir Aubrey Whitehead. Former adjutant to Lord Mountbatten. Then High Commissioner in Canada. Now living off a pension in Surrey on an estate which he cannot afford to keep up, but is too proud to give up. He's also a member of White's, which never hurts. Of course, he doesn't understand a single thing about finance."

"He's perfect," Willy said. "I assume that you will be willing to serve as company secretary."

"I'd be honored to do so," the solicitor replied. "How fast do you intend to move on all this?"

"Right away. You set up everything here, in the Channel Islands, and Liberia, so that when I press the button, we're in business right away."

"I don't want to pry, but are we going back into the junk bond business?"

"Hardly. Times have changed in America," Willy replied.

■

"Clinton promised to soak the rich, and he's kept his word. So the rich are scrambling to preserve what they've still got."

"And you're going to help them. How?"

"By putting them into the last surviving tax haven. Bonds."

"You mean like our Gilts?"

"No. Tax-exempt bonds. Municipal bonds. General obligation bonds backed by the full faith and credit of some of the finest towns and cities in the United States. Even without the tax benefits, they could interest a lot of European investors. Just look around this continent. Germany's a mess. So is Italy. Sweden's falling apart. And, if you'll pardon me, Lionel, the way your country's going, it seems destined to become the Argentina of Europe. By comparison, America looks great."

"I'm afraid I must agree with you," Latham replied. "Anything or anybody I should be wary of?"

Willy thought for a minute. "Only one comes to mind at the moment. A man by the name of Sid Ravitch. He owns the ratings agency I intend to invest in. If he ever turns up here, get hold of me immediately."

"Right," Latham replied, while glancing at his watch. "My God! It's almost noon. I've made arrangements for lunch at my club. Maybe we could stop at the bar for a quickie beforehand. I could use a bit of a picker-upper."

NINE

Willy took the early evening British Air direct flight to San Francisco, arriving at the Huntington just after midnight. There was a stack of messages in his box at the front desk. Three of them were from Denise van Bercham. All were marked urgent. He set the alarm for nine, and the first thing he did after brushing his teeth was to call her. The number she had left had a 707 prefix, which meant she must be somewhere up in the wine country.

"Where were you?" she asked, the moment he identified himself.

"London," he answered, knowing that she'd hear about it from the bishop's daughter sooner or later.

"For just two days?"

"Yes."

"That's just about right for London. Where did you stay?"

"Claridges."

"Hmm. Next time you do that, let me know."

"Why?"

"I might come along," she said. "Now to why I called you. I'm up at my ranch, where I'm putting on a little do this afternoon. Some of the people there will interest you. Like George Abbott. He's the Chief Administrative Officer of the City of San Francisco. Which means he runs it. And Marshall

■

Lane, from New York. He runs all those investment funds. He says he knows you. And . . ."

"Enough. I'll come. Where's the ranch? In Napa County?"

"No. Further north. In Mendocino County. A little over two hours' drive. I'll have a map sent over to the Huntington right away. Dress casually. Bring a swimming suit. And a girlfriend, if you'd like."

"Is that obligatory?"

"The swimming suit or the girlfriend?"

"Either."

"As far as I'm concerned, you can pass on both. As I said, dress is casual."

"Then I'll come alone."

"Plan on getting here at three o'clock or so."

"I'll be there."

He called Dan Prescott next. He'd also phoned three times, the last time leaving his home phone number, and saying that he would be there the entire weekend.

"I've tried a couple of times to get you," the investment banker said.

"I had a few out-of-town errands to take care of," Willy replied. "But now I'm back in business. Look, I've got something I want to ask you."

"Fine. But first I've got to tell you something. Our situation has changed. Their lawyers decided to play hardball. They gave us a take-it-or-leave-it settlement offer."

"How bad is it?"

"They upped the ante another five million. Which we don't have."

"Now what happens?"

"They'll seek a judgment for three times the settlement offer."

"How do they expect to collect? I thought the firm's capital was going to be wiped out in any case."

"It is. They said they intend to go after us personally."

■

"What's Bobby say?"

"His personal assets are on the line, too, you know."

"And?"

"He says it's two-to-one odds the judgment would go against us."

"That bad."

"Maybe worse."

"How come?"

"If this thing goes to trial, a lot of dirty linen is going to be washed in public. Bobby says it's bound to attract attention in some of the wrong places."

"Such as?"

"Such as the D.A.'s office."

"But not if the settlement is reached now."

"That's right."

"I'll see what I can do. Now, like I said, I've got a question. How big are you guys in municipal bonds?"

"Pretty big. We must have been involved in at least twenty underwritings so far this year. Which is about par for what we've been doing for the past five years."

"Do you trade them?"

"Yes. It's a small department. About a dozen guys. But we do a pretty good volume. And we make a market in the issues where we originate the underwiting."

"How many's that?"

"Of the twenty so far this year, five or six."

"For what municipalities?"

"In January it was Fresno. General obligation bonds. A hundred million. We did one for Salinas in March. Some kind of low-income housing project. Fifty million. In April, it was to finance an expansion of an airport up in Salem, Oregon. That one . . ."

Willie interrupted. "I get the idea. Where do you place them?"

■

"We've got a regular group of institutional clients. Bond funds. Bank Trust Department. Insurance companies. You know."

"Ever do anything for the City of San Francisco?"

"Never could break in at that level. Why?"

"Something came up that gave me an idea. Now look, before I make any final commitment I'll have to know where Prescott and Quackenbush stands. To the last penny. I'll need all the numbers. And you know me well enough to realize, Dan, that I would expect no surprises down the road. So I want you to include a hard number on every conceivable contingent liability. Plus, I'll need the firm's balance sheets and P and L statements for the past five years. And I want complete and up-to-date statements of your and Bobby's personal net worth. What you've got, and where you've got it. And I expect no errors or omissions there, either."

"By when? Time's running out on us, Willy."

"How about Monday evening?"

"You'll get them. Where?"

"Here at the Huntington."

"Bobby and I will be there. Jeezuz, Willy, how can I thank you?"

"Don't. This is strictly business, Dan. Dead serious business."

TEN

By this time it was almost nine-thirty. When he pulled the curtain to check the weather, Huntington Park was still shrouded in fog. The Chinese were doing their Oriental exercises. The Nicaraguan maids were walking their mistress' poodles. A little black boy wearing a Giants cap was playing catch with his proud father. Two bums were still fast asleep on adjacent park benches. On another bench, a man in coat and tie sat reading the Sunday paper. From the size of the pile of newspaper beside him it could only be the *New York Times.*

Despite the paper, it was a scene you could only find in one place: San Francisco. And Willy Saxon savored it all. He was like a man who could still not quite believe that he had survived a near-fatal disease.

He decided to spend the rest of the morning in bed, so he picked up the phone and ordered breakfast and his own copy of the *New York Times.* He first emerged from the Huntington at twelve-thirty and decided to walk down Taylor—straight down, it seemed—to the Hertz garage on Post Street, where he had reserved a convertible. Then he headed for the Golden Gate Bridge. The fog was gone, so he pushed the button that folded back the top. Once across the bridge and beyond the Waldo tunnel, he turned on the radio and tuned in KGO where, on Sunday mornings, they replayed the best shows of

■

his favorite talk-show host, Ronn Owens. Then he put the car on cruise control at 65 and headed up U.S. 101.

Willy Saxon was back, really back.

By two-thirty he was in Cloverdale, where he pulled over to consult Denise's map. It told him to turn left on Highway 128, just north of Cloverdale, and head for the coast. Half way there was a tiny town, Andersonville, and on its western outskirts was an Exxon gas station. Turn left there, and just follow the road to its end.

The road was marked private. After a mile, it entered a redwood forest. At first, there was a series of clearings, but then the forest became increasingly dense, the redwoods ever taller, ever more ancient. The midsummer heat, which had been rising the further north of San Francisco he had driven, hitting 100 on the car's outside temperature gauge in Cloverdale, began to fall. By the time he reached the gate, under a wooden arch that told him he had arrived at the Van Bercham Ranch, it was back to 75. A ranch hand was standing at the gate. He asked Willy's name and then waved him through. Another hundred yards down a lane and he knew he had arrived. In front of him was an immense house, incongruously built in the style of an eighteenth-century French château. In front of it, even more out of place, stood a valet dressed in the full regalia of an English butler.

"You must be Mr. Saxon," he said.

"I am."

"If you leave your keys, your car will be taken care of. Are you planning on spending the night, sir?"

"I wasn't, no."

"But you may want to change into your bathing attire."

"Perhaps."

Willy got out of the car, and retrieved a small Nike bag from the back seat. The valet immediately took it.

"If you'll accompany me, I'll show you to your cottage. Everybody is down at the swimming pool, which is just

■

beyond it." Which seemed to indicate that he was the last to arrive, even though it was barely a quarter past the hour.

The cottage, he later found out, had been done by Mark Hampton, who had gone on to redo the living quarters at the White House for Barbara Bush, as well as the American embassy in Paris for Pamela Harriman. The setting made it all the more stunning. For the cottage was dwarfed by the grove of five-hundred-year-old redwoods surrounding it.

"I'll trade this for Pleasanton any time," he said, once the valet had left. But having said it, he realized it was an exercise in pure bravado. For three years and a day he had known what, and more importantly who, to expect when he went to lunch: the same people and, often, the same food. And very little conversation. But not today.

The living room of his cottage had a fully stocked wet bar. Glasses of all types and a crystal ice bucket filled with cubes were at the ready. Maybe a quickie, as his English solicitor had termed it? No. Might as well bite the bullet. He decided to leave the "bathing attire" be until he got a better feel for the situation. An expeditious exit might be called for if the gang down at the pool turned hostile when confronted with the presence of a very recent ex-con.

The pool was situated in a clearing in the redwood forest, and its turquoise tile—it seemed like there was a half acre of it—shone like a huge jewel in the sun, which was once again hot. At the far side of the pool was an oversized cabana—a redwood cabana. Beneath the timbers were scattered groups of lounge chairs. Atop or among them, lay, sat, or stood perhaps twenty people, some in bathing suits, some in jeans, and one wrapped in what looked like an Indian sari. It was Denise. As she came forward to greet him, it became apparent that her garb was not totally up to strict Hindu standards. The diaphanous material left very little to the imagination when she moved from the shadowed area of the cabana into the afternoon sun.

■

"Darling," she exclaimed as she took his outstretched hand and pressed it to her breasts before moving in to kiss him. The etherial material between them now left nothing to his imagination.

"How nice to see you again, Denise," was the only reply he could muster under the circumstances.

"Let me introduce you to some of my friends," she then said, keeping his hand in hers as she led him toward the cabana.

"This is George Champion," she said, when they approached a man standing alone at the outer periphery of the group.

"Willy," the man said, as he extended his hand. "What a pleasant surprise!"

"I didn't know you knew each other," Denise said.

"Willy put me into Microsoft at ten," Champion replied.

"Still got it?" Willy asked.

"Still got it. Was eighty-six last time I looked."

"Still in real estate too?" Willy asked.

"Sure. Just finishing a development outside of Alamo in the East Bay. Next door to Blackhawk. Do you know the area?"

"Only too well. I used to live near there," Willy said. "In Pleasanton."

"I know," Champion replied. "Nothing like taking some time off to think. Come up with any new ideas I might be interested in?"

"I'm working on a few."

"When you're done working, give me a call."

"Will do," Willy replied. Maybe it was going to be easier than he'd thought.

"And this is Ralph Goodman," Denise said, as they turned to a man who was too fat to be in a bathing suit. "Do you also know each other?"

"Yes," the man responded. This time no hand was extended. "Excuse me, Denise, I think my wife just gave me a

■

signal that she needs another drink." He turned his back and waddled away.

"What's his problem?" Denise asked.

"As you must know, he's head of the state banking commission. He was appointed by Jerry Brown when he was governor. Before that he was an accountant."

"Figures," Denise said. "Other than that, what's his problem?"

"He thinks I screwed some of his banks. In fact, he testified against me."

"Did you?"

"Probably one or two."

Perhaps prompted by the brief scene that had just ended, it was now a man, overdressed for the occasion, right down to his black socks and shoes, who approached them.

"Remember me, Willy? Marshall Lane." And the hand that now took his took it firmly and shook it briskly, ostentatiously briskly. "Come on," he continued, "let me get you a drink. Denise's got things to take care of, I'm sure."

She took the hint.

There was a bar to the rear of the "cabana," and behind it was a second valet offering the specialty of the afternoon: a Bloody Mary made from fresh tomatoes, spiced up with jalapeño peppers, and served as ice cold as a drink can get without freezing.

"What was that all about?" Lane asked.

"You mean with Ralph Goodman? Do you know him?"

"Unfortunately, yes."

"He claims I stuck some of the state's banks with some bum investments. They wanted bonds yielding sixteen percent, so I sold them some."

"Luck of the draw I suppose. Remember those junk bonds you put us into?"

"Hardly," Willy replied, thinking that this was turning out to be a big mistake.

■

"Well if you don't remember, I do. Safeway, American Standard, Owens Illinois, to just name three. I checked the list when Denise told me you'd be here. Just two losers in the lot. I put them in our high yield fund and held on through the hard times, thank God. We had a total return of 18.6 percent on them last year. Over twenty percent the year before. Fifteen percent the year before that. You sure knew how to pick 'em, Willy."

"Not according to Ralph Goodman," Willy said.

"Fuck Ralph Goodman," Lane replied. Then came a question—the same one that had been put to Willy just minutes earlier. "Come up with any new ideas that might interest us?"

"Maybe. It's a different game out there right now."

"Don't tell me. We've got fifty-five billion under management and it keeps coming in at the rate of a half billion a month. We don't know what to do with most of it."

"How many funds have you got now?"

"Fifteen. Mostly equities. That high yield bond fund was an exception. But we're thinking of going a lot heavier into fixed-income securities in the future. Though not junk. People are getting very safety conscious. So are we. That's why we're reluctant to go much deeper into equities. They're starting to look pricey. Plus, they're getting damn expensive to manage. You've got to pay the hired help a mint these days, Willy, or they take a hike and set up their own shop."

"Then I might have an idea for you, low risk, and a lot cheaper to run than even a no-brainer index fund," Willy said. Someone behind him touched his elbow.

Denise had returned.

"You can talk business later," she said. "Right now I have some ladies who want to meet you, Willy."

The ladies—wives, it turned out—had grouped themselves around a low table where they had plunked their glasses, mostly half filled with champagne. When Denise introduced Willy, they all gave him the same curious once-over he had received a week earlier from the women Denise had gathered for lunch at Stars restaurant. The word had spread that a sex-starved ex-con was on the loose.

Willy was tempted to treat them to a leer, but decided for Denise's sake to behave. He dutifully shook hands with the lot of them, and then excused himself. His glass, it seemed, was already empty.

Three Bloody Marys later, Willy Saxon was feeling no pain. He had joined the group of men being regaled by story after story told by an English actor in their midst. Apparently, Denise was plugged in everywhere. At five o'clock he was still at it.

Then, as if by signal, one by one the wives came to fetch their husbands, and, pair by pair, they disappeared.

Fortunately for Willy, Denise appeared once again to rescue him.

"What's happening?" he asked.

"Nap time," she answered. "You see, we never eat before eight."

"Then I'm afraid I'll have pass on dinner," Willy said.

"But why?"

"It would get too late, Denise. I've got important things to do in the city tomorrow."

"So what? I'll make sure someone knocks on your door tomorrow morning in time to have you back in San Francisco by ten."

Willy's resolve weakened, but not totally. "Besides," he said, "I don't have a jacket with me."

"I'm sure there's one around here that will fit you. Go take a nap, Willy. I'll have a jacket delivered at seven-thirty. Dinner's at eight. Up in the main house. Be prompt."

The table was set for twenty-four. All twenty-three guests were there promptly at eight. They all were in compliance with the Northern California weekend dinner dress code. The

■

women were in long dresses, loaded with jewelry. The men were in slacks and jackets and loafers. Not a tie among them, except for Marshall Lane. But, being from New York, he didn't know any better, and it didn't appear to faze him one bit.

Once they were seated, six maids—all in black and white, and all Mexican—immediately began serving the first course, smoked trout. The two valets poured a 1990 Batard Montrachet. As Denise now explained to Willy, who had been given the place of honor to her right, she never served California wines with but one exception: those produced by the Jordan winery just a half hour away in the Alexander Valley. Not, she said, because she liked them that much, but because Sally Jordan was one of her best pals. Sally, however, wasn't there that night.

To Denise's left sat the black pastor of San Francisco's Glide Memorial Church, famous for its rousing music and the often outrageous sermons he preached every Sunday morning to a packed congregation of women and men of every race.

"You probably wonder what I'm doing here," he said to Willy, once Denise had explained who both of them were.

"You're right."

"Simple. For the food, the drink, and the marvelous company, like everybody else. But my real motive is money. Denise's money. And hopefully, before the evening's over, some of your money."

"You mean donations?"

"That's right. From the rich."

"How much do you raise this way?"

"In a good year, over two million dollars."

"And where does it go?"

"To feed the poor at Thanksgiving and Christmas. To provide children with clothes in the winter. To arrange temporary shelter for the homeless."

"Temporary shelter?"

■

"Yes."

"Which still leave them homeless."

"What else could we afford? You just try to get somebody to build low-cost permanent housing. Believe me, there's no way to finance that sort of thing anymore. The city's done all it can; the state doesn't have any money, since it's in a constant budget crisis. And everybody and his cousin are competing for any Federal funds that might be available."

"What about the private sector?"

"We're back to donations," the minister said.

"Not necessarily. If it's properly engineered, and the city cooperates, maybe you can get long-term financing."

Now the man sitting diagonally across the table from Willy spoke up, first introducing himself as George Abbott, San Francisco's Chief Administrative Officer—the man, Willy now realized, whom Denise had spoken about on the phone.

"What do you mean, properly engineered?" he asked.

"Piggyback it."

"What's that mean?"

"A city like San Francisco issues bonds, on a regular basis, that everybody wants. Rated Double-A. Right?"

"Right."

"So take advantage of your placement power to help out the Reverend."

"How?"

"When you go into a new underwriting, tell the buyers that to get a thousand of your Double-A bonds, they're going to have to also buy a hundred of the Reverend's unrated bonds for his housing projects."

Willy'd gotten the idea quite a while ago, when Michael Milken had referred to himself as a "social engineer" in an interview he had given to the editor of *Forbes Magazine* in the cafeteria over in Pleasanton. He had intended to save the entire Third World through junk bonds and become the Mother Theresa of high finance. But he'd been thwarted by

■

that female, anti-Semitic judge in New York, who had sent him away for ten years.

Well, Willy Saxon would leave the Third World to Milken. He would follow the stellar example set by Willy Clinton and seek to *first* take care of America's own!

By piggybacking.

"Who's doing this?" Abbott now asked, with obvious interest.

"Nobody," Willy answered, truthfully. "But I know an investment bank that might be prepared to try."

"What makes you so sure investors would go for a package like that?"

"Besides getting your Double-A's, which are in short supply, they would become one of those thousand points of light. The Do Gooders would be a cinch. Like public employees' pension funds. But even some of Mr. Ralph Goodman's California banks would probably go for it. Although they would ask for some sort of quid pro quo, like lowering the reserve requirements on these 'socially-sensitive' bonds."

"I like that," the minister said.

"So do I," the city bureaucrat echoed.

"Then why don't you all have lunch next week and talk about it," their hostess said. "I'll arrange it. On the proviso that we change the subject. Right now."

"One last question before we do," Willy said. "What happened to Ralph Goodman?"

"I sent him home," Denise replied.

"How did you manage that?"

"My dear, I can manage anything, if I put my mind to it."

They proceeded to make their way through pheasant served with spaezli and accompanied by a 1967 Lafite. Then the cheese, and finally the soufflé. And, of course, the Chateau d'Yquem.

Immediately after the final wine was poured, Denise rose to give the sole toast of the evening.

■

"To the memory of my only love, Jacob, who would have enjoyed your company as much as I did this evening."

She even managed a tear as she sank back into her chair. The room fell into a respectful silence.

It was midnight when the party finally broke up. Most of the guests were staying the night in the main house. Willy, after receiving but a perfunctory peck on the cheek by the hostess, was sent off, armed with a flashlight to make sure he found his way back to the cottage.

There he fell almost immediately into a deep sleep. The jet lag and an evening of food and drink had taken its toll. His last thought was the hope that somebody would pound on his door the next morning as Denise had promised. Otherwise he would sleep until noon.

Four hours later, he was proven wrong. Nobody had pounded on the door. But somebody was definitely in the living room of the cottage. The instincts he had quickly developed in prison brought him to full alert. When somebody lost it and went berserk, it was always in the middle of the night. Jails did that to some people.

Then he realized where he was.

And when that someone who had been in his living room now entered his bedroom he also knew who it was. She had sat beside him all evening, so her perfume gave her away.

Without a word, Denise approached his bed and slipped in beside him. He turned and put his hands on her breasts. This time there was no sari. Her hands now also moved to him. Within seconds, and without any pretense of subtlety, they went at each other. Only when she had finally brought herself to the point of exhaustion did Denise speak for the first time.

"Darling, that was the best fuck I've had in twelve years. But don't think that has anything to do with love. I only loved one man, ever."

How did one respond to such a statement?

■

"Denise," he finally whispered. "You will stay, won't you?"

"Of course I will. First we'll take a nap. Then, I have a little surprise for you. When you're ready."

These cryptic words, given the circumstances, made it difficult for Willy to go back to sleep. So he just lay there, listening to the breathing of the woman next to him. She was soon fast asleep. Finally, he also dozed off.

It was the first light of dawn that brought him back to wakefulness. With an assist from Denise, whose mouth was at his ear.

"Ready?" she asked.

She leaned over to the wall beside the bed and pushed a button on what appeared to be a light switch. She was no sooner back down beside him when it started to happen. First the glass sliding doors beyond the foot of the bed began to open. The bed began to move, down rails, through the open doors, and out onto a deck beneath the redwoods. The giant trees were now backlit by a sun which had barely begun to peek over the horizon.

"Ready," Willy answered.

When it was over he asked, "And how would you rate that one, Denise?"

"Like the redwoods. Awesome."

"By the way," Willy asked. "Who thought this one up?"

"I did," Denise answered. "I nearly tried it out once before. Without, I might add, any success. The dear boy turned out to be gorgeous but gay."

■

ELEVEN

Willy was back in San Francisco by early afternoon. At six that evening, Bobby Armacost and Dan Prescott entered the living room of his suite at the Huntington, both carrying bulging briefcases.

"In there," Willy told them, pointing to the dining room, off to the right.

"Drinks first?" he asked, after the investment banker and his attorney had laid out an array of bound documents on the dining room table.

"No thanks. Let's get right to it, Willy," Prescott answered.

They spent the next three hours poring over the documents, their silence periodically interrupted by a question from Willy.

"I think I've seen enough," he finally said. "It's not exactly a pretty picture, is it?"

"No. Not really," Prescott answered.

"What bothers me most is not that the settlement is going to completely wipe out your capital. I can replenish that. It's your current performance. You keep losing money. A quarter of a million dollars a month so far this year. And it seems to be getting progressively worse. Why?"

"Two factors," Prescott answered. "Reputation and performance."

"Explain," Willy said.

■

"That lawsuit. Everybody knows about it since the *Journal* ran that piece on the firm in January. It scares off clients."

"But that can't be the whole answer. Look at what happened at Salomon Brothers a few years ago. They got caught rigging the U.S. government bond auctions—about as big a sin as you can commit in the financial world—and yet they were back making record profits a year later. How come?"

"Simple," Prescott replied. "They kept making money for their clients. Tons of it. We're not."

"That's obvious. Because you keep doing the same old stuff, Dan. Since the M and A business dried up, all you're really doing is acting like a small run-of-the-mill brokerage house. Even big run-of-the-mill brokerages can't make money these days, as Sears found out after it bought Dean Witter. Or Prudential after it imprudently bought Bache. Because more and more people are catching on to the fact that they can get the same results at Charlie Schwab's place for half the cost. So why should I buy Prescott and Quackenbush?"

Everybody knew the answer to that one. They were all damaged goods. Thus, they needed each other. But nobody dared venture that answer out loud.

"Back to Salomon Brothers," Willy said. "How did they keep making all that money?"

"Arbitrage between the auction prices of securities on the various exchanges and their derivatives, like options and futures, or options on futures. It's another world, Willy. Understood only by rocket scientists. Salomon Brothers owns the best team of that kind of guys in the world. They're also known in the business as DGs—Derivative Geeks. They and their computers spit out profits like Mrs. Fields churns out cookies."

"So why doesn't everybody copy them?"

"Because there's only one Donald Lakewood, and Salomon Brothers has him. It's *Dr.* Donald Lakewood, by the way. He invented his own system, employing differential calculus.

■

With the help of other rocket scientists, he develops the software, and plugs it into a huge IBM mainframe, or in his case maybe even a Cray. Then they feed in the prices as they develop during the trading day, and out come the instructions for buys and sells, which, if executed instantaneously and simultaneously, take advantage of minuscule disparities in prices in different markets. They make a nickel here, a dime there. Very small potatoes, but always a sure thing. The trades are executed in such huge numbers that at the end of the day, like clockwork, Lakewood and his team of DGs have chalked up another million dollars in profits."

"What's this Lakewood guy make?"

"Ten, twelve million a year."

"But is it all legal?" Willy asked."

"As far as I know," came the assurance from Bobby. "Unless you know something I don't."

"All I know is that there was a guy like that over in Pleasanton—Fred Something-or-Other. I forget his last name. A real quiet one. Had his Ph.D. in mathematics from MIT. Used to come to the library and order really far out stuff, which we'd get from the library at the University of California in Berkeley, if it wasn't already lent out to somebody over at Lawrence Livermore Laboratory. Anyway, the word was that Fred was one of those rocket scientists on Wall Street. And look where he ended up."

"That must have been Fred Fitch," Bobby said.

"Fred Fitch. That's it. Do you know him?" Willy asked.

"No. But I know all about him," Bobby answered. "He started out as Donald Lakewood's protegé. Some say that they were really partners. That Fitch had as much to do with "inventing" the Salomon Brothers system as Lakewood. But that doesn't really matter, since they nailed Fitch on a completely unrelated matter. Counterfeiting twenty-dollar bills using one of Salomon Brother's state-of-the-art copying machines. Can you believe that?"

■

"Why not? But hold it right there for a minute," Willy said. "I want the whole story. But first let's get some food brought up. What do you guys want?"

They all wanted steak. After dinner—and the rest of the Fred Fitch story—the three got down to hard negotiations. By midnight, Bobby had drafted the basic elements of a series of agreements. The first set down the procedures under which Willy's company in Zug would put fifteen million dollars into Prescott & Quackenbush and in return get seventy-five percent of the investment bank's equity. Zug would lend an additional five million dollars to Dan Prescott, all of which would be reinvested in the firm, giving him a twenty-five percent share of ownership, and restoring the investment bank's capital to a respectable twenty million dollars. Both Prescott and Bobby Armacost—the due diligence lawyer—needed an additional two million dollars each to cover their personal share of the settlement that would open the way for the restructuring of the bank. Willy agreed to lend them the money. But both Prescott and Armacost would be required to pledge all of their personal assets as collateral for the loans.

"So how long will it take you to have these contracts in final shape?" Willy asked Armacost.

"They'll be ready on Friday. Let's say Friday afternoon, to be sure."

"What about the settlement? That's got to be wrapped up before I finalize anything."

"I'll let them know right away that they've got a done deal. I'm sure we can sign by Friday morning. Can you arrange to have that four million over here by then?"

"I'll take care of it," Willy said.

"What are you going to tell the newspapers?" he then asked.

"I'll prepare a statement to the effect that an amicable settlement of our past problem has been reached, and that a

■

major Swiss financial institution is taking a substantial stake in Prescott and Quackenbush," Bobby answered.

"Perfect," Willy said. "One last question before we break up."

"Sure," the lawyer responded, uneasily.

"Where can I find Fred Fitch?"

"I can put an investigator on it right away tomorrow," Bobby answered. "But these things normally take a while."

"Then forget it," Willy said.

TWELVE

Willy had decided that to find Fitch fast he would enlist the help of Sidney Ravitch, as much as he regretted having to do so. But he had to see Ravitch, in any case, and would try to introduce the subject as obliquely as possible.

He met Ravitch at four the next day in the offices of the Western Credit Rating Agency.

"I'll only keep you a few minutes," Willy began. "I've been over in London, and everything is ready to go from that end. On this end, the drill, as I see it, is this. My attorney—his name's Bobby Armacost—has been working on a draft agreement along the lines we discussed last Tuesday. He says he needs another two weeks."

By that time he'd have completed his takeover of Prescott & Quackenbush. If not, he'd simply walk away from any deal with Ravitch.

"I'm sure you'll then want your lawyers to go over it with Armacost. We should be able to close the deal immediately thereafter. Assuming, Sid, that you haven't changed your mind since last time we met."

"No. Quite the contrary. How do you intend to pay the ten million?"

"Wire transfer. It will come from Barclays in London. Where do you want it sent?"

"I'd prefer a check, a cashier's check. Hand delivered here."

■

"Then that's the way we'll do it," Willy said. "There are two other matters. First, the company name, "Western Credit Rating Agency." It's got to go. How about changing it to Western Financial Services? That way we can branch out in any new directions we want. What do you think?"

"I like it," Ravitch answered.

"Then there're these offices. I like the location, but the decor really sucks, Sid, if you don't mind my saying so. I'd like to bring in an interior decorator and spruce the place up."

"Fine with me, Willy. As long as it doesn't cost too much. Remember, we'll be fifty-fifty partners from now on. So I'll be paying for half of it."

"Don't worry. Before I do anything I'll get an estimate and run it by you."

"Anything else?" Ravitch asked.

"Not really," Willy said, as he got up to leave. "Come to think of it, there is one very small favor I'd like to ask of you, Sid."

"Sure."

"Do you still talk to Lenny over in Pleasanton every week?"

"Sure do. Every Tuesday. In fact," and Ravitch looked at his watch, "normally, right about now. Lenny tells me that this is the best time . . . between getting off work and dinner. Why do you ask?"

"Well, there's a guy Lenny and I both know over there. Jim Slade. He works in the warden's office. Typing, filing, that sort of thing. I want him to look up something for me."

"Sure. I'll put Lenny on it. What do you want to find out?"

"Where an ex-con is now. His name is Fred Fitch. He checked out a couple of months ago. They must have a forwarding address for him on file in Pleasanton."

"Who's this Fred Fitch?"

"Nobody special. He did a favor for me once. I'd like to reciprocate. That's all."

■

"If Lenny finds out, where can I get hold of you?"

"I'm still at the Huntington hotel," Willy answered.

Willy Saxon was barely out the door when Ravitch picked up the phone and dialed 510-833-7510, the number of the Federal Correctional Institute in Pleasanton. Lenny was on the line a minute later.

"Hey," he said, "you're right on time as usual, buddy."

"How's it going?" Ravitch asked.

"The closer the day comes, the worse it seems to get."

"How much longer you got?"

"Eleven more days. Then I'm free to go to work with you again, Sid." He paused. "It's still on, isn't it?"

"Of course, Lenny. With me a pal's a pal for life. Now look, I want you to help me out on something. Do you know a fellow by the name of Jim Slade?"

"Sure. He works in the warden's office."

"That's him. Do you think he'd do a favor for you?"

"Depends. Like what?"

"Find out the forwarding address of a guy who checked out a couple of months ago."

"Who?"

"Fred Fitch. Did you know him?"

"He was a weird one. Kept to himself. Was reading all the time."

"What was he in for?"

"Counterfeiting."

That stopped Sidney Ravitch for a moment. Was Willy Saxon thinking of getting into counterfeiting? Naw. That didn't fit. There must be something else.

"Lenny," he now said. "They must keep a pretty detailed background file on everybody over there."

"I would think so."

"Do you also think that, as long as he's at it, the guy in the

■

warden's office could lift the file on this Fred Fitch and make a copy of it?''

"That might be stretching things. I said I *know* him, Sid. But I don't *own* him or anything."

"Maybe *he* needs a favor. Anything come to mind?"

"Cigars. He loves cigars."

"I'll Fed-Ex two boxes of Partagas over to Pleasanton right away, Lenny. One for him and one for you."

■

THIRTEEN

By midafternoon the next day, Ravitch was already on the phone with the information. Fred Fitch was still in the Bay Area, living in an apartment in Livermore, the town just to the east of Pleasanton. Lenny had even gotten his phone number.

After Ravitch had hung up, Willy dialed that number. Somebody picked up on the first ring.

"Hello." It was said very hesitantly.

"Is that you, Fred?" Willy asked.

"Who's that?" Suspiciously.

"Willy Saxon. Remember me? From the library?"

"Library?"

"The library In Pleasanton, Fred. I was the librarian. Willy Saxon."

"Oh. Sure. You kind of caught me by surprise. Gee, how did you get my number anyway?"

"It's a long story. Look, I'd like to get together."

"Why?"

"I've got an idea about a job that would be perfect for you, Fred."

"What kind of a job?"

"I'll explain it when I see you."

"I don't want you to waste your time, Willy. I can't go back into the old business. The SEC has banned me for life."

"I'm fully aware of that, Fred. And it's no problem."

■

"I've already got a job, sort of. It's part time and I do it from home. Writing programs for a small software company over here. They're into computer games."

"Good for you, Fred. But believe me, the job I'm talking about will be better. A lot better. And it'll pay a lot of money, Fred. A whole lot."

If the guy had been counterfeiting the stuff, he must really like lots of money, Willy reasoned. Correctly, it turned out.

"When do you want to get together?" Fred now asked.

"Right away. Why not this evening? Are you free for dinner?"

"I guess so. Where are you calling from?"

"San Francisco."

"I don't like to drive over there at night."

"I'll send a car for you. And it will also bring you back. I'm staying at the Huntington hotel. We can eat here."

Willy was in the lobby waiting when Fred Fitch arrived at seven-thirty that evening. The gawky young man looked miserably out of place. With his long straggly hair, ill-fitting tweed jacket, slightly torn jeans, and dirty brown shoes he *was* out of place.

Whatever he'd used his counterfeit bills for, Willy thought, it sure hadn't been for clothes.

"Let's have a drink first," Willy said, leading the way into the Big Four bar, which lay off the lobby to the right.

He knew right away that having drinks had been a mistake when Fred ordered a Perrier, no ice.

He *knew* it was a mistake when Bob, the bartender, asked: "The same for you, Mr. Saxon?"

Willy decided that the better part of wisdom was to say nothing. It paid off in the form of an ice-cold Sapphire gin martini.

"You ever bet baseball, Mr. Saxon?" Bob asked.

"No. I never bet, period. Why?"

■

"We've got a big pool going on who's going to be in the World Series this year, and I thought you might want to get in."

"The Giants and the White Sox." It was Fred who said it.

"What was that, sir?" Bob asked.

"The Giants and the White Sox," Fred repeated. Then he turned to Willy. "I developed a program for this and ran the numbers through the computer just yesterday. It's kind of a hobby."

"Put me down for the Giants and White Sox," Willy said to Bob, "and see if you can get me a corner table in the restaurant."

"For how much?"

"A hundred."

"Done. For when do you want the table?"

"Right now." Willy said.

By the end of dinner, Willy knew that he had found his man.

"Assuming we go forward with this, Fred," Willy said, "what would be the start-up costs?"

"Let's begin with the hardware," Fred responded. "My recommendation is that we put in a system using Sun work stations working in tandem."

"I was somehow under the impression that you guys used big IBM mainframes," Willy said. "Or even Crays."

"Not anymore. They're not flexible enough. You need an open-ended platform . . . custom built."

"And you know how to build one?"

"Of course."

"And it would cost?"

"For a lot less than a million we could put together a really good system."

"Next question: How much working capital would you need?"

"A lot. Clients out there simply won't deal with an institu-

■

tion which is rated less than Double-A by the credit rating agencies."

"Let's say the institution in question has equity of twenty million dollars. Would that do?"

"Not these days. The best route to go would be to set up a new separate subsidiary and capitalize it with another twenty million. Then it would all depend on what rating the agency comes up with when they look at the whole picture."

But he, Willy, would soon control a credit rating agency, wouldn't he? So no big problem there.

"And how much staff?"

"Two or three professionals. I even know where I can get them. Guys that were real rocket scientists and got laid off by Lawrence Livermore Laboratories. There're three living in the same apartment complex where I am. Plus a minimal support staff. Maybe half a dozen."

Another million.

"Fred," Willy said. "I think we're in business."

"How soon can I go to work?" Fred asked.

"Soon. Very soon, I hope."

That would depend on how fast he could find a place for Fred and his team of geeks to work. A secluded place.

Denise would know. So why not call her? It was still only ten o'clock, and he knew that she never went to bed before midnight.

He went up to his room and called her San Francisco number, assuming that she too had come back from the ranch that afternoon. She answered on the second ring.

"It's Willy. Am I disturbing you?" he began.

"Don't be silly. I hope nothing's wrong," she said in a voice that was huskier than usual.

"No. Nothing's wrong with me. But you sound like you're getting a cold," Willy said.

"Maybe. If so I probably got it from sleeping outdoors."

"That's why I'm calling," Willy said. "But it's not what

■

you're thinking. I want to buy a place in the country. Like yours."

"It's not for sale, dear. What do you want it for?"

"Primarily for privacy. But ideally it would also have some guest cottages on the property, like your place."

"I thought you were interested in an apartment."

"I still am. I've decided that I want to live half the time in the city and half the time in the country."

"Good," Denise said. "Because I've been working on that apartment. I think I'll be able to free up the seventh floor pretty soon."

"Great."

"And I think I've already got an idea about the country place. It's an hour north of San Francisco. On the Russian River, outside of Healdsburg. You drove past the area on the way to my place."

"How many acres?"

"Five hundred. The main house is a beautiful old Victorian. But there are also four or five cottages on the property. It's owned by an architect who inherited it from his father, who was also an architect. I guess they just built another cottage on the place whenever the spirit moved them."

"How much would he want?"

"My guess would be around five million."

"How soon can I look at it?"

"My oh my, you are an impetuous one, aren't you, Willy."

"Not really. But every now and then most of us come up with a great idea and then do nothing about it. When that happens to me, I go for it. All out and right away."

"What's a country place got to do with this great idea?" she asked.

"I'll tell you some day. Now get hold of that architect," Willy said. "Then call me back."

The idea had been parked in the back of his mind for a couple of years. It had been inspired by Pleasanton, by the

■

very existence of the Federal Correctional Institute in Pleasanton. It was one of those "only in America" places.

For only in America did the government set up special institutions to house white-collar criminals. Every other country just dumped them in with the murderers and rapists. And it wasn't just Pleasanton. There was one exactly like it in Lompoc, in Southern California; another in Lewisburg, Pennsylvania. These places housed men who, collectively, had demonstrated more financial entrepreneurship, had thought up more innovative financial schemes, and had earned more money in a short time than any other group on earth. They represented an amazing pool of uniquely gifted men.

But all had been struck down by the cruel arm of the law at the height of their careers, only to now languish in these country clubs where all their talents and energy went completely to waste. Dennis Levine mopped floors at Lewisburg. Boesky worked on the dairy farm in Lompoc. Milken mowed the lawn at Pleasanton.

And the waste did not end there. When they were finally released, most simply disappeared. Willy remembered reading a piece in *Forbes* magazine about them. He could even remember the article's title: "Beyond the Slammer." Very few had made it even halfway back, because they remained social outcasts, pariahs in the business and financial community.

But, like Fred Fitch, they still had their mental prowess. All they needed was someone to show them a way around the prejudices of society, a way which would allow them to apply their God-given talents and reap their due rewards once again.

Well, Willy now knew such a way. He would simply make them invisible. And he would start with Fred Fitch.

But first he had to have that country place.

■

FOURTEEN

Denise picked him up at eleven the next morning. She was driving a red Porsche convertible.

"You probably have no idea how big a sacrifice I'm making for you, dear boy," she said to him, once he was in the car. "Normally I'm still in bed at this hour. But Jack—he's the architect—insisted that we be there no later than noon. He's got to leave by one."

"Can we get there by noon?" Willy asked, as he strapped himself in.

"Sure," Denise answered as she pulled away from the curb and put the Porsche directly into a U-turn, accelerating all the way. She missed the oncoming cable car by six feet, maximum, provoking the brakeman into a frenzy of bell ringing.

They arrived at the main house at noon on the dot. Willy sensed immediately that it was everything he wanted and more. Its name—River Ranch—described it perfectly.

The architect who owned it was waiting on the porch. At first he just ignored Willy.

"Denise," he said as he came down from the porch and approached them, "like I told you on the phone, I can give you one hour. What do you want to see first?"

"The main house, I guess," Denise answered, looking at Willy.

■

"Let's leave the main house until last," Willy said. "I'd like to see the other structures on the property first."

"You the one that's interested?" the architect asked, addressing Willy for the first time.

"Not exactly. It's a company that I own. By the way, my name's Willy Saxon."

"Why would a company want a place like this?" Jack asked.

"For a retreat," Willy answered. "For meetings. To entertain clients. Assuming the place has the proper facilities. We're not interested in any big building projects."

"You know," the architect said, "you just might have found the right place. My dad had these same ideas. He thought it would be a great spot for artists, artisans, and architects to get together. They'd come here for a weekend, a couple of weeks, or even a month, and just exchange ideas."

"You mean like Esalon?" Denise asked.

"No, Denise," Jack said. "At *our* place people kept their clothes on."

"So how many times a year do you do this?" Willy asked.

"None. My father died three years ago, It was his show, not mine. That's why I want to sell the place. But only to the right person," he added, looking sternly at Willy.

"Now, Jack," Denise said. "Willy is as right as they come. He's been a friend of the family for as long as I can remember."

Which was news to Willy.

There were actually six "cottages" on the property. They were spaced about a hundred yards apart, strung out along the bank of the Russian River. The bank was really more like a cliff, going almost straight down to the water sixty or seventy feet below. At one point on the tour, Willy stopped to take a better look.

"Jeez," he said. "Look at those fish. They must be three feet long." There were at least a dozen of the silvery fish taking advantage of a small inlet to swim just below the surface in

■

lazy circles around huge rocks, basking in the heat of the noonday sun.

"What kind are they?" Willy asked.

"Steelhead trout. They migrate to the sea, and then come back here to spawn and spend part of the summer. In spring you'll see salmon down there too," the architect said.

"Can we take a peek inside of one of these cottages?" Denise asked.

"Sure."

The outside was deceiving. It was built like an Alpine chalet. Inside, it was strictly California, from the huge state-of-the-art kitchen to the large-screen TV in the living room.

"What kind of reception do you get up here?" Willy asked when he saw the TV.

"From San Francisco? Lousy. But it doesn't matter. Each house has its own satellite dish. There are at least thirty satellites up there in the sky with twenty-four transponders each. So if you like TV, there's no lack of entertainment at the River Ranch. Let me show you."

He picked up a remote control, turned on the satellite receiver, and then the TV set.

"What do you want to see?"

"CNN."

"That's Galaxy Five, Transponder Five."

He clicked the remote, the screen turned green and said that the satellite was moving east. Five seconds later on came Bernard Shaw from Atlanta.

"CNBC," Willy now said.

One click and there it was, with the stock prices moving like a ticker tape across the bottom of the screen.

"Can you get the Reuters services off that thing?"

"What are they?" the architect asked.

"They provide specialized financial data. One service is for foreign exchange dealers. Another commodities. That sort of thing."

■

"Now I know what you're talking about. You in the financial business?" Jack asked.

"Not in it. But very interested in it," Willy replied.

"From what I know, that stuff's available. But you need a special descrambler, which you lease, to decode the signals. I'm told that comes very expensive."

"How's the telephone service up here?" Willy asked.

"First rate," the architect replied. "We've got sixteen lines coming in here now for both phones and fax. If you needed more, Pac Bell would have them installed within twenty-four hours. This might look awful woodsy, but it ain't."

"Is there a fax in each cottage?"

"That's right. Want to see one?"

"No. Just asking."

"Want to see the other buildings?"

"Sure. What are they for?"

"For meetings."

"Let's look."

The meeting hall was perfect. It could be easily converted into an open trading floor. The dining hall was about fifty yards away, in a clearing right on the edge of the bluff, high above the Russian River. There was a picnic area outside. Both buildings had also been done chalet-style.

"This place could just as well be in Zermatt or Gründelwald," Willy said.

"You're right. In fact, my father brought over three carpenters from Switzerland to build it. They also did the cottage you just looked at. He loved everything Swiss."

"My mother was from there," Willy said. "And I spent a year studying at the university in Zurich."

"Then you must like Swiss food."

"Of course."

"Well, we've had a Swiss cook in the family for twenty years. From Appenzel. She's really chief housekeeper and cook. Lives in a small cottage in back of the main house. In

■

fact, I should have brought this up earlier. We wouldn't want a new owner to kick her out."

Denise intervened. "Kick out? My dear Jack, if we buy your place we would *insist* that she stay. What's her name?"

"Vreni."

"Vreni?"

"It's Swiss for Veronica," Jack answered. He looked at his watch. "I've got to go in ten minutes. So let's walk back to the main house."

They got as far as the living room of the huge old Victorian when Willy decided that he had seen enough.

"I'm interested in buying this place, Jack."

"Are you sure you can afford it?"

"Pretty sure. How much do you want?" Willy asked.

"Five million."

"What if it's cash in thirty days?"

"Four and a half million."

"You've got a deal," Willy replied.

"Hold on a minute. A deal with whom?"

"You'll get a fax from one of my companies by Monday. It will make a formal offer and it will include bank references."

"Your friend doesn't fool around, does he?" Jack said to Denise.

He turned back to Saxon. "Let's shake on it, Willy." It was the first time the architect had deigned to use his name. "But now I've got to go."

"What's the big hurry?" Denise asked

"Golf. It's Thursday."

"I thought only doctors golfed on Thursday," Denise said.

"Doctors golf on Wednesdays, Denise," Jack responded, adding, "It's obvious you're not a golfer."

"But I am," Willy said. "Where do you play?"

"Fountain Grove Country Club. It's about twenty minutes from here. Want to take a look at it? As long as you're buying this place, you might as well join. It's the only decent club up here. At least it's the only club with decent members. But don't worry. If I put you up for membership, you'll be automatically in, Willy."

Minutes later they were in their cars, Denise trailing Jack's Mercedes in her Porsche.

"Don't worry, Willy. If I put you up you're automatically in," Denise said mimicking the architect's last words. "God, he's a snob. Why didn't you just tell him to shove his damn country club?"

"Because it gave me an idea. Remember your suggesting that the black Reverend, the guy that runs the city, and I get together for lunch?"

"Of course. I'll arrange it any time you want."

"I think what I've got in mind could be better accomplished during a round of golf," Willy said. "I used to do a lot of business that way. But my memberships all ran out during the past three years. And somehow I suspect that if I try to rejoin the Olympic Club, somebody's going to blackball me."

"You take advantage of every opening, don't you, Willy?" She reached over to pat his knee. "I like that."

He liked Fountain Grove Country Club a lot. Surprisingly, so did Denise. At her suggestion they stayed for lunch, eating outside on the terrace overlooking the lush Sonoma valley. During lunch he filled out a membership application form and attached his check for fifty thousand dollars, drawn on Barclay's Bank in London. As his sole sponsor he gave the name of Jack. He was assured by the general manager that it would receive the promptest attention.

On the drive back to San Francisco, Willy said very little. That fifty thousand dollar check had brought home how fast the money was pouring out. There was twenty million dollars to buy the investment bank. Another two million dollars each to bail Prescott and Armacost out of their legal problems. Then ten million dollars for his forty-nine percent stake in the ratings agency. Now he had just committed four and a half

■

million dollars to buy the River Ranch. And to get Fred Fitch going, he needed to invest a million for equipment, and another twenty million dollars for working capital. Plus staff costs.

Grand total: sixty million bucks.

As of a week ago, his stash in Liechtenstein had added up to $74,768,411.76.

Out of that would have to come at least two million for front-end costs in Switzerland—legal fees, board fees—and another half million to set up and run his offshore operations in London, the Channel Islands, and Nigeria. He had to factor in Prescott & Quackenbush losing money at the rate of two hundred thousand dollars a month for a while before it was turned around, say another million. And refurbishing costs for those lousy offices of the credit ratings agency, and now River Ranch, especially the main house, maybe another quarter of a million.

That brought his capital commitments up to $64 million. Had he overdone things?

He was way over budget for the simple reason that, originally, he had not factored in a large-scale derivatives operation like the one to which he was now committed with Fred Fitch. If Fitch's operation really clicked, he would have to put in yet more capital. Not right away, but pretty soon. There was, of course, no way he could get capital legitimately. So he would have to continue to develop his original plan.

Which meant that he had to gradually move municipal bonds from the back burner to the front burner. Get the right product, like AAA bonds issued by the City of San Francisco. Then provide the product at the right price to the right people, like Marshall Lane and his bond funds in New York. That might require a favor here, a favor there. But all legitimate. The name of the game: build up placement power, especially institutional placement power.

And *then* raise more capital.

■

But first, he had to put his money machine in motion.

"You know something?" he said.

"What?" Denise asked. "I thought you were asleep."

"No, just thinking. Thinking that I'm having more fun than I've had in my entire life. There's a phrase in German that describes what's happened to me: '*Glück in Unglück.*' "

"Which means?"

"It doesn't translate well."

"Try."

"Bad luck leads to good luck."

"I like that. Am I part of the good or the bad?"

"All good, Denise."

They were approaching the Huntington hotel. It was just after four.

"You know something?" Denise asked.

"What?"

"I'm feeling horny."

"Then how about a quickie, followed by a little nap?" Willy asked.

"You're on."

It ended up as two quickies and no nap.

As Denise dressed, she asked, "So what's next?"

"I've got to move out of here," Willy answered. "This doesn't fit your style. I apologize."

"Don't. It was my idea," she answered. "But I agree. You do have to get out of here."

"You said that apartment would be free soon."

"It will. It comes furnished, but it will still need a little fixing up. So will that Victorian at the ranch."

"I agree about the ranch. Know anybody that could help me out there?"

"Sure. The bishop's daughter. She's one of the best interior decorators in San Francisco. That's why you bumped into her in London. She's over there at least twice a year buying stuff.

■

Furniture, paintings, china. She's great. And she really likes you."

"Where can I get hold of her?"

"She'll call you."

"Tell her that I want to focus in on the River Ranch first."

"And the apartment?"

"I'll move into it as is. The sooner the better, Denise."

■

FIFTEEN

Late the next morning Denise was on the phone already.

"You can move into the apartment on Saturday," she said. "The man who leases it is packing even as we speak."

"How did you manage that?"

"Another quickie did wonders."

Which left Willy speechless.

"Just kidding," Denise said. "Did I at least have you a little worried?"

"Sure." Yet despite himself he had to admit it was true.

"I'll have one of my maids go over the place. When she's done, I'll come by with the keys. Say around three tomorrow."

"I'll want some things delivered. What's the exact address?"

"1190 Sacramento, seventh floor. The concierge's name is Bill. His number is 441-7810. Tell him what to expect, and when. Now I've got to run."

Willy remembered seeing a full page ad in the *Chronicle* that morning about a place down on Market Street that seemed to offer every type of electronic office equipment ever invented. He went to the wastepaper basket in his room and fished it out: The Whole Earth Electronic Bazaar. Only in San Francisco.

Time to go shopping. And also time to reenlist the aid of old faithful, the one guy who had stuck with him through thick,

■

99

thin, and jail. He called the offices of Prescott & Quacken-bush, and asked for Frank Lipper.

"Jeez, Willy. I thought you forgot me," he said. "I haven't heard from you since the day I picked you up over there in Pleasanton."

"I've been busy. But now I need your help. A lot of it. So come on over to the Huntington."

"When?"

"Right now."

"But I'm working."

"Frank, in a few days you'll be working for me, like the good old days. So just come right over."

Willy was waiting for Frank when he walked into the lobby of the hotel.

"Next stop is this place," Willy said, handing him the ad from the *Chronicle*.

"What you do you want to buy there?"

"A phone with all the gadgets. A Xerox plain-paper fax. A Macintosh computer. An Apple laser printer. A Sharp copy machine. A shredder."

"Where are you going to put all that stuff?" Frank asked.

"I'll show you."

Frank followed Willy out the door and onto California Street.

"Over there," Willy said, pointing. "As of tomorrow after-noon, I've got the seventh floor."

"Man, how did you manage that?"

"Connections, Frank. Connections. Now let's get a cab and visit the Whole Earth Electronic Bazaar."

It took them less than an hour to order everything.

"Now that you've got all that stuff, who's going to operate them?" Frank asked as they walked out of the store onto Market Street.

"I am, Frank."

"By yourself?"

■

"That's right. Just like I learned to do over in Pleasanton."

"Not even a secretary?"

"Nope."

"But why?"

"Because what I do from now on, Frank, and especially how I do it, is strictly my business. With one exception. You. Because you're the only person I really trust."

"What can I say, Willy?"

"Nothing. You want to shake on it, partner?"

Frank Lipper responded by damn near breaking Willy's hand.

"Enough of that," Willy said, more moved than he wanted to show. "Let's take a cab to the offices of Prescott and Quackenbush. A week ago Dan Prescott and Bobby Armacost told me they'd have papers ready for signing today. Let's see if they are."

"Do you want me to continue to work there?" Frank asked.

"More than ever. Those papers will give me ownership control of the bank. Which is just between us girls, by the way. After today, I'll need your eyes and ears to keep me informed about what's going on there."

"I can already tell you something you won't like," Frank said.

"Tell me."

"The operating losses more than doubled last month. They were up to just a shade under half a million."

"So my capital's starting to get eaten up before I even put it in," Willy said.

"The place is way overstaffed," Frank said. "And the only part of their business which is profitable is the muni bond operation."

"Your department," Willy said.

"That's right. But I'm just a salesman. What we desperately need is a rainmaker to bring in new product."

"Maybe you're about to get one," Willy said.

■

"Who?"

"Me. I'll explain over a beer. Know a bar that's close?"

The closest bar was a block away in the Sheraton Palace hotel. After ordering two Anchor Steam beers, Willy described the conversation he'd had with San Francisco's city manager and the good reverend from Glide Memorial Church.

"That's a hell of an idea," Frank said when he was done.

"Could you work out the details?" Willy asked.

"By when?"

"Next Thursday. Then we'll all go golfing."

"I'll get on it right away tomorrow," Frank said.

"Great. But tomorrow afternoon I'll need your help installing all that equipment."

"I can get back to it on Sunday."

"All right. But then on Monday you and I will be taking a little trip up to the wine country. In fact, we will probably stay a few days. You can keep working on it there. OK?"

"Are there computers up there?"

"Not yet. But that shouldn't bother us. Let's finish the beer and go back to the store quick."

There they ordered two Macintosh Power Books. To go.

Fifteen minutes later Willy entered the office of Prescott & Quackenbush with Frank at his side. Each was lugging a box containing a portable Mac.

"Would you mind telling Mr. Prescott that Mr. Saxon is here to see him?" Frank said to the receptionist.

"Who?" she asked.

"Never mind," Willy said. "Why don't you just go back to his office, Frank, and tell him I'm here."

It was a broadly smiling Dan Prescott who came out to fetch Willy less than a minute later.

"Your timing's perfect, Willy," he said. "Bobby arrived just fifteen minutes ago with the papers. Come on back."

Bobby was waiting for them in the conference room.

"There they are," the lawyer said, pointing to four sets of documents that were lined up on the conference room table. "And we're ready to go, too. The settlement went through this morning on schedule, thanks to the arrival of the four million that Dan and I needed to kick in. Thanks, Willy. We'll never forget it."

"I hope not."

"If you've got time we could review the contracts right now and get it over with."

"Let's do it."

An hour later they were done. Only seven pages needed revision.

"Who's going to get these documents on the other end?" Bobby asked.

"I'll take care of that," Willy said. "You deliver the revised documents to me at the Huntington tomorrow morning, and I'll have them in Switzerland for signature the beginning of next week."

"Don't forget to have the signatures notarized, Willy."

"I won't. By next Friday both the executed documents and the twenty million dollars that goes with them should be here. Then we can get down to business."

Willy turned to Prescott. "Speaking of business, I just heard from Frank that the place lost almost half a million last month. Is that right?"

"Unfortunately, yes," Prescott said, while giving Frank a not-too-friendly glance. "It's a little worse than we thought, Willy. But like we told you, everybody in the brokerage business is suffering."

"I don't intend to suffer at the rate of a half million a month for very long," Willy said.

"You said you'd have some ideas about bringing in new business," Prescott said. "We're ready to go with them any time you are."

■

"I'll be ready by next Friday." Willy responded. "So let's meet then at, say, four o'clock. As I recall it, you intended to announce the settlement and capital restructuring of the bank right away. Hold off on that. After you hear what I've got in mind you can include it in your release to the press."

SIXTEEN

At three the following afternoon, Denise van Bercham showed up as promised at the Huntington hotel. Willy was waiting in the lobby, packed and ready to go.

"Where's all your luggage?" she asked, after giving him a perfunctory peck on the cheek.

"Right here."

Right here were two suitcases, and a Macintosh Power Book computer.

"But where's the rest of it?"

"This is it, Denise," Willy insisted.

"But . . ."

"I was in jail for three years. Remember?"

"But what about all the stuff you had before?"

"I gave it to the Salvation Army."

"Why?"

"Because I did not want to be reminded of my old life."

"Reminded of what?"

"Of anything."

"Makes sense," she said. "So let's get to work on your new life."

This time instead of the red Porsche she had her driver and the Bentley waiting outside. All of Willy's worldly belongings did not even fill half of the trunk. Once loaded, Denise and Willy climbed into the backseat, and the Bentley started roll-

■

ing. It went three quarters of the way around the block—the block consisting of Huntington Park—and exactly three minutes later they were at their destination.

"Doesn't this strike you as slightly ridiculous?" Willy asked as they climbed out of the Bentley.

"Of course," Denise replied. "But I like the absurd."

The uniformed doorman who ushered them to the elevator was all subservience, obviously overwhelmed by Denise's presence. When they emerged onto the seventh floor from the elevator, it was Willy's turn to be overwhelmed. First came the marbled hall, then the huge living room with windows overlooking the park and Grace Cathedral. But what impressed most were the room's appointments: Louis XV furniture, Aubusson rugs, Flemish tapestries.

"It's absolutely stunning," Willy exclaimed.

"The bishop's daughter did it for me," Denise said. "Let's look at the other rooms."

The other rooms consisted of a dining room, three bedrooms, a beautiful wood-panelled study, and a maid's quarters in the rear behind the kitchen. It came with a maid.

"This is Juanita," Denise said, as they entered the kitchen. "She's going to stay for a week or two and really get this place in shape, aren't you?"

"Sí," she answered.

"This is the man who now lives here, Juanita. His name is Mr. Saxon."

Juanita curtsied.

"She also cooks," Denise said. "In fact, she's a very good cook. Her specialty is tamales. Very hot tamales. If you like, she'll cook some for you tonight."

"That would be great."

"Juanita," she said, "there's a grocery store just one block down Taylor Street. You go and get your stuff for your tamales. Mr. Saxon is going to eat here tonight. And get some beer, too."

■

She looked at her watch. "I'm afraid that you're going to have to eat alone, Willy. I've got something on this evening that's quite important to me. When will I see you again?"

"Would you be free for dinner next Friday?"

"I wasn't, but now I will be. Is next Friday something special?"

"Yes. If all goes well, it will be the day my new life *really* starts."

"And you want to celebrate that with me?" Denise asked.

"Yes."

"That's nice of you, Willy. Very nice. Now I've really got to go."

She had no sooner left than the doorman called to tell him two things: that a gentleman by the name of Frank Lipper was there, and that a number of boxes had just been delivered by the Whole Earth Electronic Bazaar. Willy told him to send both the gentleman and the boxes up.

By six o'clock that evening, with the help of Frank Lipper, all the equipment was up and running in Willy's new study. He sent Frank back to the office to work on the municipal bond package. Then Willy went to work himself.

He had decided to buy the River Ranch through his Channel Islands operation—keeping it at arm's length from Prescott & Quackenbush, which would be controlled from Liechtenstein and Switzerland. After composing the wording of the offer for the property on his new Mac, he printed it out, and faxed it to his London solicitor, with instructions that it should be faxed back to Jack, the architect, no later than Monday. Denise had supplied him with Jack's various addresses and numbers.

Then he sent a message to Dr. Guggi in Vaduz, advising him that the documents related to the takeover of Prescott & Quackenbush were on the way, and that, when executed and notarized, they should be promptly returned, along with a cashier's check for twenty million dollars drawn on the Union Bank of Switzerland.

Finally, he called Fred Fitch in Livermore, asking him if he could meet him Monday afternoon at 1190 Sacramento, and suggesting that he pack a bag for a short out-of-town stay. When Fred sounded a bit reluctant, Willy told him that his first paycheck, in the amount of ten thousand dollars, would be awaiting him. Fred then inquired about the exact time he should show up.

At 7:00, his phone rang. It was the bishop's daughter.

"I just talked to Denise and she said I should call," she began. "Normally, I wouldn't, especially on a Saturday night. But you know how Denise is."

"I know how Denise is. And I appreciate your calling. Because if you hadn't, I would have somehow gotten hold of you. By the way, thanks again for spending that evening with me in London. It made my trip."

"Mine too."

"Why don't we have dinner again?"

"Perhaps. When?"

"Tonight."

"But that's impossible. There's a big charity dinner this evening at the St. Francis. For the opera. Denise will be there, of course, along with everybody else. Including me. In fact, I've got to get off the phone pretty soon and finish dressing."

"Skip it. Call Denise back. Say you're suddenly not feeling well. We can eat here. At my new apartment. So nobody will see you."

She remained silent.

"We'll be having tamales, very hot tamales," Willy said. "And Mexican beer."

She broke her silence. "I *love* tamales. And Mexican beer."

"So you'll come?"

"I'll come."

As soon as she hung up, Willy rushed to the kitchen.

◾

"Juanita," he said. "Someone is joining me for dinner. Do you have enough for two?"

"*Sí.* For what time?"

"Nine. Did you get the beer?"

She had. But what about drinks?

"Does that store sell liquor too?" he asked.

She didn't get it.

"Whiskey. Tequila. At store?"

"*Sí, sí.*"

Margaritas! They would get the evening off to the right start. Juanita insisted on going back to the store herself. When she returned it was with a suspiciously large grocery bag, from which she extracted a bottle of Mexico's best. She presented it—triumphantly—to Willy, and then marched on to her kitchen looking all too pleased with herself.

The bishop's daughter stepped out of the elevator into his marble hall an hour later. She was taller and even better built than he had remembered. Maybe it was the Donna Karan outfit she was wearing.

And maybe he was being a bit obvious, since her first words were: "I'm not sure this was such a good idea."

"Did I leer?" Willy asked.

"You did. Or at a very minimum, you ogled."

"Then I apologize and promise to behave from now on."

"Good."

"OK. Now that we're back on the straight and narrow, would Madame care to join me in the living room and share an ice-cold margarita? But only if Madame goes for that sort of thing."

"*That* sort of thing Madame goes for," she replied.

When he presented her with her drink she said, "I see you found the bar."

After a frantic search, he had—hidden behind the doors of an eighteenth-century French armoire.

Pointing in its direction, Willy asked, "Was it your doing?"

■

"Yes. Bars belong in bars, not living rooms. Other than that, how do you like the apartment?"

"It's magnificent. And it's the reason for asking you over on such short notice. Denise told me you were a very talented lady. But it was not until I saw this place this afternoon that I really appreciated what she was talking about."

"Then why do you want to change it?"

"You misunderstand. I wouldn't change a thing here. It's at another place where I need your help."

"Where is it?"

"Up in the wine country, outside of Healdsburg. It's a five-hundred-acre spread located right on the Russian River."

"Surely not the River Ranch?" she asked.

"Yes. Do you know it?"

"Very well. Every July, for years, Jack and his father put on a big picnic up there. They always invited us. And we always went. I love the place. I'm surprised Jack's willing to sell it."

"He says it's because things changed after his father died. Jack doesn't want to use it for retreats, like his father did."

"I understand. His father and my late husband were very good friends."

"Really."

"I know what you're thinking, and you're right. My husband and Jack's father were of the same generation. They actually went to school together at Stanford. My husband studied engineering. Jack's father became an architect."

She paused. "Why am I telling you all this?"

"Maybe because in London I told you my life's history," Willy said.

She looked at her glass. "Do you have more of this stuff? I think I've run out."

"I have a whole pitcher of the stuff in the fridge in the kitchen," he replied, taking her glass. "How about some music?"

"Why not."

"The problem is I don't have the faintest clue as to how to go about getting some music."

"That's because the equipment is hidden in there." She pointed at a second armoire, opposite the one containing the bar. "Let me do it."

As he got the drink, she got some Mozart.

After he returned with her second margarita, she said, "As long as I'm at it, let's sit down and I'll tell you the rest."

She sat on the sofa while Willy took his place, carefully, on a chair that had been built around 1725, in Paris.

"Comfortable?" she asked.

"Fairly," he answered.

"You'll get used to it."

"Maybe."

"Anyway, my husband, the engineer, ended up running the largest gold mining operation in North America. Homestake Mining. He also acquired a substantial interest in the company."

That brought Willy to full alert.

"Why me as his wife? After his first wife died, I met him through my father—who was also of his generation. In fact, my father presided over his first wife's funeral. They were both devout Episcopalians. Next question: why did I marry a man of the same age as my father? Because I got sick and tired of having to put up with, and getting pawed by, the so-called men of my generation, especially those here in San Francisco. That's what I liked about you in London, Willy. No pawing. So there. Now we're even."

At that point Juanita appeared.

"La cena asta lista," she announced.

Since Willy looked confused, the bishop's daughter stepped in. *"Porque no pasamos al comedor."*

Juanita disappeared back into her kitchen.

"What's going on?" Willy asked.

"The tamales are about to be served," she replied.

■

111

When they entered the dining room, they found it bathed in soft candlelight. The table itself was set for two. But how it was set! Meissen china, and enough silverware for a five course meal. Incongruously, though, there was no crystal: just two plain beer glasses.

"I had nothing to do with this," Willy said, fearing that it might be mistaken by the bishop's daughter for a setup to a later pawing. "I really thought it was to be just tamales."

They were no sooner seated than Juanita appeared with the first course.

"De plato de entrada tenemos ensalada de langosta con adereso de guayavo," she announced before flouncing back to her kitchen.

"It's lobster salad with guava dressing," explained the bishop's daughter.

"How come you're so fluent in Spanish?" Willy asked.

"I spent a year in Mexico City," she replied, adding, "living with a writer who also drank margaritas. Too many of them, it turned out."

Now Juanita returned to offer beer: Corona, Tecate, Dos Equis, or Superior. Both went for Tecate.

"I wonder where she got all this stuff," Willy said, after she had again disappeared.

"I've been wondering where you got *her.*"

"Where else?" Willy replied.

"My God, surely not . . ."

"I'm afraid so."

"But it's bound to get back to Denise that I've been here."

"Don't worry. I'll have a word with Juanita," Willy said.

"Don't bother. After all, it was Denise who asked me to call you in the first place. Unless, of course, it would bother *you* if it got back to her."

"Hardly. Denise might own this apartment, but she sure doesn't own me," Willy responded.

"Doesn't own you *yet,*" she responded. "Anyway, you can

■

explain that this was all my idea. To find out more about the job she said you might have for me. Which brings up a question. Why exactly are you buying Jack's ranch?"

"I'm going to use it for business."

"How?"

He decided to tell her, since, after all, it was bound to come out anyway, if she took on the job of redoing the place, which would include converting the conference facility into a trading room.

"I'm going to put a team of financial people to work up there, trading financial instruments of a fairly exotic nature."

"Go on. I'm not that dumb about financial matters."

"I noticed that at the lunch Denise put on at Stars. All right, we'll be dealing especially in financial derivatives, like stock futures, puts, calls, warrants, interest rate swaps."

"For whom?"

"Initially for our own account. Then, when the word gets out, we'll put together a series of partnerships, probably in the form of hedge funds. But only for sophisticated investors with a high net worth. High rollers who are after very high rewards, but are also fully aware that high rewards require taking high risks. The returns, at times, can be staggering. A Hungarian by the name of George Soros, who operates out of London, put together something called the Quantum Fund, playing especially the currency markets. In 1992, he made one and a half billion dollars in one month."

"Wow! But you said he operated out of London, which is obviously right in the middle of things. How in the world could you do the same thing operating out of Healdsburg?" Sara asked.

"The world has changed dramatically in the past few years, especially in terms of computing power and telecommunications. I'm just taking advantage of it. We'll link our computers to satellites and tap into the myriad of information provided by services which are already available up there. Through

■

them we can track every trade of every kind on every exchange
in the world. From Healdsburg. Then we'll have Pac Bell
install dedicated hard lines tying us directly to the major
exchanges in New York, Chicago, London, Frankfurt, and
Zurich for the actual trading."

"But why not do this like everybody else does? From Wall
Street? Or Montgomery Street, if you want to stay in California?"

"Again, it's a matter of adapting to the changing times, in
this instance where people are concerned. The two guys that
started Apple figured it out first. Then the filmmaker, George
Lucas, followed their example. They recognized that, these
days, a large percentage of really brainy guys will no longer
put up with working nine to five in some office tower in the
financial district. Or wearing a tie. Or commuting on BART.
They want to work in a relaxed, loose, noncity atmosphere, to
come to work in jeans, and to have beer parties after work on
Friday. Like on a college campus.

"So Apple created its own campus down on the peninsula.
And George Lucas makes his movies, like *Raiders of the Lost
Ark,* at a completely secluded ranch in west Marin County.
His special-effects nerds love it there. I'm going to create a
campus on River Ranch up in Sonoma County. The only
difference is that, instead of designing computers or making
movies, we are going to design ways to make money."

"That's absolutely terrific!" she said. "In fact, it's one of the
most exciting ideas I've ever heard of. And you want me to
help you design the campus?"

"Exactly. If you still want to."

"I do. On one proviso," she said.

"That is?"

"That you start calling me by my name. Do you realize that
so far this evening you haven't used it once? So just in case
you've forgotten—again—it's Sara. Just plain Sara."

■

Juanita appeared with the main course. *"Pechugas de pato en salsa de chipotle."*

Sara explained: "Duck breast in chipotle sauce."

"What the hell is chipotle sauce, Sara?" he asked.

"That I don't know. The writer I was living with was into drink, not food. Why not just try it?"

He did. And while he did, he explained how he envisioned his trading room. She agreed to drive up to River Ranch with him the next day, to get things moving.

They were then offered a choice of either tequila mousse or nieve de mango for desert. They decided to try one of each.

Over her mango sorbet, Sara probed further. "Willy, I was just thinking. Doesn't all this require an awful lot of money? I don't mean just for the ranch and the computers. But also capital?"

"You're right. It does."

"And you've got enough?"

Willy wondered how to address that one.

He decided to answer it this way: "I've got friends who've got enough."

Sara for the first time looked flustered. "Willy, I'm sorry if it sounded like I was prying. I wasn't. It's just that the more I hear, the more exciting the whole thing sounds. Perhaps you were not aware of it, but I inherited a lot of money. And what you're doing sounds like something I'd like to be part of. And I'm not just talking about helping you with the campus. That too, of course. But . . . ."

Willy interrupted. "No, Sara," he said. "This is not for you."

"Why?"

How to explain it?

"Because, as I said, investing in something like this is high risk. Very high risk. Not for widows and orphans."

"So is gold mining. And that's where this widow has most of her money—invested in the shares of Homestake Mining.

■

The price of those shares, like the price of gold, has fluctuated all over the place in recent years."

As Lenny had also found out, Willy thought.

"But you can hedge against those fluctuations," he said.

"How?"

"Don't the people who now run your husband's company explain that sort of thing to you?"

"No. Maybe you can."

"Simple. You sell the gold you are scheduled to produce in the forward market, and thus lock in a price. I'm sure Homestake does that. It's just a new twist on what the farmers in the Midwest have been doing for many years at the Board of Trade in Chicago. In summer they sell their wheat or corn crops for future delivery in the fall at a guaranteed price."

"Assuming they really do this at Homestake, if I had a word with them could they now start doing it through you?"

"Definitely. At least in a week or two."

He did not exactly have a gold guy lined up, but he could certainly find one fast. Homestake was, after all, one of the world's largest producers of gold. And as long as he was at it, he might as well line up a currency trader too. Like George Soros had done and made that one and a half billion dollars in one month back in 1992—right after he had gone to jail.

The more Willy thought about these new ideas, the more he wanted to get to work on them. Giving way to an unconscious impulse, he looked at his watch. And got caught looking.

"Getting bored?" Sara asked, and then quickly went on. "I'm sorry. I shouldn't have said that. It's just that you never let up, do you?"

"I guess not. I apologize."

"Don't. That's one of the things I really like about you, Willy."

"What's the other?"

"I'm not going to tell you. Yet."

A half hour later, as she drew them to her breasts, she did.

■

"The other thing I like about you is your hands, Willy. The way they're shaped, the way you move them. The way . . ."

He moved them lower.

Minutes later in the master bedroom, it was her hands that moved on him. Shortly thereafter, it was her body that moved on top of his.

As Willy found out during the next two hours, Sara was not only a big girl, but a strong girl as well, and one with tremendous endurance. She was also noisy, as Juanita discovered, when she was awakened by a series of triumphant shrieks that echoed through the seventh floor of 1190 Sacramento. The last could be heard just as, so appropriately, the bells of neighboring Grace Cathedral, the seat of the local Episcopalian bishophric, began pealing midnight.

Soon thereafter, the bishop's daughter and an exhausted Willy sank into a deep sleep.

■

SEVENTEEN

The next morning Willy decided that they should have breakfast in bed, and that he would both make it and serve it. That way neither Sara's Episcopalian sense of propriety nor Juanita's Catholic prudery would have to be put to the test.

Willy trotted down to the corner store, returning with everything from waffles to maple syrup to eggs to bacon to croissants. At just after nine, he entered his master bedroom bearing a tray with enough food on it to feed a family of five.

The two of them ate it all, while watching the David Brinkley show on channel 7. The subject under discussion was Germany. Willy became so engrossed that, except for going to the kitchen to get more coffee during two of the commercial breaks, he paid no attention whatsoever to the woman sharing his bed. Not that it bothered her. The strenuous activities of the preceding night had left her as hungry as she had been in years. So while he watched, she ate.

When the program was finally over, she finally felt it safe to say something.

"Why the big interest in Germany?"

"Because something serious is starting to happen there," Willy replied.

"You don't mean Hitler all over again?"

"No. Not that bad. But bad enough. Nobody's sure quite

■

how long democracy can survive if tough economic times continue there. I'm sure it will, but it could be a close call."

"But I thought the Germans were among the richest people in Europe."

"They are. As a result of the *Wirtschaftswunder* that happened after World War Two. But they're not getting rich*er* anymore. In fact, their standard of living has been stagnant now for years. That has them really pissed off. So, like good Germans, they are taking it out on each other, or on the foreigners who have 'infested' their country."

"Who's to blame?"

"The government in Bonn as much as anybody. When the Berlin Wall came down, they promised that within five years they would convert what had been Communist East Germany into a model of prosperity. This would lead to a second *Wirtschaftswunder* in all of Germany, with the result that by the year two-thousand the Germans—all of them—would end up as the richest people in the *world,* not just Europe. To put the icing on the *Kuchen,* the German chancellor promised that all this could be done 'with no new taxes.' He pulled a George Bush."

"What went wrong?"

"They found out that they had totally miscalculated. Totally. To pay for reunification—to raise the standard of living in the East to that already prevailing in the West—they had to spend huge sums, hundreds and hundreds of billions of dollars. To get that money they had to borrow like crazy, which kept interest rates sky high. But even that was not enough. So, like George Bush, the German chancellor had to break his promise and raise taxes. The problem is that, despite all that borrowing and taxing, nothing has really improved in East Germany, while in West Germany the economy sank into the worst recession since the depression of the early 1930s and has remained stagnant ever since.

"The level of discontent in Germany is worse than it's been

■

since World War II. The Germans in the West are convinced that the Germans in the East are a bunch of lazy bums who were living off the state their entire lives, and in the process forgot what it means to really work for a living. The Germans in the East think that those in the West are arrogant, greedy, uncultured slobs. That all they're interested in is making money. So the social and political fabric is starting to come apart. A lot of people on both sides now regret the day the Wall came down."

"Go on, Willy. What comes next?"

"It can only get worse. And worse will not exactly be good for the German mark. Remember, the last time the Germans went into one of their manic-depressive periods was during the early 1930s. It was also brought on by severe economic hard times, which led to total disillusionment with the democratic government of the Weimar Republic. You know what happened next, Sara."

"But you started off this whole conversation by saying that you did *not* think this would lead to another Hitler."

"That's right. That's *my* opinion. But as that TV program showed, a lot of people disagree with me. And when more and more people start to think the worst, this leads to more and more people starting to think that maybe Germany is not exactly the greatest place on earth to keep their money. In fact, maybe even a lot of *Germans* are going to start thinking like that."

"Then what happens?"

"They start pulling out of the German mark. But where to go? France? Holland? Switzerland? The problem is that all of these countries are totally dependent on the German economy. What happens there is bound to spread across Europe, so the currencies of *these* countries also become suspect. In the end *no* place in Europe will be considered safe."

"And then?"

"What happens then is that the lemmings all start to swim

■

the Atlantic, headed west toward the last surviving safe haven."

"The United States."

"Right. Like so many times in the past."

"And you, of course, being Willy Saxon, know how to make money on that," Sara said.

"I do. It's pretty simple. As more and more people decide to get out of marks and buy dollars, the price of marks goes down, and the price of dollars goes up. Ditto when the fear virus spreads to the French franc, the Dutch guilder, and so forth. They go down and the dollar goes up even further. So he who buys dollars and sells marks and francs and guilders in huge quanties in the forward market—like the Midwestern farmer does with his corn—just before all this starts to happen, makes a lot of bucks."

"If it's so easy, why doesn't everybody do it?" Sara asked.

"Because it is not enough to suspect *what* is going to happen to a currency. The *when* is even more important. If you're timing is wrong, just off by a week or two, you can *lose* a bundle. Currency speculation is what they call a zero-sum game. There's always a big loser for every big winner."

"So when that Soros fellow made that billion and a half in one month, who lost it?"

"The Bank of England. Because they announced to the world that they were going to defend the pound sterling to the death. Stupid. But that's what they did. And eventually, *inevitably,* I might add, they lost. Now if you think the *British* authorities can be stubborn when it came to the value of the pound, wait until you see how the *German* authorities, especially those arch-conservatives who run the Bundesbank, will react when that very symbol of German supremacy, the deutsche mark, comes under attack. They'll promise to defend it beyond death, well into eternity. And they will also go down in flames."

"Why is that inevitable?"

■

"Because, again, the times have changed. It used to be that the central banks of the world, like the Bank of England and the German Bundesbank, had more money at their disposal than anybody, so they could fend off almost any attack. No longer. There are hundreds and hundreds of billions of hot money in private hands floating around the world, just waiting for an opportunity like I'm talking about to come along. When they collectively sense a kill, they set in motion a wall of money that comes at a central bank like a tidal wave. These days this does not create a sink-or-swim situation. Today it's sink now or sink later. In other words, faced with such a situation today it is *always* the better part of reason for a central bank to cave in and devalue almost right away, rather than trying to fight it and losing many billions of dollars in that zero-sum game. As the Bank of England found out in 1992. And as the Bundesbank is going to find out soon."

"Hm. How interesting. So when do you *think* all this is going to start happening?"

"Not tomorrow morning. But it's coming for sure. So I'm going to start getting ready for it."

"At the River Ranch?"

"That's right."

"You know something, Willy," Sara said. "I think you're probably the most intriguing man I've ever met in my entire life. I mean, here we are in bed and for the past hour all you've been doing is talking about Germany."

"Are you ready to radically change the subject?"

"I thought you'd never ask."

At eleven-thirty, Sara said she had to leave. Willy offered to drive her home until she reminded him that he didn't have a car. So he walked her across Huntington Park to the hotel, where he got the doorman to hail a cab for her. As they parted, Willy reminded Sara that he was expecting her at noon

■

the next day, at the apartment. Then it would be on to the River Ranch.

Willy walked four blocks down Taylor Street to the out-of-town newspaper store at the corner of Post and Taylor, Harold's. He bought every German newspaper and periodical they had on offer: *Der Spiegel, Die Zeit, Die Frankfurter Allgemeine, Das Handelsblatt.* He had Harold throw in a couple of German/Swiss publications too—*Die Neue Zürcher Zeitung* and *Die Wirtschaftswoche*—since the Swiss covered their big brother to the north better than anybody else. To round things out, he also bought *The Economist* of London, and three American paperback novels.

Thus armed to the teeth, Willy walked back up to 1190 Sacramento and plopped down on the sofa in his magnificent living room, ready to enjoy the afternoon doing what he liked to do best. Read.

Three articles immediately caught his attention.

The first he found in *Die Zeit,* which had a piece on Volkswagen being in deep trouble. It got Willy searching back into his memory banks for another instance of troubled times at VW. He couldn't remember the exact year, but he certainly recalled what had happened.

It had involved Volkswagen foreign exchange operations. They were huge, since VW sold all over the world, produced cars and vans in a dozen different countries, and so had money coming in and going out in a myriad of currencies. It added up to an annual volume equal to tens of billions of dollars. The guy managing VW's foreign exchange operations—a Swiss, if he recalled correctly—had developed a reputation as one of the best in the world. His department became one of VW's major profit centers. He was making as much money playing around with their cash flow as the plant managers were making by manufacturing cars.

Then, as happens so often, he went too far. He was going through a bad period, and, being an egomaniac like all hugely successful traders, decided to pep up the results in order to keep his record as a consistent money maker intact. He cooked up some huge trades with the central bank of Hungary, which brought in tens of millions of profits for VW. The problem was, these trades never took place. The paper behind them was completely fictitious. And those profits were nonexistent. This all came out, but nobody ever went to jail. No one was even charged with anything. After a burst of publicity, all had gone quiet.

Why? It was rumored that the phony trades had not just been with the Hungarians. That perhaps some of the largest banks in Germany and Switzerland had also been involved, with their traders doing a favor for one of their biggest clients, VW, in the full knowledge that the "arrangements" were only temporary. After all, the guy at VW had maybe the best track record in the business. So it would be only a matter of time—a short time—before the phony trades could be replaced by real ones with real profits. Then the fictitious trading slips would go into the shredder, and, as far as the rest of the world was concerned, nothing had ever happened.

Giving credence to these stories was the fact that the financial establishment in central Europe put the lid on this affair, and kept it there. They quietly divided up the losses among themselves, and ate them.

"So where is that guy now?" Willy asked himself.

The second article was in *The Economist* of London. It confirmed his interest in gold, which Sara had sparked the night before. It also tied in with the theory he was developing about the increasing vulnerability of not only the German mark but all the European currencies. The thesis was quite simple. Much of the gold in the world was in the hands of central banks—thirty-five thousand tons of the stuff—and much of that was owned by European central banks. It had been just sitting there in their vaults for decades, doing nobody any good. Why? Because gold was still thought of as the

■

last guarantee of the integrity of a currency, the last defense against those nasty currency speculators. But slowly it was beginning to sink in after the 1992 debacle that, ultimately, there was no defense. It was better to just give in, devalue, and get it over with as quickly and cheaply as possible. Then what to do with the gold? Well, to continue to sit on it was not only doing no good, it was actually costing the taxpayers a lot of money because it earned no interest. Better to sell gold for dollars which could then be used, if necessary, to intervene in the markets and to steady exchange rates before they began gyrating out of control. In the meantime, the dollars would earn interest.

In two cases, Belgium and Holland, the central banks had already broken the taboo of never, ever selling gold. Both had already gotten rid of a quarter of their gold holdings.

Which led Willy Saxon to this conclusion: If the German mark tanked and started to take every currency in Europe down with it, you could be sure that a lot of other central banks would dump gold to gain liquidity. Anybody who called this right, and sold gold futures ahead of time, would make a *real* ton of money!

He had to find a gold guy fast.

The third was an article in London's *Financial Times.* It's title: "A Swiss maverick exercises its muscles." It was about a tiny Swiss bank, the BZ Bank in Zurich, which, although it had a total of only twenty—twenty!—employees, was Switzerland's fourth largest bank in terms of profits. It's earnings were exceeded only by the Big Three Swiss banks. Between them those three employed one hundred fifty thousand people.

How did BZ Bank do it? By trading warrants—derivatives, managing closely held investment trusts, and dealing in foreign exchange and precious metals.

"Exactly!" Willy exclaimed.

At that moment Juanita appeared for the first time that day.

■

She bore a tray. On the tray was a plate. And on the plate were two of her famous hot tamales. There was also a bottle of Tecate beer. It came with a lime but no glass.

Willy decided it was time for a break. So he reached for one of the paperback novels he had picked up at Harold's. While he began to read, he began to munch on his tamales.

"What a life!" he exclaimed to his empty living room.

He was all set to spend the rest of that afternoon just as he had every Sunday afternoon during the past three years: all by himself, reading a good book.

Habits were hard to break.

EIGHTEEN

Willy went to bed early that night, and got up very early the next morning so as to be sure to catch Dr. Werner Guggi while he was still in his office in Vaduz.

"Salü, Werner," Willy began when Guggi came on the phone. *"Hesch du alli Document bekoh?"*

Willy had decided to use the Swiss dialect from then on when discussing "delicate" matters with his Liechtenstein lawyer. Now that he had his own phone, one never knew who might be tempted to listen in.

"Jo, alles isch in beschter ornig," Guggi replied, assuring him that the documents had indeed arrived.

"OK," Willy said, switching to English. What he now wanted to discuss was also delicate, but hardly in the class of using a Liechtenstein cover to buy an American bank with money he had never paid taxes on. "I've got a very odd request. Do you remember that big scandal maybe five years ago when Volkswagen got caught rigging phony foreign exchange transactions with the Hungarians?"

"Sure. I think it involved around a quarter of a billion dollars. Everybody here followed that very closely, especially because the chief trader involved was a Swiss."

"You're right. Now Werner, could you find out where that guy is? I'll bet anything he's back in Switzerland. And I'll also bet that if anybody knows where he is, it'll be a fellow Swiss

■

foreign exchange dealer. They all know each other. And they all stick up for each other."

"You're right. Look, I'll give a call to the bank in Liechtenstein. It's right across the street, as you must recall. But what should I tell them if they want to know why I'm trying to track him down? Like you said, these people are known for protecting each other."

"Tell them that somebody wants to offer him a job."

"You?"

"Don't tell them that. But yes. Me."

"But will the American authorities let him into the country?"

"Why not? He's no felon. He not only was never convicted of anything. As far as I know, he was never even charged with anything."

"OK. I'll make my inquiries and then I'll call you right back. What's your number?"

Guggi was back on the phone in less than five minutes.

"I've got everything," he said. "His name is Urs Bauer."

"Can't get any more Swiss than that, can you?" Willy said.

"I guess not," his lawyer replied. "He lives in Basel at 136 Bruderholzallee." Then he gave him his phone number.

"Good work, Werner. Did you find out what he's doing?"

"No."

"If I call him cold, do you think he'll know who I am?"

"Most probably. After all, you introduced the first junk bonds to be issued in Swiss francs."

"Do you think he also knows the rest of my history?"

"Maybe. Although that did not get a big play in the press here. In any case, in Swiss financial circles, as I think I've already told you, they think that sending anyone to jail for insider trading or parking a few shares is a big joke. If they did that here, they'd have to build a dozen new jails."

"All right. Thanks for the help, Werner. If anything comes of this, I'll let you know."

■

As soon as he got Guggi off the line, Willy hung up and dialed again.

A woman answered in Basel. That, Willy had not planned on, but he plunged ahead anyway.

"Ich möchte mit Herr Bauer sprechen," he said, this time in high German.

"Ein Moment," she answered.

Willy could then hear her call, "Urs! Telephone!"

As soon as Urs came on the phone, Willy decided not to play linguistic tag but move right into English.

"Mr. Bauer," he began, "I don't know if you've ever heard of me but my name's Willy Saxon. A few years ago I was underwriting junk bonds in your country, working together with the Union Bank of Switzerland."

"Sure. You're the American who started that whole business over here, right?" His English was perfect.

"That's right."

"Sure. What can I do for you?"

Apparently what happened hadn't affected his cockiness, Willy thought before continuing. "I'll tell you what you can do for me. I'm in the process of establishing a professional investors' operation here in California, dealing principally in derivatives, but operating globally. I need a foreign exchange dealer, and I'm told you're the best there is."

"Was," Bauer said. "You must know the story."

"I do. As far as I'm concerned, it's water over the dam. I've had a similar experience myself."

"So that's the other reason you're calling me?"

"Yes."

"I'll tell you right now that I have no interest whatsoever in getting connected with any shady operation. You're not the first one to come with one of those offers I wasn't supposed to be able to refuse. But so far I've refused them all."

"Fair enough. What if I have my lawyers in Zug and Vaduz

■

give you a full rundown on what I'm up to? Would you consider it?"

"Maybe. How much capital do you have to work with?"

"Initially twenty million dollars. But I fully intend to put it up to fifty million very soon. And we'll be putting together some hedge funds involving outside investors which should involve at least another hundred million."

"Who can vouch for your really having that kind of money?"

"For one, Dr. Rudolph Schweizer."

"You mean the Dr. Schweizer who is chairman of UBS?"

"That's right. Do you know him?"

"Of course. I ran his foreign exchange operations in Zurich before I moved over to Volkswagen," came the response. "What kind of foreign exchange operation did *you* have in mind?"

"Trading for our own account. And those hedge funds. You would call all the shots. We'd share the profits eighty/twenty. It's different from what you've been used to at both UBS and Volkswagen."

"I know what you're talking about. It's like the BZ Bank in Zurich. But you're doing this in California?"

"Yes. We'll be operating out of a ranch up in the wine country north of San Francisco."

"Really. That's something only you Americans could do," Urs said.

"If you wanted, you could live up there. There's a chalet on the property overlooking the Russian River that might be just right for you."

"Hold on a minute," Urs said.

When he came back on the line he said, "My wife's on the extension phone. Would you mind once again going over what you just told me about the ranch?"

"With pleasure."

She—her name was Susie—kept Willy on the line for the

∎

next twenty minutes, wanting to know every possible detail: about the chalet, the climate, the river, the town of Healdsburg; how far it was from San Francisco; how long it took to drive from the ranch up to Squaw Valley for skiing.

"You know, Mr. Saxon," Urs said, after she had finally gotten off the line. "Susie has not had it easy after what happened. We first moved from Germany back to Zurich where they treated us—both of us—like dirt. So we moved to Basel. Same thing here."

That's when Willy knew they were hooked—both of them. And that's when he decided to ask about the other matter.

"Ever been involved in precious metals? Especially gold?" Willy asked.

"Of course," came the immediate answer.

"Including derivatives?" Willy asked.

"Of course," came the answer again. "In fact, when I was working for UBS I was one of the biggest operators in the gold futures market in Zurich. In fact, we *were* the biggest. Because South Africa used UBS to market its bullion. They still do. And they often asked us—me—to hedge their positions in the futures market."

That did it. "Let me make a suggestion, Urs, if I may call you by your first name."

"Please do."

"OK. And I'm Willy. Now why don't you ask around about me right away, starting with Rudolph Schweizer? I'll have my lawyers contact you this evening, and they will meet with you any time you want."

"Agreed."

"Then if you like what you hear, why don't you and your wife just come over and have a look around."

"I think she'd like that a lot," Urs replied.

"Good. Just in case, I'll arrange to have two first-class return tickets available for you with Swissair in Basel. For this Thursday. If you don't want to come, just let my lawyer know

■

and he'll cancel them. If you do decide to come and don't like what you see here, fine. No obligation."

"You've just got yourself a deal, Willy," the Swiss said.

Willy barely caught Dr. Guggi in his office before he left for the day. He told him what had happened with Bauer, requested that he contact him right away, and asked that he arrange for those tickets with Swissair.

Then he made a local call, ordering a limo to be at 1190 Sacramento at noon. After that he took a long shower, dressed, and went out to get the *Times,* the *Journal, Barrons,* and the *Chronicle.* He read them in the dining room while eating the breakfast that Juanita had prepared without his even asking.

Frank Lipper arrived shortly before noon. He brought two things with him: the proposal for the San Francisco municipal bond underwriting and a cellular phone.

"We forgot this," he said, as he presented it to Willy.

"That's what happens when you're out of circulation for three years," Willy said.

"Do you know how to work them?" Frank asked.

"Not these new ones. Show me."

"Who do you want to call?"

"City Hall."

After Frank got the number from 411, he dialed again while Willy watched.

"Got it," Willy said, taking over the phone. When the operator at City Hall came on, he said, "I'd like to speak to the chief administrative officer."

"What's his name?" he asked Frank, after he had been put on hold.

"George Abbott."

At that moment the regular phone rang.

"Take it, Frank," Willy said.

■

Frank did, and then repeated what the concierge had told him: Sara Jones had arrived, as had a limousine driver.

"Tell them we'll be right down," Willy told him. "I wonder what happened to our rocket scientist?"

Then George Abbott's secretary came on the cellular phone. When Willy gave his name, it drew a somewhat skeptical response. There was a similar hesitancy in the voice of San Francisco's chief administrative officer when he came on the line.

But that changed immediately when Willy said, "Remember, we and the good reverend were talking about that piggyback bond issue up at Denise's ranch last weekend."

"Sure. I apologize for not recognizing your voice immediately. Look, I talked that idea over with some of our people here in both the financial and housing departments. They all loved it."

"Great. Now I know it's short notice, but I thought maybe we could get together and talk details over a round of golf tomorrow afternoon up at the Fountain Grove Country Club. Do you know it?"

"Sure. It's a great course. Let me check tomorrow's agenda with my secretary," Abbott said.

When he came back, Abbott asked, "Would a twelve o'clock tee time work out for you?"

"Perfect. We'll be a foursome. Dan Prescott, the chairman and CEO of Prescott and Quackenbush, and Frank Lipper, who runs their municipal bond operation, will be joining us."

"And the Reverend?"

"I thought it best that we can include him later—after we know whether or not we've got something concrete going."

"I agree. OK. I'll see you tomorrow, Willy," Abbott said, and hung up.

Frank Lipper had, of course, heard the entire conversation, at least Willy's end of it. "I didn't know you were a member of the Fountain Grove Country Club."

■

"I'm not."

"So how can you invite three guests to play up there tomorrow?"

"Don't worry. I'll work on it while we drive up 101. I can
already tell, Frank, this cellular phone is going to change my
life!"

The other phone rang again. Fred Fitch had just arrived.

"Everybody that's supposed to be here is here, Frank,"
Willy said. "So let's go."

"Where are we going?" Frank asked.

"I'll tell you in the car."

■

Nineteen

The four of them climbed into the stretch limo shortly after noon. Everybody had packed a small suitcase. Fred, however, also had a big box and a bulging briefcase.

The first thing Willy did was slip Fred Fitch an envelope containing his first pay, in the amount of $10,000 cash, which he'd brought back from Europe. Then, after he had made introductions all around, he explained about River Ranch—where it was, and what was going to happen up there. When he was done, Frank Lipper asked the first question.

"So the operation will be really, essentially, a branch of Prescott and Quackenbush?"

"Wrong, Frank. River Ranch is going to be a *stand-alone* operation that will be *advising* Prescott and Quackenbush."

"All right. So if I'm a client and I want to trade some stock options, where do I call? San Francisco or Healdsburg?"

"San Francisco. Never Healdsburg," Willy replied.

"But nobody in our office in San Francisco has a clue about options. If they call us, we'd have to call Healdsburg. Healdsburg would have to give us a quote on the trade, then we'd have to relay it back to the client to see if the price was right. Then . . ." Frank just threw up his hands. "That'll never work, Willy."

"What if you call San Francisco but you get Healdsburg?" Willy said.

■

"Can't be done. San Francisco's area code is 415. Healdsburg's is 707," Frank said.

"Wanna bet?" Willy asked. "Believe me, it can be done. I checked with Pac Bell."

"No shit!" Frank explained. He then looked at the bishop's daughter, and said, "Sorry."

"Of course it can be done," Fred Fitch said.

And now that he had their attention, Fred began talking a blue streak. As he talked, he kept yanking memos out of his briefcase and giving them to Willy.

"These," he said, handing Willy the first one, "are the type of computers we're going to get. They're Sparcserver One Thousand work stations made by Sun Microsystems down in Mountain View. The memo explains what they can do. To put it in perspective, each has ten times the computing power of the average IBM mainframe system shipped in 1991, yet they're the size of a desktop printer."

"How many will we need?"

"Not many. I'd say four to start with. We'll be three professionals, and five or six staff."

Another memo appeared. "Their job descriptions," Fred explained.

As Willy scanned the memo he said, "Make it five computers." In case Urs Bauer came through. "No, make it six."

"Why?" Fred asked.

"I'm going to be bringing in a foreign exchange dealer who also trades precious metals. He'll need support staff too."

"Do you think he can handle this sort of equipment?"

"If not, you'll teach him."

"Fine with me. So six it is. But just so that we agree on what we're talking about, this is the price list." He fished out yet another memo. "The version of the Sparcserver One Thousand we need lists at 86,300 dollars, but I can probably work out a ten percent discount."

■

"Order them," Willy said, although it did add up to a little more than he had thought. It seemed like everything did.

Fred had noticed the cellular phone that Willy had with him.

"May I?" he asked.

"Sure."

He obviously had the number of Sun Microsystems in his head. He spent only ten minutes on the phone, interrupted once when he asked Willy to write down both the exact name and address of the buyer and where he wanted the computers delivered.

When he gave the phone back to Willy, he said, "They'll be there on Wednesday morning."

"I thought there was a waiting period for those computers?"

"There is. But I helped Sun out a few years ago when they were developing the architecture for the Sparcserver workstation."

"Oh. OK, now that we've got the computers, what's next?"

"I program them."

"With what?"

"It's all ready to go—on disks. And the disks are in that box we put in the trunk. But without data, neither the hard- nor software is going to do us much good, are they?" Fred smiled. Apparently he had just indulged in a bit of geek humor. "What kind of communications systems do you have up there?"

Willy repeated what the architect had told him about both the satellite receivers and Pac Bell's ability to immediately install dedicated land lines.

"We'll go the satellite route for information," Fred declared. "Here are the data services we will have to buy."

Willy read the names, and then said, "Reuters I know. What's Telerate?"

■

"It's the leading carrier of price information and news for the U.S. financial markets."

"Topic and Telekurs?"

"Topic covers the markets in the U.K. Telekurs, which is Swiss-based, does the same for the continent of Europe."

"What about Tokyo and Hong Kong?"

"Reuters covers that, too."

"Does Reuters also cover American municipal bonds?" Willy asked.

"Why in the world would we be interested in municipal bonds?" Fred asked. "They're for little old ladies."

"Maybe. But we are going to be interested in them."

"Fine with me. Muni bonds are covered by a service provided by Bloomberg Financial Markets."

"How do we subscribe?"

"Just call up the same way you call HBO. Like HBO, all of these services scramble their signals. The problem is that you can't use the Videocipher Two system that HBO uses to descramble them because it's too easy to rig the Videocipher and tap in for free. So each service has its own encryption system and its own descrambler hardware that will have to be installed. Which is a pain in the neck. I'll have to find a way to get them up to Healdsburg fast."

While he was mulling that one over, Frank Lipper decided to take advantage of this pause in Fred's colloquy to jump in.

"Remember, Willy, you'd better take care of that country club matter. And don't you think you'd better tell Dan Prescott that he's expected to be playing golf with us tomorrow?"

"I'll take care of the country club. You take care of Prescott."

Willy consulted his little black book—which he had brought up to date the day before—and got the architect's number and dialed it.

"This is Willy Saxon," he said, "Did you get my offer?"

"It was on my desk when I got to the office."

■

"What do you think?"

"You've got a deal."

"Do you have a title company that can handle this?" Willy asked.

"Sure. In Santa Rosa."

"You fax their name and address back to London, and I'll have London wire them the full purchase amount immediately. They should be able to put it in escrow by tomorrow afternoon."

"Consider it done."

"Do you mind if we start moving in right away?"

"Hell, no. I'll arrange for my personal stuff to be taken out of the main house right away. Everything else you can keep." Then he added, "I like the way you do business, Willy. No screwing around, right?"

"That's the idea. Speaking of doing business, I'd like to do a little tomorrow on the golf course at Fountain Grove. We'll be a foursome. I know it's awfully short notice."

"No problem. What time?"

"As close to noon as you could make it."

"A foursome at noon tomorrow. You've got it."

After he hung up, Willy turned to Frank Lipper. "You know something? This is the greatest toy yet."

"I saw that black book of yours," Frank said. "Why don't you go through it and mark the phone numbers you use most. Then I'll put them into the memory of the cellular. It'll make life easier still."

"Great idea!" Willy said, and being Willy he immediately whipped out his black book and began marking it. "But you'd better call Prescott first."

"What if he can't make it?" Frank asked.

"He'll make it," Willy answered.

Willy was right.

"Hey, Sara," he said, after Frank had finished his brief conversation with Dan Prescott, "why so quiet?"

■

"Because you guys never stop talking. You're like a bunch of women."

"Fair enough. Now it's your turn."

She looked at Fred. "What are you going to put all those computers on?"

"Desks."

"What kind of desks? Wood? Metal?"

Fred look baffled. Who cared? A desk was a desk.

"And how many desks?" she asked Willy.

"Twenty," he answered, without the slightest hesitation. If the BZ Bank in Zurich could become the fourth most profitable bank in Switzerland with just twenty people, that was going to be his target too—no, his *limit*. "And make them wood. After all, it is a ranch."

They passed through the gates of River Ranch around one-thirty that afternoon, and minutes later the four stepped out in front of the nineteenth-century Victorian that served as its main house.

"All right, first the grand tour," Willy said. "And then we assign bunks."

Their first stop was the conference center, soon to be a trading center. There, Willy explained what he had in mind. Sara took notes while he talked.

"What do you think, Fred?" Willy asked, when he was done.

"Couldn't be better. I see a phone over there. Does it work?"

"I'm sure it does."

"I want to get moving right away on those information services. Then I want to get somebody from Pac Bell over here right away. Is that all right?"

"Sure. But don't you want to look at where you'll be spending the night?" Willy asked.

"Later," Fred said.

At that moment, Jack walked in.

■

"I thought I'd find you here," he said.

Willy appeared disconcerted. "Has anything changed?"

"No, no. I just decided to get my stuff out of the main house right away. A moving van's on the way. They should be out of your hair by four."

Willy looked relieved.

"There is one other thing that I think we should take care of as long as I'm here," Jack said. "The housekeeper."

"Sure. What do you have in mind?" Willy asked.

"That you give her the same deal that I do. She gets her little house and a car, plus three thousand a month. You've also got to pick up her Social Security and all that stuff. In return, she takes care of the main house and cooks."

"Agreed."

"I think it best you tell her that directly," Jack said.

"Then let's do it right now."

Fred was already on the phone, and Sara was busy sketching out her plans for the place. Frank Lipper, however, looked a bit underutilized, which gave Willy an idea.

"Jack," he said to the architect, "do you know many people in Healdsburg?"

"What kind of people?"

"The ones who run it. Like at City Hall."

"Sure. I designed a new high school for them just last year."

"Who handles their finances?"

"A man by the name of Abner Root. Not a great name, but that's what he's stuck with. His title is Director of Finance. I can give him a call if you'd like."

"I'd appreciate that. But it's not for me. It's for my friend here. Frank heads the bond department at Prescott and Quackenbush. Who knows? He and Abner Root might find something of mutual interest to talk about. Right Frank?"

All this was news to Frank, but whatever Willy Saxon wanted him to do, for whatever reason, he would go along with it.

■

When the three men got back to the main house, the moving van was already there. So was the housekeeper. She was supervising things in a firm way.

"No, no, that stays," she said, as the movers were about to pick up a sofa.

"If it's all right with you," Jack said, "I'll leave stuff like sofas and beds and dishes here. I just want the antiques and the paintings and, I guess, the silverware. No. Keep the silverware."

"Leave whatever you want," Willy said. "Sara is going to redo the place, and so I'll leave it up to her what she does with the stuff."

"It kind of needs a little redoing, doesn't it?" Jack said. "Say, I just thought of something else. You're going golfing tomorrow, right?"

"Yes, and thanks again for fixing it up, Jack," Willy said.

"But I'll bet you don't have any clubs with you, do you?"

"No. I thought . . ."

"Don't think. I've got two sets of clubs in the garage—MacGregors and Callaways. Both come with a Ping putter. I haven't used them in years. They're also yours if you want them."

"You're sure you want to part with your Callaway Big Bertha?" Willy asked.

"Of course not. But when you live in the city full time—like I now intend to do—going golfing gets to be too much of a hassle."

"OK," Willy said, "I accept with thanks. Now let's have that word with Vreni."

They took the housekeeper out onto the porch and five minutes later she agreed to stay on.

"But how can I cook dinner for you, Mr. Saxon, when I have to watch these movers? Because if you don't watch them, you know what happens."

"Forget dinner, Vreni," Willy said. "We'll fend for ourselves."

"No, Mr. Saxon. I'll make sandwiches. How many will you be?"

"Four."

"I'll have everything ready at seven. Is that all right?"

"Certainly."

Vreni went back into the living room. Jack looked at his watch. "There's no sense my hanging around any longer. I'll just get depressed," he said.

"Would you mind making that phone call before you leave?" Willy asked.

"Not at all."

"And I changed my mind. If you can arrange something, I think I'll tag along with Frank."

Jack went into the living room to phone, and when he returned to the porch he said, "He's expecting you in his office at eleven. It's in the City Hall, which is on the south side of the main square. They call it the Plaza. Don't expect too much of either Abner Root or his office."

"Thanks, Jack," Willy said.

"My pleasure. I'm off. I'm sure that title company will want both of us to come in before this thing is settled. But don't worry. I don't plan on going anywhere in the immediate future."

"Great."

The two men shook hands, and Jack walked down the stairs to his car and took off in a cloud of dust. Willy and Frank went back to the conference center, where they found both Fred Fitch and Sara Jones hard at work, Fred working the phone, Sara busy sketching. But as soon as Fred spotted them, he quickly finished his phone conversation, and came over to Willy.

"The computers will arrive tomorrow morning. I've got a satellite communications service coming up early tomorrow afternoon from L.A. They've already signed us up with those services we discussed in the car, and they'll be bringing all the black boxes we'll need. Pac Bell is coming first thing tomorrow morning, right after eight, to put in those land lines we'll need. We'll also have to get them to rig that arrangement we discussed in the car—where you call San Francisco, but get Healdsburg. They'll probably have to know what the phone setup is in San Francisco."

"Frank can explain that," Willy said. "He'll be here at eight, won't you Frank?"

"I'll be here." Frank replied.

"Anything else?" Willy asked.

"Yes. We forgot one thing," Fred said.

"What's that?"

"A backup generator. If the power goes out—I called PG and E and they told me that it does on a regular basis around here—we would be in very deep shit. So I've ordered one. OK?"

"If you say we need it Fred, let's get it."

"I've also hired two guys, subject to your approval, of course."

"Professionals?" Willy asked.

"Sort of."

"Where are they working now?"

"They're not working anywhere right now. Both *used* to be with Lawrence Livermore Laboratories, which is attached to the University of California in Berkeley, but located in Pleasanton. I got to know them when I lived in Pleasanton—not in that prison, Willy, but after I got out. Both were in the Star Wars program that was centered there. One was in their nuclear weapons development program—making prototype warheads for missiles that were very small and thus easily deployed in space. The other was working on 'brilliant pebbles.' That's a really far-out program. It reminds me of the Middle Ages, when they would put cities under siege and then hurl huge rocks over the city walls, hoping to get lucky inside."

This caused even Sara who was working nearby, but obviously listening, to pause.

"Brilliant pebbles?" she asked.

"Yeah. For the past five years Glenn has been trying to figure out a way to hurl a bunch of little bitty rocks—they're actually pellets—at incoming missiles and break them up in space. It was an idea thought up originally by Edward Teller, who, as you may remember, was also the father of the hydrogen bomb. This new idea is really good stuff. But it requires the development of mathematical models of phenomenal complexity. The math was beyond even Teller, so he brought in Glenn."

"So why don't they work there anymore?"

"Because both programs were shot down by Clinton. And these guys—both in the top ten in the world in their fields of mathematics—are out of work. Bob—he's the nuclear warhead guy—believe it or not, is working in a video store. Glenn just stays at home and sulks."

"But can they adapt to doing your sort of stuff in the financial field?"

"Sure. It's not that different. On Wall Street they don't call us rocket scientists for nothing, you know. It'll take a little time to bring them up to speed. Maybe a week. But then look out!"

"So do I get to see them before I hire them?" Willy asked.

"Absolutely," Fred answered. "They'll be coming tomorrow afternoon, too. Can we put them up for the night?"

"Yes. But you'd better tell that to the housekeeper. No, scratch that, Fred. I'll talk to her." Willy wasn't sure whether the Swiss housekeeper, after spending much of her life in the service of architects, was quite ready for Fred, the geek.

Then it was Sara's turn. She showed Willy her sketches of how she envisioned the trading room.

■

"Fred helped me," she admitted. "Fred also insisted that he must have desks here by tomorrow afternoon. So I ordered them and talked the supplier into bringing them up from San Francisco tomorrow morning. All right?"

"Absolutely."

"The next thing that has to be changed right away is the lighting," Sara said. She went on to explain what she had in mind.

By six-thirty they were ready to call it quits. A small buffet, consisting of salads and sandwiches, had been set out in the dining room of the main house. To the Swiss housekeeper's satisfaction, it all disappeared in short order.

"Now for the sleeping arrangements," Willy said, when they all had retired to the living room of the old Victorian for a glass of wine. "Vreni has decided that we are all going to stay here in the main house tonight. Whenever you are ready to retire, just let her know—she'll be out in the kitchen—and she'll show you to your room."

Sara was the first to go. Then Fred Fitch pleaded a long day, and likewise disappeared.

"Well, Frank," Willy said, once they were alone, "what do you think so far?"

"So far I think that it's going to be the best thing you've ever undertaken, Willy. But there's still one thing that I can't really figure out."

"You mean those derivatives?"

"No. Something very basic."

"So what is it?"

"Why are you doing it? I mean it's obvious that you socked away a pretty big stash, Willy. Otherwise you couldn't begin to afford all this. But why run the risk of blowing your entire nest egg? Why not just retire, and live the good life with no risk, no hassle?"

"For God's sake, Frank. I'm only forty-six years old! So what if I did retire? Then what would I do all day? Play golf?

■

Sure, we're going to play golf tomorrow, but the real fun of it will be whether or not we succeed in what we're trying to accomplish *while* we play golf."

"Yeah, I see that one," Frank replied, "although we're only talking about a sales job that's not going to cost anybody anything if it doesn't work out. But what about Prescott and Quackenbush? You're putting twenty million dollars into what is in essence an investment bank that's broke, and still losing money. The only difference is that now it's going to be *your* money. Who says we can turn that place around?"

"I say, Frank," Willy said. "I say. And not by playing any games like last time around. *This* time it's going to be all brains and high tech. We are going to outsmart the rest of them—you, me, Fred and his two rocket scientists, and another guy who's probably coming over from Switzerland this week. Come on, Frank, this is what the 1990s are all about. And it's *fun!*"

"I won't argue with that, Willy. I mean just the idea of setting this place up, and then directing the business through Prescott and Quackenbush without anybody knowing what's really going on—it's an absolute fucking stroke of genius. But there's still one thing I *really* don't get."

"What's that?"

"Why, when we're going hi-tech, are we going to still be fooling around with municipal bonds? I mean Willy, that's about as *low*-tech as you can get."

Willy sat back and thought for a bit before answering that one.

"You're absolutely right," he finally said. "It's an anomaly. But that's precisely the point. Underwriting municipal bonds is so . . . so mundane, so tedious, so *pedestrian.*" Willy paused. "Therefore it's also the *last* place that anybody would look."

"What's that mean?" Frank asked.

"You'll find out in due time. Maybe. Because maybe we can manage without."

■

"Without what?"

"Later, Frank, later." Willy looked at his watch. "Want to try to get some TV off the satellite, or are you ready to call it an evening?"

"If you don't mind, I think I'll hit the hay, Willy," Frank said. "What's the drill tomorrow?"

"Fred said he'll need you at eight, when the Pac Bell people get here. We won't have to leave for the golf course until eleven. That'll still leave us enough time to hit a bucket of balls on the driving range before we tee off. OK?"

"Sure. Good night, Willy," Fred said, as he got up. "I can't tell you how much I enjoy working together with you again."

"Same here, pal. Sleep well."

After Frank had disappeared up the stairs, Willy went out into the huge kitchen and scrounged around in the cupboards until he came up with a bottle of cognac bearing the label of Gallo of Modesto, California. It was obviously there for cooking purposes—but what the hell. After he had poured himself a half glass of the stuff, he went back into the living room, and then, changing his mind, out onto the porch. He had noticed that there was a swing there, and it was directly to it that he now went.

Frank's question was still bothering him. Why *was* he doing all this?

He rocked for a while, taking a sip of the cognac now and then, thinking.

Frank was right. He could have checked out of Pleasanton, gotten on an Air France 747 a few hours later, and right now he'd be sitting at a table in a sidewalk cafe in Nice or Cannes, sipping a Campari and soda and watching the girls in their skimpy summer outfits parade by. Six months later he'd be sitting at the bar of the Palace hotel in St. Moritz, being watched by ski bunnies from a half dozen different countries—watched because the word would have gotten out by

■

then that an expatriate, single American millionaire was in Europe and on the prowl.

That's how Bernie Cornfeld had ended up, and he was *damned* if he was going to go *that* route.

No, he had no plans to become an expatriate. He liked America, dammit! And somehow he'd get right back on top again—the old-fashioned way. By proving that, when he really put his mind to it, there was *nobody* in America or any place else who knew how to make money with money like Willy Saxon. Not a Bernie Cornfeld, nor that guy from Omaha whose name he always forgot—no, now he remembered: Warren Buffet. Not even that Hungarian, George Soros.

Now he felt better. And tired. So Willy Saxon went to bed, and that night he slept like a baby—a contented baby.

■

TWENTY

He was awoken at six by the phone. It was Dr. Guggi, calling from Vaduz.

"I'm so glad I got through to you, Willy. I called your number in San Francisco and got a woman who spoke Spanish. It took me five minutes before she understood what I wanted."

"What's the big problem?" Willy asked, impatiently.

"Urs and Susie Bauer."

"They changed their minds, I guess."

"No. Quite the contrary. What happened is this. Yesterday afternoon I called Bauer just like you asked me to do and he insisted that I come over to Basel immediately. So, reluctantly, I might add, I drove over to Basel, which takes two hours, since it seemed that this Bauer man is very important to you."

"He is."

"I explained what you intend to do, how much funding you have available to back the project, and who is on the Board of Directors of the holding company in Zug. He knew all the names, and he asked especially about your relationship with Dr. Schweizer of UBS. I told him about our joint venture with him in the junk bond business in the 1980s, and suggested that he call Schweizer directly. He thought that unnecessary. He's a very quick study, you know."

"I sensed that when I spoke to him on the phone."

■

"Anyway, after I had finished my pitch, his wife, who was in on our entire conversation—which, as you know, Willy, is rather unusual in Switzerland when business is being discussed—drew him aside. After about five minutes, Urs came back alone and told me that he would have preferred to mull it over for a week or two, but that his wife was of a different opinion. She wanted to do what you suggested—go over to California and take a look."

"Great."

"Now what I've been leading up to is this, Willy. She wanted to go right away. So I stayed overnight in Basel, drove them to Kloten airport in Zurich early this morning, and personally put the two of them on a Swissair flight to Los Angeles about six hours ago. I would have called you then, but it was the middle of the night where you are and I didn't want to wake you up. As it is, I think it's rather early to be calling.

"You're right. It's six o'clock. But don't worry."

"They'll be transferring to a United flight in Los Angeles, which is scheduled to arrive in San Francisco at two o'clock this afternoon your time. The flight number is UA 759."

"I'll have them met there," Willy responded.

Then, following the precedent Willy had set in their prior conversation, Dr. Guggi switched to the Swiss German dialect as he switched to a more "delicate" subject.

"Hesch du die Document zruck bekoh? Und die zwanzig millione Dollar?" he asked.

"Das weiss ich nonit. Aber wenn nit, dueni-dr wieder alüte," Willy replied.

Until he talked to either Bobby Armacost or Dan Prescott, he would not know whether the documents related to his purchase of Prescott & Quackenbush, and the twenty million dollars needed to close the deal, had arrived. If not, he'd call Guggi back.

After Willy hung up the phone, his mind immediately

■

switched to another subject: Sid Ravitch. Now that the take-over of Prescott & Quackenbush was a sure thing, there was no reason to hold back any longer on his investment in the Western Credit Rating Agency. So he picked up the phone and dialed the number of his solicitor's office in London.

"It's Willy Saxon," he said, once Lionel Latham was on the line.

"My God," his solicitor exclaimed, "what time is it there?"

"A little after six."

"You Americans never cease to amaze me. What could possibly be that important to get you out of bed at this ungodly hour?"

"Actually, I'm still in bed," Willy replied, an answer that seemed to mollify the party on the other end. "I'm calling about that matter we discussed in your office a week ago Saturday."

"I recall it vividly."

"Good. I told you that I'd press the button when it was ready to go."

"And you are now pressing it."

"Yes. Is everything ready on your end?"

"All set, exactly as discussed."

"And the funding?"

"Ditto," Latham replied.

"You'll be hearing from an attorney in San Francisco within a day or two. His name is Bobby Armacost. He's prepared all the documents. They have to be reviewed by the seller, and I'll arrange that that be done today. I see no reason why we can't close this deal early next week."

"I can assure you that where this end is concerned, we could close tomorrow."

"Good. Now in case there are any loose ends that need discussing, or any major screwups, call or fax me immediately. I'll give you my new numbers."

After Willy hung up for the second time already that morn-

■

ing, he looked at his watch. It was still only six-thirty, too early for any local calls, unfortunately. So he might as well have breakfast.

He put on his bathrobe and slippers and padded down the stairs, through the living room, into the kitchen. Sara was already there—likewise in bathrobe and slippers.

"Coffee's just done," she said as soon as she saw him.

"Why don't we drink it out on the porch?" Willy suggested.

"You carry the cups, and I'll bring the coffee," Sara said. "Take cream or sugar?"

"Just cream."

It's was about as domestic a scene as you could get, Willy thought, as he carried two mugs out onto the porch and put them on top of a low wicker table which stood in front of the porch swing, where he sat down and waited for Sara.

When Sara came and stooped down to pour the coffee, however, the display of her very ample decolletage turned Willy's thoughts in another direction.

"I know what you're thinking," Sara said, without even looking up at him, "and the answer is no."

"Well, that takes care of that," Willy said.

"But I would like to join you on the swing, if you don't mind," she said.

When she did, she sat as close to Willy as possible without physically touching. So he put his arm around her, gave her a peck on the cheek, and said, "You know something? I could easily get used to this."

Suddenly noises came from within the house, causing Willy to take his arm back like a teenager who had almost been caught in the act by parents arriving home earlier than expected.

It was the housekeeper, who came out the front door onto the porch.

She offered to make them a real breakfast, but both Willy and Sara declined.

■

"I could use your help on something else, however," Willy said. "That chalet by the river. Would you mind arranging to have it cleaned from top to bottom, and then thoroughly aired out? I assume you can mobilize some help."

"Certainly, Mr. Saxon. The wives of the Mexicans who work in the vineyards around here are more than happy to help out doing such things. By when must it be done?"

"Preferably by four, but no later than five. And make sure there are flowers in the living room and especially the master bedroom."

That caused Sara's eyebrows to rise slightly.

This time it was Willy who said, "I know what you're thinking, and you're wrong."

"You mean Denise is not coming up to check out the arrangements?"

"You never know. She might," Willy said. "But in this instance it is a couple—a fairly young couple—who is coming over from Switzerland today, and planning on spending a few nights here. Which leads me to a favor I would like to ask of *you*, Sara. Would you mind picking them up at the San Francisco airport?"

"Of course not. But how?"

"Rent a car. I can take you to Hertz in Santa Rosa on the way to the country club. I'm leaving here at eleven. They're arriving at SFO at two. So it should be a perfect fit."

"Are they expecting me?"

"Good question. As far as I know, they don't know what to expect when they get here."

"Give me the airline and flight number and I'll meet them at the gate with a sign, like the limo driver's do. I'll make the sign right away. What's their names?"

"Urs and Susie Bauer," Willy replied.

"Excuse me for intruding, Mr. Saxon," Vreni said, "but those sound like Swiss names."

"They are. They're coming from Basel."

■

"Oh, how wonderful! Then I'll cook a real Swiss dinner for them tonight."

"No, Vreni, you take care of the chalet. I'll take care of dinner." Willy suspected that the last thing Susie wanted after escaping from Switzerland was to have to eat Swiss food as her first meal in California.

Vreni looked skeptical, but excused herself. She had to arrange for that help.

"Hold on, Vreni," Willy called out. "I forgot something. We've got two other guests coming in today." Fred's two rocket scientists. "Could you fix up one of those other houses the same way. Except you can forget about the flowers."

Vreni disappeared back into the house.

"What about me?" Sara asked. "Don't I get a house, too?"

"We're running low on houses. So you stay here," Willy said, adding, "if you don't mind."

"Quite the contrary," and now it was she who moved over to kiss him on the cheek. "But now I've got to get dressed."

Willy decided to do the same.

He then impatiently waited for eight o'clock to come along, since he knew that Bobby Armacost always arrived at his office early.

When he finally got him, Armacost said, "I'm glad you called. I hope you haven't forgotten that Friday afternoon we are all going to meet at Prescott and Quackenbush to finalize the deal."

"How could I forget that?" Willy said. "I assume from what you say that all the documents have come back from Switzerland in good order."

"They're here. So is the twenty million."

"Good. Now as to why I called. I want to move forward as rapidly as possible on the other deal. I assume those papers are ready to go?"

"They have been for quite a while."

"OK. Then I'd appreciate it if you could call Sid Ravitch

■

right away and arrange to go over the papers with him and his attorney. Then get hold of Lionel Latham in London to coordinate things on that end. I'd like to close that deal early next week."

"That's do-able," Armacost said, "unless Ravitch or his lawyer give me trouble."

"They won't," Willy said.

■

TWENTY-ONE

Willy was right. Ravitch told Armacost to come right over with the documents. His attorney would be there within the half hour.

By nine-thirty they were already done. Ravitch did not change a word. Every time his attorney raised objections, Ravitch said to let it ride.

After Armacost had left, the attorney just sat there shaking his head.

"What's wrong with you?" Ravitch asked.

"I don't get it," his attorney said. "I've never seen you act like this. They could have asked for your dick on a platter and you would have said fine. What's going on?"

"I'm getting ten million dollars in cash," Ravitch said, "that's what's going on."

"But you're giving away control of your company. Their buying just forty-nine percent is bullshit. You gave them an option to buy the other fifty-one percent *at their discretion* for Christ's sake, and you didn't even demand extra compensation for giving them the option. Why?"

"Because they'll never exercise it."

"Why not?"

"Because the client that the fancy Mr. Armacost represents is not Veritas, Ltd., of London. *That* is bullshit. It's a front, pure and simple, for the real buyer."

■

"So who is the real buyer?"

"A convicted felon by the name of Willy Saxon."

"Jeezus, Sid," the attorney said.

"I hardly need mention that this information comes under the protection of our attorney-client relationship. Right?"

"Of course. But do you know what you're doing?"

"Absolutely. I'm going to get my ten million dollars in cash now. And I'm going to get back one-hundred percent of my company later. For free. It's what you call having your cake and eating it too."

"And how do you intend to do this?"

"With the help of a friend."

"Which friend?"

"It doesn't matter. He's tied up until the end of this week."

Lenny Wilkins was due to check out of the Federal Correctional Institution in Pleasanton on noon that Friday. When he got done with him, Lenny would be so damned mad he'd be ready to kill.

Ravitch sincerely hoped, however, that killing would not be necessary.

TWENTY-TWO

At 9:45 on that same Tuesday morning, Willy looked at his watch for already the tenth time that day. There was *still* an hour to waste before they left for the country club. How to kill it?

Dinner!

He immediately took off for the conference center—now trading center—at a fast walk. Inside he found Fred and Frank discussing things with three men who must have been from Pacific Bell, from the truck that was standing outside.

"How's it going?" he asked.

"They've already got all they need from me about our setup in San Francisco," Frank said. "And it's just like you said, Willy. Calls made to any numbers we so designate there will automatically end up here."

"And how soon can they get that working?"

"By Friday," one of the Pac Bell men said.

"Then he's excused?" Willy asked, pointing at Frank.

"As far as we're concerned."

"So Frank," Willy said, "why don't you come with me and we'll start to work on dinner."

"Isn't this a bit early to start work on dinner? What kind of dinner?"

"A barbecue. There's a big barbecue pit up here, picnic

■

tables, the whole deal. It's fifty yards down the lane, in a clearing overlooking the river. Let me show you."

After they had inspected the facilities, Willy said, "Now all we need are the makings."

"That woman back at the main house should be able to help us there," Frank said.

"No. She's busy with other things today. I'll just ask her where to go to get the stuff we need. And then we'll go get it, Frank."

"But who's going to cook it?" Frank asked.

"I am," Willy said.

The place to go was the Safeway in Healdsburg, Vreni told them, which turned out to be the best Safeway any of them had seen in their lives. The reason, Willy found out later, was that the ex-chairman of Safeway had retired in nearby Alexander Valley, and had had the store built as one of his last official acts before leaving.

An hour later, the two emerged pushing shopping carts loaded with bags of charcoal, a package containing eighteen pounds of ribs, four different bottles of barbecue sauce, a bag filled with a two dozen cobs of corn, two pounds of butter, three large containers full of ready-made potato salad, macaroni salad and cole slaw, a box containing a cheese cake, and two cases of Heineken beer. They had also bought two aprons.

As the driver helped them load all the stuff into the limo, Willy said, "We forgot the hors d'oeuvres!"

So back into the safeway they went, this time to the deli counter. A few minutes Willy had what he wanted: a pound of Scottish smoked salmon, twenty-four ounces of Beluga caviar, and three bottles of "J" champagne, made just a few miles west of the store by the same people who produced the Jordan wine.

Back at the ranch, they unloaded the charcoal outside the

■

old conference center, and put the rest of the stuff in the fridge—fortunately, a huge one—of the main house.

When they were done, Willy said, "I'm hot. You too?"

"Yeah," Frank said. "It's going to be a scorcher. At least a hundred. It must be in the nineties already."

"Which means we have to be careful about dehydration," Willy said.

"I would think so."

"So how about a beer?"

When Sara arrived at eleven, she found them contentedly rocking on the porch swing, beer cans in hand.

"Bit early for that, isn't it?" she said.

"Not for two growing boys like us, ma'am," Willy replied. "But now duty calls. Off to the country club, Frank."

■

TWENTY-THREE

They dropped Sara off at the Hertz office in Santa Rosa, and arrived at the Fountain Grove Country Club at eleven-thirty. The parking attendant loaded Jack's two sets of clubs onto a waiting cart, and Willy and Frank climbed in and headed for the pro shop.

They were obviously expected. Bruce Bennett, the manager, was waiting—waiting to present Willy with his brand new membership card, and to tell him that all guest greens fees were waived that day and that lunch would be on him. Which caused Willy to think that either Jack was one of the nicest guys in the world to set all this up, including throwing in those golf clubs, or *he* was greatly overpaying Jack for his ranch.

"The other fellows are obviously not here yet," Willy said, "so I think we'll hit a few balls on the range."

Out came a handful of tokens for the ball vending machine, this time compliments of Mike, the club professional.

Willy hadn't hit a golf ball in over three years, so it was with some trepidation that he teed up the first ball. He decided to go for broke—with the Big Bertha. He swung, and the ball exploded at least 250 yards down the range, straight as an arrow. Willy teed up a second ball. Wham! Same result.

"You've still got it, Willy," Frank said.

"You know, they always say that the first time you play

■

after a long hiatus, everything seems to work. I'm starting to believe it," Willy said.

Both he and Frank went through a bucket of balls and then took the cart back to the pro shop. Dan Prescott and George Abbott had just arrived.

At noon the foursome was on the first tee. Willy suggested that he and Abbott would team up against the two investment bankers. That way they would share the same cart. Frank volunteered to act as the scorekeeper. Both Frank and Prescott sported a 15 handicap, Abbott's was a 17, and, since Willy had no idea what his would be after the long layoff, they agreed to split it down the middle and assign him a 16. They also agreed to play a modified Nassau.

By one-thirty they were back at the clubhouse, having finished the front nine, and decided to park their carts at the turn and head for Bogey's bar for that free lunch. So far, all that Willy and George Abbott had discussed during the time they had shared their cart was the game itself and the Giants, who were in first place. Now the subject of Denise van Bercham and her friends came up—which gave Willy the opening he'd been searching for.

George, it soon became obvious, was a social climber, and his wife even pushier.

"She *really* regretted missing that weekend up at Denise van Bercham's ranch," the Chief Administrative Officer of the City and County of San Francisco said. "She was visiting her mother in Iowa. She and Denise have never actually met, but I think that when they do, they'll find out that they've got a lot in common. My wife's originally from one of Yugoslavia's leading families, and I understand that the same is true of Denise, only her family were Romanians. Aristocrats I am told."

"Well, that has to be rectified," Willy responded. "Denise is very fond of you, and I'm sure, from what you've told me, she and your wife will get along great."

■

"You seem to know Denise rather well."

"Yes."

"And also her friends in the so-called social scene in San Francisco?" Abbott was nothing if not obvious.

"Some of them. In fact one of her best friends, Sara Jones, and I have gotten to be rather close of late." Although this morning it had not been quite close enough.

"My wife knows all about them since she subscribes to WWD and reads Suzy religiously. Suzy's the columnist who always writes about Denise and her friends. My wife would just love to meet some of them in person."

So now Willy knew what kind of bait to use. All he had to do was bait the hook.

He set that up in the men's room of Bogey's bar after having first made sure that he and Dan Prescott were alone.

"Look," he said, "this guy and his wife are hot to trot with high society in San Francisco. You see a lot of them, don't you?"

"Don't ask. My wife drags me to one of those dinners in Pacific Heights at least once a week. Same crowd every time, although not quite in the same league as your new pal Denise van Bercham."

"Not to worry. This guy's wife probably can't even differentiate between the A and B crowd. She no doubt just wants Suzy and Pat Steger to put her name in the paper." Willy alluded here to the San Francisco *Chronicle*'s society columnist, who could make or break anybody with social ambitions in that city.

"So you want me to fix something up?" Prescott asked.

"Yes. Next week, if possible. If you get your wife to set up a dinner party with some of the B crowd, I'll produce both Denise van Bercham and Sara Jones and get them to provide a list of some of their 'A' crowd friends you might also invite."

"I'll talk to my wife as soon as I get home."

"Great. By the way, one other thing."

■

"Sure. What is it?"

"Take it easy out there," Willy said. "You and Frank are up by six bucks. That won't do."

"I'll have a word with Frank," Dan said.

The word worked, culminating on the 17th hole. Prior to that, Dan Prescott had managed to go out of bounds on 15, while Frank Lipper had done likewise on the 16th. So they went into the 17th tied with Willy and his partner.

The 17th hole was a long par three—195 yards. It seemed even longer since 165 of those 195 yards were over water. And on this very hot summer day a cross-breeze had started coming in from the ocean, making it still more difficult. Willy, as usual, had the honors, and, using a five-iron, came within six yards of the pin. Next up was Frank. He plunked his ball in the middle of the lake, damn near hitting a Canada goose. Dan was next. His ball sailed over the green and buried itself in the sand of a deep bunker behind.

"Seems like I used a bit too much club," he commented innocently.

The Chief Administrative Officer of the City and County of San Francisco was up next, and, as everybody else held their breath, he made it over the lake, and ended up to the left of the green, an easy twenty-yard chip shot from the pin. He holed out two shots later with a par. Willy had a birdie. Both of their opponents had double bogeys.

That did it. After going through the motions of playing out the 18th hole, they ended up back at Bogey's bar.

Willy went directly to the bar and brought four Heinekens back to their table. "What's the damage, Frank?" he asked.

"We owe you guys eight bucks," Frank answered as he reached for his wallet, with Dan Prescott immediately following suit.

George Abbott was all smiles as he raked in his share of the dough. "The next drinks are on me," he offered magnanimously.

■

"No, partner," Willy said. "At my club, I pay." After all, he had been a member now for more than four hours.

"Well, I hope you don't mind if I spoil the fun by bringing up business," George Abbott said.

"No, go ahead," Willy said.

"Are your colleagues aware of what we discussed up at Denise van Bercham's ranch?" He obviously loved dropping *that* name.

"Absolutely. Actually, they're not colleagues in the strict sense of the word. But I do give them a bit of advice now and then," Willy said before continuing. "In fact, Frank here has worked up a proposal, haven't you Frank?"

"In fact, I've got it in the car," Frank replied. "Should I go get it?"

"Absolutely," Abbott said.

After Frank had left for the parking lot, George Abbott turned his attention to Dan Prescott. They'd met on a couple of occasions—official city functions—so Abbott knew who he was.

"Willy explained that you are in the process of greatly expanding your operations, Dan," he said.

"That's right. We're bringing in a lot of new capital, and moving into new areas. But municipal bonds have always been one of our strengths, and we intend to get stronger and bigger in that field."

"What do you think of Willy's idea to piggyback financing of a major low-income housing project onto an issue of revenue bonds?"

"It's a good one. In essence, it's the equivalent of a tactic that underwriters have used before when they issue two classes of debt simultaneously and tell the buyers: either you take some of that junior debt or you don't get any of the senior. As long as the ratio was right, the underwritings succeeded."

"And what would be the right ratio on this type of deal?"

"Frank's worked that out. He'll explain when he gets back.

■

But before he does, I'd like to bring up a nonbusiness matter. My wife and I are giving a dinner party this Friday, and when I mentioned to her this morning that we'd be playing golf together, she suggested that I ask you and your wife to come. I know it's short notice, but we would certainly be honored if you'd join us."

Willy now jumped in. "I'll be escorting *two* ladies to the dinner, Denise, of course, and her friend Sara Jones."

"We'd be *delighted* to join you," Abbott said.

"Then there'll be an invitation in the mail tomorrow morning. I believe it's black tie," Dan said, making it up as he went along.

Frank returned, and immediately took over the conversation, much to Dan's relief. He had a briefcase with him, and extracted two copies of his proposal, one of which he shoved across the table to George Abbott.

"You'll have to fill in the blanks where the exact numbers are concerned," he began, "but I figured we could piggyback that junior debt onto the senior at a four-to-one ratio. So if you need twenty-five million dollars for that housing project, you'd go with one-hundred-million dollar general obligation bonds."

George nodded, so Frank plunged ahead.

A half hour later George Abbott seemed to be sold.

"I noticed you left a blank space for the underwriting fee."

"That's right. On purpose. Because we first wanted to get an indication of your interest, in principle, before filling it in."

"Well, you've got that interest, in principle."

"It will be just one half of one percent."

George whistled softly.

"Yes, I know," Dan said, interrupting Frank for the first time. "But, after a long discussion at the firm, we figured we'd have to come in with a really attractive proposal if we were to break into your underwriting group."

"You're right there. Goldman, Sachs, Lehman Brothers,

■

Merrill Lynch—they'll all scream when they hear about this," Abbott said. "Their standard fee these days is a full percent."

"We know."

Now it was Willy who broke in. "I think I've got another idea that might save you some money."

"How?" Abbott asked.

"By cutting back on what you would have to shell out for a credit rating on these issues."

"But Standard and Poors and Moody's more or less have a lock on that."

"Why? As I understand it, you always use one or the other or both, depending on the nature of the issue. This time why not take on one of them, and bring in another agency . . . one that's going to cost you a lot less money."

"Who do you have in mind?"

"A local firm, which should make it all the more attractive to the city fathers—they'd be taking care of their own. I know the city of Chicago always brings in Duff and Phelps for that reason. I'm talking about the Western Credit Rating Agency. They're headquartered in the Russ Building."

"I've heard of them, but we've never been approached by them."

"They've got a new man running their operations. Used to be at Moody's. His name's Sid Ravitch. I'll have him give you a call," Willy said.

Fifteen minutes later, after George Abbott had finished loading his golf bag into the trunk of his car and was about to head back to the city, he turned to Dan Prescott and said, "You won't forget about that invitation for Friday, will you?"

"Certainly not," Dan replied. "We really look forward to being able to greet you in our home, George."

"I'll look forward to see you there, too," Willy added, "and I'll tell Denise that your wife will be with you this time. I'm sure she'll be pleased."

It was a beaming Chief Administrative Officer of the City

and County of San Francisco who then drove off, leaving Willy and his two cronies standing at the bag drop.

"Are you sure you can produce Denise van Bercham and her friends?" Dan asked.

"One way or the other, yes," Willy replied.

Neither of the other two men asked what that was supposed to mean.

"Hey," Willy then said, "what are you doing for dinner, Dan?"

"Nothing special as far as I know," Prescott replied.

"Then why don't you join Frank and me and a few other people for a barbecue?"

"Sure. Where?"

"It's a surprise. Just follow our limo. It's about twenty minutes from here."

When they were back inside their limo, it was Frank who immediately asked a question. "Was that wise to invite him to the ranch?"

"He'll have to find out sooner or later. Better sooner."

"Yeah, but doesn't this pull the rug out from under his position of authority in the firm?"

"So what? *Without* us, he'd be broke, and either on the street without a job or in jail. *With* us, he and his wife can continue to live the good life, putting on their dinner parties for the Pacific Heights set to their heart's content—if that's their thing."

"Does he know this?"

"So dumb he's not." Willy said. Add the fact that he held Prescott's personal note, where he'd pledged everything he's got. His wife had to co-sign that note, so there could be no doubt that she also knew the score. And the score was quite simply this: without Willy Saxon, Mr. and Mrs. Dan Prescott were washed up for the rest of their days. They'd end up in a trailer park in South Florida.

And ditto for my due diligence lawyer, Bobby Armacost, come to think of it, Willy thought.

■

TWENTY-FOUR

Twenty minutes later, they were back at River Ranch. As soon as they climbed out of their cars, Willy took charge of Dan Prescott.

"Remember that conversation we had at the Huntington hotel a couple of weeks ago?" he began. "About the changing nature of investment banking?"

"Sure. Derivatives and all that. I remember that you used Salomon Brothers as an example."

"Right. The name of a guy who used to work there came up. Fred Fitch. Remember?"

"If I recall correctly, you wanted me to track him down for you. Then you changed your mind."

"Well, I found him. And he's here."

That stopped Prescott for a moment.

"What do you mean, here?"

"Here. Or to be even more precise, about five hundred yards that way." Willy pointed down the lane that paralleled the path of the Russian River as it flowed west through the redwood trees toward the Pacific Ocean.

"Why here? Who owns this place?"

"I do, Dan. Or to again be more precise, I will own it by next week."

"But I still don't get it," Prescott said.

So Willy explained. That this operation had to be one step

removed from Prescott & Armacost. Because of Fred Fitch's "problem." That there might be a similar "problem" with a hot-shot foreign exchange-cum-gold guy that he wanted to bring in from Europe. Willy failed to bring up his own "problem," which was hardly necessary.

"But how will it work in practical terms?" Prescott asked.

Willy explained the telephone setup. "The lid had to be put on the existence of that arrangement, and kept on. Understood?"

"I understand," Prescott answered. "But still, something's bound to leak out about the presence of these guys up here in the middle of nowhere. What then?"

"They are independent contractors. Ready to offer their advice—their *software*—to any respectable client who might need their services. In the meantime, they have one client, Prescott and Armacost."

"And Prescott and Armacost will pay for these services?"

"Of course. But that pay will depend on how valuable their 'services' prove to be."

"How valuable do *you* expect their services to be?"

"I wouldn't be surprised if they would produce ten million dollars, maybe even twenty million dollars net in the first six months."

"Holy shit!" Prescott exclaimed. "But if you're talking about that level of trading activity, where's the working capital going to come from? We're going to need all of that twenty million that's coming into Prescott and Quackenbush on Friday to fund our municipal bond operations, especially now, if that deal with the City of San Francisco comes through."

"I'm aware of that," Willy said. "So I'm prepared to put in another twenty million dollars. Right away. It will come in the form of a five-year loan from the Swiss holding company and be convertible into equity at its option. We'll use it to capitalize a new wholly-owned subsidiary of Prescott and Quackenbush devoted exclusively to derivatives and trading foreign exchange and precious metals. We'll call it P and Q Financial Products."

"Can I announce that on Friday too?" Prescott asked.

"Absolutely," Willy said.

"Holy shit," Prescott said again. "This is going to fucking knock them dead when the boys in the financial district hear about this."

At this point Sara appeared on the porch of the old Victorian.

"Did I just hear some naughty words out here?" she asked.

"Come on down, Sara," Willy said. "I want you to meet one of my oldest friends. And for him to meet one of my newest."

Sara came down and properly shook hands with the newcomer.

"You don't know this yet, Sara, but we are going to Mr. Prescott's home for dinner this Friday—if you are free, which I very much hope you are."

"Why?" Sara asked.

"To impress the Chief Administrative Officer of the City and County of San Francisco. And his pushy wife. It's for a good cause. To arrange financing for some low-cost housing in the city. The good Reverend from Glide Memorial will also be involved."

"In that case, I'll come," said the bishop's daughter. "What time and exactly where?"

"2725 Broadway at seven-thirty," Dan said.

"I hope Denise will agree to come and entice some of her friends to come also," Willy added. "She knows him, somehow. I met him up at her ranch a couple of weekends ago."

"What's she working on?"

"Got me. But knowing Denise, there's bound to be something she needs him for."

"In that case, she'll come. I'll call her," Sara offered.

"Now," she continued, "about dinner."

∎

"We're taking care of that," Willy said. "But first tell me about what happened. Did they show up?"

"Right on time. And as we speak, Vreni is installing them in their chalet. She's in seventh heaven, jabbering away in that odd Swiss dialect."

"And how are they?"

"Susie is an absolute doll. And Urs, well, he's a Swiss version of Fred."

"Wow."

"Not only that, but Fred's two friends have also arrived."

"The same?"

"The same."

"Vreni installed them earlier in the house next door to the chalet. Fred moved in there, too."

"So that means how many for dinner?" Willy asked.

"Let's see," Sara said. She squinted as she mentally counted. "Nine. And by the way, since it was starting to get late, I decided to get the charcoal going about twenty minutes ago. All right?"

"Perfect."

"Vreni set the picnic table for eight, which I will now change to nine," she said. "Another thing: I spotted the caviar and smoked salmon in the fridge alongside with the ribs. I must admit, Willy, that you have good though strange tastes. You forgot bread and a few other things, so I went into Healdsburg to shop. If you agree, since you and Frank are going be doing the barbecuing, I will take care of the hors d'oeuvres."

■

TWENTY-FIVE

At seven, they all began to gravitate toward the picnic area. Willy, in white apron and wearing a chef's hat that he had found in a cupboard in what had been Jack's kitchen, was there to greet them.

Susie and Urs Bauer were the first to arrive. They were dressed in Levi's and plaid shirts. Sara explained later that she had stopped at the Gap in San Rafael, on the way back from the airport, to get them "properly" attired for the occasion. Sara, who had fetched them from their chalet, introduced them. Urs firmly shook hands with Willy like a good Swiss. Susie was less restrained.

"Oh, Mr. Saxon," she said. "This is the most fantastic place I've ever seen in my life! I'm going to *love* it here."

She then proceeded to throw her arms around him in a spontaneous hug that was so robust it almost knocked the breath from him. This caused Sara, who was standing beside Willy, to murmur, "I said you'd like her."

Willy demonstrated that he indeed did, by taking Susie's arm and leading her to a table that was serving as the bar. Behind the table was the bartender, Frank Lipper, and in his hand was a glass of ice-cold "J" champagne, which he presented to Susie. Then he poured a glass for Willy, and one for himself.

"Welcome to California, Susie," Willy said, as he raised his

■

glass. "I can tell already that you're going to fit in perfectly."

In the meantime Fred Fitch, accompanied by the two physicists from Livermore, had arrived. Sara again took over, and introduced them to Urs Bauer. From the first moment on, she sensed that she was in the company of kindred spirits. For when Urs Bauer had explained that he had just come over from Basel, Fred seized on this opening to say that all he really knew about Basel was that it had been the home of the Bernoulli family.

Sara didn't quite know who they were, so, being Sara, she asked. "What's so special about the Bernoulli family? Or maybe I should ask what they are famous for?"

It was one of the visitors from Livermore who offered the first answer. "Chiefly for the Bernoulli theorem."

"And what is that theorem?"

Fred Fitch said, "Most people know it as the law of averages. It states that there is a more or less predictable ratio between the number of random trials of an event and its occurrences. It was Jacob Bernoulli who discovered it."

"When was that?" Sara asked.

"Around 1680."

The second man from Livermore, who had been in the Star Wars program there, provided further information. "There are actually two Bernoulli theorems. The second is key to understanding hydrodynamics. It's an expression of the conversion of energy in streamline, fluid flow, and states that the sum of the ratio of the pressure to the mass density, the product of the gravitational constant and the vertical height, and the square of the velocity divided by 2, are constant."

"And Jacob Bernoulli thought that one up, too?" Sara asked.

"Yes. I remember that when I studied at MIT some students used to confuse him with Daniel Bernoulli, who was Jacob's nephew. But Daniel discovered what came to be known as the Bernoulli *equation.*"

■

"Exactly," Urs Bauer said. "It states that dy/dx + f(x)y = g(x)y n where n is any number other than 0 or 1."

The other three men all nodded in agreement.

"Come," Sara said, "let's move on and join Mr. Saxon. I'm sure he wants to meet your colleagues, Fred. Then I'm going to get things moving on the food front."

The sun was just setting and a full moon rising when they sat down for dinner. It was still warm, in the eighties, so Sara had kept the hors d'oeuvres in the fridge in the main house. A phone call to it soon produced Vreni and the first course. Vreni had insisted that she, not Sara, would serve that evening.

They began with caviar and smoked salmon, accompanied by the usual capers, onions, lemon, and toast, which was the result of Sara's shopping trip. Frank continued to play bartender, and opened two more bottles of "J," to make sure there was enough to go around.

Sara disappeared for a few minutes to turn on the switch that provided electricity to the lanterns that were strung around and over the picnic area. A few seconds later music came on—country and western. She had found a sound system, in the dining hall on the edge of the picnic area, which fed speakers situated behind a small wooden dance floor beside the barbecue pit.

Then it was Willy's turn. He removed the first rack of ribs from the barbecue grill, placed them on the butcher block table beside it, and carved off the first rib.

"Who wants to try it?" he asked.

"Me!" Susie said.

"So come on up," Willy said.

She did. "But how do I eat it?" she asked.

"With your fingers. Like this," said Willy, as he carved off a second rib and took a big bite.

She did the same. "It's absolutely wonderful!"

■

"Now try this," Willy said, carefully handing her a cob of corn after putting on some butter and salt.

"How do I eat this?" Susie asked.

"Same way," Willy replied. He waited. "How is it?"

"Terrific!" she answered.

"Susie says it OK," Willy announced to the rest of the table, "so come and get it."

Vreni had mustered some huge Mexican plates, and as they came up Willy plunked down half a dozen huge ribs on each and handed it over. The salads had been set up buffet-style on the bar table, and Vreni stood behind it, serving. Frank exchanged the champagne glasses for large frosted beer mugs, into which he poured an equally large quantity of Heineken beer.

The nerds, who had changed places and been babbling away among themselves at the far end of the picnic table, welcomed the change. They were all beer guys. Also rib guys. All four of them went back for seconds, another half dozen each. Then they were back at it.

"What the hell are they talking about?" Willy asked Dan Prescott, who had moved and was now sitting next to Willy.

"I listened in for a while, but, frankly, they lost me."

"What do you mean?"

"Well the Swiss guy knows Germany like the back of his hand. He thinks that Germany's going to sink into a double-dip recession. Not now, but in half a year or so."

"I agree," Willy said.

"Then Fred told Urs that, if he's right, then inverse floaters denominated in DM would represent a great play. Urs agreed."

"What are inverse floaters?" Willy asked.

"I'm obviously out of my depth where this stuff is concerned too, Willy, but this much I do know. They take a bond issue paying, say eight percent over thirty years, and split it in two. On one part the investor gets a guaranteed rate that

■

177

moves with money market rates, say four percent. The inverse floaters get all the rest of the bond's interest. This means that if short rates drop from four percent to two percent, the yield on those inverse floaters doubles, and investors make a killing."

"And if short term rates go from four percent to eight percent?" Willy asked.

"Then the yield on the inverse floaters goes to zero."

"Not good," Willy said.

"Right. But Fred said he'd figured out a way to 'tweak' them so that the downside risk on the inverse floaters could be limited. To demonstrate it, he started scribbling mathematical formulas on the table cloth. I'm not sure your housekeeper's going to be too thrilled about that."

Dan Prescott continued, "Then one of the rocket scientists from Livermore said that he had an idea about how to build in a further tilt—which would eliminate the foreign exchange risk. And *he* started scribbling numbers on the table cloth."

"Tilt?"

"Yeah, Willy. That's when I decided to change places."

"It's a new world out there, Dan," Willy said.

"And how," Prescott replied.

"But we've got to go with the flow."

About then—it was Sara's doing—the music changed from country and western to old time rock 'n' roll. Susie was on her feet like a flash.

"Can you dance to that?" she asked Willy, from across the table.

"Try me," Willy said.

Sara reappeared, and Dan immediately asked her to dance. So, just for the hell of it, Frank asked Vreni if she was up to it. She was. The nerds paid no attention to all this. They were too busy tweaking and tilting inverse floaters.

At ten o'clock, Willy concluded that since it had been a long day for everybody, it was time to call it quits. But before he

■

did, he went over to the nerds' end of the table to spend a few minutes there in order to get a better feel for how he should proceed with them, especially the three potential recruits. He ended up spending a half hour listening.

Fred was their spokesman. They had agreed, he explained, to suggest two paths of immediate action. First, to accumulate options on a selected number of German inverse floaters. Urs Bauer interrupted by recommending two in particular—those just issued by Daimler Benz and the DG Bank. Then, Fred said they should organize an underwriting on their own, building in the new features they had just come up with. Of course, they would first have to test their model on the Sun computers, which they intended to do right away in the morning. If it worked out, Urs Bauer said he could line up an issuer in Germany almost immediately. Fred said that, on this end, they'd have to organize the placement, ideally with some international bond funds in the East. Willy told them that he could probably be of some help.

Fred suggested that the five of them get together later the next day to get an estimate of their capital requirements for the first stage of their operations. Urs said that he had some quite concrete ideas that he had brought with him as to what funding would be necessary to start up his foreign exchange operations. They'd also have to talk about support staff, he said. And one more piece of equipment that they would have to have.

In essence Willy was faced with a fait accompli. It was almost as an afterthought that he brought up the subject of employment contracts and compensation. It would take a few days, he said, but he would try to come up with individual proposals by the middle of next week. Frank Lipper would work with each of them in order to work out conditions that were mutually acceptable. They all agreed in what seemed like one voice.

"So how about a beer for the road?" Willy asked. "Then

we'll sit down together again tomorrow afternoon—at let's say two o'clock, in the trading center—and discuss funding, staff, and equipment."

While they drank, Sara, Vreni, and Susie were busy cleaning up, chattering away among themselves. When they were done, Susie came over and sat on Urs's lap.

"We're staying, aren't we?" she whispered in his ear.

"We're staying," her husband whispered back.

She responded by enveloping him in another of her hugs, this one culminated by a big kiss, smack on his lips.

"We're staying!" she now announced to the rest of them. And led by Sara, they all applauded.

By eleven o'clock, total stillness had descended upon the River Ranch. Willy Saxon was already in bed, but not asleep. It had been the fullest day that he had spent in over three years, and he could not help but relish it by once again going over everything in his mind—from those early phone calls to Europe to the eighteen holes of golf to inverse floaters.

At eleven-fifteen there was a very slight knock on his bedroom door. It was Sara.

"Mind?" she whispered, as she moved under the single sheet which covered him on this hot California night.

"Are you kidding?" Willy answered, as he turned to hold her.

"I didn't come here for that," Sara said. "Although . . ."

"I know," Willy said, relaxing his embrace. "It's not easy to just end an evening like that without talking to somebody about it. Right?"

"Exactly. What nice young people they all are! Especially that Susie. I know you will find this really silly, but if I had ever had children I would have hoped to have had a daughter like her. She is *so* unspoiled, so enthusiastic about everything, so nice."

"Her husband's quite different, though," Willy said. "Reserved. But smart as hell."

■

"Like those other two. By the way, are they married?"

"Damned if I know."

"You better find out."

They chatted softly for another fifteen minutes.

"You know, Willy," Sara then said. "I think you've had enough."

"I'm afraid you're right."

"So let's call it a night."

They exchanged a chaste kiss, and minutes later both were asleep.

■

TWENTY-SIX

At eleven the next morning, Willy Saxon and Frank Lipper walked into the City Hall, just off the plaza in the center of the town of Healdsburg. Willy went to the receptionist and asked for Abner Root, the director of finance.

She said that Mr. Root was expecting them, and then came out from behind her desk. "I'll show you to his office."

His office was fifteen feet long and ten feet wide, maximum. Abner Root, who stood up behind his metal desk as they entered the room, was well over six feet tall and, it seemed, about three feet wide. It turned out that he had a booming voice that matched his size.

"Welcome to the city of Healdsburg," he proclaimed, as he stuck out his paw, first to Willy, then Frank. "Jack told me all about you folks buying his ranch and all. You're going to love it around here. No better place to live in California, or any-place else. Take a seat."

There were two old wooden chairs situated right in front of his desk. Both creaked as Willy and Frank sat down.

"Now what can I do for you?" Abner asked.

"Nothing, really," Willy said. "We just thought that since we're going to be neighbors we'd drop in and get acquainted. Although I think we do have an area of mutual interest."

"What's that?"

■

182

"Municipal finance. Frank here runs the muni bond department of an investment bank in San Francisco that you might have heard of, Prescott and Quackenbush."

"Yeah, I've heard of them. Not that big is it?" he asked Frank.

"Getting a lot bigger," Frank answered. "So we're going to be out and around trying to drum up business."

"Well, right now there's nothing to drum up in Healdsburg. We rammed through the financing of that new school that Jack built for us. Fine school, by the way. Now we'll have to wait a few years before proposing anything else. This is a conservative, some say a redneck, town, gentlemen. People here don't like change."

"Can't blame 'em," Willy said. "Why change it if it doesn't need it."

"Yeah, but there's some things that we're going to be forced to do. By Big Brother in Sacramento."

"Like what?" Willy asked.

"Ever heard of AB 939?"

"No. What's that?"

"Assembly Bill 939, passed last year by the state assembly in Sacramento and then signed and put into law by our beloved governor."

"I have heard of it," Frank now said. "Doesn't it deal with waste disposal?"

"Exactly. It says that every municipality in California must have what they term a Materials Recycling Facility—otherwise known as MRF, in caps, gentlemen—which will recycle fifty percent of its solid waste. Or else."

"Or else what?" Willy asked.

"A fine of ten thousand dollars a day. A fucking day, gentlemen!"

"By when?"

"It must be in the works within two years."

■

"So what is Healdsburg going to do?"

"We can't afford it right now. So we're looking for a joint venture with another community. No luck so far."

"How much does one of those things cost?" Willy asked.

"Fifteen, twenty million."

"Wow."

"Exactly. Ukiah—that's the town about fifty miles north of here, in case you're not that familiar with the territory—came up with that ballpark number. In fact, they did a complete feasibility study—what an MRF would cost, what kind of payback the city could expect, possible ways to finance it. Want to see it?"

"Sure," Frank said.

Abner struggled out of his chair, reached up to the bookshelf behind his chair, and retrieved the three-inch-thick bound report.

"Here it is. We chipped in to help pay for the cost of it. You see, we've got what you might term a league of small cities here in the north of the state. It includes the towns in Sonoma, Mendocino, and Lake counties, in fact, all the counties right up to the Oregon border. We get together on insurance and a lot of other things. Like trying to find a way to deal with the requirements of that goddamn AB 939."

Frank took the study in hand, and asked. "What's the biggest problem besides the cost itself?"

"The rate of payback. It's bound to be very, very slow."

"Out of curiosity," Willy said, "just where would the payback come from?"

"From dump fees. You'll pay five bucks every time you unload a pickup truck full of crap at the goddamn twenty-million-dollar MRF. Just like you do now at a normal landfill dump. There's no way we could raise that fee. People simply wouldn't put up with it. They'd start dumping their garbage along the freeway. So it would take forty years to pay the sucker off, according to that study. More important, there is no way that the interest on a municipal bond that you'd have to issue to finance such a facility could possibly be covered during the first five, maybe even seven years."

This was music to Willy Saxon's ears.

"Run that by me again, if you don't mind," he said.

Abner ran it by.

"All right. I get it," Willy said. "I've also got the solution to the financing problem."

"Which is?" Abner asked.

"A forty-year zero coupon municipal bond. With no sinking fund for at least the first seven years."

Abner had a stunned look on his face, as the import of Willy's suggestion sank in.

"You are absolutely right, sir," he said. "Why didn't any of us come up with that idea? Shit, I can hardly wait to tell those guys in Ukiah."

"I wouldn't do that if I were you," Willy said. "I'd keep this idea in the drawer. For Healdsburg, if and when the time comes that you'll have to finance one of those MRFs on your own."

"You're absolutely right," Abner said.

"But just to make sure that my thinking's right," Willy continued, "would you mind if we took this report home for a few days and really studied it?"

"Hell, no. It's just going to gather dust here. Keep it as long as you want."

A few minutes later Abner walked them to the front entrance of City Hall. "Come back again, fellows. Next time we'll go over to Zeke's and hoist a few brews together."

As soon as he had disappeared, Frank asked: "What's Zeke's?"

Willy pointed across the plaza at an establishment that had a neon sign outside, telling what was on offer within:

■

BEER, SPIRITS, POOL
SATURDAY NIGHTS MUSIC,
EXOTIC DANCERS.

"It has a certain appeal, don't you agree?" Willy said. "But Zeke's will have to wait. We've got to go back to the ranch and sit down with the four nerds. But it does raise the subject of places to eat and drink in this town, other than Zeke's. I'm going to go back into City Hall and ask for a few names."

■

TWENTY-SEVEN

The limo dropped them off in front of the old conference center of River Ranch. When they walked in they saw all four men hunched over their computers. The moment Fred Fitch saw them he came over to greet them.

"That idea we had last night—it works," he said. "We'll combine calls on those DM inverse floaters with long-term deutsche mark/dollar currency puts. It should be a very attractive product."

"Great," Willy said. "Have you guys also had time to assess what your capital needs will be?"

"Yes."

"OK. Then why don't we all sit at that table over there and discuss it."

When they were all there, Willy explained what the capital structure of the new Prescott & Quackenbush would look like. The parent firm would be capitalized at twenty million dollars and another twenty million dollars would be brought in immediately from the Swiss holding company to capitalize the derivatives subsidiary, which would be called P & Q Financial Products.

Fred Fitch immediately responded. "I recall that twenty million dollars was the figure I originally gave you, Mr. Saxon. But now we're adding Urs's trading operation."

"I realize that," Willy said.

■

"We can *both* probably get by for a while on that twenty million. But if things work out like we hope they will, we're going to need more capital. Don't you agree Urs?"

"I agree. My guess is that we'll need another fifteen to twenty million dollars pretty soon."

All then fell silent. But everybody knew that a key issue had been raised. Could Willy Saxon really produce an additional fifteen or twenty million dollars if and when it was required?

Willy realized that his answer to this question was absolutely crucial. He had to convince them that he had real financial staying power—and convince them right now. Otherwise, this whole thing would be over before it even started. They'd all take a hike, including Urs, despite the assurances to the contrary that he had given his wife the previous evening.

And they would be right. In their business, it took a lot of money to make a lot of money. Without it, forget it.

Willy looked them in the eye, one by one, and then said: "Let me assure all of you that *if* your performance requires it, if things work out, as Fred put it—which I interpret as making a damn good return on the twenty million you've already got—then you have my personal guarantee that you'll get another twenty million."

"Even if we demonstrate the need for it within a month or two?" Fred asked.

"Yes. You prove that you really know how to make money, and within thirty days of that you'll get the additional funding you need."

Willy could tell from the looks on all four faces that he had won the day.

This was confirmed when Fred said, "In that case, you can count us all in. Right Urs?"

"Right."

"I couldn't be more pleased. So let's move on to the next subject. Like I said last night, during the next couple of days

■

Frank will talk to each of you regarding employment contracts, salary, profit sharing—the whole compensation package. OK?"

Murmurs of agreement were heard all around.

"Then let's discuss staffing," Willy said. "I'll tell you right now that I've decided that twenty bodies is all we'll need—now, or ever. Like that BC Bank in Switzerland, Urs. If they can do what they did with twenty people, total, so can we."

After a half-hour discussion, they decided that twelve would suffice for the time being.

"Now some mention was made of equipment last night," Willy said. "Somehow I had the impression that with all those Sun workstations we were set to go."

"We are," Fred said, "but where development of new derivative products is concerned, we have come to the conclusion that we are going to have to have a whole lot more computing power than they can provide."

"You're not talking about a twenty-million-dollar Cray?" Willy asked, visibly startled.

"No. Crays are outdated. We're talking about a MasPar MP-two. It's a parallel computer and costs only five hundred thousand dollars. They've got them at Lawrence Livermore, at NASA down in Sunnyvale, at Lockheed's Palo Alto Research Lab. It runs circles around a conventional supercomputer like Cray. And I don't know if you remember, Mr. Saxon, but when you asked in the beginning how much equipment costs would be, I guessed about a million dollars. If we include an MP-two along with the Sun workstations and the satellite stuff, the bill will come to almost exactly that million."

Willy had no choice but to agree.

Then came the housing issue. It seemed that neither of Fred's new colleagues had wives. Both had been divorced after very brief marriages. Willy fully understood *that*. So it

■

was agreed that the three bachelors would permanently take over the house in which they had been temporarily staying.

The four then went back to their computers. Willy, accompanied as always by Frank Lipper, headed for the main house. Frank had the City of Ukiah's three-inch-thick feasibility study tucked under his right arm. Both remained silent for a long time. Both had the same thing on their minds, however.

It was Frank who finally voiced it. "How much are you committed to putting in already, Willy?"

"Sixty-four million, give or take a million."

"Not counting that extra twenty million dollars these guys were talking about?"

"Not counting it. Right."

"That worries me, Willy. Don't get me wrong. It's not just you. A couple of years ago Kidder Peabody wanted to set up a derivatives unit, and it was nixed by their parent company because they were afraid it would eat up too much capital. As you know, Willy, their parent company is General Electric. My point is that even you will be hard-pressed to come up with the kind of money this derivatives operation will need one of these days, Willy."

"I guess so."

"Then what?"

"I'll have to consider the options."

"What options?"

"You've got one of them under your arm, Frank."

"What the hell's that supposed to mean, Willy?" Frank said. "There's nothing like that kind of money to be earned underwriting municipal bonds. Believe me, that's been my business now for quite a while."

"I believe you, Frank."

Frank decided to leave it there. He knew from years of experience that, when Willy Saxon went enigmatic, there was no use pushing him any further.

"Now what?" he asked.

■

"Is there a swimming pool here somewhere?" Willy asked.

"Yeah. I took a long exploratory walk early this morning. There's one just the other side of that picnic area where we were last night."

"How come I didn't see it before?"

"There's a high hedge around it. Maybe Jack liked to skinny dip there."

"Wanna give it a try?"

"I'm a little old for skinny dipping, Willy."

"Me too. But I'm sure Jack left some swimming suits along with everything else. Let's go look."

They found a half dozen wildly Hawaiian swimming trunks in an upstairs chest. When they tried on a couple, they discovered that, like Bermuda shorts, they all stretched below their knees.

"We look ridiculous," Frank said.

"So what?" Willy replied. "Nobody's going to see us. Let's get some towels."

As they approached the picnic area, Willy suddenly heard what sounded like a shriek and stopped.

"Where did that come from?"

Frank pointed at the hedge on the far side of the area.

Both broke into a trot. When they got to the other side of the hedge, the source of the shriek was poised on top of a diving board, clad in the skimpiest bathing suit that either of them had ever seen. It was Susie. Sara was standing at the side of the pool, watching her. Both now turned toward the two intruders, and this time it was Sara who shrieked—in laughter.

"Jeez," Frank said. "This is embarrassing."

"Yeah," Willy said. "But it's too late to turn back now." He broke back into a trot and dived into the pool. So did Frank. Then Susie jumped in. As did Sara.

For the next fifteen minutes the four of them fooled around

■

in the pool, diving under each other, pushing, pulling, and all the while screaming and giggling like little kids.

"Time out!" Sara finally yelled.

They then all sat down at a table shaded by a huge beach umbrella.

"What's that?" Willy asked, pointing at a pitcher full of something.

"Lemonade," Sara replied. "Want some?"

"I guess so," Willy replied, regretting that he had passed up Zeke's for this.

As Sara filled a paper cup with lemonade, she asked, "Where've you been?"

"Healdsburg's City Hall."

"Why?"

"Talking municipal bonds with the town's finance director."

"What's a bond?" Susie asked.

"They're what you call *'Obligationen,'* " Willy replied.

"How do you know that?" Susie asked.

"I studied at the university in Zurich for a while."

"Oh."

"So did you make any progress at City Hall?" Sara asked.

"Maybe."

Frank broke in. "Willy, as usual, came up with a great idea."

"And that was?"

"They couldn't figure out a way to finance a certain project. Willy told them how. With a forty-year zero coupon bond."

"If bonds are *Obligationen,*" Susie asked, "what are zero coupon bonds in German?"

"I don't know," Willy said. "When I studied in Zurich, they hadn't been invented yet."

"Really," said Sara. "When were they invented?"

"They were invented, perhaps I should say reinvented, in the early 1980s."

"What's so different about them?" Sara asked.

"They provide a way for governments or corporations to raise capital without having to make interest payments."

"I don't get it," Sara said.

"Well normally, bonds have coupons. Every year you clip the coupon, send it in, and you get your annual interest payment. Right?"

"That we get, don't we Susie?" Sara said.

Susie nodded.

"Zero coupon bonds don't have coupons."

"Makes sense. Then how do you get your interest?"

"It's all paid in a lump sum at the end. If it's a twenty-year bond, you get all the accumulated interest at the end of those twenty years. Plus your initial investment. It's like those World War Two Victory Bonds. Your father bought a one hundred-dollar bond, but he only paid fifty dollars. He put it in the safe and forgot about it. Then when the war was over he went to the post office and cashed it in . . . for one hundred dollars. In the 1980s the guys on Wall Street took that basic concept and applied it first to U.S. government securities, when primary dealers in those bonds started stripping the coupons. Then it spread to corporate financing and finally to municipal bonds."

"There is one slight difference where municipal zero coupon bonds are concerned," Frank said.

This puzzled Willy. "What do you mean?"

"That's my field, as you know, Willy," Frank said, obviously embarrassed at having to correct Willy, "and we sometimes use terminology of our own."

Willy was still puzzled.

"What I mean," Frank said, "is that in the muni field we call zero coupon bonds 'Capital Appreciation Bonds.' Which makes sense when you think about it. Take those war bonds. Your father's fifty-dollar capital appreciated to one hundred dollars. Right?"

■

"My mistake, Frank," Willy said. "Somehow to me a zero coupon is a zero coupon. Period."

"Let's change the subject," Sara said. "Susie needs some clothes. Where around here should she go?"

"I would think to Santa Rosa. What kind of clothes?"

All eyes now turned to Susie. Both Willy and Frank didn't quite know where to look, since only about three percent of Susie's body was covered by her bathing suit. But she seemed perfectly comfortable that way.

"I want a real American summer frock," she said. "And shoes to match."

"Why don't you take her to Santa Rosa, Sara," Willy said, "and then join the rest of us for dinner. There's a great little restaurant in Healdsburg which they told me about at City Hall. It's called Tre Scalini, which means three steps, because it's just three steps around the corner from the Healdsburg Plaza. Let's say seven o'clock. I'll make the arrangements."

At seven, Susie walked into the restaurant wearing her new frock, new shoes, and a smile that wouldn't stop. The six men who had been awaiting their arrival joined in a round of applause. Sara stood behind Susie, beaming.

But the moment they sat down to eat their crostini appetizers, the talk turned to business—derivatives. They moved from differential swaps, to municipal bond index futures, to equity index swaps, to options on swaps, or swaptions, and finally discussed yet more ideas on how to tweak and tilt inverse floaters.

They broke up early, and by eleven o'clock, like the night before, Willy was in bed and ready to go to sleep. But like the night before, there was a knock on his door.

"All that talk about derivatives got me worked up," Sara whispered as she slid in beside him. Unlike the previous night, she wore no nightgown.

"Feeling a little kinky, huh?" Willy asked.

"Maybe."

■

"Then how about an inverse floater?"

"Not that kinky. Perhaps a tweak, a tilt, or even a swap."

"Let's start with a tilt. Then maybe a swap."

Just before she fell asleep she told Willy that she liked the tilt, but that the swap had been even more fun.

■

TWENTY-EIGHT

Frank Lipper and Willy spent the next morning working on compensation packages. After sitting down with their new team, one by one, Frank would shuttle back to the main house to get the go ahead, or not, from Willy. By two o'clock, they had draft agreements with all four men who would be running the River Ranch operation. Their employer would be the dummy corporation in the British Channel Islands, which was part of the elaborate string of companies that his London solicitor had set up with the dual purpose of hiding the true beneficial ownership of any and all of Willy's operations, as well as avoiding taxes. He had already arranged for the Channel Islands company to be the purchaser of River Ranch. Now he would simply take it the next logical step. P & Q Financial Products would contract for the services provided by the Channel Island company in regard to developing derivative products, and would pay it fees based on the profits such derivatives generated for the San Francisco investment bank. All Healdsburg expenses would be covered from the Channel Islands, including the payment of a rather hefty emolument to Willy Saxon. The difference between those fees coming in and the expenses in Healdsburg going out would stay as profit in the Channel Islands—where the corporate tax rate was zero. It was complicated as hell, which is why he did things this way.

■

Nobody from the SEC to the IRS could possibly find their way through this maze.

They decided to skip lunch and head back to San Francisco right away. Sara offered to stay another day. There was still a lot of work to do on the trading room. And she had not even begun to develop plans for the refurbishing of the old Victorian. But she would drive back down to the city Friday afternoon, so she could make Dan Prescott's dinner party that evening. She'd talked to Denise about it, and they had decided that they would go together and meet Willy there.

Willy was barely inside the car when he pulled out his cellular phone.

"Did you put Marshall Lane's number in here?" Willy asked Frank.

"Would I forget to put in the name of a guy who runs over fifty billion dollars?" Frank replied.

"It's five o'clock back there, but if I know Marshall he's still in the office," Willy said.

He was.

"Marshall, this is Willy Saxon," he began, when the New York money manager came on the phone. "Remember our little talk a few weeks ago up at Denise van Bercham's ranch?"

"Sure. So you've come up with an idea I can use?"

"Maybe. You got an international bond fund?"

"Of course."

"Then I've got an idea for you. Options on DM inverse floaters, with the currency risk fully hedged."

"So you figure both German interest rates and the DM are headed lower?"

"That's right."

"I think we agree with you. In which case that product would be a great buy. But who's offering it?"

"Nobody yet. But they will on Monday."

"Pals of yours?"

"Yes. Prescott and Quackenbush here in San Francisco."

■

"I didn't know they did derivatives."

"They will, starting Monday."

"Can you fax me the details?"

"Right away tomorrow morning. How much might you be interested in?"

"A hundred million, for openers."

"That fax will be waiting for you when you get to the office tomorrow."

"Thanks, Willy. Anything else?"

"Yeah, maybe. A rather unique municipal bond offering with a pretty high yield. I'll know for sure by Monday."

"Call me."

"Will do," Willy said.

As soon as the connection was broken, Willy called one of the brand-new numbers at the trading center at River Ranch and asked for Fred Fitch.

"Just lined up your first customer for those inverse floaters," Willy said. He gave Fred the details, and then asked, "Will that phone system hookup with San Francisco be working by tomorrow morning?"

"Pac Bell is here right now. They're testing it."

"On an outgoing fax, where does the machine say it's originating?"

"I've already thought of that," Fred answered. "P and Q Financial Products—San Francisco"

"Perfect. What time do you expect to get to work tomorrow?" Willy asked.

"Now that everything's up and running—the satellite feeds started coming in an hour ago—we'll all be here at least an hour before the markets open in New York. That gives us time to catch Europe before it closes there. We're going to give everything a test run today and tomorrow so we'll be ready to get down to real business next Monday."

"Great." Willy asked, "So that will put you at work around five?"

■

"That's right."

"Then, if you don't mind, I'd appreciate it if you'd get that fax off to Marshall Lane first thing."

"Consider it done," Fred replied.

"Your turn," he said to Frank after he had hung up.

Frank called three bond fund managers, one in Boston, one in Los Angeles, and one in Atlanta, and all three went for the inverse floater concept.

"We're cooking," Willy said. "Now I'm going to call Sidney Ravitch."

"What's going on with him?" Frank asked. "I intended to ask you that question earlier, after hearing you recommend his credit rating agency to the honcho from the City of San Francisco. Why did you do that?"

"First slide shut that panel," Willy said, pointing to the glass partition behind the limo driver. Frank did.

"Here's why," Willy continued. "Because I'm buying forty-nine percent of his operation."

"Do you trust Ravitch?"

"Of course not. So I've got an option to buy the rest."

"Oh," Frank said. "That's different, I guess. Who else knows about this?"

"Nobody but Bobby Armacost. He's handling the legal side of the deal. In fact, I'd better call him right now to see how it's coming along."

He did, and Armacost assured him that everything was completely on track and on schedule. Sidney Ravitch and his attorney could not have been more cooperative.

"Then it's safe for me to call him?" Willy asked.

"I don't see any reason why not. This is a done, done deal." Armacost responded.

So Willy did.

Bobbie Armacost had been right Ravitch was all sweetness and light—ready to sign on the dotted line any time the papers and Willy were ready.

■

"We're actually ready right now," Willy said.

"Then let's do it tomorrow."

Willy thought, Why not. That way both acquisitions, the investment bank and the ratings agency, could be consummated on the same day. That could be a good omen for the future.

"All right," Willy said, "Bobby Armacost and I will show up at noon at your place with all the papers—and your ten million dollars."

"Could you make it a little earlier?" Ravitch asked.

"Why not. What suits you?"

"How long will it take?"

"An hour."

"So how about ten o'clock?"

"Done. We'll see you then."

After he hung up, Frank said, "Odd conversation."

"What was so odd about it?"

"His telling *you* what time to be there."

"Maybe he's got something very important scheduled at noon," Willy responded.

"What could be more important than selling half his company and getting ten million dollars?"

Willy shrugged. "We'll never know, will we?"

Willy made one last phone call, back to Bobby Armacost, to inform him about the 10 a.m. meeting.

"So that's it," he said to Frank. "Everything's set. And it's not even three o'clock. What will we do now?"

"There's a game at Candlestick starting at five-fifteen. The Giants are playing the Braves."

"Now that's what I call a hell of a good idea. But what about tickets?"

"Don't worry. We've got a box there."

"Who's we?"

"Prescott and Quackenbush. Dan Prescott takes his pals there all the time. I've got a pass for the box too."

■

"What's *that* cost?"

"You don't want to know," Frank replied.

"No wonder they've been losing money. Where's the box situated?"

"Almost right behind home plate."

"Let's go. It's almost three. Tell the driver to step on it so that we can make Candlestick by five."

Willy slid the glass partition open and gave the driver Willy's instructions. "I'd better call Dan to make sure he's not going," he then said.

"If he was, he's not now," Willy said.

Traffic on 19th Avenue was worse than normal, so they entered their box high above the playing field in Candlestick Park just as the national anthem was being played. Nobody else was there.

"Don't tell me you've got the *whole* box," Willy asked.

"No. We've got the four front-row seats," Frank said.

"Who's got the rest?"

"Wells Fargo bank."

"We used to do a lot of good business with them," Willy said.

"I know. And they know."

"So you still get along, despite my fall from grace?"

"Sure. You'll see if any of them show up for the game."

Five minutes later they did show. And just as Frank had indicated, the vice-chairman of the bank and two of his colleagues immediately came down to say hello. Two other men who were with them did not.

After they had all sat down to watch the game, Willy leaned over to Frank and said, "Don't look now, but one of those guys with the Wells Fargo people is that prick, Ralph Goodman, who runs the state banking commission."

"I know," Frank said. "The other one is the new state attorney general. I noticed them watching us."

"Exactly. And that asshole Goodman was talking into the

■

other guy's ear the entire time—no doubt bringing him up to date on my life history. This is the second time I've run into that bastard since I got out. He stiffed me in front of twenty people a couple of weeks ago up at Denise van Bercham's ranch. Guys like that make me so goddamn mad. Who in the fuck do they think they are?"

"Don't let it bother you, Willy," Frank said. "What can he do to you now?"

"Nothing. But that doesn't mean he won't try," Willy said, adding, "in which case I'm not so sure it's so healthy us being seen together like this."

"Why? Everybody knows we used to work together."

"Sure. But now you're with Prescott and Quackenbush, and I'm banned for life from the securities business."

"Come on, Willy," Frank said. "I'm going to get us some hot dogs and chili and beer so we can start enjoying ourselves. Don't let this spoil the game for you."

But it did. When Barry Bonds hit a grand slam home run in the seventh, putting the Giants up by four runs, Willy immediately said. "That does it. Let's go."

They said goodbye to the Wells Fargo guys on the way out. While they did, the banking commissioner and the attorney general pointedly looked the other way.

"How about a nightcap at the Big Four?" Frank asked, when they were back in the limo.

"Naw, not tonight," Willy said. "I've got maybe the biggest day of my life tomorrow. I want to get a good night's sleep."

He was back in his Nob Hill apartment by eight, in bed by nine, but he didn't fall asleep until eleven.

■

TWENTY-NINE

At ten the next morning, Willy and Bobby Armacost met with Sidney Ravitch and his attorney in the conference room of the Western Credit Rating Agency. The signing of the agreements which gave Willy co-ownership of the Western Credit Rating Agency went off without a hitch. Willy was merely a spectator to that. The signatures of the buyer, Veritas, Ltd., had been executed in London by the Company Secretary, Lionel Latham, and by Sir Aubrey Whitehead, former adjutant to Lord Mountbatten, who served as its Chairman of the Board. But the final act was Willy's, when he stood up and handed a cashier's cheque issued by Barclays Bank over to Sid Ravitch. It was for exactly $10,000,000.00.

"Now that that's done," Willy said to Ravitch, as the two lawyers went into a huddle at the other end of the conference room table to go through the documents once more to make sure that everything had been properly executed, "let's sit down and talk about a few things I've lined up. The first is the City and County of San Francisco. I think I've talked them into taking you on as one of their credit rating agencies."

"No shit!" Ravitch exclaimed. "I thought Moody's and Standard and Poors had an absolute lock on them. That's why I never even approached them."

"No more. And I'll explain how this developed."

Willy told him about his idea to piggyback the financing of

■

a public housing project onto the issue of some general obligation bonds. That Prescott and Quackenbush were prepared to do the underwriting. And that the chief administrative officers seemed ready to give it the green light.

"So while I was at it," Willy continued, "I threw in your name, suggesting that he could get a much better deal on fees from you than he could from Moody's or S and P. I also pushed the point that you are local, and they're not. He seemed to buy the idea. So he's expecting your call."

"His name's George Abbott, right?"

"That's right. I think he's expecting you to come in at half what they've been paying."

"No sweat. To break into that league, I'd do it for nothing."

"Let's not get *too* carried away, partner," Willy said.

Sid liked that.

"How about a cigar?" he asked. "We've now got two things to celebrate."

"Sure. Why not."

While they were lighting up two of Cuba's finest, Willy continued. "There's another project. It's not in the same league, but they'll pay the full price if it comes off. The City of Ukiah. They're seriously considering building a solid waste disposal facility and . . ."

Ravitch interrupted. "Sure. That's because of AB 939. The state's forcing all those little cities to put them in. They cost about twenty million dollars a pop, as I understand it."

"Exactly. Prescott and Quackenbush are thinking of putting a proposal in to the City of Ukiah for the financing. They are thinking in terms of a forty-year zero coupon bond. I know—you guys call them Capital Appreciation Bonds."

"CABs, actually," Ravitch replied.

"Fine. I'll stick to zero coupon."

"Who should I contact in Ukiah?" Ravitch asked.

"Nobody. They'll come to you, if and when this thing jells."

■

"I could maybe at least make a preliminary contact."

"Nope. They'll come to you."

Ravitch shrugged. "Fine with me." Then: "You know, everybody always said that you were a rainmaker, Willy, and by God you sure are. Between the two of us, this thing's really going to fly."

"That's the idea, Sid," Willy said.

The lawyers had finished their review of the documents and came over to join the two principals. Sid offered both a celebratory cigar. Both declined.

"But I still want to celebrate," Armacost said. "How about all of us reconvening somewhere for lunch? Say around noon?"

"I can't," Ravitch said. "Unfortunately, I've got something scheduled. But you guys go ahead without me."

Ravitch's lawyer, who had acted rather strange the entire time, also declined, saying he had a court appointment later that day. So after handshakes all around, Willy and Bobby left by themselves.

"Still want to do lunch?" Willy asked as they rode down the elevator.

"Sure. Where?"

"Why not Moose's, where this whole thing started."

"It's a bit early," Bobby said.

"Yeah, but we could have a couple of bloody Mary's first."

"I'm game. Then we take a break and reconvene at Prescott and Quackenbush at four to wrap up that deal. And don't forget—there's dinner at our place at seven-thirty."

"I'd hardly forget that. If I don't show up Denise and Sara will kill me," Willy said.

"So would my wife," Dan said. "By the way, where's Frank? I thought he'd be here with you."

"He intended to, but then changed his mind. Said he had to prepare something for that press conference this afternoon."

While they were trying to hail a cab on Montgomery Street,

they saw Sid Ravitch hurry out the door of the Russ Building and disappear down the street.

"I wonder what he's up to," Bobby said.

"Who knows," Willy replied "But it must be important."

THIRTY

It was exactly noon when Sidney Ravitch pulled up in front of the Federal Correctional Institution in Pleasanton. He was driving a Hertz rental car. One couldn't be too careful.

Lenny was waiting outside on the porch. He didn't wait for Ravitch to get out. He came right to the car, threw his suitcase onto the backseat, climbed in the front, and said, "Let's get out of here."

"What's the hurry?" Ravitch asked.

"If you had been in there for three years, you'd be in a hurry, too."

"I guess so." He put the car into a U-turn and sped off.

"So where are we headed?" Lenny asked. "Back to your office, I hope. I can hardly wait to get to work. Just the prospect of that has done wonders for me in recent months."

"I understand, Lenny. But let me tell you right away that it's not going to be exactly like we've been discussing."

Ravitch did not dare to look at Lenny when he said this.

There was now a tremble in Lenny's voice when he spoke. "Sid, don't tell me . . ."

Ravitch interrupted. "Let me finish, Lenny. You've got a job working for me. Starting right now. OK?"

"OK. Doing what?"

"First let me explain what's happened. Exactly one hour

■

ago our mutual friend Willy Saxon bought forty-nine percent of my company."

"That's great," Lenny said. "He's one hell of a smart guy."

"That he is. But so great it isn't for you, Lenny."

"How come?"

"Well, when I told him I was coming over to pick you up, and that you'd be working for the firm from now on, he nixed the idea."

"He what?"

"He said he didn't want you working in any company he was affiliated with."

"I thought he liked me."

"I think you thought wrong."

"Then why, if he's such a jerk, did you sell out to him?"

"I didn't sell out. I've still got fifty-one percent of the company. But to answer your question, I sold half of it to him because of you."

That stopped Lenny dead in his tracks.

"Now how the fuck could *I* have anything to do with *his* buying into *your* company. I've been locked up in that goddamn place for three years!"

"Yeah. But during those three years you kept a few mementos of your past exploits, it seems."

"What's that mean?"

"The prospectus."

"So that's where it went!" Lenny exclaimed. "I looked all over the fucking place for it yesterday, when I was packing to leave."

"It went with Willy when he left Pleasanton. And he used it to blackmail me into selling half my place to him for a song," Sid said, deciding that it would be the better part of wisdom not to mention that ten-million-dollar check he had received from Willy just over an hour ago.

"But how did he know that you put that prospectus together?" Lenny asked.

■

"Because, according to him, you told him so." Sid replied.

"No wonder he doesn't want me around," Lenny said. "I might kill the lying cocksucker!"

"I figured he was lying," Sid said, lying a bit himself. "But that doesn't change things. He knows."

"OK. That explains why *you* sold," Lenny said. "But it hardly explains why *he* bought."

"Now we're getting to the heart of the matter. Why indeed? We both know Willy well enough to realize that he must have an angle. A very crooked self-serving angle. But so far, I haven't figured it out," Sid said. "Sure, he used some Mickey Mouse setup in England to buy into my company, but that's hardly a Federal offense. Even if it were, he's got a damn good lawyer covering his ass. Then this morning he came through with two new clients for me. One is the City of San Francisco, which, believe me, is big time where a firm our size is concerned. He's also bringing in the City of Ukiah, which is no big deal in itself, but it could lead to other cities in California signing up with us."

Lenny was getting impatient. "So where does all that leave me?"

"With a full-time, well-paying job finding out what Willy's up to."

"How well-paying?"

"A hundred thousand a year."

"A hundred and fifty and I'll do it."

"You got it," Ravitch said.

"When do I start?"

"The moment you've moved into a hotel and unpacked. I've got you fixed up at the Holiday Inn on Van Ness."

"OK. That takes care of the when. What about the where?"

"I found out that he just moved into an apartment at the corner of Sacramento and Taylor, overlooking Huntington Park. That would be as good a place to start as any."

"You mean you want me to break into the place?"

■

"No, no. At least not yet. Just follow him around a bit. See who his new pals are. He's bound to show up there sometime this afternoon."

"What about expenses?"

"You keep track. I'll reimburse you."

Ravitch then fished an envelope out of his breast pocket and handed it to Lenny. "You'll need some money to start. It's in there."

Lenny opened the envelope, took out a wad of bills, and counted. There were forty fifties.

"You know something, Sid," he then said, "I'm starting to like this job already."

■

THIRTY-ONE

At two o'clock, Willy and Bobby Armacost finished lunch.

"I totally forgot something," Willy said, as they walked out of Moose's restaurant.

"What?"

"I gave away my tux and everything that goes with it to the Salvation Army three years ago. And I've got to go to a formal dinner tonight."

"I've got a tailor at Brooks Brothers who has taken care of me for years," Armacost said. "It's on the way to my office. So let's take a cab. I'll go into the store with you. I'm sure they'll fix you up."

They did, and at three o'clock Willy was back in his apartment at 1190 Sacramento Street. Forty-five minutes later, after a brief nap—he did take one now and then but never admitted to it—Willy walked out the door and headed across the park for the Huntington hotel, where he would get a cab.

Lenny had arrived about a half hour earlier, and had taken his place on one of the benches that encircled the fountain in the middle of the park. It offered a clear unobstructed view of the seventh floor of 1190 Sacramento. The curtains were drawn across most of its windows to keep out the hot afternoon sun, which bore directly down on them. But then, around three-thirty, the curtains on what was obviously the living room were pulled open. And there, beyond any doubt,

■

stood Willy Saxon, clad in what appeared to be a Japanese-type dressing gown.

"Bingo!" Lenny said.

Lenny stayed on the bench as Willy crossed the square fifteen minutes later, and watched as the doorman at the Huntington put him into a taxi. Minutes later, Lenny approached the doorman.

"Was that Mr. Saxon who just went off in that cab?" he asked.

"Yes, sir." Willy was by now well known to the people at the hotel after having stayed there so long.

"Damn!" Lenny exclaimed. "I was supposed to meet him here. He must have forgotten. And I've got to get a six o'clock plane back to L.A."

"Maybe you can still catch him. He told the cab driver to take him to 501 California Street."

"Can you get me another cab fast?"

"Right away."

As the doorman opened the back door of the cab for Lenny while telling the driver where to go, Lenny slipped him a twenty.

"Good luck!" the doorman called out, as the cab pulled away.

At 501 California, headquarters of Prescott & Quackenbush, the closing of the deal in which International Bank Holdings of Zug, Switzerland, bought a dominant share of that investment bank involved the merest of formalities. The real show started fifteen minutes later, when, one by one, the arriving press was ushered into the bank's conference room. They included reporters from both the San Francisco *Chronicle* and *Examiner,* as well as representatives from the local offices of the *Wall Street Journal,* the *L.A. Times,* the *Journal of Commerce,* and Reuters.

Willy had left the room well before they arrived. He sat in

■

Dan Prescott's office listening in on the speaker phone. The line from the conference room had been left open.

Prescott got things going by reading from a prepared script, announcing the infusion of twenty million dollars of new equity, which had been consummated that afternoon.

"But that's just the first step in the expansion plans of Prescott and Quackenbush," he went on to say. "Our new partner in Switzerland has indicated its intention to put in an additional twenty million dollars in long-term capital next week, to fund the startup of a totally new activity, P and Q Financial Products, which will operate under the auspices of a wholly-owned subsidiary of our bank. It will offer a full range of derivative products. Here is Frank Lipper, our Executive Vice-President, who will oversee those operations, to explain."

"So that's what Frank was up to," Willy said, as he listened in.

"Gentlemen," Frank said, "As Mr. Prescott said, it will be my responsibility to oversee these new operations. But the actual development of the products will be handled by others. I'd like to introduce one of them to you now. He's Dr. Glenn Godwin, formerly of Lawrence Livermore Laboratories. Dr. Godwin."

"I'll be damned," Willy said.

"As you know, gentlemen," the ex-physicist from the Star Wars program began, "techniques in this field are rapidly changing. Heretofore they have revolved around linear methods of analyzing economic and financial data. The aim was always to detect patterns or structures in financial markets that could be isolated and then used as the basis for investment or trading."

He paused to let that sink in.

"However, we are taking a different approach, involving *non*linear methods. They include neural networks and genetic algorithms. We are also attempting to apply chaos theory. I

■

think you will be surprised at some of the results we have already come up with. Thank you."

There was total silence in the conference room, but not in the adjoining office of Dan Prescott, where Willy sat.

"Absolutely perfect," Willy said. "They didn't understand one fucking word he said."

There were two feeble questions asked.

"What exactly are neural networks?" This came from the woman who ran the business section of the *Examiner*.

"They are networks of computer processing units, like Sun workstations, whose interaction is designed to replicate the learning processes of the human brain," was the answer.

"Oh," the woman said.

"Maybe you could bring us up to date on chaos theory," asked the man from the *Journal*.

"Certainly. It simply holds that it is often possible to identify short-term patterns in apparently random data. Which, if true, pulls the rug from under those who insist that changes in market prices resemble a random walk and are therefore inherently unpredictable."

"Thank you," the man said.

And that was that, where Dr. Glenn Godwin was concerned. This sudden hiatus prompted Frank Lipper and Dan Prescott to hurry back to the front of the class to fill the awkward void.

"What this will do," Frank said, "is for the first time really put San Francisco on the map, where derivatives are concerned. To be sure, Morgan Stanley has a pretty good operation going here. But our intention is to go way beyond what they are doing at present."

Then Prescott broke in. "But lest we forget, the principal business of Prescott and Quackenbush has been the underwriting of municipal bonds. And there we also have big plans."

■

As he droned on, Willy Saxon decided to quietly slip out. He had to pick up his tux at Brooks Brothers before it closed. He decided to walk.

So Lenny did the same. From a safe distance.

■

THIRTY-TWO

Denise van Bercham and Sara Jones were already there when Willy Saxon arrived at the dinner party on outer Broadway in his brand new tuxedo. He was immediately greeted by the hostess and her husband, Dan Prescott, who was now his new partner in the investment banking business.

As he moved on into the main living room, he saw Denise and Sara standing by themselves in front of the fireplace. Denise was dressed in a stunning green floor-length Givenchy; Sara in an azure blue Gianfranco Ferre. They had obviously gone all out for the cause.

"We weren't sure you'd make it," Denise said, as he sidled up to them. She then added, "It's been a long time."

"A whole week," Willy said.

"I hear from Sara that we've been a very busy boy."

Sara just stood there, listening.

"Very."

"Also a good boy?"

"Fairly. Anybody interesting here?"

"No. Although most of my friends came, just as I promised. Prentis Cobb Hale and Denise, Charlotte Maillard, the Rosenkranzes, Frances Bowes and her husband, Matthew Kelly and Diane."

Sara finally decided to say something. "Did you hear the latest one about Matthew?"

■

216

"No."

"That he's the only man in San Francisco who's been living exclusively on hors d'oeuvres for over thirty years."

"You could probably say the same of most of the women here," Denise said, her eyes constantly on the move. "Oh, here comes the guest of honor."

It was indeed the Chief Administrative Officer of the City and County of San Francisco with his bride of twenty years.

Denise immediately took charge. First she kissed George Abbott on both cheeks. Then she turned to his wife.

"You must be Lisa," she said. Denise caught her in an ostentatiously affectionate embrace in full view of the watching crowd, which included first and foremost her beaming husband.

Lisa Abbott knew that she had just been catapulted from obscurity into the A level of San Francisco society.

Willy Saxon knew that he had just been assured that the underwriting project he had proposed to the City and County of San Francisco was in the bag.

"By the way," Denise said, focusing once again on the guest of honor, "have you made any progress on that suggestion of mine?"

"The problem is the mayor," Abbott replied. "He feels that until his first term runs out he should stick with the current chief of protocol."

"But my dear George," Denise said, "there is no guarantee that the mayor will be reelected, is there?"

"I guess not."

"But his chances would certainly improve if his campaign was adequately financed."

"No doubt about that, Denise."

"Maybe I and some of my friends might be of some help there."

"That would certainly help a lot."

■

"I think the mayor should be reminded of an old Romanian saying," Denise said. "One hand washes the other."

"I'll have another word with him tomorrow morning," Abbott said, fully aware of the fact that his wife had been listening in on the entire conversation.

"I'll remind you," Lisa said, and was immediately rewarded with the most appreciative smile that Denise van Bercham could muster.

Denise then took the arms of both Sara and Willy and guided them in the direction of a couple whom she introduced as Carol and Robert McNeil. Real estate and money. Beside them were Walter Shorenstein and Phyllis. More real estate and a *lot* more money. Then they moved on to Ingrid and Reuben Hills. Coffee and money. Further on was Nini Martin—newspapers and money—talking to the Pelosis, politics and money. Next the Getty's. Music and *big* money. Denise worked the room like a political operative, making sure at each "stop" that everyone was aware of the fact that she had a new best friend, Willy Saxon, and that Willy was the smartest man she'd ever met, where making money with money was concerned. On a couple of occasions, Willy noticed a glimmer of recognition when his name was mentioned. But now that he had Denise's endorsement, the issue of past indiscretions had been rendered moot.

Sara just tagged along. She knew that it was showtime and that Denise was in charge.

The dinner was over by ten-thirty. Sara, Denise, and Willy left the house together. Denise offered him a ride home, but since he had his limo waiting, he declined. So Sara and Denise left as they had come—all by themselves in the backseat of her Bentley.

As Willy rode back to his apartment alone in the backseat of his stretch Cadillac, he could not help but congratulate himself on how he had handled what could have been a touchy situation. It was apparent that Denise had sniffed something in the air where Sara and he were concerned. Sara, on the other hand, had reverted to her usual aloof self. In fact, she and Willy had barely had any eye contact the entire evening. She had not touched him even once. So there was nothing that could even remotely confirm Denise's suspicions. Which was important, since he liked both women. And both obviously liked him, as well as each other. So why rock the boat?

Not rocking the boat meant, however, that Willy was going to spend the night alone in his apartment. Which was fine with him. It had been probably the fullest week in his entire life—a week that called for a moment of quiet reflection. So the first thing he did after getting back to his apartment was to take off the damn tuxedo and everything else, and put on his favorite Japanese-style silk robe. Then he poured himself a generous Jack Daniel's with a touch of water, turned on some soft rock music on KABL, and plunked himself down on the living room sofa, savoring the quiet solitude.

At midnight, just as he had decided to head for bed, he heard the elevator and then a key turning the lock on the door. He went on full alert. But not for long.

"I couldn't sleep," the owner of his apartment house said, as she entered the living room. "It must have been the coffee."

Willy stood up as she came over to him.

"I hope you're not mad at me for just busting in like this. Are you?"

"Of course not," Willy said, and caught her in a full embrace.

Her hand went inside his robe to his chest. Then it moved down. Then she moved down. Later, he returned the compliment in his bedroom.

"I like you Willy Saxon," were Denise's last words before she went to sleep.

When she left the next morning at eleven, Lenny, from his bench in Huntington Park, took note of the time and the license number of the Bentley that picked her up.

■

Thirty-Three

Willy spent the rest of Saturday and much of Sunday alone, reading most of the time. When the concierge phoned at five Sunday afternoon, telling him that his limo driver had arrived, Willy was ready to go again. In fact, he was eager to go. Because Monday was going to be the first day that the Healdsburg derivatives team went into action. And he wanted to be there in the trading room when it started.

If it started.

For Willy had to admit to himself that, deep down, he was worried that this whole thing might turn out to be the bust of all time, or at least a sixty-four-million-dollar bust.

So it was with a sense of foreboding that he walked into the trading room at five a.m.

He knew immediately that his worries had been for naught. From the cacophony in the room it was apparent that the action had not only started, but that it was already hot and heavy. *At five a.m.!*

Urs Bauer was screaming into two phones in Italian. Deal done with the party on phone number 1, he went directly to his computer to confirm the transaction to his counterparty in Milan, the Banca Nationale del Lavoro. The new derivatives unit of Prescott & Quackenbush had just gone short ten billion lira. Five minutes later, he had concluded another transaction, this time with Barclays in London. P & Q Financial

■

Products was now long ten million pounds sterling. The next ten minutes were spent haggling in French with a fellow foreign exchange dealer in Paris. No deal was struck here.

What was noticeable, even to a bystander, was the apparent welcome that greeted Urs Bauer with each phone call he made to Europe. With a pause in the action, he saw Willy standing behind him, for the first time.

"They're all glad I'm back," he said, beaming from ear to ear. "Isn't that great!"

"Terrific," Willy said.

"There's only one problem," Bauer then said. "They all want to see our balance sheet. So I've faxed probably at least two dozen to Europe already."

"I trust you faxed the new pro forma one that reflects the capital restructuring we did last week."

"Of course. But I'll be blunt, Mr. Saxon. They're not happy. They're doing business with me, sure. They're my friends and we foreign exchange dealers stick together. But they all must work within the credit limits their managements lay on them. And with the forty-million-dollar long-term capital we've got, even after the restructuring, we're going to hit those limits very quickly. That's just where I'm concerned. Those guys," and Bauer now pointed in the direction of Fred Fitch and his two colleagues, "are soon going to face exactly the same problem."

"I understand," Willy said. "Don't worry. You make money and I'll back you up with capital. I'll take another look after I see where we stand at the end of this first week."

Willy then walked over to the corner of the trading room that Fred Fitch had taken over. Fitch, who had also been on the phone the entire time, hung up just as Willy arrived in front of his desk.

"That's was the Deutsche Bank. We've been able to buy fifty million marks worth of German inverse floaters. We're trying to get another fifty million from Dresdner. Urs is work-

■

ing on the currency swap. If he can cut a deal before they close in Frankfurt, then we can try to sell the package in New York later today. They're not open there yet."

"So it's working out just like you predicted."

"Yes, but frankly, Deutsche Bank wasn't going to do the deal until I told them that Urs Bauer was now with us. Apparently Urs had a little trouble in Germany a few years back, but everybody says he got screwed, and they all still have an enormous respect for him."

"What was Deutche Bank's problem before you told them about Urs?"

"They don't know Prescott and Quackenbush from Adam. And their balance sheet—I guess I'd better get used to saying *our* balance sheet—is not exactly overly impressive. Forty million capital, for them, is just not enough. It's like we discussed last week, Mr. Saxon, we're going to have get more."

"Urs raised the same point. And I'll give you the same answer I gave him. Let's see where we stand at the end of the week. Then I'll decide what to do."

"One other thing, Mr. Saxon. We put an ad in yesterday's *Santa Rosa Press Democrat* and the *Healdsburg Tribune* for clerks. We'll probably start getting calls in a few hours. Do you want to interview them too, or will you leave that to us?"

"You take care of it," Willy said.

"Thanks," Fred said, just as his phone rang.

Willy decided that he had already seen—and heard—all that he had to. This operation was doomed to success. Probably enormous success. Probably *immediate* enormous success.

"You can't fucking win," he muttered to himself as he left the trading room and began walking toward the main house in the dawn light. "Now I've got no choice."

As soon as he got back to the main house he called the Vintage Inn in Healdsburg, where his driver stayed. The man first answered on the sixth ring. It was, after all, five-thirty a.m.

■

"This is Willy Saxon. We're going back to San Francisco. I'd appreciate your picking me up at the ranch as soon as possible."

The car was there at six, and it pulled up in front of 1190 Sacramento an hour and a half later. Willy waited until five after eight and then called Frank Lipper at his office at Prescott & Quackenbush.

"Frank, it's Willy. I need some help. Could you come over to the apartment right away?"

"Sure."

"Have you still got that feasibility study we borrowed from Healdsburg's director of finance?"

"It's right here on my desk."

"Bring it along."

Frank was there twenty minutes later.

"Let's sit in the living room, Frank," Willy began. "I've got something serious that I want to talk over with you. But first I've got a few questions about Bobby Armacost."

"Sure. I brought the feasibility study," Frank said, reaching into his briefcase.

"Just leave it on the coffee table for the moment. Speaking of coffee, would you like some?"

"Yeah. It's still pretty early."

"I'll get some from the kitchen. Go ahead and sit down."

After Willy had returned with two cups, he said. "You and I have known Bobby Armacost for more than ten years. As you know, it all started when I hired his firm as bond counsels when we first got started in the junk bond business."

"1984," Frank said.

"Exactly. I know he is involved in other things, but does his law firm still act chiefly as bond counsel?"

"Yes. That's why Dan and he are so close. More often than not Armacost and Slater act as bond counsel to the towns and cities that we—Prescott and Quackenbush—float bonds for as underwriters. We feed him business and he feeds us."

■

"Is the Slater in Armacost and Slater still around?"

"No. Bobby is the sole boss in his firm. He runs it like a dictator, too."

"And how's the firm been doing?"

"Lousy. Bobby won't admit it but when he got involved in that scandal where Dan Prescott and he were on the board of that biotech that was caught doctoring its books, things went from bad to worse at Armacost and Slater. If you hadn't bailed him out, Willy, his law firm would be history by now. He owes you a big one."

"But the firm's reputation as a bond counsel is still good?"

"That it is. The biotech situation that got him in trouble didn't involve bonds. The problem is that almost all law firms are in trouble, so there's lots of competition among bond counsels for whatever business is out there."

"All right. That clears that up. Now let me ask a couple of more questions that might sound really dumb. But bear with me. OK?

"Whatever you say, Willy."

"Now, during the past three or four years you've been primarily involved in underwriting municipal bonds with Prescott and Quackenbush."

"That's right."

"When you develop such an underwriting, who are the key players?"

Frank thought that one over for a minute before answering.

"There are always four. First, the finance director of the city that's trying to raise the money."

"OK."

"Second, the underwriting group, led by what we call the Managing Underwriter—firms like Prescott and Quackenbush—that commits to buy the bonds from the municipality and then resell them to the public or institutions like bond funds."

"Right."

"Third, the bond counsel, who puts his name on the line on all the basic legal issues. That ranges from confirming that the municipality has the legal authority to issue the bonds to guaranteeing the tax-exempt status of the bonds they want to sell. The buyer of the bonds relies totally on the soundness of these opinions."

"And, as you just confirmed, this is the principle activity of Armacost and Slater."

"Right."

"And the fourth?"

"The ratings agency, which, in essence, makes a judgment concerning the ability of the borrower to pay the interest and repay the principle when the bond comes due."

"Like our friend Sidney Ravitch."

"Your friend, Willy. Not mine."

"Yeah, I know what you mean. But there's a reason behind my having anything to do with Ravitch—a reason I'm about to come to. And I'd appreciate it if you'd hear me completely out before commenting. OK?"

"Sure."

"I just got back from the ranch, Frank. They started trading at four this morning—with Europe—and it's already going like gangbusters. Incredible. It's going to be a huge success, Frank. Huge."

"That's great."

"But—and there's always a 'but' in our business—what they do requires capital. Big capital."

"But you've already put in forty million."

"That's not enough."

"What is enough?"

"I don't know yet. What I do know is that we'll need another twenty million dollars almost right away."

"You got that in reserve?"

"No. I've got a reserve, but not that big. And I want that reserve to stay a reserve." He was down to eleven million

■

dollars in Liechtenstein, but that was nobody else's business, not even Frank's.

"So where are you going to get it?"

"That's the problem. Until Prescott and Quackenbush can show that they're really making money, with their track record during the past few years, no financial institution is going to lend them the sort of big money we're going to need. For the same reason, there's no way they can tap the commercial paper market."

"Agreed."

"With my track record—especially how I spent the last three years—there's not a chance in hell that anybody would lend *me* any money."

"Unless somebody was willing to come in as a partner on a purely personal basis," Frank suggested.

"I've thought of that," Frank said. Both Denise and Sara were loaded, in fact, lonely and loaded. "But I decided not to go that route."

"What's left?"

"Ukiah."

"What's that supposed to mean?"

"First, another question. With that in hand," and Willy now pointed at the feasibility study for a Materials Recycling Facility, which had been prepared by the City of Ukiah, "could you write a prospectus for the underwriting?"

"We call it an Official Statement in the muni bond underwriting business, not a prospectus, but the answer is yes. With two exceptions. I would need an opinion from bond counsel, as well as a rating."

"Let's stop for a minute at the rating. How is that usually presented in a muni bond Official Statement?"

Frank reached into the briefcase he had brought with him. "Here's a draft of the one we're working on now—the one you set up, Willy, for the City and County of San Francisco. It's at the top of page thirty-six. Here. Read it."

■

Frank handed the document over to Willy. The paragraph on page 36, read as follows:

RATINGS

Moody's Investor Services and the Western Credit Rating Agency have both assigned the Series 1995 Bonds the rating of AA. These ratings reflect only the views of Moody's and the Western Credit Rating Agency at the date of the delivery of the Series 1995 Bonds. An explanation of these ratings can be obtained from Moody's and the Western Credit Rating Agency. There is no assurance that these ratings will remain in effect for any given period of time or that they will not be revised downward or withdrawn entirely.

"Two more questions, Frank," Willy said, still holding the document. "How come you already filled in the Double-A rating? Neither Moody's nor the Western Credit Rating Agency have prepared anything on this new issue, have they?"

"Of course not. But that's the rating both Moody's and Standard and Poors gave to the last five general obligation bonds issued by the City and County of San Francisco. So it's as good as a cinch that Moody's will go with Double-A again. That leaves your pal at the Western Credit Rating Agency with no choice but to follow suit."

"Makes sense. Now I'll refer back to the text of your draft prospectus. The third sentence reads: 'An explanation of these ratings can be obtained from Moody's and the Western Credit Rating Agency,' " Willy said.

"That's standard boilerplate language," Frank said.

"Understood. But does anybody actually *approach* them for that explanation? And then actually *read* it before they buy the bonds?"

■

"Normally they read it only if the rating has changed—especially if it has been lowered. But otherwise, as part of their practicing due diligence, most institutions that buy the bonds would merely go through the motions. They'd get the report—with no big hurry—and it would get buried in a dossier. They rely primarily on what's in the prospectus."

"Would it look funny if *you* provided that 'explanation' directly to an institutional buyer?"

Frank thought about that one for a while.

"I guess not. As long as it ended up in their due diligence dossier, I don't see why anybody should care how it got there."

It was now a visibly satisfied Willy Saxon who leaned back in his overstuffed eighteenth-century chair.

"Does this mean that over the weekend you signed up the City of Ukiah for this underwriting?" Frank asked.

"No, it doesn't," Willy replied. "It means that we are going to go ahead with the underwriting anyway."

"You can't do that, Willy," Frank said.

"Why not? Just because nobody's ever done it before?"

"No. Of course not. You can't do it because if you do, Willy, you go back to jail. And so will I—in my case, for the first time."

"Who says? First somebody has to catch on. And the way I've got it figured, nobody will until the year 2035. By that time we'll all be dead."

"Hold on. Why would this stay undetected for forty years?"

"Because we'll be underwriting a forty-year zero coupon bond."

Frank just sat there, thinking.

"And I'll place the whole issue with one institution," Willy continued. "Nobody else will even hear about it. Especially the city fathers in Ukiah."

Frank still sat there, thinking.

■

"And if the buyer keeps the bonds, they just remain buried at the bottom of the pile in their vault," Frank said, finally.

"Exactly. On a forty-year zero coupon no money changes hands for forty years. On a forty-year zero coupon municipal bond no taxes are paid, ever. So it's a one-time transaction. After that one time, no money, no coupons, no nothing ever changes hands. So there is absolutely no reason for an institutional buyer to even think about them until maturity, by which time, as I've already pointed out, we're both dead and buried."

"But what if five years from now your buyer tries to unload the bonds?" Frank asked.

"They always approach the underwriter first, don't they? In five years we'd be in a position to work something out."

"You've thought of everything, haven't you Willy?" Frank said.

"I had three years and one day to think. So, yes, I believe I have thought of everything," Willy replied.

"But why run this crazy risk?"

"We went through that just a few days ago, Frank. I'm onto the biggest thing I've ever done in my entire life. I'm getting near fifty. So this is the *last* time I'll ever have a chance to go really big time. The last chance. And I'm not going to blow it because I can't raise enough capital to see it through. If I don't get more capital, the boys in Healdsburg are going to take a hike, and I'm going to be stuck with a moribund investment bank and a credit agency which, as I now realize, I never should have bought into in the first place."

Willy paused.

"But if you want out, Frank, so be it. I'll understand and there will be no hard feelings," he then said.

"It won't be me who wants *out,* Willy." Frank said. "But I'm not so sure that Dan Prescott and Bobby Armacost will want *in.* And you'll need them both."

■

"Without me they'll both go down the tubes," Frank said. "But you always need both a stick and a carrot."

"What's the carrot?"

"Everybody, including you, gets one million dollars, cash, off the top, at the bank of your choice anywhere on earth. The rest stays with Prescott and Quackenbush as capital."

"What about Sid Ravitch?"

"He'll stay outside the loop. As I said, he was a mistake. We'll go around him. As to how, I think you already know what I've got in mind."

"So when are you going to talk to Bobby and Dan?" Frank asked.

"Right away today."

"I'm meeting with George Abbott at City Hall at ten. I think I can sew up that deal then and there."

"Then I'll wait here until I hear from you after that meeting. It will give me yet more ammunition when I have my little talk with Dan and Bobby."

Frank called just before noon.

"It's a done deal," he said.

■

THIRTY-FOUR

It was a knockdown, drag out confrontation that occurred later that day in the conference room of Prescott & Quackenbush.

The meeting started on a high note. All the newspapers in the Bay Area were lying on the conference table, opened to the business section. The *Chronicle,* the *Examiner,* the Oakland *Tribune,* even the San Jose *Mercury News* had given prominent space to the "new" Prescott & Quackenbush. All referred to it as the local investment bank that had fallen on hard times and had been rumored to be near collapse. But now, as announced in a Friday press conference, not only was it to receive a fresh injection of forty million dollars in new capital, but it was launching a derivatives unit staffed by true rocket scientists. It was just another symptom, the *Chronicle* said, of the renaissance of San Francisco as the leading financial center in the West.

"The phones have been ringing off the hook all day," Dan Prescott said. "And now, to top it off, Frank met with City Hall this morning, and they've agreed to the underwriting project we proposed. They also agreed to take on Bobby as Bond Counsel. We'll make sure that all of this hits tomorrow's papers."

"How much capital will that underwriting tie up?" Willy asked.

■

"We generally figure it on a one to ten ratio. It's a hundred and fifteen million dollars all told, including both issues. We're putting together an underwriting group that we expect will take half of it. So we're talking six million dollars, more or less. But, thanks to you Willy, we've now got that and a lot more."

"And it all comes back when we resell the bonds," Armacost added.

"Until the next one," Willy said.

"True. But nobody claims that you can operate in the big leagues in the municipal bond business as senior managing underwriter, like we're now doing for the first time, without capital," Prescott said.

"I agree," Willy said. "Now before I get to the problem that made it necessary for me to call this meeting, let me tell you what's already started to happen in Healdsburg."

When he was done describing the successful launching of the DM-inverse-floaters-cum-currency-swap package, Prescott said. "But that's all great stuff. What's the problem?"

"We're buying one hundred million deutsche marks in inverse floaters from two German banks. Right? That's sixty-five million dollars commitment right there. The problem is that the Deutsche Bank was even reticent about doing half of that, when they heard that our capital base was just forty-million dollars. Then there's the one hundred million deutsche mark currency swap. Again, the problem is to find a counter-party who is willing to do that type of business with what is, in the view of the financial community, an undercapitalized investment bank like us. If we face obstacles like this already on the first day, what do you think will happen a few weeks or months down the road?"

"So they'll have to take it easier in Healdsburg during the next weeks and months," Prescott said, "until we start building up some retained earnings."

"If I tell them that, they all quit. Tomorrow morning. And then what do we do? Call another press conference? Tell the

■

Chronicle it was all a big mistake? That everybody can forget about any "new" Prescott and Quackenbush?"

"It's that serious?" Bobby asked.

"That serious," Willy said. "And believe me, word of our debacle in derivatives would come out whether we wanted it to or not. Then how many more municipal bond underwritings would you expect to come in? Today's deal with the City and County of San Francisco would end up being the first *and* last of its kind. And the number of times that we could feed *you* any more business, Bobby, would gradually sink toward zero. Which, I am told, is where your law firm was sinking anyway before all this started to happen."

"Why are you telling us all this?" Armacost asked, visibly alarmed.

"To inform you that we absolutely must have more capital. Now," Willy replied.

"From Switzerland?" Dan asked.

"Not from Switzerland. That well has gone dry," Willy said.

"Then where?"

"Maybe you can find some, Dan," Willy said.

"As I told you at Moose's the first day we met there, I tried everything. No dice. Without your money, Prescott and Quackenbush could never have survived."

"Bobby?"

"I'm a lawyer, not a fund-raiser. And as you full well know, Willy, I'm also broke. More than broke," Armacost replied.

"All right. We are in total agreement. We need capital to save what could be the best thing any of us has ever been involved in. But none of us knows how to raise it. Would you say that describes the situation correctly?"

"Yes," Dan said.

"I agree," Bobby said.

"Then we need a fresh approach," Willy said. "One that is

■

innovative, raises a lot of money fast, and gets around the fact that none of us can raise a nickel on our own."

"How?" Bobby asked.

"We do something that I am told involves a new technique in financing. We 'source' the credit risk elsewhere."

"What's that mean?" Bobby asked.

"We temporarily borrow another party's good credit to raise money for ourselves."

"Who would do that?" Bobby asked.

"Usually it's cash-rich companies that have huge unused lines of credit," Willy said.

"I've heard about that," Dan said. "But even if any such company would be willing to do that—which is highly doubtful—they would charge an enormous fee. Furthermore, it would only be a very temporary expedient," Dan said.

"I agree with every word you said, Dan. However, I've come up with something that is slightly different—one might call it unconventional," Willy said. "We would 'source' our credit not with a company but with a municipality. And we would be talking not weeks or months but years, many years."

"That I've never heard of," the investment banker admitted. "Do you have a particular municipality in mind?"

"Yes. Ukiah."

"Ukiah?" Bobby asked, "You mean that little city way up US 101, half way to the Oregon border?"

"Exactly," Willy replied.

"Why would they agree to it?"

"They wouldn't. We'd borrow their credit on the sly, so to say. Let me explain," Willy said. "And I'd appreciate it if neither of you interrupted me until I'm done."

So for the next ten minutes Willy spoke without interruption, ending with his offer of one million dollars each, front end, anywhere they wanted it.

He could immediately see that Dan Prescott was on board. But Bobby Armacost's face had turned near-ashen.

■

That was when Willy reached into a large yellow envelope he had brought with him and withdrew two documents on legal-size paper.

"Recognize these? They're the notes you and your wives signed. Two million dollars each. I'm prepared to literally tear them up here and now and give you both a total release as of today."

Bobby Armacost finally spoke. "We're damned if we don't, and damned if we do, if I understand you correctly."

"No, no." Willy said. *"You're* damned *now* if we don't. *We're* damned, *maybe,* if we do, but only in forty years."

"Why maybe?"

"How old will you be in forty years, Bobby?"

"Let's see. Ninety-three."

"You think anybody's going to put a ninety-three-year-old in jail?"

"What about Leona Helmsley?"

"She wasn't ninety-three. She was barely over seventy when they sent her off. But look what happened to her husband, Harry. Nothing. *He* was damn near ninety, so they let him go."

"As long as we're being silly," Dan Prescott said, "there's another precedent for Willy's theory that immunity from prosecution becomes automatic after a certain age—the BCCI case a few years ago. If you recall, those two big-time Washington lawyers, Clifford and Altman, were accused of concealing the fact that a bunch of Pakistani crooks who were their clients had secretly bought control of the largest bank in D.C. The difference was that Clark Clifford was eighty-five, while his law partner—also the husband of TV's Wonder Woman, which probably didn't help him—was only forty-six. So they tried to nail Altman. Clark Clifford they didn't even bring to trial."

The room lapsed into silence. All three men knew that this interlude of gallows humor had been a rather crude diversion from the issue at hand.

■

Bobby Armacost finally broke the impasse.

"You can tear up my note, Willy," he said.

"Mine too," said Dan Prescott. "I assume that Frank is already in?"

"He is," Willy said.

"What about the ratings agency guy, Sid Ravitch?" Bobby asked.

"He's not in the loop. But he'll be no problem, Willy replied.

"Why not?" Bobby asked.

"For reasons I won't go into further. Suffice it to say that when I say jump, Sid Ravitch jumps real high."

Dan Prescott got up, and as he did he looked down once more at the newspapers that were still spread out across the conference table.

"I guess this means we can frame these stories and hang them up on the wall," he said.

"Let's hope they stay there for forty years," Armacost said.

"I'll second that," Willy said.

"I'd say this calls for a drink," Bobby said, "a strong drink. Got any Jack Daniel's?"

"A brand new bottle. I think we'll need all of it."

Two drinks later, Willy left for his apartment. He had to arrange to meet with Sid Ravitch early the next morning, he explained, and that would require a very clear head.

As soon as the door had closed behind him, Dan Prescott spoke to Bobby Armacost in a low voice—just in case for some reason Willy came back.

"What do you think?" he asked.

"Let's face it," Bobby replied. "He's got both of us by the balls. And therein lies salvation—if salvation ever becomes necessary."

"What's that mean?"

"We have been coerced into this, pure and simple."

"So?"

"So if this all comes out this side of forty years, we plead that we were victims as much as was the City of Ukiah, or, even more so, the poor sucker he sells these zero coupons to."

"But would a court buy it?"

"The D.A. would. Ever heard of plea bargaining? It's well known that there are people in this town who would love to nail Willy Saxon for the rest of his life—the D.A. for one, the head of the state banking commission for another."

"And what about Frank?"

"I'm afraid we'd have to throw Frank to the wolves, too."

"Jeezus, what a day!" the investment banker said. "How about another Jack Daniel's?"

"Make it a big one this time," the bond counsel replied.

■

THIRTY-FIVE

That Monday evening, Lenny Newsom was also having a Jack Daniel's—at Zeke's in the heart of downtown Healdsburg. He and Willy Saxon's limo driver had discovered the joint the night before.

They had checked into the Vintage Inn at the same time, and when the limo driver had asked the desk clerk where he could have a few drinks on a Sunday night, the only answer had been Zeke's. When Lenny asked if he could tag along, the driver had been more than happy to have found a drinking buddy in this God-forsaken town in the middle of Sonoma County.

Following Saxon's limo had required some fast footwork on Lenny's part. The moment he saw the car pull up in front of 1190 Sacramento earlier that Sunday afternoon, he knew that Willy Saxon was once again on the move. Lenny had parked his car half a block down Sacramento Street, and was barely inside it when the limo had begun pulling away from the curb with Willy inside. After that it had been easy as they headed toward the Golden Gate Bridge, and then north on U.S 101. The Sunday afternoon traffic was all headed south, as the city people returned from their weekend or day trips to the Wine Country in Napa and Sonoma counties. So Lenny could keep well back of the limo all the way up. That changed when the limo left the

■

freeway at Chalk Hill Road, just north of Santa Rosa, and ten miles later ended up turning onto a narrow lane that led into a heavily wooded area. Lenny could hardly follow it any further. So he had gone a half mile further, parked, and then walked back to the lane. He even ventured up the lane on foot until he came to a locked gate and a sign that told him he was about to enter River Ranch. He then decided to go back to the car and wait.

Fifteen minutes later the limo emerged from the lane, and then turned north, headed toward Healdsburg, passing Lenny's car in the process. He arrived at the Vintage Inn just minutes after the limo did. Thus, the driver and he checked in at the same time.

That Sunday night drink with the driver at Zeke's—actually it was four drinks—had paid off like nothing so far in Lenny's new job. He'd wanted to get even more information from the guy, but when he had gotten up that morning it was to discover that the limo was gone. The desk clerk had told him that the driver had checked out before six a.m.

Lenny had decided to stay in Healdsburg looking for another opening. But so far that day he had been more or less just spinning his wheels—both figuratively and literally. For he had come up with the idea—for the sake of "security"—to leave his car at the motel, and rent a bicycle from one of the shops in Healdsburg. He had noticed the day before that, even as dusk had approached, the area was still full of tourists on bikes pedaling past the vineyards in their gaudy outfits.

It had only taken him a half hour to pedal his way out of town to Chalk Hill Road. Equipped with blanket, thermos bottle, and camera, he had spent most of the day playing the lover of nature, lying beside his bike under a grove of trees immediately adjacent to the lane leading off Chalk Hill Road into River Ranch.

Instead of watching for birds, Lenny's interest was in any

■

traffic that might use the lane. There had not been much—a
total of eleven cars. Oddly, all eleven had been driven by
women. One had been a beat-up Honda driven by an old gal
who looked like a peasant. She left the ranch by nine and came
back an hour later. That was the last he saw of her, so Lenny
assumed she must work there.

The other ten were young women, all but one in their twen-
ties. Also odd was the fact that each of those ten was impecca-
bly coiffed, and, from what he could see, also well-dressed.
Peasants or wives of farm hands they were not. They came—
and went—in a procession that had them spaced almost exactly a half-hour apart. Lenny got a Polaroid picture of each
car and driver taken through a zoom lens with what he hoped
passed for his bird-watcher's camera. At five he had pedaled
back to town.

Now at Zeke's bar, for lack of anything else to do, he
shuffled through the photographs for the fifth time. It was
Monday night, and thus quiet, so, since he was one of only
two customers at the bar, the bartender hovered near him.

"What kind of pictures you got there?" he asked.

"Pictures of girls," Lenny said.

"Dirty pictures?"

"Not yet," Lenny replied. "I'm more or less just interview-
ing them at this point."

That was it! Somebody at River Ranch had been interview-
ing those girls for a job.

"You with *Playboy* or something?" the bartender asked.

"I wish," Lenny replied. "No. I'm just a buyer for a chain
of food and wine stores in Canada. I'm down here checking
out the local wineries."

"I thought I noticed a slight accent," the bartender said.
"From Vancouver?"

"No, a place near Toronto," and Lenny pronounced it
"Tronna" like a good Canadian would. After all, he still *was*

■

a Canadian, although he'd hadn't been home for a few years now, due to that prior engagement in Pleasanton.

"You were also in here last night, weren't you?"

"Yeah, with another guy. He drives the limo for the new owner of River Ranch out on Chalk Hill Road."

"Yeah, I heard the place just changed hands. I don't know what they're doing out there, but there was an ad in the local paper Sunday where they were looking for office help—for people used to computers and stuff like that. Big ad. My wife showed it to me, since she's looking for a job."

"She knows how to use computers?"

"Naw. She's looking for a job as a waitress."

Lenny went back to looking at his pictures. It was all starting to come together. The limo driver had told him about those computers and the satellite dishes and the really oddball guys—computer freaks—who were moving in at the ranch. He'd driven them all up from San Francisco. A very high-class dame from the city had come along, too, although, apparently, she wasn't moving in.

So what the fuck were they up to? Developing an atomic bomb for the Arabs? Communicating with little green men in outer space?

Lenny laughed out loud at his clever little jokes. He was liking this job more and more.

"Gimme another one," he said to the bartender.

When it arrived, he said, "Where do the girls hang out around here?"

"Depends what kind of girls you're talking about," the bartender answered.

"Let's say nice ones, like the kind that know how to work computers."

"Not here, that's for damn sure. The really local ones sometimes have a drink after work over at the place across the plaza—Jacob Horner's. In Santa Rosa there's a slew of places they hang around, but one of the most popular ones is a

■

Tex-Mex place called Chevys. It's in the old town, across from what used to be the railroad station."

At eleven Lenny went back to the motel.

When he woke up the next morning at 6:30 and looked out the window, the limo was back in the parking lot.

■

THIRTY-SIX

It was there because late the following evening Willy had decided to leave his city apartment and head north to the ranch.

The reason was a phone call he had received the prior evening from Jack, the architect. The title company, Jack had explained, had everything together, and there was now no reason to further delay the final act in the sale of the ranch. So he had arranged an eleven a.m. meeting at the title company, in Santa Rosa. It was really nothing more than a formality, but Jack wanted to do things properly. Willy told him he'd be there.

But then what to do about Sid Ravitch?

The more Willy had thought about it, the more he had come to the conclusion that, in any case, Frank could probably handle him a lot better. First, Frank could tell how he had *personally* talked City Hall into taking on Ravitch's company as one of the city's ratings agencies, right alongside Moody's and Standard & Poors. Then, almost as an afterthought, he could bring up Ukiah.

So Willy's final act before leaving for the ranch Monday evening had been to call Frank and ask him to meet with Ravitch as soon as possible, the next day. He explained that both Dan and Bobby were on board where Ukiah was concerned, and that the only element of the deal that was still

■

missing was the bond rating documentation. He'd leave it to
Frank as to how to get it from Ravitch without letting any
cats out of the bag.

So Willy had spent the night at River Ranch, and as he was
more and more prone to do, was up very early the next morning.

"Gee, Mr. Saxon," Fred Fitch said, the moment Willy
walked into the trading room, "we weren't expecting you back
so soon. But you couldn't have arrived at a better time. We're
launching a new product that the boys have been working on
ever since they got here. They love it out there."

"What kind of product?"

"I dubbed it an 'ICON,' " Fred said.

He then called across the room to his colleague who was at
work at their brand new Sparcserver 1000 computer. "Hey,
Glenn, come on over and explain the new one."

Dr. Glenn Godwin first shook Willy's hand, and then
asked, "How was that press conference last Friday received?"

"Didn't you see the papers?"

"No. We've been pretty busy."

"You went over like gangbusters, Glenn."

"I'm glad. I was a little nervous. I'm not used to that sort
of thing."

"Don't worry. That's probably the last time we'll ask you
to do that. Now what's this 'ICON' all about?"

"It's just an acronym for a new type of financial product."

"You invented them?"

"Well, yes and no. The idea originally came from Urs
Bauer." He pointed across the room to the Swiss foreign
exchange dealer who, as usual, was talking into two phones at
the same time.

"He pointed out that a lot of institutions in both Europe
and the U.S., especially pension funds, can't get involved in
the foreign exchange markets. Pension plans, as you know,

control hundreds of billions of dollars, so they represent a huge untapped market."

"Why can't they deal in foreign exchange?"

"Because, according to Urs, the laws in almost all European countries preclude pension funds from engaging in speculation. And dealing in currencies, at least in the forward markets in currencies, is considered to be outright speculation. Yet, everybody knows that George Soros made one and a half billion dollars in one month speculating in currencies. So every pension plan manager, from Madrid to Frankfurt to Zurich, is looking for a way to get around the laws so they can do the same thing. Pension fund managers in New York are also hot to trot, since usually their bylaws preclude them from trading currencies also."

"And you found a way around all that?" Willy said.

"Right. ICONs. That's the acronym that Fred came up with. It stands for "Index Currency Option Notes.""

"I love it already," Willy said. "Explain it."

"Well, we—or one of our clients—issue notes. We decided to start with one-year and two-year notes. What's different about these notes is that they do not carry any given interest rate. Instead, when one of those notes comes due at the end of, say, two years, the payback is contingent upon the spot price of the dollar vis-a-vis another currency then, as compared to when the note was issued."

"You lost me."

"OK. Let's use the German mark. Currently the spot rate is about DM 1.50 to the dollar. That's 100 on the index the note's price is tied to. Say in two years it's DM 2.00 to the dollar. That puts the index at 133. If you bought one million dollars worth of these notes, you get back $1,333,000. That's a hell of a lot better than the five percent per annum you would have been able to earn on 'normal' two year notes."

"And if the DM goes to 1.25 to the dollar?"

"He gets back a lot less than he put in."

■

"So it is still highly speculative."

"Of course, but that's what derivatives are all about."

"But what about us, if we are the ones that issue these 'ICONs'?"

"Well, we have two choices. To enter into separate forward contracts with third parties—which cover our ass no matter which way the DM goes. Or to not cover our risk and hope that the mark goes the other way. We'll cover, since we agree with you, Mr. Saxon, that in the long range, the DM's going down, not up. Which would make our clients very happy, and, since we covered ourselves, somebody else, not us, will be paying for that happiness."

"How many have you sold so far?"

"We have commitments for almost one hundred million in dollar notes tied to deutsche marks, and another fifty million tied to the Swiss franc."

"Where do you find the buyers?"

"For these particular ones, mostly in New York. For Frankfurt and Zurich, we custom design notes that do exactly the opposite—they go up if the dollar goes down, since most Germans and the Swiss are still convinced that they have the hardest currencies on earth. We stress that it's a proprietary financial product available only here."

"Sounds great. Thanks for the explanation," Willy said, and Glenn went back to his computer, while Willy turned his attention back to Fred Fitch.

"How are the inverse floaters doing?" he asked.

"Selling like hotcakes," Fred said.

"So how are you keeping up with the paperwork?"

"That's already a problem. Susie, Ur's wife, is helping us out. She should be here in an hour or so. We also hired five local girls yesterday. They should be coming in at eight."

"I'm glad to hear that. Frank and I are going to be working on something up in the main house later today and probably

■

for the rest of the week. Could we borrow one of them just for the time being?"

"Of course. Let me know when you need her," Fred said.

"By the way," Willy said. "I've already arranged for another seventeen million dollars in long-term capital."

"Jeez, that was fast. The way things are going here, we'll need almost all of it right away."

"That's what I figured."

"Urs will be tickled pink," Fred said. "You want to tell him or should I?"

"You tell him later. He looks awful busy right now."

Willy decided he'd seen enough, so he headed back to the main house. Now all he had to do was to call the limo driver, meet Jack at eleven in Santa Rosa, and then come back and wait for Frank's phone call telling him how his meeting with Ravitch had gone.

THIRTY-SEVEN

Willy's driver left the Vintage Inn at ten-thirty, which left Lenny Newsom a decision. To follow now, and risk being detected by the limo guy, or even worse, by Willy Saxon. Or to play it safe, and go out to River Ranch later that day. He decided to stay put for a while.

Jack was already there when Willy arrived at the title company in Santa Rosa. There was really no need for his being there. All the papers had already been duly signed and notarized by the buyer in London. It was Jack who had to now sign the same papers as the seller. It was a laborious process, but by noon it was all wrapped up.

"How about lunch at the country club?" Jack asked.

Willy was not nuts about the idea, but Jack obviously felt that the occasion called for it. However, this all changed when, near the end of lunch, Jack, for some reason began talking about his career as an architect.

"You know, Willy," he said, "people always ask me which building or project I'm most proud of. Well, you know, Jack Kennedy and I were pretty close, so I got to do some big government projects, including the new Senate Office Building in Washington. I like it, but the critics think it's a pile of crap.

"I did some work for both the shah of Iran and King Fahd of Saudi Arabia in the 1970s, big projects usually involving whole clusters of government buildings. Now those buildings

■

were piles of crap, big piles. But I made a lot of money on them. The shah and the king are both long dead and gone, and when they went, so did my business over there. By the way, I liked the shah. I guess I'm the only American who ever did, or at least the only one who still admits it."

He rambled on.

"But the project I liked best was never built. It was commissioned by Bill Gates—the one who owns Microsoft. Actually, it was jointly sponsored by a Japanese company called Fujitsu. They're in computer hardware and wanted to get into software in a joint venture with Gates. Just like Toyota did with General Motors down in Fremont, where they assemble some kind of hybrid car using Japanese management, American workers, and parts from a half dozen countries. I bid on the assembly plant, and lost. Where was I?"

"With Microsoft and Fujitsu."

"Right. They wanted me to design a town. A whole new town. Along the lines of Levittown—the city they built from scratch in Pennsylvania after World War Two. They named it after the developer. This one was going to be a lot different than Levittown, however. They wanted to go first class all the way. The idea was to have a place that would attract the best people in the field from around the world. I hear from my former housekeeper that you're apparently using my ranch for the same purpose."

Jack saw the surprised look on Willy's face.

"Don't worry," he said. "That's between us girls. But I'm telling you about this new town project because I thought you'd appreciate it.

"They even had a name. Sun River City. Gawd, even the name was great, don't you think? It was to be built just outside of Bend, Oregon. It's a most glorious part of America, with mountains and streams, forests and vineyards, eagles and bears. And hardly anybody lives there. In fact, very few tourists even visit it. Too remote, I guess. It's one of the last unspoiled paradises left in America. And relatively close to Microsoft's headquarters in Redmond, Washington, at least by plane. Naturally, my plans included an airstrip that could take even small jets.

"Well, I spent damn near two years and they spent damn near six million bucks developing the plans for that little city. And then they decided not to do it."

"Why?"

"I think IBM—it's their PCs that use most of Microsoft's products—scuttled the idea of any joint venture with the Japanese. What really got to me was that this project was not just some utopian idea, one that you would never build since you could never get financing. This one would have been easier to finance than any project I've ever been involved with in this country in my entire career. I talked to a couple of investment banks in New York about it. Every one was ready to go the moment I pushed the button. They could have resold the bonds ten times over."

"So how long ago was this?"

"The project was killed just last year."

"How come I never heard about it?"

"You don't know Bill Gates. Or the guys that run Fujitsu. They make the Sphinx look like a blabbermouth."

"Had the way been cleared for the financing?"

"Of course. The Oregon Legislature already passed legislation amending the Oregon Economic Development Authority Act two years ago. It established a separate agency for this project, the Sun River City Economic Development Authority. The funds generated by the initial bond issue would have been allocated to the building of the basic infrastructure, plus the financing of educational and cultural facilities. The next issue would have provided funds to cover the first stage of housing development. And so forth."

"But all you'd have had to show at the initial offering would have been bare, undeveloped land outside of Bend, Oregon."

■

"Plus six million bucks worth of plans, and the backing of the State of Oregon. Hard to beat that."

"Who owns the land?"

"Some guy who is also on the County Board of Supervisors up there. We had an option to buy thirty thousand acres. As far as I know, he still owns it."

"And how much did the option cost?"

"Once he found out that Gates was involved, way too much. You could probably get the same option today for a song."

"Back to that initial financing. How much were they going to go for?"

"One hundred million dollars. Because of the nature of the project, there would have been no cash flow to service the bonds for quite a few years. It takes time to develop a brand-new city to the point where it starts generating tax revenue. So the idea was to go with a thirty-year Capital Appreciation Bond. Probably you're not that much at home in public finance, Willy, but that's the term they use for zero coupon bonds."

Bingo!!!

"You know," Willy said, "this is the most interesting thing I've heard about in one hell of a long time. You think I could see those plans?"

"Jeezus, Willy. It would take you a month to go through just half of them. But I've got a half a dozen copies of the summary back in the office. We would have used it for the drafting of the Official Statement—that's what they call a prospectus in public finance circles—for the initial underwriting. It's got all the numbers projected out to eternity and beyond. If you're really that interested, I could send a copy to you at the ranch. Then if you want to look at the plans proper, I'll send them over."

"I'd really appreciate that," Willy said.

"Thinking of maybe building Sun River City yourself?"

■

"Maybe," Willy said.

And also maybe not.

Willy insisted on putting the lunch on his bill, and by two o'clock was already back at the ranch. Frank called at four.

"How did it go?" Willy immediately asked.

"Perfect. I came up with an idea after I talked to you last night. I arranged for Ravitch and myself to have lunch with George Abbott and two of his minions from City Hall. That way he could hear it from the horse's mouth that the Western Credit Ratings Agency was now part of the financial establishment serving the City and County of San Francisco. He lapped it up."

"How soon will that San Francisco prospectus be ready to go?"

"Within days. Abbott wants to move on it right away."

"Great. Now what about Ukiah?"

"That turned out to be easy, too. After we got back to his office, I told Ravitch that Ukiah also wanted to move right away. I hinted—more than hinted—that I had something going on the side with the finance director of Ukiah. The reason he wanted to move fast, I told Ravitch, was my suspicion that he needed money rather desperately. You could see it in his eyes, I told him. Probably gambling debts, or something. Anyway, Ravitch bought the story and agreed to do his ratings report on the basis of the numbers I provided him. I'll have it by tomorrow."

"Good for you, Frank. Thank God I changed my mind and asked you to take care of him."

"What did *not* go over too big was my request for a small office at his place. I hope you will understand this, Willy, but when he asked why, I told him that it was you who insisted."

"And how did he react to that?"

"I think I can repeat his exact words, which were: 'Doesn't that fucker trust me?' "

"And what did you then say?"

■

"I just shrugged."

"Did you get the office?"

"Yes. Including a key. It's the shittiest office in the place, and right next to the elevator shaft. But at least we're inside now."

"So you batted a thousand today. Nice going."

"Now what?" Frank asked.

"Let's draft that Ukiah prospectus. I don't want anybody in San Francisco involved, for obvious reasons. So let's do the whole thing up here. I can arrange for secretarial help, and I'm sure we can find a local printer. How long will it take?"

"Hell, it'll be ready to go by the end of the week. Back in December of 1985, right before they changed the law on the issue of housing bonds, we once did three in twenty-four hours, in order to beat the deadline."

"Perfect."

"What about the placement of the bonds?"

"I'll take care of that," Willy said. "What I've got in mind is essentially a private placement. The Ukiah zero coupons will all be tucked away in the portfolio of a six billion-dollar bond fund. They will disappear like a few grains of sand on the beach."

■

THIRTY-EIGHT

While Willy was on the phone, a procession of cars moved up the lane from the trading center past the main house, then out the gate of River Ranch and onto Chalk Hill Road. The five brand-new employees of P & Q Financial Products were leaving after their first day's work. The first four cars turned right and headed toward Santa Rosa. The fifth turned left, in the direction of Healdsburg.

Lenny Newsom, who had arrived in his rental car an hour earlier, decided to follow the last one back into town. And sure enough, she drove to the Plaza and parked in front of Jacob Horner's—the place where nice girls hung out, according to the bartender at Zeke's. When Lenny walked in five minutes later, she was sitting at the bar, chatting with two other young women.

Lenny knew that the ladies went for him. He had discovered that very early on, when he played Junior hockey in Canada, for a town in Ontario, called Kitchener. He was a defenseman, and a good one. So he spent a lot of time in the penalty box for fighting. But that seemed to make him all the more attractive to the Canadian girls. And he soon found out that it worked in Healdsburg, California, too.

"Gimme a Labatt's beer, if you've got some," Lenny said, after sidling up alongside the three girls, who were giggling among themselves at the end of the bar.

■

"We've got some, although there's not that much call for Canadian beer around here," the bartender said.

"Well, I'm Canadian, and I drink it because it reminds me of home."

"What brings you here?"

"I'm in the food and wine business now. But I used to be a hockey player."

"Did you play in the National Hockey League?"

"Almost. For a while I did play for Team Canada in international competition."

"Is that how you got banged up?"

That always did it. The three girls now stopped talking to look at Lenny, more specifically to look at what he called "The Scar." It was mean looking, and ran across half of his forehead. Except for that, he was an exceptionally handsome man in his midforties.

"Yeah. A highstick in a game with the Czechs in Prague. Deliberate, too."

"Wow, you mean somebody did that to you on purpose?" the girl next to him asked.

"Yes, ma'am."

"What did you do?"

"Hit him. But fair. No stick. I just took off my gloves and even though I could barely see him for all the blood that was coming down my face, I slugged him. He was out cold before he hit the ice."

It was actually true.

"Wow," the girl said again. "Then what?"

"I got kicked out of the game and sent back to Canada the next day."

"Did you still play after that?" the girl asked.

"Yeah, but somehow my heart wasn't really in it as much as before."

He could see the sympathy in her eyes.

"By the way," he said, "my name's Lenny."

■

Her name—the one he had followed here, and the one who
had been asking him the questions—was Pam. Pam Pederson.
She was blond, tall, maybe twenty-five, and built like an ath-
lete. He liked big girls.

"So what's a Canadian hockey player doing here in little
old Healdsburg?" she asked.

"I'm in the wine business now," Lenny answered.

"But you still drink beer," Pam said.

"All Canadians drink beer—Canadian beer. You girls want
to try one?"

"Sure. Why not?"

He ordered four Labatt's—all that was left.

Then he offered to take the girls to an early dinner. They
stayed at Jacob Horner's, where, it turned out, the food was
excellent. By eight, they were already done. As they were
leaving, a party of three men was just arriving. Pam stopped
to talk to them, while Lenny and the other two girls waited
outside on the sidewalk.

Lenny, who had been jabbering away for the last two hours,
fell strangely silent. When Pam finally caught up with them,
she explained that they were her three new bosses. She also
said she had to go right home and get some sleep, since they'd
asked her to come in early the next morning. At six, for God's
sake.

Back in his car, Lenny could not help but talk aloud to
himself. "One of those guys was Fred fucking Fitch."

For a while, Fitch's room had been next door to his at the
Federal Correctional Institution in Pleasanton.

"Fred Fitch, the counterfeiter. Working at River Ranch!
Wait until Sid hears about this."

The first thing he did when he got back to the motel was to
call Sid Ravitch's private number. So far Lenny had reported
in twice a day, but this was the first time he had called Ravitch
so late. When Ravitch answered, Lenny immediately blurted
out the news of his startling discovery.

■

Sid cut him off in midsentence.

"Lenny, you've got to do better than this. If you recall, you dumb fuck, it was you who helped me track Fitch down. Because Willy Saxon asked me to."

"But Sid, maybe that's what's going on up here. They're making funny money."

"Forget it. Willy's not that stupid. Fitch is a computer freak. Just like those other two guys. They're obviously the ones Willy's driver told you about. *That's* why he's there. But he's a computer freak doing what? That's what I want you to find out, Lenny."

"All right. I think I now know how," Lenny said.

"How?"

Lenny was really pissed after being cut down that way by Ravitch. So he said, "I'll tell you how if and when it works."

"All right. And stop drinking so much, Lenny. You sound half looped every time I talk to you."

"Anything you say, Sid," Lenny answered, and then he just hung up.

Sometimes that Ravitch really got on his nerves. Who the hell did he think he was, treating him that way? After all, they'd been in that gold thing together. Yet he had served time, and Ravitch hadn't.

Fucking ingrate.

He spent the rest of the evening watching TV alone in his room and thinking about Pam Pederson. Thinking that next time he'd like to mix a little pleasure with business, where she was concerned.

■

THIRTY-NINE

Frank Lipper was already there at eight the next morning. By nine he had commandeered his own corner of the trading room, and had enlisted the help of Pam Pederson to help him put together the Ukiah CAB (Zero Coupon) Official Statement.

Willy arrived shortly after nine. He sat down at an empty desk and was immediately on the phone to New York, talking to Marshall Lane.

"I hear those inverse floaters you bought are already up ten percent," Willy said for openers.

"Yeah. Not bad for three days," Lane said. "Got something else?"

"Depends. You managing any funds that can't deal in foreign exchange?"

"My management company controls thirteen funds, Willy. Three of them were designed exclusively for pension fund money. All three are precluded from speculating in currencies and commodities."

"Then I got something for you. ICONs."

"What the fuck are ICONs?"

"Index Currency Option Notes."

"What do they do?"

"Go up and down with the currency they're tied to. You can play it either way."

"Now that's a new twist."

■

"And perfectly legal."

"And timely," Lane said. "One of these months all hell is going to break loose in the currency markets, just like it did in the fall of 1992."

"There we agree."

"Can you get the details to me right away?"

"You'll have a fax coming your way the moment after I hang up."

"Don't hang up yet. If I recall correctly, you said that by now you might have worked out that piggyback muni bond deal with the City and County of San Francisco—the one you brought up at Denise's ranch."

"It's a done deal. We'll have a red herring coming your way early next week. I mean a Preliminary Official Statement. I keep forgetting."

"What yield?"

"On the general obligation bond, 5.5 percent. On the housing development bond, 6.4 percent."

"That's a nice package. How do I get some? As I told you at Denise's ranch, my fixed-income funds all have a lot of cash lying around."

"Call Dan Prescott. He'll take care of you."

"Great. Anything else?"

"Yes. Something really special. The City of Ukiah—it's about thirty miles to the north and east of Denise's ranch—is coming out with a real dandy. Ukiah, by the way, was just rated as Number three in the country, in terms of the all-around quality of living it offers."

"Maybe I'll move there," said the New York money manager.

Willy winced. "Naw, it's way too tame for you. In fact, it's so dull you'd be wasting your time even visiting it. But though dull, it's fiscally sound. They're going to be raising twenty million dollars to build a Materials Recycling Facility."

"Whatever that is," Lane said.

■

"It's a mechanical dump, I guess. The bond's a forty-year zero coupon offering a yield of eight percent."

"Wow! How much of *that* can I get?"

"All of it, if you want. You're my best customer, Marshall. I'll admit it. This is the kind of deal that can really sweeten a portfolio. So if you want it, it's yours."

"I'll take it, Willy."

"OK. I'll handle it personally. That is, my friend Frank Lipper and I will. You remember Frank, don't you?"

"Of course. He organized that famous junk bond junket for you back in the mid-1980s. Right?

"Exactly. He's now with Prescott and Quackenbush and it was Frank who organized the Ukiah underwriting. With my help, of course."

"I understand, Willy. Now don't forget to send that fax on those ICONs."

"You'll have it in five minutes. Talk to you later, Marshall," Willy said, and hung up.

Frank Lipper had been listening to the whole conversation from his desk beside the one where Willy was sitting.

"You're unbelievable, Willy," he said. "It's all working out exactly like you said. By next week, we can just forget about zero coupons and move on."

"Not exactly," Willy said. "One more, and *then* we move on. But first let's put Ukiah away for forty years. I want that prospectus in my hands by Friday afternoon."

FORTY

The prospectus describing the imminent issue of bonds by the City of Ukiah to finance the building of a twenty-million-dollar Materials Recycling Facility was in Willy's hands by three o'clock that Friday afternoon. It had required almost nonstop work on the part of Frank Lipper and his assistant, Pam Pederson, during the preceding forty-eight hours.

Willy personally shook Pam's hand in thanks, told her to go home early and also to take Monday off, too. On the way home, she should drop off a copy of the prospectus at the printers in Healdsburg. They had instructions as to what to do with it.

She took along two copies of the Ukiah prospectus. One she dropped off at the printer. The other she kept. She wanted to show it off to her prospective new boyfriend, the hockey player from Canada. He'd called her twice at home since they had met at Jacob Horner's, asking for a date. She'd had to turn him down each time, due to having to work with Frank Lipper day *and* night on that bond project. Lenny had sounded skeptical after the second turndown. Now she could provide the evidence of what had kept her so busy. He was always asking about her work, anyway.

But she did not exactly trot it out immediately. After all, she'd seen Lenny but once, and who knew how long *this* relationship would last. So she left it on the kitchen table.

■

Lenny picked her up at exactly seven o'clock, and by seven-thirty they were on the terrace of Chevys in Santa Rosa, eating guacamole dip and drinking their first margarita. She had watched and listened to him the entire time, saying very little. He wasn't perfect—a little too slick, a bit too crude—but he was a hunk, there was no doubt about that.

That he was a hunk had been verified the moment they had entered Chevys restaurant. The eyes of almost every eighteen-year-old, full-breasted, short-skirted Mexican tramp in the place—there must have been a dozen of them with their Anglo dates—had shifted to Lenny, when he walked in at her side. The scar must be turning them on even more, she thought, as she held on to the arm of her escort all the more firmly.

"How come you're so tall?" he asked, once they were settled in.

"You mean big and tall, I think," she said. "Because both of my parents are of Swedish ancestry."

"Mine were Irish and French. Maybe the French is why I ended up in the wine business. But I think the Irish side predominated. That's why I always used to get into fights."

"Did you fight with your wife too?" she asked.

"Probably would have, if I'd ever been married."

"Never?"

"That's right. Never found the right girl in Canada."

Pam Pederson's interest in Lenny Newsom rose by a quantum leap after hearing these words. He might be slick and crude and not the youngest, but he was a hunk and single.

At eleven-thirty they were back in Healdsburg, parked in front of Pam's home. Her parents, she assured him, being Scandinavian, had been asleep for hours.

"So if you want to come in for coffee," she said, "you don't have to worry about them."

They had coffee in the living room, as they sat side by side on the sofa. At midnight he put his arm around her. At 12:05 she turned some music on and the lights off.

■

At two a.m., a rather spent Lenny Newsom walked out of the Pederson home carrying a prospectus bearing the name of the City of Ukiah.

At eight the next morning, Lenny was already in his car, headed for San Francisco. He had just spoken to Sid Ravitch who said that if it was *that* important, he'd meet him at the office. Lenny had not wanted to discuss any details on the phone. There could be somebody at the front desk who might be listening in. There was little else to do in a little dump like Healdsburg.

Two hours later, Lenny first explained about how his new girl was now doing his work for him inside River Ranch. Ravitch liked it. However, when Lenny triumphantly handed over the draft of the Official Statement, describing the bond issue that would fund the construction of a Materials Recycling Facility in the City of Ukiah, Sid Ravitch took one look at it and threw it back in his face.

"*This* is why you dragged me out of bed on a Saturday morning?"

"That's the secret project they've been working on."

"Secret?"

"Sure. I got it from that girl. She said they had told her at least ten times not to talk about it with outsiders. So there must be something very fishy about it."

"The only thing that's 'fishy' is that they don't want anybody to make a connection between the investment bank that's issuing these bonds, and Willy Saxon. But *you* should have been able to figure *that* out. You followed him to the offices of Prescott and Quackenbush last week, for Christ's sake."

"Maybe, but did you know about this secret project?" Lenny asked, getting more burned up by the minute.

"Turn to the index of that prospectus. It's always on page three. Then look up 'Rating.' "

"It says it's on page thirty-one."

■

"Go to it. Then read it. It's just one paragraph so it shouldn't take you too long."

Lenny did as told.

"It says that the Western Credit Rating Agency has given an A rating to the bonds."

"The Western Credit Rating Agency is me, Lenny. Well, not quite anymore. As you know, it's now me and Willy. I got paid twenty-five thousand dollars for that one paragraph. I got fifty thousand dollars for another paragraph that will appear in another prospectus they're doing for the City and County of San Francisco. That was also set up by Willy Saxon."

"So what you're saying is that this is all perfectly legit?" Lenny said.

"That's right. There's something going on. There's *got* to be something going on. But we're missing it. And missing it is costing me almost a thousand dollars a day with expenses. So it's time to give it a rest, Lenny. Go back to Toronto for a while—say a couple of months—and visit your friends and relatives. I'll call you when I'm ready to start over. OK?"

"You mean leave, starting now?"

"Starting whenever it's convenient for you. I want your forwarding address, too, so I can arrange to have your checks sent. Here," Ravitch said, as he shoved first a pad of notepaper, then a pencil, across the desk, "write them down."

Minutes later Lenny Newsom was back down on Montgomery Street, deserted since it was Saturday morning.

His mind was going like crazy. "First Fred Fitch, and now this. That's the last time I tell or show him *anything* before I know for absolutely goddamned sure we've got Willy nailed to the cross."

He drove straight back to Healdsburg. Three days later, after a very long Monday night spent mostly in his room at the Vintage Inn with Pam Pederson, Lenny Newsom flew off to Canada.

■

If he would have stayed a month longer he no doubt would have gotten hold of a copy of yet another prospectus—describing a new bond about to be issued by the Sun River City Economic Development Authority.

A zero coupon bond.

■

FORTY-ONE

"It's the last one, believe me," Willy said to Frank Lipper. They were at thirty-three thousand feet, in the third row of a United Airlines 767, headed for JFK.

"The Ukiah thing was like a test," he continued. "You have to admit, Frank, that it worked like a charm. Even the SEC swallowed it hook, line, and sinker. They didn't come back with a single question. So those bonds are as good as buried for forty years."

"Agreed," Frank said. "But why another one? Why Sun River City and not another Materials Recycling Facility somewhere else? And why right away?"

"Three very good questions, Frank. You ought to be on *Meet the Press*. I will answer them one by one. But are we going to just talk? Or are we going to attempt to both talk and drink at the same time?"

"I'm for number two."

"You're a good traveling companion, Frank."

After the bloody Mary's had arrived and been duly tested, Willy said. "Now for question number one: Why another one? Answer: Because with an additional hundred million dollars in capital, we will finally have arrived in the big-time. Not in the same league as Morgan Stanley or Lehman Brothers, but big enough so that we can now bid against them on deals."

He took a sip of very slightly diluted tomato juice.

■

"Now as to why not another MRF in another city, believe me, I thought of that. I even had the next city picked out—Eureka, way up the coast. But another twenty million dollars wasn't worth the risk."

He ate some peanuts.

"Which brings us to Sun River City. It's so well set up—even you have to admit it, Frank—that it's certainly worth the risk, since it represents one hundred million dollars in the pot, our pot, or the equivalent of a Ukiah, a Eureka, a Fresno, a Modesto, and a San Luis Obispo. You see? I've given it a lot of thought."

"As always, Willy, you're right. But why now?"

" 'Strike while the iron's hot,' " Willy said. "Sure it's a cliché. But clichés become clichés because there's something to them. Right now P and Q Financial Products is so hot that I could sell the Bay Bridge, especially in New York. I think most of them have caught on to the Brooklyn Bridge by now, due to propinquity, but the Bay Bridge is two thousand five hundred miles away. Like Sun River City. But I digress."

He took another sip of what United passed off as a bloody Mary.

"What I'm referring to is, first, our inverse floaters. Then our ICONs. And finally, last week, our LIBOR Turbos."

"Who figured that one out?"

"It was a joint venture of all three derivative geeks."

"The money market fund guys are going ape over that one."

"Wouldn't you? Instead of getting the current London Inter-Bank Offer Rate of three and a half percent, they'll get five times that."

"If they're lucky," Frank said.

"Hope springs eternal," Willy said.

"But back to Sun River City for a minute, Willy," Frank said. "Sure, we're hot in derivatives. So whatever we offer those guys in New York they're going to buy. But these bonds

■

are different. This time we can't stash them all with your buddy, Marshall Lane. What if *afterwards* some lawyer at one of the other funds in New York decides to get tough and really check things out?"

"We've got three lines of defense. First, our bond counsel, Bobbie Armacost. He's known on both coasts as one of the best. I'll make sure that he gets on the phone or plane if any serious questions start being asked."

"Number two?" Frank asked.

Willy pointed to the luggage bin above.

"We've got four ten-pound packages of Jack Warneke's plans for Sun River City. We're going to be talking to three, maximum four, bond fund managers. Each one gets ten pounds designated 'For Internal Distribution Only.' Just the sheer quantity will blow the minds of their due diligence attorneys, especially when they see Jack's name on it. Everybody knows he's an asshole buddy of all the Kennedys. That makes them stand up and salute even in New York."

"I'll grant that one. Especially since they'll be dealing here with a relatively small commitment."

"Exactly. I hope that Marshall takes down half, and that we find two other funds that will commit for twenty-five million dollars each. And now for the last line of defense—our councilman and real estate developer in Oregon. The one we paid a million for a two-year option on his useless thirty thousand acres. Or is it forty thousand?"

"Thirty thousand. I did the deal with him last week," Frank said, "so I ought to at least remember that."

"Anyway, if some hotshot New York due diligence attorney wants to go to Bend, Oregon, to check things out, we are no doubt in very deep doo-doo, Frank. But at least we would have a fighting chance as long as we have our Councilman in there exercising damage control."

"A very weak third line of defense," Frank said. "But it is highly doubtful whether anybody will try to go past the first

■

two. Due diligence lawyers cost two hundred fifty dollars an hour. You hardly want them spending a couple of weeks thousands of miles away, chalking up hours like crazy, because of a lousy twenty-five-million-dollar bond investment that's going into a three-billion-dollar portfolio."

"My sentiments exactly."

"You know, Willy," Frank then said, "this is just like it used to be. Here we are, on our way to New York, peddling our wares. Remember the last time we put on a road show together?"

"How can I forget," Willy answered. "1986. Our last big junk bond deal. It's funny that you mention it. Marshall Lane brought it up recently, too. I guess it was what you call a memorable event."

"I'll always remember the moment when you told me to charter a 747. A fucking 747!" Frank said.

"Well, we had to have room for the rock band. And the dance floor."

"It cost a fortune to get the plane configured the way we wanted."

"It was worth it, though."

"If you recall, our first pickup was in Frankfurt, then London, then New York. That's where the biggest bunch came on board, including Marshall Lane, as well as the other three guys we're scheduled to meet with tomorrow."

"I didn't pick them out at random, you know," Willy said.

"And finally, San Francisco, before going on to the Big Island."

"In retrospect, that stop in San Francisco was a mistake. Too many California bank trust officers joined the party."

"Why was that a mistake?"

"Because it made enemies for life out of half of the banking establishment in California, led by the guy in charge of the California Banking Commission. He told all about that junket when he testified against me and it sure didn't help my case.

■

But that's water over the damn dam. Go back to the story of that junket, Frank. I love to hear you tell it."

"Sure. Remember when we finally got to that hotel in Kona?"

"That was a big moment."

"There, right next to the luau pit, was that canoe, or outrigger—whatever they call those things in Hawaii—filled with fucking Mai Tai's!"

"There must have been a hundred gallons of rum in there."

"And a little pineapple juice."

"Each guy got a big silver mug with his name engraved on it. Remember?"

"Of course. But when the hookers from Honolulu arrived—that was the high point. Forty fucking hookers in grass skirts and that's all."

"It sold a lot of junk bonds," Willy said.

"Especially when most of the hookers agreed to join us on the flight back."

"That final gesture when we finally unloaded our colleagues at each stop didn't hurt either."

"You mean those gold Rolex watches? Yeah, it was a good idea. The only disappointment was when I made my presentation on those junk bonds—a very convincing one too, I thought—only seven guys showed up."

"What's that bond selling for now?" Frank asked

"The last time I looked it was 152 compared to the new issue price of 98. And it's been paying twelve percent interest every year since 1986. That's one reason why, when I called up those guys in New York, they all agreed to meet us any time, any place," Willy said.

"How come Dan Prescott didn't come along?"

"You want the truth?" Willy said.

"Sure."

■

"I think he—in fact, both he and Bobby—want to put some distance between themselves and us, Frank."

"Did they drag their feet on this one?"

"Sure. But in the end, what choice did they have? Although I did have to swear on a Bible that this was absolutely the last one. Which it is. Don't worry, they'll calm down when they see the profits our geeks are generating."

"How much so far?"

"We're ahead almost twelve million dollars already."

"Jeezus, Willy. Did you tell Dan and Bobby that this time we're totally bypassing Sid Ravitch?"

"Yeah. I had to, lest somehow it came up in casual conversation when Ravitch was in the same room. I trust that the ratings report you drafted is also up there in the luggage rack?"

"It's there. On the official stationery of the Western Credit Rating Agency. Insisting that I get that office there was a stroke of genius, Willy. And by the way, I gave instructions to their mail room that any queries regarding underwritings that were done by Prescott and Quackenbush should be routed directly to my little office there."

"As usual, Frank, our minds think alike."

"But if something goes astray and ends up on Ravitch's desk, what then? I don't want to pry, but I assume you've got something on him. Right?"

"Yep."

The movie had just started.

"Wanna watch?" Willy asked.

"Why not," Frank answered. He closed the window shade and started to put on his headphones.

"One last thing, Frank, before you do that," Willy said. "That talk about our last junket gave me an idea."

"I'm not sure a repeat of that one would go over in the 1990s," Frank said.

"No. I'm thinking of something totally different. A skiing

junket to Switzerland at Christmas time. Can't get any more wholesome than that."

"Who'd be invited?"

"Wait and see. I want it to be a surprise.

■

FORTY-TWO

It was just after dawn on the second day after Christmas, a Tuesday, when the Swissair jumbo jet carrying the entire staff of P and Q Financial Products in its first-class cabin landed at Kloten airport, just outside of Zurich. Just one girl had been left behind to man the phones and faxes at River Ranch. A chartered bus was waiting to take them on to St. Moritz.

Five hours later they arrived. The bus pulled up in front of the station of the funicular railroad that transported skiers from the valley floor to Piz Nair, the mountain peak towering high above. It took awhile to unload, but by one o'clock all seventeen passengers and their gear were jammed inside the funicular's single car, and it soon began to glide up the mountain. There was one intermediary stop—where the ascending and descending cars passed each other—at the plateau half way up. It was called the Chanterella. There everybody got out. Waiting for them were four horse-drawn sleighs, which took them a half kilometer along the plateau to their final destination, a huge private chalet known as the Villa Engadin, named after the valley that now lay stretched out below them. Willy's Liechtenstein attorney, Dr. Guggi, had arranged to rent it through New Year's Day. Guggi had been waiting to greet them at the airport and had come along in the bus to make sure that everything was in order at their destination.

It was a glorious winter day, the first such, they were told,

■

in more than two weeks. For that year the snow had come early and heavy. There was already a meter of it on the valley floor, at least two meters on the Chanterella, and well over three on top of Piz Nair.

Susie Bauer could hardly wait to put on her skies, but was hesitant to do so before everything had been unpacked inside the chalet. Vreni, the River Ranch housekeeper, who had also come along, intervened.

"You young people go ahead," she said. "I'll take care of things here."

Susie, her husband Urs, Pam Pederson, all the other girls, and even Sara Jones—who had decided at the last moment to accept Willy's invitation—were on their skis within twenty minutes. Led by Susie, they were soon off on their first trial run down to the valley floor.

The derivative geeks, needless to say, stayed behind, as did Frank Lipper and Willy Saxon. The latter two installed themselves on lying chairs on the deck in front of the chalet. Vreni, somehow, had conjured up a cold bottle of Aigle, and poured each a glass of that Swiss white wine while they began to soak up the winter sun.

"Is this the fucking life or what?" Willy said, once the housekeeper had disappeared back into the house.

"You know something," Frank said. "I think I'm going to like this junket even more than the last one."

"Yeah, we're getting old, I guess. Anyway, I prefer to think of this as an outing. Like Sunday Schools used to put on for nice little girls like Susie and Pam."

"That Susie is something, isn't she?" Frank said. "Always cheerful, helpful, and ready to go."

"I agree. How lucky we are to have such a group of fine young people with us this time around."

"They all sure look up to you, Willy," Frank said.

An embarrassed Willy was saved from having to reply by

■

the appearance on the deck of Dr. Guggi, still dressed in his lawyer clothes.

"Everything all right?" he asked, anxiously.

"Perfect," Willy said. "Pull up a chair. I'm sure Vreni will be back soon with some more wine."

"I was talking with Urs Bauer on the bus," Guggi said. "He couldn't be happier working with you, Willy."

"I was just telling Willy the same thing," Frank said.

"We're the ones that should be happy with *them,"* Willy said. "Do you know how much money they've made so far?"

He waited before springing it on them.

"Twenty-seven point six million dollars."

"That's amazing," the lawyer said. "What is just as amazing is how much capital you've been able to round up, Willy. I just received the new consolidated balance sheet of Prescott and Quackenbush. You've got a capital base now of around a hundred-fifty million dollars. How did you do it?"

"It wasn't easy," Willy said. "But I'll tell you this. Without that amount of capital there was no way that we could have made that twenty-seven million in profits."

"I assume that this trip is your way of rewarding your people?"

"And myself. This is the first vacation I've had in many a year," Willy said. "So I intend to enjoy it to the hilt."

At four o'clock they took the funicular back down to St. Moritz and then walked through the village to Hanselmann's, where they all had the tearoom's famous hot chocolate and patisserie, even Willy. By six-thirty, they were back up in the villa, and at seven they gathered around a huge wooden table in the kitchen for dinner. It was fondue, personally prepared by Vreni, their own Swiss housekeeper and cook. Naturally, there was lots of Aigle wine to go with it, as well as Kirschwasser. It was a perfect way to start a Swiss Alpine vacation. By eleven all seventeen were in bed, snuggled under their featherbeds.

■

Susie was up at dawn the next day, ready to go. By eight, everybody was gathered outside the chalet. This time both Willy and Frank had joined the rest of them, as had Dr. Werner Guggi. They walked over to the funicular station, and took the mountain train up to the Piz Nair this time.

Guggi, surprisingly, was the first to push off from the icy mountain peak. It was soon obvious that he was the best skier in the group. By noon, they had done the run three times and were ready for a more difficult challenge.

"We'll go over to Pontresino and try the Diavolezza," Guggi suggested.

There was a public bus waiting at a stop in the center of St. Moritz that made the fifteen-minute run over to Pontresino every hour. By two, the gondola had taken them to over ten thousand feet. There, after pushing off, they immediately found themselves on a piste, which plummeted while also curving sharply to the left in order to skirt an Alpine glacier. Willy decided that the better part of wisdom would be to stick pretty close to one of the Swiss skiers, and so he stayed right behind Susie during this initial stage of the descent. After about five minutes it began to level off and she veered over to the extreme right side of the piste, where she pulled up just before a row of markers which spelled out a warning in huge red letters: GEFAHR DANGER ATTENZIONE

"Look behind those markers," she said. They had pulled up no more than five meters short of the edge of a cliff that plunged at least three hundred meters straight down to a group of huge boulders below.

"Scary," Willy said.

"Years ago, shortly after they installed the lifts and opened the Diavolezza, five skiers, including a famous German sports star, went over this cliff in a snowstorm. That was when they put up those signs," Susie said. "It reminds me of that spot at River Ranch along the walk between the main house and the rest of the buildings."

■

"You mean where it passes just by the edge of the precipice overlooking the Russian River?"

"Exactly. It's right near the house where we now live. It also goes straight down, though not so far. But like here, there's a pile of huge boulders in the river below. When I walk by that point I always get the creeps," she said.

"You should have told me earlier," Willy said. "When we get back, I'll do something about it."

"I'd like to tell you something else, Mr. Saxon. Which is one of the reasons why I brought this up. Something very private."

"Sure. Go ahead."

"Urs and I are going to have a baby. We want to have it born in California so that he will be an American. We checked and already know it's a he. We've decided to name him after you."

For a moment, Willy was at a loss for words. He finally leaned over and kissed the young Swiss woman on the cheek.

"Congratulations," he said. "We'll all look out for both you and him. I'll take care of that danger spot at the ranch right away." Then he shoved off, with Susie behind.

That evening at six, the four sleighs, piled high with hay, pulled up in front of the Villa Engadin. By torch light they traversed the plateau and then followed a trail that led gently down to the Suvretta House, the ultra-luxurious, yet rustic hotel that lay nestled in a forest of fir trees. The restaurant there was expecting them. It had been forewarned about how they would be dressed, so they were discreetly ushered into a private dining room. Willy took his place at the dining table beside Sara.

"Wasn't that a day?" he said.

"I'm pooped like I've never been in years," Sara replied.

"Me too. And tomorrow Guggi has something planned that's even more difficult. The Corvatsch."

"I'm not sure I'm up to that."

■

"I'm probably going to pass on that one too," Willy said.

"That might be a good idea in any case," Sara said.

"Why?"

"I think you'd better have a word with Denise. She called me at the villa right before we left."

"How'd she get the number?"

"I called her and left it."

"Why did you call her?"

"Just to say hello."

"And that's the only reason she called back?"

"No. She's a little worried."

"About what?"

"About you. She was at a dinner party last night and got into a conversation with a man who is head of the California Banking Commission, Ralph Goodman. She said you'd know that name."

"All too well," Willy said. He reached for a glass of water and found that his hand was not totally steady.

"Go on," he said, after carefully taking a sip.

"You'd better talk directly to her, Willy," Sara said.

"What time is it in San Francisco?" he asked.

Sara looked at her watch.

"You have to subtract either eight or nine hours," she said. "I always forget."

"Doesn't matter. It would make it either ten or eleven in the morning."

"Call her when we get back to the villa. I told her we'd be having dinner together. She'll still be there, since I'm sure she's expecting your call. Otherwise she wouldn't have brought this up with me in the first place."

For Willy, the next two hours seemed like an eternity. He ate very little, and talked even less. But no one, except Sara, seemed to notice. The men and women had somehow managed to segregate themselves at the dinner table. The women, led by Susie, spent the evening replaying their day on the ski slopes. Frank and Werner Guggi spent most of their time at dinner talking to each other. The four younger men, led by Susie's husband, were in a deep, sometimes highly agitated, discussion of what was happening in Germany. In fact, when Willy announced at nine-thirty that the sleighs had arrived and were ready to take them back, they were relieved. That would allow them to catch the ten o'clock news on television back at the chalet.

The phone in Denise's apartment in San Francisco rang seven times before she finally picked up.

"It's Willy," he said.

"I'm glad you called," she said in a husky voice. "Hold on. I'm going to get a fresh cup of coffee from the kitchen. It will take thirty seconds."

He waited.

"There," she said upon returning. "When I'm nervous I always seem to drink a lot of coffee."

"Sara told me about your earlier conversation with her," Willy began.

"That's why I'm nervous. It's really none of my business, I suppose, but that awful Ralph Goodman deliberately took me aside before dinner at the Getty's last night. Why they even invited him I don't know. Anyway, he started on you right away. About how, through deception and bribery, you had loaded up California S and L's and banks with your junk bonds in the 1980s, had made a billion dollars personally in the process, and had only gotten three years in prison. It was a travesty of justice, he said."

"Nothing new there, Denise." Willy said.

"Hold on, I'm getting to the point. Goodman then said that he had sworn to get you, Willy, really get you this time, if you ever tried to get back into the bond business."

"And?"

"He said that a few months ago he saw you with Dan Prescott at Candlestick Park. But after checking around, he determined that no one has ever even seen you inside his investment bank, so he forgot about it. Then, the day before Christmas Eve, he bumped into Jack at the Pacific Union Club. Jack told him that you had bought his place and that he was glad you did, because it was finally being put to good use again."

"Good old Jack," Willy said.

"I'm sure he meant well," Denise said.

"You're right. What else did he tell Goodman?"

"That you had moved into the main house, and that the old conference center was now full of computers and telephones and people."

"Shit," Willy said. "And how did he connect that with my getting back into the bond business?"

"He didn't. He just said that it sounded might fishy."

"And why is that his business?"

"Goodman said that you were banned from the securities industry in this country for life. Is that true?"

"Partly true. I can't act as a broker/dealer. I can act as an advisor to anybody I want. But anyway, what's Goodman going to do about it? Did he tell you?"

"Yes. And that's why I brought it up with Sara. He said that as soon as the holidays are over, the first thing he's going to do is to start asking a lot more questions. This is his turf, he said, and he won't abide criminals like you messing it up again like you did in the 1980s. Those were his final words before I finally turned my back on him." Denise said. She then asked, "Is this as serious as it sounds?"

"Not yet," Willy said.

"If it does get serious, and if I can be of any help, call me right away. Even in the morning. If you don't, I'll never talk to you again. Promise?"

"I promise, Denise."

"And remember, I've got ten times more clout in this town

■

than that Ralph Goldman will ever have. Now to change the subject. How are you and Sara getting along?" she asked.

"Pretty good," Willy said.

"She sounded a bit tired."

"From skiing, Denise," Willy said.

"When are you coming back?"

"That's hard to say now. We're scheduled to fly back from Zurich late New Year's Day."

"You'll call me as soon as you're back, won't you?"

"I will, Denise. You're a good pal."

"So are you."

Willy had made the phone call from his bedroom. After he hung up, Willy decided he needed a cognac and a cigar. Both, he knew, were available from a cupboard downstairs in the living room.

All six men were still there. The TV was on, and all were watching, even Frank Lipper.

Willy went over to him after getting himself the drink and smoke. "What's going on?"

"It's in German so you're asking the wrong guy," Frank said. "But apparently, according to that German magazine that makes a habit of bringing down big-time German politicians, the German chancellor has been caught with his hand—in fact his whole fat arm—in the cookie jar. As much as I can understand of it, they claim he's been feeding confidential information to the head of one of Germany's biggest banks for years—in essence, tipping him off in advance on where interest rates are headed. It's also claimed that the bank's been taking care of him to the tune of a million DM a year. Cash. His personal secretary went to *Der Spiegel* magazine and spilled the beans. Have I got it right?" he then asked, turning to his new buddy, Werner Guggi, who was sitting beside him.

"You summed it up perfectly, except for two additional matters. The Chancellor vehemently denies this, claiming that *Der Spiegel* is run by a bunch of Socialists that are out to get

■

him, just like they got Franz Josef Strauss a decade ago. Secondly, it is claimed that the head of the German central bank, the Bundesbank, believes the story and feels he has been betrayed. There are now rumors that he, also, might resign."

Urs Bauer, who had been sitting right in front of the TV set, now got up and came over to Willy.

"Have you heard what's happening in Germany, Mr. Saxon?" he asked.

"Just now," Willy said.

"I think I should go to Frankfurt immediately and find out as much as I can about all this," Urs said.

"Whatever you think," Willy said.

"Everything's closed between Christmas Eve and the second of January all over Europe," Urs said. "That means that nobody over here is going to be able to do anything about this for quite a few days. All the bankers and traders that count are either skiing in the Alps or lying on the beach in the Canary Islands or Mombasa. So Europe's down."

Willy was only listening with half an ear.

"But not the United States," Urs said. "The banks and futures exchanges are all operating."

"I know, Urs. What are you leading up to?"

"I want to short the German mark in New York at the opening tomorrow morning. OK?"

"Go ahead."

"I'll do it from the Frankfurterhof. I know the hotel and it's even got a fax in every room," Urs said.

"When are you going?"

"At dawn. I've tentatively arranged to charter a plane, if that's all right. I should be back here by six in the evening, if the weather holds."

"Go to it," Willy said.

He waited for Urs to go back to the TV, and then he turned to Werner Guggi.

■

"I want to discuss something with you in private," he said. "Maybe we could sit down somewhere else."

Frank looked at him in a strange way, but said nothing.

"The women have taken over the kitchen," Guggi said.

"There's a small den just off the living room. Let's go there," Willy said.

After Willy had closed the door to the den behind them, he said, "Let's sit over there on the sofa. It will only take a few minutes."

Once they were seated, he continued. "I'm going to ask what may appear to be some strange questions, but I have my reasons. OK?"

"Of course," the Liechtenstein attorney said.

"All right. First, how much do I still have in my personal account with you?"

"Just about eleven million dollars. As you know it's not actually with me. It's at the Union Bank of Switzerland. I just administer it."

"I know. Second question: What do you know about the extradition arrangements between the United States and Switzerland?"

Guggi did not bat an eye. "They are spelled out in a bilateral treaty between our two countries. Switzerland has over a hundred such treaties, each one different."

"Can you get hold of the text of the treaty with the United States?"

"Sure. How soon do you want it?"

"Tomorrow."

"I'll contact a colleague in Bern. He can make a copy at your embassy there—they'll have the English text—and fax it here. But this is Switzerland, where things move at a very deliberate pace, so don't expect it before tomorrow afternoon."

"Do we have a fax here?"

■

"I haven't seen one. Maybe Urs got one and has it in his room. If not, I'll buy one first thing tomorrow."

"OK. Now just so you don't get the wrong idea, something just came up that may or may not spell trouble. I'm just checking out my insurance policies, that's all," Willy said.

"Fair enough."

"So let's rejoin the other guys."

Willy went to bed at midnight, but it was two in the morning before he finally fell asleep.

■

FORTY-THREE

Nine time zones to the west in Healdsburg, California, it was five in the afternoon and Lenny Newsom was sitting alone at the bar in Zeke's saloon. He was alone because his new girlfriend had gone off skiing in Switzerland—despite the fact that she had known he would be coming back from Toronto right after Christmas.

They had kept in touch during the past couple of months, phoning each other at least three times a week. Due to his persistence, she had kept him up to date on what was happening at River Ranch. Most of it had been pure gobbledegook—involving financial products with weird names like inverse floaters and turbos. She did the back office work for the guys that were trading this stuff using their computers and satellite links. It was all too far out for him. The only exception had been the second bond issue. She'd sent him a copy of that prospectus, too. Just like the Ukiah one, only bigger. There, also on page 31, was the same paragraph that Sid Ravitch had made him read in his office. The Western Credit Rating Agency had given an A rating to this one too.

So far he still hadn't come up with a goddamn thing that could be used to nail Willy Saxon. But that was soon to change.

The man who came in just after five and sat beside him at the crowded bar was a big man, also a talkative one.

■

"My name's Abner Root," he said, stretching out his big hand, "and I work at City Hall right across the plaza. I like to come in here after work now and then for a beer. I don't think I've seen you before. From here?"

"Not really. I'm in the food and wine business in Canada. I come through these parts every now and then to buy some of your fine local wines."

"Well, well, you're the type of person we need more of. Let me buy you another beer compliments of the City of Healdsburg. What are you drinking?"

"Labatt's. It's Canadian."

"Then I'll try one, too."

"What do you do at City Hall?" Lenny asked.

"I'm the finance director. If the city needs money, I go out and try to raise it any way I can."

"Including bonds?"

"If it's a big project, sure."

"Like what?"

"Schools. Hospital. New low-income housing development, that sort of thing."

"Have you had to build one of those Waste Recycling Plants yet?"

"You mean a Materials Recycling Facility—an MRF. How in the world would you, as a Canadian, know about something like that? It's only a state like California that would pass a goddamn law making those things mandatory. Fucking environmentalists have gone nuts here. Do you know what one of those things costs?"

"Yeah. Twenty million dollars."

"How in the hell would you know *that?*" Root asked.

"I saw a study on one of those things—the one that Ukiah's building."

"Ukiah ain't building no MRF. Who told you that bullshit? And who gave you that study? I know the one you mean and it was confidential."

■

Lenny decided to back off. "Well, I didn't exactly *see* it. I just heard about it from one of the girls who works out at River Ranch."

"OK, that makes sense. Clears it all up too. A couple of months ago I lent a copy of that study to the fellow who bought River Ranch from that architect, Jack Warneke. He gave it back, too."

"You sure Ukiah isn't building one of those things?" Lenny asked.

"As sure as we're sitting here having some holiday cheer. If you don't believe me, call my counterpart up in Ukiah. His name's Al Friendly. And he's as friendly as his name. Can't forget that, can you, so I won't have to write it down. Now tell me, how did you get that god-awful scar? Were you in the war, like me?"

"You mean Vietnam? No Canada stayed out of that one, thank God. Were you there?"

Abner Root had been there for two full years. So, between his war stories and Lenny's hockey stories, they spent a pleasant evening together.

At eight the next morning, Lenny called Al Friendly from his motel. He introduced himself as a civil engineer looking for work. He'd heard that Ukiah was soon going to be building a Materials Recycling Facility, and thought he'd inquire if there might be any job openings.

Abner Root had been right. Friendly was very friendly. But he was afraid that Lenny had gotten some false information. Sure, they had done a pilot study. But no MRF was being built in Ukiah. Why? Way too expensive for a small city like Ukiah. Maybe sometime down the road they'd build one in cooperation with some other small cities like Healdsburg and Cloverdale.

By the time he hung up, Lenny's mind was working overtime. If Ukiah was a scam—and there could be no doubt now that it was—it bore a remarkable resemblance to the scam he

■

had worked together with Sid Ravitch and that other guy. The only real difference was that, in his case, instead of no MRF there had been no gold bullion. The paper he and Willy had issued based on these "assets" was, however, exactly the same. Worthless.

Then his mind skipped back to the conversation at the bar the prior evening. To a name—Jack Warneke, the guy that Abner Root said had sold River Ranch to Willy. Where had he heard that name before? Or seen?

"Jeezus H. Christ!" Lenny said. "Abner said he was an architect."

He went to one of his suitcases and scrambled through it until he found what he was looking for, right at the bottom. It was the prospectus which Pam Pederson had sent him, describing the zero coupon bond that would finance the building of Sun River City up in Oregon. He'd gone through it at least a dozen times. The project was based on a city plan developed by a famous architectural firm in San Francisco. He paged through the prospectus until he found the spot. He was right. The firm was Jack Warneke & Associates. The city they intended to build sounded like an ideal place to work and live. In fact, Pam had told him on the phone that if she could, she'd move there in a minute. Once it was finished, of course.

Lenny was already prepared to bet his life that it would not only never be finished. It would never be started. But how to make sure?

He dialed information in San Francisco, and immediately had the number of Jack Warneke & Associates.

He didn't get Jack Warneke, but he did get one of the associates—a very junior one from the sound of his voice. Again Lenny was the civil engineer looking for work and ready to move anywhere if a job was available, even Bend, Oregon, to work on the building of Sun River City.

Same response.

No Sun River City either.

■

Ten minutes later, Lenny was in his car headed toward San Francisco. By nine-thirty, he was sitting in the office of Sid Ravitch, talking a blue streak. During the next half hour, Ravitch did not interrupt him even once.

■

FORTY-FOUR

By this time it was seven in the evening in St. Moritz, and everybody was still down in the village for an après ski aperitif or hot chocolate—everybody but Werner Guggi and Willy Saxon. They were sitting behind closed doors in the study of the Villa Engadin.

Guggi had finally received the long-awaited fax from his colleague in Bern, and Willy was now sitting behind the desk in the study, reading it.

1900
EXTRADITION TREATY
Concluded 14 May 1900;
ratified by Senate June 5, 1900;
signed by President February 25, 1901;
ratified by Switzerland, January 21, 1901;
proclaimed February 28, 1901.

ARTICLES

I. Delivery of accused.
II. Extraditable crimes.
III. Attempts to commit extraditable crimes.
IV. Special Court

V. Procedure
VI. Provisional Detention
VII. Political Offenses
VIII. Limitations

■

ARTICLE I

The government of the United States of America and the Swiss Federal Council bind themselves mutually to surrender such persons as, being charged with or convicted of the crimes enumerated hereafter in Article II, committed in the territory of one of the contracting States, shall be found in the territory of the other State: Provided that this shall be done by the United States only upon evidence of criminality as, according to the laws of the place where the fugitive or person shall be found, would justify his apprehension and commitment for trial if the crime or offense had been there committed.

ARTICLE II

Extradition shall be granted for the following crimes and offenses, provided they are punishable both under the laws of the place of refuge and under those of the State making the requisition, to wit:

1. Murder, including assassination, paracide, infanticide and poisoning; voluntary manslaughter.

2. Arson.

3. Robbery; burglary; house-breaking or shop-breaking.

4. The counterfeiting or forgery of public or private instruments; the fraudulent use of counterfeited or forged instruments.

■

5. *The forgery, counterfeiting or alteration of coin, paper-money, public bonds and coupons thereof, bank notes, obligations, or other certificates or instruments of credit; the emission or circulation of such instruments of credit, with fraudulent intent.*

6. *Embezzlement by public officials.*

7. *Fraud or breach of trust, committed by a fiduciary, attorney, banker, administrator of the estate of a third party, or by the president, a member or an officer of a corporation or association, when the loss involved exceeds 1000 francs.*

8. *Perjury; subornation of perjury.*

9. *Abduction; rape; kidnapping of minors; bigamy.*

10. *Wilful and unlawful destruction or obstruction of railroads, endangering human life.*

11. *Piracy.*

Willy stopped reading at this point. Guggi just sat there on the sofa, saying nothing.

"At least they can't get me on murder, arson, piracy, rape, or wilful destruction of any railroads," Willy said. "But the rest?" He sighed. "I guess four out of ten's not *that* bad."

His attorney finally spoke up.

"I don't know what you're talking about exactly, Willy. We can get into it later if it becomes necessary. As I understood it, all you're looking for is insurance at this point."

"That's right."

The phone rang. Willy decided to ignore it. After the third ring it stopped. Almost immediately, there was a knock on the study door.

"Yes?" Willy said.

The door opened ever so slightly. It was Vreni, the housekeeper. "Phone call for you, Mr. Saxon," she said, "from San Francisco. It's a man."

He picked up the phone.

"Hi Willy, it's Sid Ravitch. Remember me?"

"Very funny, Sid. I assume you've got a good reason for calling."

"I'll get to that in a minute. I know you're on vacation, Willy, but something came up that I thought you would want to hear about sooner rather than later. By the way, I got your number from Dan Prescott, which shows that it always pays to stay in touch."

"Get to the point, Sid."

"In a minute. But before I do I should tell you that I've got a mutual friend right here with me in my office. Lenny Newsom."

"He's out?"

"Yes. He's paid his debt to society."

"Give him my best wishes," Willy said.

"I will. And I'm sure it will make his day."

Willy did not like the way this conversation was developing.

"Sid," he said, "either get to the point or get off the phone."

"If you insist."

"I do."

"OK. I know all about Ukiah. How I let you con me into signing off on that rating is beyond me. The point is I now know that no Materials Recycling Facility is being built by Ukiah. It was a phantom project created by you for the sole purpose of stealing money through the issue of twenty million dollars of phony zero coupon bonds. I even know where you put it all together—at the River Ranch outside of Healdsburg, with the help, of course, of your buddy Frank Lipper. By the way, it was very clever of you to have him get an office here. No wonder they call you Slick Willy."

Willy chose to remain silent.

"Which brings me to Sun River City. What a beautiful

■

Paul Erdman

concept! And what a wonderful prospectus! A thing of beauty. Where did you flog those bonds, Willy? And what happened to the hundred million dollars? I hope it is still intact, because I'm going to want some of it."

Ravitch paused.

"I was hoping you'd ask how much, Willy. But since you didn't, I'll just tell you. I want half of the twenty million, half of the hundred million, plus the return of that half of my company that your phony company in London bought."

Willy decided that enough was enough.

"Gee, Sid," he said. "Why not take one of my balls, too?"

"Why just one? I've got you by both balls, my friend, so unless you want to go back to the slammer for the rest of your life, don't *ever* get smartass with me again. Hear?"

"Look, Sid," Willy said, fighting to stay calm, "you're catching me completely by surprise. One question. Who besides you knows this?"

"Just Lenny. Nobody else."

"Keep it that way."

"Willy, watch it! I give the orders now, not you. OK? Anyway, why should I tell anybody else? Unless you turn out to be a much dumber fuck than I think you are."

"Look, Sid," Willy said. "There's no use us talking any more right now. I've got some thinking to do."

"I understand. But I'm not a patient man. I'm giving you thirty days, my friend. Thirty days. No extensions. And lest you get too clever and think that this is a bluff, consider this. In the worst case scenario, after I turn you over to the D.A., I'll at the very least get back control of my company, and keep the ten million you paid me to boot."

"You're forgetting one little thing—my friend," Willy said. "Yet another thing of beauty."

"What the fuck are you talking about?"

"A third prospectus. The one you put together for Lenny. The one that I now have a copy of. The one that can put *you*

294

into the place that Lenny and I just got out of. What I'm telling you, Sid, is that if I go down, I'll make sure you go down with me. You could probably use a few years rest. I sense from this conversation that you've lost touch with reality."

"I really don't have the faintest idea what you're talking about," Ravitch said. "Who told you a fairy tale like that?"

"You know damn well who," Willy said. And the moment he said it he knew he was making a mistake.

"Surely you're not referring to Lenny?" Ravitch said.

Willy didn't answer.

"Reality, my friend," Ravitch said, "is that Lenny now works for me. In other words, Willy, you are now up that famous creek without a paddle. The paddle belongs to me. So no more threats, hear?"

Willy said nothing.

"You know where to reach me, Willy," Ravitch said. "From now on I won't be calling you—you call me. Understood? And remember—thirty days."

With that, Sid Ravitch hung up. Willy had no choice but to do the same. Then he just sat there, motionless, his eyes squinting, deep in thought.

Finally Werner Guggi broke the painful silence. "I couldn't help but overhear that conversation," he said. "I should have left the room. I apologize."

It took a while before Willy responded. "No need for apologies, Werner," he said. "In fact, I'm afraid that you are exactly the right man in the right place. The need for that insurance policy has just become acute."

"You're talking about seeking safe haven here in Switzerland."

"Right. Like Marc Rich did. Tell me, how does he get away with it? In the States they say he made off with at least a billion dollars. He's charged with fraud, tax evasion, racketeering, even trading with the enemy—specifically, Iran. In other

■

words, according to what I have just been reading, he's about as extraditable as one can get. Yet, as far as I know, he and his family have been living comfortably in Switzerland ever since he fled New York over ten years ago. How did *he* do it?"

"Easy. He transferred his business to the canton of Zug. Rich controls one of the largest commodity trading operations on earth. They have a turnover that runs to billions of dollars a month. In the process, he makes hundreds of millions of dollars in profits. On this he pays taxes in one place only—the canton of Zug. Marc Rich is by far and away its biggest taxpayer. Do you think the authorities there would ever let him be extradited back to the United States?"

"But what about this treaty?"

"The authorities in Zug say that none of Switzerland's extradition treaties list tax evasion as an extraditable offense, which is true, since tax evasion is not considered a crime in Switzerland. They also claim that the trading with the enemy thing is political and therefore also outside of the scope of such treaties, which is also true. The other charges, they go on to say, devolve from these two primary charges, and are therefore likewise not grounds for extradition. All this is, of course, just an exercise in sophistry. Rich simply bought them."

"So maybe we could follow his example," Willy said.

"I'll be blunt, Willy. In this country, especially in Zug, the eleven million dollars you've got left won't get you very far."

At this point there was suddenly a lot of noise coming from the living room next door. The gang had obviously just got back from town. Then there was another knock on the door. It was again Vreni.

"Excuse me, Mr. Saxon, but they asked me to tell you that Urs Bauer is safely back from Germany. They met him at the little airport in Samedan. That's why they're so late getting back. But don't worry, I'll have dinner ready in half an hour."

"Thanks, Vreni. Maybe I'll skip dinner tonight. Tell them to go ahead without me."

■

The housekeeper looked at him rather carefully, and then withdrew.

Willy turned his attention back to Guggi. "Don't let me keep you from enjoying the evening, Werner. It's just that I've lost my appetite. Go ahead, join the rest of them."

"Not yet, if you don't mind," Guggi said. "I might be able to revive your appetite—if my memory serves me correctly."

"How?"

"Let's go back a bit. If you recall, we first met in February of 1985. We had dinner in Vaduz, at the Gasthof zum Sternen. One of the first things you told me was that you knew Switzerland reasonably well, since you had studied at the university in Zurich for a few semesters. Remember?"

"Vaguely."

"I remember very clearly. Then you mentioned that the main reason why you chose the University of Zurich was that your mother was Swiss. She is, isn't she?"

"She was. She died five years ago."

"Sorry," Guggi said, but then he immediately plunged on. "Now I want you to think back very carefully, Willy. Did your mother ever register you with a Swiss consulate?"

"Yes."

"Where?"

"The consulate in San Francisco."

"You're absolutely sure of that?"

"Positive. I had to go with her. The consul general handled it personally. I remember sitting in his office. He was very stiff, very formal. Smoked a pipe."

"All right. Under Swiss law, then, you are Swiss. Do you remember the canton your mother came from?"

"Why?"

"Because in Switzerland your citizenship is registered in the canton of your birth, or in your case, the canton of your mother's birth."

"It was Aarau."

■

"That's all I have to know, Willy. You are literally home free."

"Explain."

"Go back to the treaty. I read it twice before giving it to you, but I don't recall the exact page I want you to now look at. Just go to the section under the heading "Limitations." I think it was Section Eight."

Willy did as told, and then read the text of Section VIII aloud. It consisted of a single sentence.

SECTION VIII

Neither of the two governments shall be required to surrender its own citizens.

"Can't be any clearer than that, can it?" Guggi said.

"You mean I cannot be extradited by the United States? Period?"

"Period. End of story."

"But I'm also an American," Willy said.

"In Switzerland's eyes, you're Swiss, Willy. That's all that counts here. First thing tomorrow morning I'll phone a colleague in Aarau and have him get an official excerpt from the canton's registry—just in case something comes up unexpectedly. With that in hand, I, as your attorney, can guarantee that no American authority will be able to get at you. Ever."

"I'll be damned," Willy said. "I'll be damned. If I would have known that I could have saved myself three years and one day in the slammer." Then he added a word. "Maybe."

"Got your appetite back?" Guggi asked.

"And how. Let's get out of here and join the rest of the gang. Otherwise they're going to start wondering what's going on."

Urs Bauer came up to Willy the moment they stepped into the living room. He was flushed with excitement.

■

"I want to tell you what happened right away, Mr. Saxon," he said, "if you now have time."

"I'm all yours, Urs," Willy said.

"I think Fred Fitch and his colleagues would like to listen in, too," Urs said. "And so would Frank."

The other men were all sitting in front of the fireplace.

"OK. Let's join them by the fire. Am I wrong or is it getting cold in here?"

"You're right. The wind is starting to howl out there. The landing tonight was pretty rough," Urs said.

"What kind of plane did you have?"

"An old Lear jet," Urs said.

"Better you than me," Willy said.

Then Urs explained. He had met with the chief foreign exchange dealer of the Bundesbank in his hotel room at the Frankfurterhof. They had known and traded with each other for ten years. The man said that he had never seen such turmoil in that bank. He and most of the other people there believed what *Der Spiegel* said. If it's true, he told me, it was a foregone conclusion that the central bank's president was going to resign. Nobody knew who would then succeed him. In the meantime everything had been put on hold. All official intervention in the credit markets had effectively come to a halt. All foreign exchange trading by the German central bank had stopped.

"The paralysis of the Bundesbank," Urs explained, "has gone unnoticed so far, since, as I explained to you last night, Mr. Saxon, all the financial markets and institutions in Germany are essentially closed down until January second."

"What's going to happen then?"

"In my opinion, and his, all hell is going to break loose. Germany will be in the biggest economic and political crisis it has faced since World War Two, as a result of the forced resignation of the Chancellor. It's like what happened to America when Nixon had to resign. But on top of that, just when a very sure, steady hand would be necessary at the Bundesbank to calm the financial markets when they open, there's going to be a vacuum at the top there. So things could very easily start to spin out of control."

"Which means?"

"A capital flight from Germany. Investors controlling tens of billions of marks will seek a safe haven elsewhere."

"Where?"

"The United States, primarily. Which means a flight from the mark into the dollar. Also gold, maybe."

"Why gold, maybe?" Willy asked.

"If a run starts on the DM it will probably spread to what was Europe's hard currency bloc—one that included Belgium and the Netherlands. To protect their own currencies, the central banks there might sell gold to raise dollars, which they would then deploy in the foreign exchange markets in an attempt to keep their currencies from collapsing. Both countries have done it before. That would stop, or at least slow, any rise in the gold price, and the speculators would then turn their full attention to the dollar/DM relationship."

"So what do you propose we do about all this?" Willy asked.

"Sell DM against dollars in the forward markets. I've already started. But it is not easy. I tried to get off as much as I could with the big American banks in New York. But the market is simply not there. A lot of the foreign exchange departments in those banks have in essence closed their books for the year, and their dealers don't want do any big trades that might queer their year-end results. The branches of the big European banks in New York won't trade much either, since their parent banks over here are closed for the holidays."

"So you were stymied."

"I *was* stymied. Until Fred here found me a way out," Urs said. "I'll explain. When I do forward currency transactions, normally it is always with banks. And I do it on credit. With

■

our new balance sheet, I've been able to open up large credit lines—usually fifty million dollars—with a half dozen banks, including Chase and Citibank in New York, and the Deutsche Bank in Frankfurt. But for the reasons I've already explained, they won't enter into any big DM trades until the new year. When I told Fred this same story on the way back from the airport, he said the only place in the world that was able and willing to handle big volume in DM today and tomorrow was the Mercantile Exchange in Chicago. And that's why I wanted to talk to you right away, Mr. Saxon."

"What do you and Fred want to do?" Willy asked.

"Bypass the banks by going to the options market in Chicago. The problem there is that we have to go through a broker, like Merrill Lynch. Fred has credit lines with them, but at present, because of the volume of business he's been doing, they're all used up. So now they'll want cash as protection. In fact, they won't even make the slightest move until they have the cash literally in hand."

"How much are we talking about?"

"It depends on how far you are ready to go against the DM."

Willy saw a way out. Maybe.

"It depends on how much we could potentially make in thirty days."

"What would be your target?"

"One hundred twenty million dollars." Willy said.

That was a show stopper. Every face in the room registered shock, except one—that of Fred Fitch, the chief derivatives geek.

"Let's figure that out," he said. "We'd be buying March DM puts—March because there's no liquidity for February puts, and we're talking big numbers. But we can cash out any time we want between now and then. One contract costs $1,250. Ten thousand contracts cost $12.5 million. The DM is now at 1.7250 to the dollar, or seen from the other side, one

■

DM is worth just under fifty-eight American cents. We could probably start buying at a striking price of fifty-eight cents even. If the DM goes down, say, ten pfennig to 1.8250 to the dollar within thirty days, we would make . . . hold on a minute."

He punched some numbers into the pocket calculator he had conjured up.

"We could make roughly thirty million dollars. So, to make one hundred twenty million, we'd have to buy forty thousand contracts. Which would require fifty million dollars."

"Cash?" Willy asked.

"Cash," Fred said.

"And if all these rumors prove false, and the DM goes up instead of down?" Frank Lipper asked, speaking for the first time.

"Well, we could very well lose it all," Fred said. "That's what makes dealing in derivatives so much fun."

That produced a brief lull.

Urs Bauer broke the silence. "There's another problem," he said. "We've only got very little time to work—the rest of today, tomorrow, and part of the next day, which is New Year's Eve, when everybody will be going home early. After that, when the holidays are over, the forward trading between banks will be back in full swing. That run out of the DM could very well start right in earnest at the very beginning of trading, pushing the mark straight down. And we would then have missed the boat."

"What time is it in Chicago?" Willy asked.

"Twelve-thirty in the afternoon," Fred said.

Vreni came out of the kitchen and announced that dinner was ready.

"You all go eat," Willy said. "I'm going to think."

"Do you need me," Guggi asked.

"Not this time," Willy said, as he disappeared into the study.

■

FORTY-FIVE

It was decision time for Willy Saxon.

The situation had reduced itself to very few options. Willy decided to write them down. He pulled open the desk drawer and took out a pen and a single piece of paper.

1. Do a Marc Rich. Stay in Switzerland. Transfer the River Ranch operation to Zug.

There were problems with that.

To start the River Ranch operation over here from scratch, he would need capital—a lot more than the eleven million dollars that was still left from his original stash in Liechtenstein. The rest of his money was stuck inside Prescott & Quackenbush. He could try to raid it, but it wouldn't be easy and it would certainly take time. In the meantime that maniac Ravitch might blow the whistle, Prescott & Quackenbush would be immediately taken over by the authorities, and all his assets in the United States would be frozen instantaneously by court order.

Bad idea.

2. Stay in Switzerland. Live off the $11 million. Abandon everything in the United States.

■

That was an even worse idea. How could he abandon all these young people who were knocking themselves out for him? Or worse—who looked up to him? And what would he do with the rest of his life in Switzerland?

3. Cut a deal with Sid Ravitch.

This would mean giving him half of everything he owned. That he could live with. Having Sid Ravitch calling the shots from now on—that he definitely could *not* live with. Anyway, even if he did cut a deal with Ravitch, there was no guarantee that that would be the end of it. Denise's phone call had changed that.

4. Go for it. Bet the ranch.

Provided he could come up with that one hundred twenty million dollars in thirty days, he knew exactly what to do next. He would still need some help from Denise, but not even that much. He would also need some help from Sara—and right away. He had sworn never to do it. But . . .

■

FORTY-SIX

They were all sitting at the kitchen table when Willy walked in.

"We're going for it," he announced. The words produced a buzz of excitement around the table.

"When?" Urs asked.

"Now."

"Where is the cash going to come from?"

"How much cash can you raise if you totally liquidate our position in those DM inverse floaters?" Willy asked Fred Fitch.

Fred had the answer immediately. "A little over fifteen million."

"How long would it take you?"

"Maybe ten phone calls. Say, half an hour."

"Do it."

"Are you sure? We've made a ton of money so far on that position," Fred said.

"If Urs is right—and I'm totally convinced he is—those floaters will sink like a rock," Willy answered. "They go up when interest rates go down, only they do so in a highly exaggerated way. Right?"

"Right," Fred said.

"If a run on the DM starts, what will be the first move that

■

305

the Bundesbank will have to make to try to stop it?" This time Willy addressed his question to Urs Bauer.

Urs answered. "First, they'll start to sell dollars and buy marks—to counteract what we and everybody else will be doing."

"And then?"

"They'll put short-term German interest rates way up."

"Why?" The question came from Sara who, like the rest of the women, had so far been following all this in silence.

"To entice investors to stay in Germany and the mark. If the Bundesbank makes it possible to earn ten percent, maybe fifteen percent on three-month DM CDs in Germany, when you can only get three percent on dollar CDs in New York, it will make a lot of people think twice."

"It will also cause DM inverse floaters to fall out of bed," Willy said.

"Got it," Sara said.

"I'll get right on the phone," Fred said.

"Hold on. We put a lot of other people—like Marshall Lane—into those DM inverse floaters. We'll want to warn them about what might happen. Are you able to do that from here?"

"Easily. Each of us brought a Mac PowerBook along. In their memories, we've got all the information we need—names, addresses, phone and fax numbers, how much we sold to whom, when, and at what price. But I think we should liquidate *our* position first. *Then* I call them. OK?" Fred said.

"Of course," Willy said. "But there's one other thing. Some of those same clients have our Index Currency Option Notes. Tell them to hang on to them for dear life. *They* are going to go through the roof."

"May we use your study, Mr. Saxon?" Fred said.

"It's all yours."

Fred and his two colleagues all got up and left the room.

"What time is it now in Chicago?" Willy asked Urs.

■

"Going on one o'clock in the afternoon," he replied.

"Do you think we can still accumulate our first ten thousand contracts before they close down there?"

"It will be a close call, but I think we can just make it," Urs answered. "Fred can hardly clear all those sales of the inverse floaters today, so it's going to take some fast talking to convince the broker that handles the purchase of those DM puts for us that he's covered. So I'd better get on the phone, too."

Urs got up from the table and started to leave the kitchen.

Then he turned back to Willy. "Are we still talking forty thousand contracts?"

"We are," Willy answered.

"Where are we going to get the cash to buy the rest of them?"

"I've got an idea, which I'll explain later. But first, let's see how you guys do on the first round. In the meantime, let's eat. I'm suddenly hungry as a bear. What's on the menu?"

"Fondue Bourguignonne," Sara said. "In fact, we've all been waiting for the oil to get hot. Come, Willy, sit down beside me. I'll do it for you."

"First let me test it, Miss Sara," Vreni said.

She took a long fork, speared a small piece of beef from a mound in a huge wooden bowl, and then immersed it in the oil inside one of the six small copper pots sitting atop alcohol burners that were lined up in the middle of the kitchen table. After five seconds she withdrew the fork and looked at the meat.

"Perfect," she said. "So we better turn down the burners and keep the temperature exactly where it is."

"Dive in," Sara said, as she began to pass the bowl full of beef chunks around the table. The sauces followed, ranging from three types of mustard to pickled mayonnaise to—since most of the people at the table were American—Heinz ketchup.

■

Vreni poured the wine, a dark red Dole from the Valais, starting of course, with Willy.

"Perfect," he said, after trying it.

"I'm really excited about what you're doing, Willy," Sara said. "So is everybody else. I'm sure you can sense it."

"I do. But now I'm going to need your help, Sara."

"Tell me what you need and I'll try my best to do it."

"It will need not just your help, but also that of your late husband's company. How much influence do you have there?"

"I really don't know. I never tried to ever exercise any influence."

"But you do own what is in essence a controlling interest in Homestake Mining?"

"Yes."

"I think you've heard enough to understand our problem. We have to raise another forty million dollars in cash within twenty-four hours. No commercial bank in the world could act that fast even if they considered us good for that amount—which is highly unlikely once they found out what we intended to do with it."

"I agree. So much about banks I know, Willy," Sara said.

"Homestake Mining is as cash-rich a corporation as there is in the United States. On top of that, when the gold price shoots up as a result of everything that's going to happen, it will have almost unlimited credit at its disposal."

"For a while I thought you thought gold would go down," she said.

"I changed my mind."

"Then why not invest in gold too?"

"Because DM puts are even better."

"All right. I'm sorry. I got you off the track. You were talking about Homestake having almost unlimited credit at its disposal."

"Yes. And I would like to 'borrow' some of that credit for thirty days."

"Can you do that?"

"Yes, it's a new technique. You source the credit away. For a price, of course."

"But who at Homestake would understand this?"

"Your treasurer. Otherwise, Frank Lipper can bring him up to speed fast. I asked him to look into this a few months ago."

"Well," Sara said, "I can sure try. But how in the world could it be done within twenty-four hours?"

"We'd all have to meet in Chicago tomorrow. By noon."

"How could we get there that fast?"

"Do you want to try to do it?"

"Damn right," said the bishop's daughter.

"Susie," Willy then called down the table.

"Yes, Mr. Saxon," she answered.

"Do you know where Urs got that Lear Jet?"

"Yes. Alpine Aviation in Geneva."

"Do you think it's still here?"

"I think so. As far as I know they won't fly either in or out of this valley at night. It's too dangerous. But I'll call them to make sure.

"Please do. And if it's still here, tell them to hold it for me. We'll be taking it to Geneva—or Zurich—at dawn tomorrow. Hold on a minute," Willy said.

He then called down the table to Werner Guggi. "Werner, does Swissair fly directly to Chicago?"

"Yes. Leaves at eight every morning from Zurich."

"What time does it get there?"

"I forget exactly. Either ten or eleven in the morning, Chicago time."

"Perfect. Do you think we could get four seats on it tomorrow?

"You're not going to Chicago, surely?" the attorney said.

■

"I am. And now that I think about it, so are you. Make it five seats."

He turned back to Susie. "Tell them we'll be five, leaving Samedan at six for Kloten airport in Zurich."

Now she left the kitchen, as did Werner Guggi.

"Getting empty in here," Sara said. "I guess it's going to be my turn next."

"If you don't mind."

"It's eleven-thirty in the morning in San Francisco, so chances are that our treasurer will be in his office."

"Frank and I will go on the phone with you, Sara, so don't worry about having to explain any technical details."

"I couldn't even if I wanted to," she answered.

"I've just got another idea. I'm sure the first thing your treasurer is going to ask about is what kind of collateral we will be able to put up."

"I know enough about finance to understand that," Sara said. "What collateral can you offer him?"

"There's a holding company in Zug that owns ninety-five percent of the outstanding shares of Prescott and Quackenbush. That investment bank currently has a net worth well in excess of one hundred fifty million dollars. Werner Guggi, who just left the room, has those shares in his vault in Liechtenstein. He'll call over there as soon as I explain all this to him, to make sure that someone from his office hand-delivers those shares at Kloten airport before the plane leaves for Chicago."

"Willy," Sara said. "You've got a mind like a steel trap. That's why you're always such fun to be around. Now let's go and make that phone call to San Francisco before everybody there goes to lunch."

■

FORTY-SEVEN

Swissair flight 37 landed at O'Hare airport in Chicago exactly on time the next morning.

The treasurer of Homestake Mining, accompanied by his attorney, was there to greet them. So was Bobby Armacost. Willy had gotten hold of Bobby at noon, California time, the prior day, to get him to draft the basic contract setting up the credit arrangement between Prescott & Quackenbush and Homestake Mining. All three had come out together in Homestake's corporate jet, working all the way. They had agreed that Willy's idea about "sourcing the credit away" was too complicated. Homestake would agree to simply lend the forty million dollars for thirty days, provided it was fully collateralized. When Werner Guggi handed over the shares of Prescott & Quackenbush that would serve as collateral for the arrangement, both parties—with Frank Lipper representing the investment bank—and their attorneys attached their signatures to the documents in the Swissair lounge at the airport.

They then climbed into two waiting stretch limousines and headed downtown. The Merrill Lynch people were ready to go as soon as they walked into their offices, in the same building as the Mercantile Exchange on South Wacker. So was a senior vice president of Continental Bank. He had been alerted by a phone call from Homestake's jet to be there at one o'clock with a cashier's check in the amount of forty million

■

dollars. That barely made a dent in the credit line that Homestake had with that Chicago bank. The check was handed over to Merrill Lynch at 1:15 p.m. It was cashed five minutes later. At 1:30 p.m. on that second to last day of the year, Fred Fitch was able to go back into the market buying March DM puts. Urs Bauer stayed at his side. The rest of them went down to South Wacker and got back into their limousines, which took them to the Ritz Carlton hotel, where nine suites had been reserved.

The first thousand March 58 DM puts traded at 100. But then the cost started to inch up. On the second thousand, it was 105. On the third it was 107.

"Hit it harder," Fred said to Alex Trzesniewski, Merrill Lynch's chief trader, known to be the very best in the business.

On the next trade, Alex bought 5,000 more contracts at 115.

"The word's getting out," he said.

"Or maybe some more people are starting to catch on to the meaning of what's happening in Germany," Fred said. "Hit it still harder, Alex."

By the closing they had bought another 30,000 DM puts, raising the grand total to 40,000.

Willy, Frank, Werner Guggi, Bobby Armacost, and Sara were waiting for them in the bar of the hotel's lobby on the eleventh floor.

"How did you do?" Willy immediately asked them.

"We are now short five billion German marks," Urs said.

"Holy Mother of God," Bobby Armacost exclaimed. "I sure hope you know what you're doing, Willy."

"It's all in the hands of the Germans now," Willy responded.

"Urs," he then said, "What time is it in Germany?"

"It's one o'clock in the morning, and, since tomorrow's New Year's Eve, I'm sure everybody in the country went to bed early."

"I hope a couple of them are still up worrying," Guggi said.

■

"What's going to happen next over there?" Willy asked.

"Hard to say," Guggi said, "but my guess is this. It's a tradition in Germany that on New Year's Day the President of Germany—not to be confused with the Chancellor—always addresses the German people by radio and television. According to the German constitution, if a Chancellor resigns, it is to the President that he must submit his resignation. The President would have to announce it and simultaneously call for an emergency meeting of the German parliament. When parliament meets, the government would then have no choice but to resign en masse, which would mean a national election. This has never happened before in Germany. So there's no way the President could allow a thing like this to drag on."

"And if *Der Spiegel* was full of baloney and nobody resigns?" Bobby Armacost asked.

"Then the President would reaffirm his confidence in the Chancellor and his government and tell the German people that in the New Year they can go back to business as usual," Guggi answered.

"And we would have a big problem," Bobby Armacost said.

Bigger than you think, Willy thought.

■

FORTY-EIGHT

The next morning—New Year's Eve, which that year fell on a Saturday—they all left the hotel at seven. The Homestake jet was waiting for them at O'Hare. The only one who did not board was Werner Guggi. He was taking the noon Swissair flight back to Zurich.

Guggi's last words to Willy were: "A final word of advice. If this does go wrong, I sense that whatever it is that has you so worried will follow like night follows day. Then get out right away, Willy. Don't even wait for a scheduled airline. Hire a private jet and head directly for Switzerland."

These warning words punctured the mood of euphoria that Willy had been in. By going against the German mark, he was essentially taking on the Bundesbank—which was the second most powerful financial institution on earth, outranked only by the Federal Reserve. All logic dictated that he didn't really have a chance. Nor, then, would his faithful friend, Frank Lipper.

"Sit with me, Frank," Willy said to him as they were boarding. "I've got a few things I must tell you."

After they had leveled out at thirty-two thousand feet, and everybody else appeared settled in and talking to each other, Willy leaned close to Frank.

"Sid Ravitch knows everything," he said.

"How do you know?"

■

"He called me the night before last, in St. Moritz."

"How did he find out?"

"Somehow he got hold of the Sun River City prospectus. Then he must have worked his way back to Ukiah."

"What's he want?"

"Half of everything."

"I thought you had something on him?"

"I did. He was involved in a gold scam. But the only link between Ravitch and that scam is a guy I met in prison. His name's Lenny Newsom. He just got out, and Ravitch appears to have a lock on him. He was in Ravitch's office when he called me."

"But how in the world did Ravitch get hold of that Sun River City prospectus? Only four guys in New York got it. There's not even a copy of it at our San Francisco office."

"The only explanation I've been able to come up with is that it was an inside job. Ravitch must have gotten to somebody at River Ranch. He knows we put it together there. He even knows about your involvement."

"Who? Even the geeks were kept out of it."

"It doesn't really matter now," Willy said.

"Maybe it does," Frank said. "I know. The printer in Healdsburg. Remember how years ago some printer in New York who did prospectuses got caught using the advance information for insider trading?"

"That was New York. We're talking Healdsburg," Willy said.

"You've got a point," Frank said, "but who else was in on this?"

He thought for a while.

"Pam Pederson," he then said. "She was the only girl I used. She typed it. She delivered it to the printer."

"Come on, Frank," Willy said. "There's no way she could be in cahoots with Sid Ravitch. Unless she's the world's greatest actress."

■

"There's no other answer," Frank said.

"Maybe. But like I said, it doesn't really matter now."

"So what's the game plan?"

"There's something else you've got to know about. Remember Ralph Goodman, the prick who runs the state banking commission?"

"Sure. He testified against you."

"He's apparently starting to nose around."

"How far's he gotten?"

"Not very. But the game plan has to take account of him, too."

"So what's the plan?"

Willy told him.

When he was done, the first question Frank asked was: "How do we take care of Ravitch?"

"We get to Lenny."

"How?"

"I haven't figured that out yet," Willy said.

"How they got ahold of our stuff still bugs me," Frank said. "It's got to be Pam Pederson."

"Then I'll have a word with Sara. She can talk to her next week," Willy said. "Maybe if it's just between girls, Pam—assuming it was Pam—will 'fess up."

After they landed in San Francisco, they said their good-byes to the Homestake men. Sara decided to go home for a change of clothes and a rest. Bobby Armacost said his wife was waiting for him. The remaining six men went directly to River Ranch. They intended to wait there, together, to see what would happen next in Germany.

On the way, Urs Bauer explained that the German president's New Year's Day address was carried by every TV channel in Germany, and was always delivered from his residence in the Villa Hammerschmidt, outside of Bonn, at ten in the morning. That translated into 1 a.m. California time. Urs

■

even knew how to tune it in. The programs of German Public Television, known as the *Deutsche Welle,* were carried world-wide by satellite and could be seen in the United States on Satcom F 4, Transponder 5.

One thing River Ranch had enough of was satellite dishes.

The first thing Willy did after he was back at the ranch was to call Denise van Bercham as he had promised. She was bubbling over with the latest news.

"I just heard today, Willy, that I will officially become the Chief of Protocol of the City of San Francisco on January first. Isn't that marvelous?"

"Wonderful," Willy replied, trying to sound enthusiastic.

"You must come to my first big function. I'm already starting to plan for it," she continued.

"When will it be?"

"January sixth. It's a reception in the rotunda of City Hall for the President of Brazil and his smashing wife. He's sixty-six and she's twenty-three."

"Oh to be Brazilian!" Willy said.

"You'll come?"

"I'll come if I can," he said.

"How's Sara?" Denise asked.

"Fine. She's at home. Why don't you call her, Denise? I'm sure she'd love to talk to you."

"I will," she said, adding, "You sound a little—well, restrained. Is everything all right?"

"Everything's just fine, Denise," Willy said.

"Remember what I told you last time we talked. If you need me, call. OK?"

"OK. And happy New Year."

After he hung up, Willy suddenly had a thought. He immediately phoned over to Urs Bauer who, he knew, was in the trading room. His wife, Susie, and the rest of the women were first expected back early January 3.

"Are you friendly with some of the local foreign exchange dealers?" he asked.

"Sure. Enrico Riva at Bank of America. Gerry Göhler at Bank of California. And the guy at Wells Fargo."

"Do you have their home phone numbers?"

"I think so."

"Would you mind calling them up and letting them know what you think will happen to the DM at the opening on Monday?"

"Sure. Why not? We've got our position locked in."

"Thanks."

The rest of the day seemed to drag on forever. Finally, night fell, and since Vreni, the cook, was also not back, Willy invited everybody to join him for dinner at Tre Scalini in Healdsburg. He had to do some fast talking with the owner/ chef to get them in. When they returned to the main house at the River Ranch at eleven, Willy broke out the champagne— the "J" champagne of Jordan, as usual.

They were all sitting in front of the TV in the living room, watching a replay of what had happened on Times Square three hours earlier, when midnight arrived. The New Year was greeted with muted cheers.

"You'd better see if you can tune in Germany," Willy said to Urs.

"I've done it many times, Mr. Saxon," the Swiss foreign exchange dealer said. "I just punch F4 on the remote to get the right satellite, and when I get it, punch in a five to get the *Deutsche Welle.*"

"So do it again. Now."

He did, and within seconds they were watching the Vienna Philharmonic playing Strauss waltzes before an enthusiastic audience in Austria's capital.

"You sure you got the right station?" Willy asked.

"Yes," Urs answered. "This is also a New Year's tradition on German TV."

■

"It's probably better than Guy Lombardo," Frank said.

At 12.58 a.m., after the concert had finished with a rousing rendition of "The Blue Danube," the picture faded, and what appeared now was the somber face of a German announcer speaking from the *Deutsche Welle*'s studio in Berlin.

"Meine Damen und Herren, wir schalten zur Villa Hammerschmidt in Bonn."

"They're switching to the President's residence in Bonn," Urs said.

The next picture was that of an elderly man in formal dress, sitting behind an ornate desk. His face was haggard.

"Sehr geehrte Mitbürger, Ich wünche Euch allen ein Gutes Neues Jahr," he said. He then appeared to pause deliberately.

"What did he say?" Willy asked.

"He just wished everybody a Happy New Year," Urs replied. "But here it comes."

"Zu meinem grossen Bedauern muss ich Euch leider mitteilen, dass sich unser Land in einer grossen Krise befindet. Der Bundeskanzler hat vor einer Stunde sein Amt niedergelegt."

Urs was immediately on his feet.

"He resigned! The Chancellor resigned. An hour ago."

The cheer that now went up in the main house on River Ranch was anything but muted. Nor were the hugs that followed.

"We're on our way," Willy said to Frank.

Although it was late, everybody at the River Ranch had trouble falling asleep that night. But it didn't matter. For the next twenty-two hours all the banks and exchanges in both Europe and the United States would remain closed. So everybody slept in late, and then went their separate ways. Frank and Willy played eighteen holes at Fountain Grove, had an early dinner in Santa Rosa, and then decided to take a nap. They knew they would be up all night.

■

FORTY-NINE

By eleven that night they had all gathered together again—
this time in the trading room. The first real action would be
in interbank trading in Europe, especially in London and
Frankfurt. They could follow it on the computer screens in
Urs Bauer's corner of the room.

The initial response that Monday morning in Europe was
not very encouraging. The DM/$ rate opened at 1.74, down
only one and a half pfennig. It seemed that foreign exchange
dealers at the banks there had decided to wait and see.

"What are they waiting for?" Willy asked.

"For the next shoe to drop when the Bundestag, the German parliament, meets in emergency session in two hours.
That will be one a.m., our time."

"Could you call your friend—the one you met in Frankfurt—and try to get an advance reading?" Willy asked.

"I already tried. At the Bundesbank, they say he's in a
meeting and cannot be disturbed. He's got to be very careful."

"So what do we do?"

"Wait and do nothing. Just like everybody else's going to
do," Urs said.

He was soon proven right. During the next two hours the
DM had slipped another half pfennig, but that was all. Trading in Europe had almost come to a halt.

"We're not going to make anything near that one hundred

■

twenty million dollars the way this thing's going," Willy said to Frank, as they walked back to the main house, where they would resume their vigil before the TV set. The rest of the men were right behind them, except for Urs. He had gone ahead to make sure that the satellite link with Germany was working.

As they walked, they passed the spot where the path barely skirted the edge of the cliff, which dropped vertically to the river and rocks below.

"She was right," Willy said.

"Who was right?"

"Susie. She's having a baby, and was worried about this spot."

"Then put up a fence," Frank said.

Once they were all again huddled in front of the big-screen TV in the living room of the main house, Urs Bauer began to give a running commentary on what they were seeing and hearing.

"The emergency meeting of parliament is scheduled to begin in exactly one minute," he said.

At one a.m.—ten a.m. in central Europe—the German TV began broadcasting directly from the parliament building in Bonn.

By 1:15 a.m., the government had officially resigned. At 1:30 it was announced that national elections would be held within thirty days. At 1:45 the leader of the Free Democratic Party, which had been part of the ruling coalition for well over a decade, announced that they now intended to form a coalition with the Socialists. At 2 a.m. the president of the Bundesbank came on the screen. He stated that, on the one hand, he felt betrayed by the Chancellor and his party. On the other hand, he had no intention of serving under a Socialist government. So he was resigning immediately.

At 2:05 a.m., California time—11:05 a.m. German time—the German mark went into free fall.

By now everybody at River Ranch had raced back to the

trading room to again watch the action on the computer screens there.

By 2:10 a.m. in Healdsburg, nine time zones away in Frankfurt the mark was down four pfennig to 178. Four hours later it was trading at 180.50. By now it was nine in the morning on the East Coast of the United States and interbank trading had started in New York.

Within minutes the DM was down another two pfennig. It was at 182.50.

"That's it," Frank said, as he and everybody else watched the numbers change on the computer screens. "We've made it, Willy. Your target was 182.50. We've just made one hundred twenty million dollars."

"Not yet," Fred Fitch said. "It's still an hour before Chicago opens."

Ten minutes later, the DM started to recover.

181.50 . . . 180.50 . . . 179.75.

"What's going on?" Willy asked.

Urs Bauer was on three different phone calls.

"Both the Bundesbank and the New York Fed are intervening," he said. "They say the Bundesbank is buying in marks at a rate that nobody has ever seen before."

"I thought the Bundesbank was paralyzed?"

"Obviously, no longer. They've got an interim president now."

"But why is the Fed intervening?"

"Because the Germans asked for help. Central bankers always stick together. I don't think it's more than a token gesture. This is a German problem, not an American one."

By dawn in California, when two time zones to the east trading in options started on the Mercantile Exchange in Chicago, the mark had recovered to 179. even.

"We're still ahead at least ninety million dollars," Fred told Willy. "Should I start covering in Chicago?"

"No."

■

"But . . ."

"You heard me, Fred," Willy said. "No."

Everybody in the room had also heard Willy. Nobody even dared look at him.

For the next twenty minutes, the mark stabilized at 178.50. Suddenly Fred Fitch, who was also constantly on the phone, yelled out. "Somebody turn on CNBC. Right now."

There was a small TV monitor on Urs Bauer's desk. He switched it on.

Dan Dorfman's face appeared. Another man was sitting next to him in CNBC's New Jersey studio, a dark-haired, dark-complexioned, stocky man wearing glasses.

"Who's he?" Willy asked.

"It's George Soros," somebody replied.

In the trading room at River Ranch everybody now stopped whatever they had been doing and watched. Except Fred Fitch. His eyes stayed glued to the computer screen, which displayed what was happening in Chicago.

"What's going on with the German mark?" Dorfman asked his guest.

"Everything," Soros replied. "And its all bad."

"Why?"

"Because Germany is now the sick man of Europe. They've made a total mess of reunification. Their budget's out of control, as a result. So is the money supply. They've priced themselves out of world markets. Wages there are almost double those in the United States. And now the country's falling apart politically. So something had to give. And it's the German mark."

"So is the mark in the process of going the way sterling did in the fall of 1992?"

"Precisely."

"And what are you doing about it?"

Soros just grinned. "I think you ought to be able to figure that one out, Dan."

■

"In case they can't figure it out, I think I should remind the audience, Mr. Soros, that a lot of people say that you are the man with the Midas touch. You made over a billion dollars speculating against the pound sterling in September of 1992. Right?"

"That's what they say."

"Then you went into gold in the spring of 1993, drove the price up fifty dollars an ounce, and made another bundle."

"They also say that."

"And now you're trying to bring down the German mark?"

"I don't have to. The Germans are doing a very good job of it all by themselves."

"How much further can it drop?"

"A lot. I've heard that the Bundesbank has already lost almost thirty billion dollars in an attempt to stop the hemorrhaging. But all they've done is temporarily stabilized it."

"Temporarily, you said. So it's going to drop further?"

"A lot further."

"Thank you, Mr. Soros."

Ten seconds later Fred Fitch called out again.

"They just started to go absolutely bananas in Chicago."

Urs Bauer's attention now returned to his computer screen, where he could watch what was happening in forward trading all around the globe.

"The same thing's happening in New York."

Every speculator in the world, it seemed, was now getting on the bandwagon. It was as if a huge dam had suddenly burst, unleashing a tidal wave of money, hundreds of billions of dollars, all seeking to make millions, no tens of millions in a few hours, on the collapse of what had once been the world's strongest currency.

It was a rout like nobody had ever seen before.

Within two hours the DM had sunk to 2.01. It was said that during those two hours the men running the Bundesbank had again massively intervened, dumping another thirty billion dollars into the DM spot market on the buy side, in a last-ditch attempt to turn the speculative tide. They failed. They lost it all and the mark kept falling.

Again Fred Fitch approached Willy Saxon. Again he asked the question in a very quiet voice. "Want me to start covering?"

"No," Willy said.

"But soon?"

"Maybe."

Just then everybody in the trading room was distracted. The women had arrived back from Switzerland. They all looked dog-tired.

"Shall I tell them to go home?" Fred Fitch asked Willy.

"You might need some help before long," Willy said.

"Then I'll ask two to stay," Fitch replied.

Frank Lipper was standing beside Willy. "Make sure that Pam Pederson's not one of them," he said.

Fitch did as he was told, and then went back to his vigil in front of the Sun workstation.

Ten minutes later, it was Urs Bauer who yelled out.

"A flash from Frankfurt. It's rumored that the interim head of the Bundesbank has just shot himself."

"Why would he do that?" somebody asked.

"Because it was his duty to save the German mark from collapse, and he failed."

That did it.

A half hour later the DM had sunk to 2.1250 to the dollar.

"Cover," Willy said.

"How much?" Fred asked.

"All of it."

"Sell all forty thousand puts?"

"All of them."

"You've got it, Mr. Saxon."

He had Alex Trzesniewski at Merrill Lynch in Chicago on the phone within five seconds.

■

"Can you sell them all today?" was his immediate question.

"In this madhouse, I could sell twice as many," came the reply.

Now the trading room at River Ranch became as silent as a tomb. Nobody dared say a word. Everybody watched their screen. At one point Fred Fitch had to rush to the bathroom, where he threw up.

Finally, at one p.m., the call they had all been waiting for came through to Fred. He listened and wrote down a number on a note pad.

After he hung up he said just two words. "We're covered."

Nobody dared ask him the next question, even Willy.

"And here's what we made, Mr. Saxon," Fred Fitch said. He tore off the note and handed it to Willy. On it was a dollar sign followed by nine digits:

$501,695,400.

Frank Lipper came over to look.

"A half fucking billion dollars?" he asked.

"That's right," Fred said. "That includes the margin we get back."

"Not bad for a week's work," Willy said to Frank.

Then the two men embraced. Willy was shaking like a leaf.

"Come on, Willy," Frank said. "I'm going to take you home."

■

FIFTY

The first thing Willy did the next morning was call Marshall Lane in New York.

"Willy, it's good to hear from you," Lane said immediately. "You saved our ass on those DM inverse floaters. We dumped them all at a twenty-four percent profit before they fell out of bed. And we're up thirty-six percent on those ICONs of yours. Thanks a lot, pal."

"That's OK Marshall. We're here to please."

"What have you got now? Another good deal I hope?"

"Not too bad a deal. Those zero coupon muni's that you bought—Ukiah and Sun River City?"

"What about them?"

"I want to buy them back. At a premium."

"So soon? Why?"

"Our clients feel we priced them wrong."

"They probably think that with all this money pouring in from Germany that interest rates here are bound to move a lot lower. Right?"

"As usual, Marshall, you're way ahead of me. Let's just say that there's a link between what's happening in the currency markets and this buy-back offer."

"Fair enough. What kind of premium are we talking about?"

■

"It's usually ten percent in cases like this, I'm told. We're offering twenty percent."

"Twenty-five percent and you've got a deal," Lane said.

"Done," said Willy.

"Where do you want the bonds sent?" Lane asked.

"Nowhere. Frank Lipper's coming to New York tomorrow. He'll be in your office at nine tomorrow morning. He'll have a cashier's check with him. When you get the check, you give him the bonds."

"Tell Frank I'll take him to lunch."

"I'll tell him. And Marshall," Willy said, "I'd appreciate it if you'd keep quiet on this. Otherwise it might embarrass me. If the word gets out how badly we misjudged the pricing on these two issues . . ."

"Don't worry. I fully understand. My lips are sealed forever," Lane replied. And Willy knew that they were.

He made three more calls to New York. The response in each case was exactly the same. Nobody in the financial business in New York ever looks a gift horse in the mouth. Besides, they all liked Willy's style.

By noon Frank Lipper was already on the plane to New York.

At the same time, Willy was on the phone with Sara Jones.

"It's Willy," he said as soon as she came on the line. "Are you rested up?"

"I'm totally back in shape. I'll never be able to thank you enough for that trip, Willy. Not just the skiing, but all that excitement in Chicago."

"That's one reason why I called, Sara. Everything worked out. In spades. So Homestake will have its forty million dollars back already tomorrow. Maybe you could call up the treasurer and tell him the good news. After all, you got him into this in the first place."

"I'll call him right way, Willy. But he wasn't worried for one minute. In fact, on the way home from the airport we kept

■

talking about what you had done—and he was especially interested in your views on gold. After all, that's their business."

"So what did you tell him?"

"What you said. That it was going up."

"What did he say?"

"That he might follow your example and buy some gold calls in New York. And I even knew what I was talking about. Finally, for the first time in my life, I understand the difference between puts and calls."

"I hope he followed through," Willy said. "Gold is up almost seventy dollars an ounce."

"I know. I've been watching CNN and CNBC constantly the past two days—from bed. Now what's the other reason you called?"

"We're a little worried about one of the girls who works here at River Ranch. Pam Pederson."

"Really? I got to know Pam rather well in Switzerland. She's a lovely girl. And a fantastic skier."

"Well, we're not sure, but we think she's been leaking inside information to somebody."

"Who?"

"We don't know. But maybe you could find out."

"How?"

"Take her to lunch tomorrow. Find out if she has any fairly new acquaintances. Then we'd at least have something to work on. Would you mind?"

"Of course not. Is she working today?"

"Yes. She's no doubt in the trading room right now."

"I've got the number. I'll call her right away."

"You're a pal, Sara."

"So are you, Willy."

An hour later, Dan Prescott and Bobby Armacost arrived at the River Ranch. Willy had called them first thing that morning to invite them up. He immediately took them into his

■

study and began briefing them on what had happened during the preceding twenty-four hours. He ended up with a description of his phone calls to New York, and the fact that even as they spoke, Frank Lipper was on the way to get back every single zero coupon bond that had been issued by Ukiah and Sun River City and underwritten by Prescott & Quackenbush.

"What do we do with them then?" Prescott asked.

"We burn them."

"When all is finally said and done, where will we stand financially?" Dan Prescott asked.

"We started with one hundred fifty million dollars capital. We now have additional retained earnings of another five hundred million dollars, bringing the total to six hundred fifty million dollars. On those earnings, we are going to have to pay corporate income tax of roughly one third. So there goes one hundred seventy million. We are now buying back those zero coupon bonds at a twenty-five percent premium. Which means that we are going to have to pay twenty-five million dollars to get back and 'retire' those Ukiah bonds, and one hundred twenty-five million dollars to do the same for Sun River City. So there goes another one hundred fifty million. And we have to pay back forty million to Homestake."

"Which means we end up where?"

"As an investment bank with a capital of two hundred ninety million dollars. I'd say, gentlemen, that we are now definitely here to stay."

The two men were almost overcome with relief.

"There is one more item that will have to be taken care of later on," Willy said. "My consulting fee. I figure that ten percent of what we made during the past week will be about right. That's fifty million dollars. But I figure our derivative geeks will make at least that much during the balance of this year. So I think Prescott and Quackenbush will be able to afford it. Any objections?"

There was not even the slightest murmur of dissent.

■

"How are we going to celebrate all this?" Bobby asked.

"We'll find a way," Willy said.

"Maybe we could start on the seventh," Bobby said.

"What's going on then?"

"Denise van Bercham sent both of us an invitation for a big reception she's putting on for the President of Brazil. I assume you'll be coming too."

"Probably."

"Then we can all go on to dinner together. I'll make a reservation at the Fleur de Lys," Bobby said.

There was no sense, Willy thought, in bringing up the subject of Sid Ravitch. He would have to take care of that himself.

■

FIFTY-ONE

The next day Sara Jones came back from lunch at shortly after two. Willy was waiting for her in the main house.

"How did it go?" he immediately asked.

"I'm not sure," Sara answered.

"How did you explain why you wanted to take her to lunch?"

"I started out by telling her that I thought all of us should somehow find a way to thank you for that wonderful ski trip to Switzerland. Like a little surprise party."

"And?"

"She loved the idea. She said she'll talk to the other girls—and guys—and then we'll set a date."

"Then what happened?"

"You suggested I try to find out if she had struck up any new friendships lately."

"And?"

"She has. One. With a hockey player."

"Big help that," Willy said. "What's a hockey player doing in Healdsburg?"

"Apparently he's no longer a hockey player. In fact, I got the impression that he's quite a bit older than Pam. To answer your question, he comes to Healdsburg on a regular basis to buy wines. He's in the food and wine business in Canada. In Toronto."

■

"Hold it right there," Willy said. "I think we've lucked out. There sure as hell can't be many Canadians hanging around Healdsburg. How did she meet him?"

"At the bar of the restaurant where we ate today. Jacob Horner."

"OK. Is his name Lenny?"

Sara looked at Willy in awe. "How in the world could you know that?"

"We were in prison together."

"My Gawd," said the bishop's daughter. "I'm sure Pam doesn't know that."

"Where is he now?"

"She didn't say."

"We've got to find out immediately."

"How?"

"Tell her you want to invite him to the surprise party."

"You're going to have to do better than that, Willy," Sara said.

"OK. Play the worried surrogate mother. Tell her that you didn't like what you'd heard about her Lenny. That you want to check him out. And that she should stay away from him in the meantime."

"That's better. I'll go right over to the trading room and do it."

She was back a half hour later.

"He's staying at the Holiday Inn on Van Ness."

An hour later Frank Lipper called from New York.

"I got them all back," he said immediately.

"Great," Willy said. "Where are you?"

"At Kennedy. I've got a flight back leaving in twenty minutes."

"When you're back, come right to the ranch, Frank. I'm going to need you here tomorrow."

"Will do."

Willy waited until four that afternoon before calling the

■

Holiday Inn on Van Ness in San Francisco. The phone in Lenny Newsom's room rang three times before he answered.

"Hello?" he said.

"Is that you, Lenny?"

"Who's that?"

"Your old pal Willy Saxon."

"What do you want?"

"Nothing really, Lenny. Just to have a little talk with you."

"No dice, Willy. Sid told me to stay away from you."

"That's precisely why I think you should talk to me, Lenny. I think Sid is leading you down the garden path."

"What's that mean?"

"That he used you once—and you went to jail. And that he's about to do it again. Only this time it might not be just jail."

Willy could almost hear Lenny's brain working.

"I guess it can't hurt having a talk. Where?"

"I've got a ranch about an hour north of the city. Up here nobody can see us or disturb us, Lenny."

"How do I get there?"

"I'll give you directions." Willy said. As if he needed to. Lenny had probably been sneaking around the place many times.

"What time?" Lenny then asked.

"How about around five tomorrow afternoon? If you leave at three-thirty it will put you up here just before it gets dark."

"All right. Where can I reach you if I change my mind?"

"My number's 707-433-9057. Got it?"

"Got it."

"See you tomorrow, Lenny."

"Maybe," he said, and hung up.

Willy waited for five minutes before making the next call. It was to Sid Ravitch's direct line at the Western Credit Rating Agency.

"It's Willy," he began, after Ravitch had picked up.

■

"What a pleasant surprise. I said thirty days, and here you are after only, let's see, eight days. Ready to do business?"

"I'm ready."

"When?"

"Let's say tomorrow."

"When?"

"When do you usually leave the office?"

"Five. But for you I might consider leaving early."

"If you leave at four-thirty, that will put you here around six," Willy said.

"Where is here?" Ravitch asked.

"The ranch. I think you've been fully briefed on where it is."

"Maybe. But give me directions anyway."

Willy did, for the second time now in ten minutes.

"Until tomorrow, my friend," Ravitch said when he was done. "And don't plan on playing any more games with me. Hear?"

He hung up.

Willy stayed up until midnight, waiting for the return of Frank Lipper.

"It's showtime tomorrow, Frank," he said, once his friend and he were settled down in front of the fireplace, nightcaps in hand.

"What's that mean?"

Willy explained.

When he was done, Frank asked, "Have you got a gun around here in case something goes radically wrong?"

"Jack left a shotgun and a twenty-two rifle in an upstairs closet."

"Any ammunition?"

"No idea."

"Let's check before we turn in. Otherwise, I'll get some tomorrow in Healdsburg."

■

"But why would Sid even think of killing the golden goose that I represent?" Willy asked.

"Because from everything I've heard about him, he's a mean, vindictive son of a bitch. He's now playing for stakes that he never even dreamed of before. If it looks like the golden goose is getting away, he might just shoot it. That's the American way. Willy."

"Can't argue with that," Willy said.

■

FIFTY-TWO

Lenny arrived at a quarter past five the next day in a dirty Ford. Willy watched it pull up in front of the main house from his vantage point in the living room.

The first big winter storm of the season was coming in from the Pacific and the wind had already begun to pick up. So Willy decided to stay inside and greet Lenny Newsom at the door.

It was an extremely wary Lenny.

"Long time, no see," Willy said.

"Yeah," Lenny said, as he stepped into the house, looking around as he did so.

"We alone, I hope?" he then asked.

"Just the two of us, Lenny. Come on into the living room and warm up. It's starting to get nasty out there. How about a Scotch?"

"No. I'm a beer guy."

"So how about a Molson's?"

"How did you know I drink that?"

"You're Canadian, so it wasn't that hard to figure out. Stay here. I'll get two, so that we can drink to better days."

When he returned, Lenny was still looking—and prowling—around. Willy could see that he could have been a hockey player. Lenny was a big man.

■

"Come on, let's sit down," Willy said, offering Lenny the beer bottle and a glass.

"Don't need the glass, Willy," Lenny said. He took a big slug from the bottle. Then he sat down. He was obviously nervous. "So what do you want to tell me about Sid Ravitch? What's this crap about Sid leading me down the garden path?"

"He's going to screw you out of a lot of money and probably have you killed."

Lenny stared at Willy a long, hard moment.

"You've known him and you've known me. What do you think?"

"Okay, what do you want to know?"

"I'd like to back up a bit. Where did you meet Ravitch in the first place?"

"Toronto," Lenny answered.

"What was he doing in Toronto?"

"He was working for another ratings agency. Moody's."

"I thought he worked out of San Francisco?"

"He did. And one of his special areas was gold-mining companies. He always did Homestake when they came out with some stock or bond issue. Same with the gold mining companies in Colorado and Nevada. So when Moody's had something they had to do for a gold mine in Ontario or Quebec, they brought him East."

"Makes sense. So how did you meet him?"

"I was doing PR for one of the gold mining companies in Northern Ontario, plus acting as an all-around gofer and bodyguard for the president of the company, who, by the way, was bent as hell."

"What kind of PR did you do?"

"Mostly hyping the stock of the company with guys who put out financial newsletters. A whole slew of them are gold bugs, so their newsletters were ideal places to push the stock of gold mines."

■

"How did you get them to do that?"

"Are you kidding? Pay 'em. One of the biggest newsletters of that type is published in Switzerland. We flew the publisher over to Toronto from Zurich on a regular basis. One evening we ended up in the same hotel where Ravitch was staying, the Queen Elizabeth. Moody's had sent him there to work on a new rating for my boss's company. Which made my boss happy as hell, since it was generally known in the industry that if Ravitch came in to do a rating, ten thousand dollars on the side would get you one that was a hell of a lot better than you deserved. No doubt that's why Moody's eventually got rid of him. Anyway, we all got together for dinner one night—my bent boss, that newsletter jerk who was on the take, and Sid Ravitch, who was likewise on the take. It was a PR man's dream."

"But how did you two get into that gold scam together?"

"It started the next day at the bar of the Queen Elizabeth with just Ravitch, the newsletter guy, and me—kindred souls, and we all knew it. The newsletter publisher had the basic idea. To sell options on gold warehoused in Canada. Except there would be no gold and no warehouse. The Swiss guy put up the seed money and Sid wrote the prospectus—the one you stole from me, Willy. I became the salesman in the United States. Why here? Because this country has by far and away the greatest concentration of suckers on earth. You couldn't find a better place to market a get-rich-quick financial scam."

"And you got caught."

"That's why we met, Willy," Lenny replied.

"But why did you protect both Sid and that guy from Zurich?"

"I didn't protect the guy from Zurich. I told the FBI all about him, but they said they couldn't bring him back to the States even if they tried. Something to do with the extradition treaty."

■

"They told you the truth," Willy said. "But why did you protect Sid?"

"You want the real truth? Because I was afraid of him. He's got a very, very mean streak in him. If I would have finked on him, I might have ended up dead."

"Have you thought over the significance of that for you now? Right now?" Willy asked.

"What do you mean?"

"That you are literally the only guy alive who *still* knows enough about that mean bastard to send him to prison."

"I've thought of it, sure. No doubt, so has Ravitch. Why do you think he gave me the job spying on you, Willy?"

"What's he paying you?"

"One hundred fifty thousand dollars a year."

"For how long?"

"What's that supposed to mean?"

"You're what they call expendable, Lenny. You know way, way too much. But there is one thing I'm sure you don't know."

"What's that?"

"How much Ravitch is expecting from me as a result of what you found out where I'm concerned."

"You're right."

"Half of that investment bank in San Francisco, which is worth a quarter of a billion dollars."

"Jeezus, Willy. I had no idea."

"What's worse," Willy said, "nobody can stop him. Nobody but one guy."

"Who's that?"

"You, Lenny."

Lenny thought that one over for a while.

"I guess you're right."

"So maybe you're worth a hell of a lot more than that lousy one hundred fifty thousand dollars a year."

"That's for sure."

■

"You might want to talk to Sid about it."

"I will. What should I tell him?"

"That if he gets half of what I have, you want half of what he gets. After all, it was you who did all the work."

"How much would that be again?"

"Sixty or seventy million dollars."

"And if he refuses?"

"I'll put you on the payroll at one million dollars a year, starting tomorrow."

"Then he'd come and get me, Willy."

"No way. In contrast to Sid Ravitch, Lenny, I want you *alive,* not *dead.* You've haven't seen this place, Lenny. I'll put you up in a house right here on the ranch and arrange to guard you like Fort Knox."

"How can I know that you're telling me the truth?" Lenny asked.

"Would you rather trust me—or Sid Ravitch?"

"I'll talk to him."

"Now I'm going to have to tell you something that I probably should have at the outset, but I think you'll understand why now. Sid Ravitch will be here in about a half hour. He does *not,* stress *not,* know you're here, Lenny. So if you want to go back to San Francisco, and just forget the whole thing, go ahead. But I thought that after we talked, you might want to bring this to a head right away. I know I do."

Lenny said nothing.

"That wasn't fair, Willy."

"I know. And I apologize."

"You've always been a square shooter. Everybody that knew you inside said that. Do you really mean it about that million dollars?"

"If this all works out tonight, Lenny. I'll give you an advance on that million of two hundred and fifty thousand dollars in cash."

Lenny's eyes squinted.

■

"And the protection?"

"I'll have one of my associates show you the house I've got in mind. Right now. As long as he's at it, he might as well show you our trading operation up here. If you stay, Lenny, you'll probably want to get involved."

That did it. A quarter of a million cash. A house. A real job. And staying alive.

"How will I get to talk to Sid?"

"I'll bring him over to the trading room. You and Sid can go off into a corner by yourselves. OK?"

"OK."

"All right. I'll go get my colleague who will show you around. His name's Frank Lipper. I'm sure you'll get along."

Frank was waiting in the kitchen.

"How's it going?" he immediately asked.

"Perfect. I now know enough about Sid Ravitch to keep him under control with or without Lenny. But it will be safer with him. Take him to that empty house, then the trading room. But on the way to the house, go into the trading room and tell everybody that I said they should go home early. Like right away. Because a big storm's coming in. I want them out of there by six. Make sure Lenny stays outside while you do it."

Five minutes later Willy was alone in the main house at River Ranch, waiting for the imminent arrival of Sid Ravitch.

At six on the dot a big new Cadillac pulled up in front of the old Victorian. Again, Willy was watching from the living room. This time, however, he went out onto the porch to meet his guest.

He held out his hand as Ravitch came up the porch steps. It was accepted—barely.

"Good to see you, Sid," Willy said, "Come on in."

"Sure."

Once inside, Sid started to take off his trench coat, but Willy interrupted him.

■

"Might as well leave it on, Sid. We're not staying here. We're going to our trading room, which is about a two-hundred-yard walk from here. That's where I've got all the numbers. And I think it's numbers you are going to want to discuss."

"That's right," Sid said. "The word's going around that you made a big killing in the currency market. Will the numbers reflect that?"

"And how. I think that now there's more than enough to go around, Sid."

Willy could see Ravitch visibly relax.

"Hold on," Willy said, "I'm going to get a raincoat, too. Out on the porch it felt like it's going to start coming down any minute."

The night was dark and the path dimly lit. So when they entered the trading room the glare of the lights momentarily blinded them.

Then Ravitch saw Lenny standing beside Frank Lipper. They were the only two people in the trading room.

"What the fuck are you trying to pull?" he asked Willy in a strained voice. "I'm getting out of here, and I'm taking Lenny with me."

He looked across the room

"Lenny!" he yelled. "Get your ass over here! We're leaving. NOW!"

Lenny moved toward him as if in a trance. Sid met him half way, grabbed his arm, and steered him toward the door.

"You follow us and you're dead," he said, looking back but once.

Then they disappeared into the night.

"He's packing a gun, just like I thought," Frank said. "I'm afraid, Willy, that we blew it."

Two minutes later they heard a muffled gun shot, and, despite Ravitch's warning, both Frank and Willy rushed out the door of the trading room and ran up the path that led to

■

the main house and the parking lot there. Fifty yards later
they saw the figure of just one man. It was Lenny.

"He went over," Lenny said. "I told him what you said I
should tell him, Willy. He pulled a gun. I pushed him. And he
went over the fucking cliff."

"Get Lenny out of here," Willy said to Frank. "Right now.
GO!"

"But where to?"

"SFO. Put him on the next plane to Canada. Vancouver,
Edmonton, Toronto, it doesn't matter. Get him out of here.
And Frank, on the way back, stop in Ravitch's offices. You
must have the keys. There are two items there that you want
to find and bring back here. Understand?"

"Perfectly," Frank answered, as he reached out for Lenny's
elbow.

"What's going to happen to me, Willy?" Lenny asked. He
was near tears.

"Exactly what I promised, Lenny. I'm going to take care of
you. In style. But first you've got to disappear for a while."

Frank led him away. Willy, now all alone, moved to the
edge of the cliff and knelt down. Carefully he began to search
the ground with both hands. Almost immediately, he found
the gun. He stood up and stuck it under his belt.

"Susie was right," he said. "This is a dangerous spot."

He listened. Not a sound. Neither from the Russian River
below, nor from the houses nearby. Only the wind.

"The bastard's got to be dead," Willy said to nobody but
himself. "If not, then I am. So I might as well find out which."

He ran back to the main house, picked up the phone in the
kitchen, and dialed the number of the Sonoma County Sheriff.

"We've just had a terrible accident out at River Ranch," he
said.

Ten minutes later two sheriff's cars slid to a halt in front of
Willy's Victorian. He rushed out to meet them.

"Where did it happen?" one deputy asked.

■

"I'll show you."

In less than a minute all three men were at the spot.

"Who was it?"

"A business friend from San Francisco," Willy answered. "He had been with me in my offices just down the path from here. We were walking back to the main house together to have a drink, when, for some reason, he stumbled, lurched to the left, and disappeared over the edge." Willy managed to shudder. "It's something I will never forget for the rest of my life."

"How far down does it go?"

"A hundred feet at least. And there are boulders in the river at the bottom."

"Not good. But there's nothing we can do right now. I'm going to radio in for help. Normally, I'd get our helicopter. But it's too windy for that. You two stay here. Maybe you'll hear something."

At midnight they found the body. It was wedged under a boulder in five feet of water.

The next day everybody who lived or worked at River Ranch was questioned. Nobody had heard or seen anything suspicious. Nobody even knew who Sid Ravitch was.

The next day Willy went to the trading room at noon and announced that, out of respect for the dead, they would close for the rest of the day.

At three that afternoon, after they had made sure that all the employees and all the sheriff's men were gone, Frank Lipper and Willy Saxon took turns pushing a wheel barrel to the incinerator situated next to the trading room. After opening the cover, they began throwing in the wheel barrel's load. It consisted of a few thousand zero coupon bonds and two prospectuses.

"What do we do about Lenny?" Frank asked.

"He'll call one of these days. And I'll arrange for him to get the two hundred fifty thousand dollars up-front money I

■

promised him. Then I'll tell him to stay away from here and me for the rest of his life. Otherwise, I'll make sure he faces murder charges. That will mean Death Row in San Quentin, not that country club in Pleasanton," Willy said. "And that will be the last time we will ever hear from Lenny Newsom."

■

FIFTY-THREE

Willy picked up Sara Jones at six the next evening, and together they rode in his limo to City Hall.

As soon as they were inside, they found themselves at the end of a long receiving line. Ten minutes later, under the City Hall's magnificent rotunda, they were introduced to the President of Brazil and his lovely wife by the new chief of protocol of the City of San Francisco, Denise van Bercham.

Afterwards, they were given a glass of champagne, and offered some caviar.

"She's gone all out," Willy said.

"Of course," Sara said.

Willy immediately spotted Dan Prescott and Bobby Armacost in deep conversation with, of all people, Ralph Goodman, the prick who ran the California State Banking Commission.

Almost immediately, they also spotted him. Willy watched as Goodman excused himself and started walking directly toward them.

"Oh, oh," Willy said. "And just when I thought I was home free."

Goodman shook hands with Sara, and then turned to Willy. To Willy's great surprise, Goodman now also extended his hand to him.

"I won't take much of your time, Willy. I just wanted to

■

stop by and say that I misjudged you. I thought you were in the process of getting back into the bond business. I've since found out that you're now into foreign exchange, and that the people you advise just made a bundle. I've also heard, from another source, that you helped some of our California banks make a bundle, too. I appreciate it."

He then turned and walked away.

"That must have taken something out of him," Sara said.

"For a minute, before I heard what he was going to say, it took even more out of me," Willy said. "But now it's over. All over."

"I won't ask what it is that's all over, but I sense, Willy, that you've been a bad boy."

"You're right."

"Did my bad boy at least learn a lesson from all this?" asked the bishop's daughter.

"Yes. Do you embroider?"

"I know how."

"Do you remember how our grandmothers had embroidered sayings framed and hung up in the living room to remind everybody about how they should behave?"

"You mean like 'Waste not, want not?' "

"Exactly."

"What do you want embroidered?"

"Another saying. A reminder. Better yet, an admonition."

"Which is?"

"I'll tell you."

And he did.

■

Epilogue

One month later, at noon exactly, Sara Jones walked into the main house at River Ranch. Willy was waiting for her.

"The surprise party starts in fifteen minutes over in the trading room. So when we get there, be surprised," she said.

"Don't worry, I will."

She than handed him a thin, gift-wrapped package.

"It's my small token of thanks for the skiing trip, Willy," she said. "I thought you would prefer to unwrap it in private."

He unwrapped it immediately.

HE WHO SELLS WHAT ISN'T HIS'N MUST BUY IT BACK OR GO TO PRISON

■

"It's not perfect, I know," Sara said, "but it's the thought that counts."

"I'm going to hang it up immediately," Willy said.

He did, and to this day if you ever visit the main house of River Ranch outside of Healdsburg, California, you'll see it above the mantel piece in his private study, displayed in all its embroidered glory.

■